THE NEMESIS

BOOK 3 OF THE DIABOLIC TRILOGY

S. J. KINCAID

SIMON & SCHUSTER BFYR

NEW YORK   LONDON   TORONTO   SYDNEY   NEW DELHI

SIMON & SCHUSTER BFYR

An imprint of Simon & Schuster Children's Publishing Division
1230 Avenue of the Americas, New York, New York 10020

For information about special discounts for bulk purchases, please contact Simon & Schuster
Special Sales at 1-866-506-1949 or business@simonandschuster.com.
The Simon & Schuster Speakers Bureau can bring authors to your live event.
For more information or to book an event, contact the Simon & Schuster
Speakers Bureau at 1-866-248-3049 or visit our website at www.simonspeakers.com.
Also available in a SIMON & SCHUSTER BFYR hardcover edition
Interior design by Lizzy Bromley
The text for this book was set in Bell MT Std.
Manufactured in the United States of America
First SIMON & SCHUSTER BFYR paperback edition November 2021
10 9 8 7 6 5 4 3 2 1
The Library of Congress has cataloged the hardcover edition as follows:
Names: Kincaid, S. J., author.
Title: The nemesis / S. J. Kincaid.
Description: First edition. | New York : SSBFYR, [2020] | Series: The Diabolic ; 3 |
Audience: Ages 14 up. | Audience: Grades 10–12. | Summary: "In the final book in the
Diabolic trilogy, Nemesis must choose between love and justice as she watches her once-
idealistic husband ravage the galaxy through his tyrannical rule" — Provided by publisher.
Identifiers: LCCN 2019050872 (print) | LCCN 2019050873 (eBook) | ISBN 9781534409958
(hardcover) | ISBN 9781534409965 (paperback) | ISBN 9781534409972 (eBook)
Subjects: CYAC: Science fiction. | Kings, queens, rulers, etc.—Fiction. |
Courts and courtiers—Fiction.
Classification: LCC PZ7.K61926 Nem 2020 (print) | LCC PZ7.K61926 (eBook) |
DDC [Fic]—dc23
LC record available at https://lccn.loc.gov/2019050872
LC ebook record available at https://lccn.loc.gov/2019050873

05448508

ALSO BY S. J. KINCAID

THE DIABOLIC TRILOGY

The Diabolic

The Empress

THE INSIGNIA TRILOGY

Insignia

Vortex

Catalyst

In memory of Jan Whyllson,
*who lived a life dedicated to her art
and showed me that was a possibility*

The strongest poison ever known
came from Caesar's laurel crown.
—WILLIAM BLAKE

AT NIGHT, the sky ignited in stark crimson. It forewarned of the threat approaching them from space.

Few in the galaxy had heard of Anagnoresis, a small planet on the frontier of the Empire. Its nearby patch of malignant space had been growing slowly, unnoticed for decades. That malignancy was the forgotten, glowing gravestone of a long-ago vessel that had been lost while trying to enter hyperspace.

The start of the rupture had been small, a virtual splinter. It would have remained there forgotten if not for the existence of Eros.

Eros was a gas giant that had sheltered Anagnoresis from incoming asteroids. Over the course of three hundred years, it swept around the Anagnoresian star—until its orbit rammed it straight into that pinprick malignancy.

Eros's clouds swallowed the hint of light, and like that, the malignant space seemed to vanish.

Until weeks passed, and then the light swelled from within Eros's clouds, steadily devouring more and more of the gas giant's atmosphere. Within months, there no longer was a planet called Eros. In its place spread a massive and vibrant band of white and purple light—the gravestone of a gas giant, expanding with every second that slipped past.

On Anagnoresis, the tiny population of human settlers gathered to survey the new light in their skies. Distorted by atmosphere, the vibrant ribbon resembled a small moon or an asteroid. The locals were anxious—but they did not yet know to be afraid.

The boy noticed only after the malignant space swelled into a secondary sun in the sky of Anagnoresis, one that lit the night.

He was the only one on the entire planet who knew the truth: they were already doomed.

The citizenry of Anagnoresis had never faced a crisis of such proportions. They didn't properly fear it because they didn't understand what it was. Their response was misdirected. Without Eros, they worried about asteroids and comets. They gathered together to organize a new defense grid to protect Anagnoresis's skies from astral assault.

Secrecy was necessary. They'd heard stories of decadent Domitrian Emperors who used any pretense to strip planets from their citizenry and gift them to favored sycophants. So they agreed not to speak of the strange happenings in nearby space. "We'll deal with it on our own. The Empire can't learn of it, or it will be used against us."

They didn't know that among their number was one of the very Domitrians they feared. Tyrus Domitrian had sought refuge on Anagnoresis. He'd planned to escape his true identity and become just another eight-year-old among the Excess.

It had felt at first like a game—a deadly game, but a game regardless.

How to become invisible, here, at the edge of the known universe? He had studied the mannerisms and speech of the local populace. Had learned to slur his consonants and mimic the lilting rhythms of Anagnoresian speech. The people here were gentle, not like any he'd known on the Chrysanthemum. He learned how to fake gentleness like theirs, and in faking it, he discovered that it actually existed within him; it had existed there all along. He could be a good kid like any other. He could play games, and think of small matters, and worry about nothing under the safe guardianship of his father.

It had seemed a wonder to the heir to the galactic throne: that life could be so simple, and so kind.

Until today, when he had realized what it was that he saw in the sky.

Malignant space!

He tried to explain to his father, Arion, why this was a catastrophe. "Your Viceroy clearly knows nothing of it," he said. In his fear, he sounded like himself for the first time in months, his accent that of the Grandiloquy, the vocabulary of space dwellers infiltrating his speech. "Father, he's afraid an asteroid might hit us? He's insane! Don't you see, that's the least of our worries! That anomaly will keep growing until there's no escaping it. We have to leave this planet. Speak to him. He must order an evacuation."

Growing up at the center of the Empire, Tyrus had taken for granted that those near him had the power to effect change. But his father, Arion, was not a Domitrian. He was a mere worker, a mechanic who maintained the service bots for local mining machines. He'd been chosen arbitrarily by Tyrus's mother for her child's DNA.

He'd taken Tyrus in anyway and had done his best to understand the boy. But now, confronted by his son's demand for action, Arion was reminded of the difference between their worlds. Arion knew he had no power to issue orders. Nor would he wish to have such power. Unlike his son, he had no clear view of what should be done. He trusted the judgment of his rulers, that they knew more than he did and could be expected to act in the best interests of all.

But he saw his son's anxiety and wanted to relieve it. "There is an entire committee of experts with the Viceroy at this very moment," he told Tyrus, "and I promise you they're working on a way to save us. They know what they're dealing with."

"How can they possibly?"

"Tyrus," Arion said firmly, "remember which of us is the adult here."

"But . . ." Tyrus's voice faded.

Arion caught Tyrus's chin. It was a trespass none would dare do to an heir to the throne, but to Arion, he was a child. Tyrus found it more comforting than he should. His father held his eyes firmly. "Think about this: you're a smart boy, you grew up in space. You're seeing that malignant space through our atmosphere. Don't you see how that changes things? The clouds distort the light. It's not as close as it looks."

"Is that . . . is it true?" Tyrus was desperate to believe him.

"You see the same thing at sunrise, don't you? The light is everywhere, not just in one spot. The atmosphere amplifies and spreads it. Same thing is happening here. We have far more time than you think."

Later, Tyrus would hate himself for the hope that had shivered up within him. He'd wanted so desperately to believe his father's claims.

And so he did. He put his trust in this beautiful idea that there was someone else who held answers, who would act on them, who would protect them all. He wanted to have faith that other people could be right.

Two days later he awoke early to a distant buzzing sound that had disturbed the morning birds into noisy protest. Tyrus peered out the window to see supply transports launching themselves back up into the clouds. Later he learned that their captains had been bribed into keeping the star system's secrets. A mandatory evacuation still seemed the worst outcome of all to the people of Anagnoresis.

When Tyrus heard those whispers, he could not help but think, *If we had a chance to survive, we lost it when those ships left.*

He forced away his doubts. They did not return until the worst way doubts can come—far too late.

Anagnoresis was supposed to be safe.

His mother had implored him to find his way there if anything happened to her.

"Leave the Empire. Leave the sun-scorned throne. You do not want it," she'd told Tyrus, again and again. "Our family is radioactive. The power we hold will cost you your soul. Swear to me that if anything happens, you will flee. Never return to the Chrysanthemum."

"I will. I swear it, Mother."

Tyrus found his father and vowed never to return to the Empire.

At the time, he meant that vow. He meant it until malignant space invaded the sky, until the night when he could no longer sleep because the crimson glow grew so bright it flooded his dreams. He pulled on his coat and strode out into the red-stained night.

The air was chill. His breath made pink-tinted clouds, and his boots crunched over dying grass. Overhead, the bloody wound of malignant space glowered and pulsed. As he stared into it, he saw the truth.

They were doomed.

He'd been lying to himself.

His father, the local government—they were fools, and their assurances were worth nothing. This planet was doomed. *Soon,* Tyrus knew with a cold certainty. *We missed our escape window with the transports.*

Only one person could save the inhabitants of this planet now.

He swallowed and made himself look away from the heavens, down to the living world. A soft, cold breeze was brushing through the trees, carrying with it the smells of soil and sap, of fragrant blossoms and things that could die.

His uncle, the Emperor Randevald von Domitrian, could save this planet. But who would ask him to do so?

He believed Tyrus to be dead. That was important; that was good. Only this year, at the age of nine, had Tyrus discovered how good it was to be an ordinary boy—*not* the Emperor's heir, but a simple child of no importance. An ordinary child obeyed and was guided by his elders. In return, he was given the freedom to explore, to make mistakes, to ask questions, to play. An ordinary child fell asleep without fear and woke up carefree.

But an ordinary child could not ask the Emperor to save a planet.

Tyrus made himself sit on the scratchy grass, which was something he'd had to work up the courage to do when first he lived on Anagnoresis. The space dweller in him had always recoiled at the thought of the microorganisms and bacteria within natural fauna. Now he made himself lie down and stare into the bloody ribbon overhead. His awareness of the skin-crawling dirt and vegetation faded as he remained there, his gaze trained up. His eyes burned and watered, but he did not let himself blink.

I have only been pretending to be ordinary, he thought. For he could not obey or believe his elders. His father and the government had told him not to worry. But Tyrus knew more than all of them. They were the ones misguided here.

Father. Arion was a mere worker. If the Domitrians learned Tyrus was alive, they would have no mercy on an Excess man who had interfered in their affairs by daring to hide a Domitrian from them.

6

This planet's survival would come at the cost of his father's life.

At daybreak his heart felt weighted by stone, but he had reached no decision. And so the next night, and several nights thereafter, he walked through the blood-tinted darkness. His thoughts cast about for clarity, for the right decision, which he no longer believed any adult could provide him.

Until a night came when Tyrus at last made the decision the people on Anagnoresis refused to make for themselves.

That sixth night, Arion discovered his absence and found him lying again in the long grass.

Tyrus made to rise, but Arion surprised him by taking a seat beside him. "What's been keeping you awake, Tyrus?"

Tyrus noticed that Arion had not looked up. He never looked up overlong. Once, Tyrus might have called this an example of his father's optimism, but now it seemed deeply childish.

And so, he did not apologize. He did not put on the local accent, or adopt the sheepish, slouched posture of an ordinary boy caught breaking curfew by his dad. Tyrus the Excess had been such a comfortable skin to wear. He could not afford to be that person anymore.

Now, once more, he was a Domitrian.

He met Arion's eyes. "I'm done with having a bedtime, Father."

"I see," his father mumbled.

The red-hued light deepened the lines in Arion's brow. And Tyrus felt something in himself soften and yearn—a weakness he could not afford. But it did creep into his voice, lending it that gentleness he had learned on this planet over the last year, which no Domitrian should rightfully possess. "I have not been playacting your son these last months," he said slowly, "or attempting to deceive you. I . . . I wished to be Tyrus of Anagnoresis."

His father let out a short, almost soundless laugh. Not unkind, but somehow despairing. "And I wished it for you. Tyrus, before you do anything rash, *think*—"

"I owe you my gratitude," Tyrus cut in. "I have never known peace as I knew it here. But . . ." He let the Grandiloquy accent slip into the local vowels, into the cadence and rhythm that his father would best hear. "Oh, Dad, don't you see?" He pointed upward. "That's going to devour us! Malignant space does not shrink. It will not be willed away if you close your eyes. It will decimate this star system. Every single person on this planet *will* die—unless they escape. And time is running out."

Arion's jaw squared. "You want to contact your uncle."

"*Want?* No. But *must*—yes." Tyrus exhaled. "And I've already done it." Silence.

He made himself say it: "He knows where I am. That I live."

Arion reached out to grope at the grass, like a drunkard seeking some handhold for balance. "He'll come for you."

Tyrus tried to swallow. His throat felt so tight. "Yes. There was—there was no time to delay. Do you see? If the planet is to be saved, action must be taken *now*."

Another beat of silence. "And the transports left," Arion said dully.

Tyrus had examined his options time and again. There was no other route. And yet the guilt still struck. It pierced him through.

"Yes," he said flatly. "The transports are gone and won't return for months. He'll be here well before that."

And so he will kill you. And it will have been my fault.

Arion took a ragged breath and staggered to his feet. Tyrus did not move—but discovered that at some point he had drawn his own knees to his chest, as though bracing himself against something.

His father had every cause to rage at him.

"Here," Arion said, and when Tyrus blinked to clear his vision, he saw that Arion had offered a hand to him.

Taking it was the hardest thing he'd ever done.

Arion pulled him up to his feet, then let go. Tyrus stood shivering. The night air felt so much colder than it had minutes ago. *For the planet,* he thought, but could not make himself say. *For the planet's sake, I had to—*

"You go back there," said Arion softly, "and you're right back in the thick of it. You'll be in the same danger that you left behind."

The prick of tears alarmed Tyrus. He never cried. He would not cry now.

But he had expected his father to worry for himself. Instead, Arion's fears were for his son.

Shame thickened his voice. "Of course. I've no doubt my grandmother will try to kill me, just as she did my mother. Perhaps I'll manage to kill her first."

Others might have scoffed at these words from a nine-year-old. Arion knew him better. "Perhaps you will," he said quietly. Then, after a pause, and for the first time in Tyrus's viewing, he looked up toward the malignancy, studying it. "How long do we have?"

Tyrus shook his head. He did not know. His stomach felt unsettled, his limbs twitchy. He wanted to get away—not to face this any longer. What had he done? *My own father.* Arion should rightly hate him. A child who would murder his own parent. A Domitrian, through and through. "I will find some other lodging," he said, "while I wait for the Emperor's arrival."

But when he turned away, his father caught his shoulder and swung him back around. "Tyrus." He tilted up Tyrus's chin, forcing their eyes to meet, his own dark and unreadable, his skin deeply lined in the red light. "I know why you did this."

I saw no alternative. Tyrus would not speak those words, though. They seemed to ask for forgiveness, and he did not deserve any.

"I understand," his father said. "You think you're going to fix this."

"Someone *has* to fix it." Had the Grandiloquy, had any of the Emperors cared, they might have solved the problem of malignant space centuries before. Instead they had let it fester—and thereby spread. Even the most obscure corner of the Empire was no longer safe. "If it continues—it will never stop on its own, do you understand? But if I become Emperor . . . if I seek the throne . . . Father, I can fix it." This was his true purpose: he knew it in his bones. "And I won't be like the others who come to power, Father. I won't forget what I'm meant to do."

"I know you won't," said Arion. "You're my son."

"I'm sorry." His voice broke. Suddenly he felt the full weight of his grief, and he could not breathe. "Dad, I am so sorry!"

His father's arms were strong and thick, the arms of a worker for whom labor was life. They pulled him tightly against a broad, warm chest. For a brief moment, Tyrus felt once more what it was to be an ordinary child: protected and cherished by someone stronger who wanted only his safety and joy.

But even as he hugged his father back, he knew he would never feel safe again. For the purpose of his existence had been made clear under the bloody light of the malignancy, and there was only one way to achieve it.

He would claim the throne and become the Emperor.

Then he would save the galaxy.

FIFTEEN YEARS LATER

"Wait for it."

The Emperor Tyrus von Domitrian's voice was quiet, but it rang over the gathering in the presence chamber.

For the last several weeks, the Chrysanthemum had been traveling in hyperspace. The thousand vessels that had been linked for centuries had disassembled. They moved in tandem to this new star system, far from the destruction of the six-star home of the Domitrians.

Now the Emperor stood before the great windows, gazing out at that distant speck of light that had once been the heart of the Empire. All present knew what had come to pass: the Emperor had somehow created malignant space, unleashed it, and allowed it to tear through his own home system.

Today would mark the culmination of those efforts.

Long-range satellites projected a holographic image into the very center of the presence chamber. It glowed in imposing size amid the gathered Grandiloquy. The image was a live feed of the hypergiant, Hephaestus, the largest and most powerful of those six stars. Malignant space reached for it in ever-multiplying tendrils, stripping away layer after layer of hydrogen.

"Any moment now," breathed the Emperor, staring entranced out at space.

He stood at a remove from the company of the others. His Grandiloquy exchanged uneasy glances behind his back but dared do nothing more. The security bots linked to the Emperor's mind were arrayed above the company's heads, mechanized eyes fixed unblinkingly on all the faces in the chamber, watching for any threats to the Emperor's person. The Grandiloquy had not yet gauged the extent of their Emperor's control over the machines.

For some Domitrians, keying into the scepter gave them voice command over the bots in direct sight.

For others, they could peer straight across star systems as though they were machine men themselves, looking through virtual eyes, issuing commands to distant weapons.

The assembled group had no illusions of their Emperor's mercy. They had assisted him in killing thousands of their political rivals. The most prominent Grandiloquy had choked to death on Resolvent Mist, or been cast into malignant space to die. They'd assisted the Emperor in bringing about the destruction in hopes of gaining more influence and power.

Instead they now stood as virtual prisoners of the security bots overhead, silent and petrified. For their young Emperor had turned into a terror, a creature of unpredictable moods and merciless whims. He was awaiting the catastrophe to come with an air of calm expectation. Even the hint of a smile.

That smile widened as it happened: Hephaestus hemorrhaged the last of its hydrogen.

On the holographic image between them, the vast star abruptly shrank and collapsed inward. A collective cry—a mingling of awe and horror—rose from the observers.

Then the star exploded outward, and in the window beyond the Emperor, a great explosion of light swelled across the blackness.

"There it is!" The Emperor broke into a laugh as Hephaestus went supernova against the vast tapestry of darkness. The vivid explosion fanned larger and larger. Rays of light ballooned outward, the most ferocious of nature's phenomena lighting up the great void. Pitch darkness lit to blinding light and drowned away the stars, before fading once more.

The Emperor turned to look upon the observers, his form rendered a dark silhouette against the great destruction blooming behind him. He spread his arms expectantly, invitingly.

"Behold," said the Emperor. "Our triumph."

For a long, frozen moment, a horrified silence hung in the air. There was no triumph here, just pure destruction.

"You who fear the Excess," jeered the Emperor, "can you imagine them ever defeating such might? I wielded malignant space. I ignited a supernova. The power over the Cosmos belongs to me now. And my loyal few—to *us*."

At last, understanding sank into the assembled Grandiloquy . . . awe. Then one or two of their number, clever and ambitious, realized the proper response. They began to applaud.

As soon as that first smattering of applause filled the air, more hands joined into a chorus of approval. The Emperor broke into a broad, self-satisfied grin.

As if by instruction, the clapping swelled to wild cheers, to toasts with glasses of wine. The Grandiloquy shouted themselves hoarse in praise of the "most glorious light show" in imperial history. They hailed their young Emperor for this remarkable feat.

The Emperor spoke: "Most Ascendant One, come forth."

The Vicar Fustian nan Domitrian—an imposter currently pretending to be the Interdict, the highest-ranking member of the Helionic faith—stepped out of the crowd and threw himself to his knees at the Emperor's feet, pawing forward for his ruler's knuckles to draw them to his cheeks.

The Interdict would never bow to an Emperor.

But the real Interdict was dead. *This* was a puppet wearing the face of a holy man, here to speak the words the Emperor wished, and do as the Emperor bade.

"Tell me something," the Emperor said softly. "The stars reflect the will of our divine Cosmos, do they not?"

"Indeed, they do, Your Supreme Reverence." Fustian's voice shook a little.

"So it might be said, the sacred is what influences the stars."

"Indeed, that is true."

13

The Emperor's lips curved into an odd smile. "Most Ascendant One, *I* just influenced the stars."

Fustian opened his mouth but had no reply. He gawked up at the Emperor, no doubt trying to divine from that mysterious smile what he was supposed to say.

"I created malignant space. I caused a supernova. *I*." Tyrus stared down at him expectantly.

"In-indeed, you did."

"So what is the meaning of that, Most Ascendant One?"

Fustian began to tremble. "I . . . I know not."

The Emperor's unblinking stare was as empty and flat as a reptile's. A building hum came from the security bots overhead, causing many in the room to gasp and shrink into themselves. The lethal killing machines began to crowd together over the Emperor's head, their mechanized eyes fixed on the cowering Fustian.

"Hazard a guess," the Emperor suggested.

He spoke very blandly, but the words themselves were the warning. The wrong answer would mean death. None here doubted it. After all, in the ball dome of this very starship, they had watched him drive a sword through his wife—the woman he'd valued above all others, for whom he'd gambled everything.

They had hated her. Detested and feared her. Yet they had not celebrated her death for very long before a new understanding had set in.

If the Emperor could murder his own wife, then their lives would be nothing to him.

Though Tyrus von Domitrian had beamed upon them all but a moment ago, a swift undercurrent of fear stole through their ranks at the realization of what he could do to them if they gave him cause to frown.

Fustian bowed his head, deathly pale, and took a deep, audible breath. Then his gaze shot up, milky and desperate—eager. Yes, he knew just what to stay.

"You influenced the stars, Your Supremacy, so you must be a . . . a god!"

Only the greatest fools in the room let their incredulity show.

But their Emperor gave a maddening smile, his eyes warm with approval. "Think you so, truly?"

"I am certain. I am absolutely certain," burbled Fustian. "You are a god!" He rose and turned to the others. "Do you not see it? Do you not understand?" Desperation frayed his voice. "How . . . how he glows with a holy light? How he shines with it?"

Stunned silence answered him.

"You *must* see it!" Fustian shielded his eyes, as though blinded by Tyrus's essence. "Oh, it is inspiring! How lucky we are! There is a living god in our midst!" He fell to his knees again, then fell flat on his belly, his diaphanous ceremonial robes spilling around him. "Hail! Hail, Divine Emperor Tyrus! Hail to the Divine Emperor!"

The Emperor despised Fustian nan Domitrian. In the past, he'd been seen kicking away the puppet Interdict's hands as they pawed at his feet, sneering at his captive vicar's simpering reverence.

Today, though, the Emperor smiled at him broadly, fondly—like a parent to a child who'd offered some small gift.

"You see it truly, then," Tyrus said tenderly. He reached down to raise up Fustian's trembling form, and cupped the man's shoulders gently. "I will see you rewarded beyond your dreams for this . . . understanding."

"Your Supreme . . . Divine Reverence, I thank you," Fustian whispered, awestruck.

The Emperor turned his expectant gaze toward the rest of the Grandiloquy.

"Hail!" Fustian bellowed at them, chest puffed out now—emboldened. "Hail! As Interdict, I command you all to hail our Divine Emperor Tyrus!"

Behind the Emperor, the window still bloomed with the vast glow of the supernova, while the star-shaped metal security bots re-formed themselves into a circle above Tyrus's head, a crown made of deadly weaponry, awaiting a single thought from their master.

But it was Tyrus von Domitrian's next utterance that at last stirred them: "If I am indeed a divine being, I must need my most favored subjects. My most valued of disciples. What say you?" His gaze traveled over the Grandiloquy, glittering with a promise the courtiers of his Empire could not dare to resist.

Many of them had, in the past, clashed with Tyrus—back in those idealistic days when he'd been swept up in youthful dreams, in love with a Diabolic, ready to sacrifice them on the altar of some egalitarian vision for the galaxy. Yet the creature—the Emperor—before them now was shaped by cynicism, by Venalox, and yes, by avarice into a form they could clearly discern, for at last, this Tyrus von Domitrian was an Emperor they could understand.

In his demand for worship, there was a promise in return:

Profane yourselves for me and I will reward you beyond your wildest dreams.

And so came the first: "Hail!"

"Hail!" came another voice.

"Why, the light is blinding!" cried a third. "He is a god!"

"Our Divine Emperor!"

"The Divine Emperor Tyrus!"

As a wave, the Grandiloquy threw themselves to the floor, crying, "Hail to the Divine Emperor! Hail!"

Soon there was no question of remaining silent, no restraint to temper the Grandiloquy in gleefully prostrating themselves before Tyrus, because he seemed to have at last been born to their ranks. *This* was no god, but it was certainly a cynical, power-grasping megalomaniac, and the Empire had long shaped itself around just such tyrants.

What was a god, after all, but the arbiter of destiny? One who could ignite a supernova, who could kill a man with a single thought, who held the entirety of the galaxy and the Helionic faith in his hands: Was that not a god? His power over their lives was complete and unbreakable. Was that not a kind of divinity?

Tyrus gave a laugh as they knelt, and he began to call out promises: "A monopoly on the Novashine trade to you, Senator von Sornyx! And you—Credenza von Fordyce—I mean to give you Gorgon's Arm for this show of faith!"

The shouts and cheers grew louder. As the presence chamber at the heart of the galactic Empire filled with voices crying, "Our Divine Emperor! Hail to our God-Emperor!" the Emperor passed through their midst, giving favors even as he graciously allowed them to clutch at his feet, receiving their reverence as his right, and after all, was it not all his? He had triggered a supernova, and even the most restive of the Excess would quail before an Emperor—united with his Grandiloquy—with such destructive power at his fingertips.

Overhead, below, all around, the Chrysanthemum's surveillance machines recorded this moment, capturing it for posterity. And for eons to come, historians of the tragic and violent reign of Tyrus von Domitrian would debate the significance of this day. Was it here that the Emperor's madness had truly begun? Was this the defining moment of his reign?

Some would argue vociferously against it. They would point instead to an earlier time, to the years Tyrus spent under the control of

Alectar von Pasus. The Senator had forced upon his captive Emperor the neurotoxic drug Venalox, one notorious for its deleterious effects upon character—one that eroded one's empathy, one's conscience. *This*, they would argue, was the formative period that turned a young idealist into a brutal tyrant.

But gradually, over the centuries, a consensus would form. Neither von Pasus nor delusions of divinity could account for what the Emperor became. The key to that transformation was found elsewhere, in the single person who influenced his rise, his degeneration, and then his fall.

She alone had the influence to oppose the mad Emperor. She alone had the will and strength to speak when others were silent, and the ferocity to attack when none other dared raise arms.

The historians did not know as much as they thought, nor were their records as complete as they assumed. Nevertheless, they knew enough.

And so they looked to Nemesis.

1

I HAD THE MOST FAMOUS face in the galaxy, but no one recognized me.

Today, there were eyes on me. I felt them.

My feet scuffed to a stop.

A split second later, another pair of footsteps halted.

I was being followed.

My steps resumed their smooth stride down the street. *Interesting*. It had been months since I'd faced a threat. In truth, I'd grown rather restless with boredom.

Misery was a constant of life on Devil's Shade. In this most distant and hopeless of provinces, frustration boiled in every heart, leaked through every strident voice. Anger sought an outlet.

A lone young woman drew predators.

I could have avoided trouble, if I'd tried to blend in. I could have cut my long locks, worn large jackets, ducked my head . . . my size alone could have convinced hostile eyes that I was a decently muscled male. But something hard and vicious in me took pleasure in refusing to hide.

Instead I wore my long white-blond hair down. I'd made the color fashionable and saw it everywhere now, so why change it? When I walked down the street, I did not slouch. I made no effort whatsoever to avoid strangers' attention. I met every stare with a stare.

They were just humans. Let them hide from *me*.

The only disguise that obscured me was the burn across the right side of my face. I had Neveni Sagnau to thank for that tiny scrap of anonymity. If I ever met her again, I meant to return the favor.

My steps slowed again so I could gauge how many pursued me. The subtle pause between the steps grinding to a halt . . .

Three.

Pity.

I'd been hoping for a challenge.

My mind rushed over the rules I'd laid out for myself: no attacking without provocation, and no chasing however much it entertained me. After all, it was never fair, and giving chase stoked a dark instinct in me, one I had resolved to battle.

I was a Diabolic engineered for murder, but I was not some crazed beast.

A rational being did not chase one who fled, nor could I assume anyone's motives without evidence. Yet even as I reminded myself, I strained my ears for the shuffling of footsteps, and a pleasant excitement began to shiver through my limbs.

Stop. Do not indulge this, I told myself, and stopped walking.

It took several lingering, sloppy seconds for my pursuers to catch up to me.

The trio of shadowy men broke into jeering smiles as they

fanned out around me. "You look lost," called the largest of them.

I regarded them for a long moment.

My total lack of fear often frightened away those men who sniffed about for the vulnerable. Most heeded their instincts that something was "off" about me and escaped with their lives.

"Understand me," I said quietly and clearly. "I don't want to be followed. I am going to walk away and you will go in another direction. I will show no mercy on you otherwise."

Then I turned my back to them. A dank alleyway presented itself, and I swerved into it. A dead end: *perfect*. I leaned against a wall to wait.

They followed.

"You looked better from behind," called the scraggly-haired one, and the other two laughed. "What's that on your face, a disease?"

I could have lied about my scars and said it was a disease. Skin-rot, maybe. It might have driven them away.

But I was not in the mood to be kind. I just waited.

"Answer me, you ugly bitch," the man snarled. "I'm being nice to you."

"Yeah, we're real nice," said the largest of them, elbowing the third, the quiet one hanging back. "Aren't we?"

Uneasy laughter and a muttered, "Maybe we should go," from the third.

"No, no, she's got to tell us we're nice," said the scraggly one. "Actually, maybe thank us. Thank us for being nice to such an ugly bitch."

The scraggly one crossed the distance to me and invaded my space, until I could smell his body odor, until I could see the pores on his nose, the missing teeth bared by his smile. He planted one palm on the wall next to my head, and then the other.

"Well? Gonna say anything now?" he said. "How about . . . *now?*"

Then he laid his hands on me.

I'd warned them.

I rammed an uppercut into his jaw, and his bones gave a satisfying crunch as his neck fractured, killing him instantly. Forward I shot, snagging the arms of both his companions before they could react, dragging them bodily closer to me.

"Who's next?" I roared, my voice bestial.

Panic lit their faces. I crashed my head into the larger man's face, then sank a roundhouse into the ribs of the other, hearing the splinter on impact.

The larger one had stumbled back from me, clutching his head, and now he stumbled over his dead friend. He gave a squawk of anger at the sight of him. . . . "Murph? Murph! She killed him! She . . ." His hand dove into his jacket and withdrew a blade that gleamed in the light.

It slashed at my face. Too easy. I caught his wrist. His eyes met mine, disbelief ablaze in his face as I slowly twisted his arm about to turn his blade back toward him. This man was so large, he'd likely never been overpowered in his life, and now he found himself at my mercy.

"Having second thoughts?" I whispered.

"You bitch—" he rasped, and sealed his fate.

Enough. I stopped holding back and stabbed the blade through his eye.

Then I turned on the third man, the most hesitant of the three, who was sprawled on the concrete of the alley.

"Well?" I spread my arms invitingly.

He gawked up at me, wild-eyed with terror, and he finally saw me.

My size. The white-blond of my hair. The dead men behind me, battered with my unnatural strength, murdered so easily with an unnatural skill . . .

"It's you. It has to be you." He said the words with a sort of wonder. He raised his shaking hand and gestured to something behind me.

I could guess what it was before I looked, but I did so anyway, just hoping he'd try to strike at my back and give me an excuse to kill him.

Sure enough, there was graffiti on the wall amid the indecipherable messages of the dispossessed, a single stark image of that cruel and lion-haired goddess, white fire seeming to scorch up around her hard, precise features fixed in promise of revenge.

Above and below her, that familiar phrase:

NEMESIS LIVES

The pathetic wretch was scurrying back, still on the ground, scooting like a crab across the alley.

"Don't hurt me," he said to me. "I didn't want to do this. I swear to you, I didn't. Please, Nemesis. Please."

Yes. Now that he knew precisely what I was, he knew this was what he should have been doing from the start: begging me for his life. And I should not listen to him. He had seen me. He would give me away. He would endanger me.

I had promised no mercy.

He knew there was no escaping a Diabolic.

As I stalked after this weak, pitiful thing, a memory tickled at the back of my mind—another man, so many years ago, pleading with me to spare his life. I'd made one decision then as a young Diabolic desperate to escape a lifelong cage.

But I was not that frightened child now. I was not a trapped creature, at the mercy of others. There was no Matriarch here to make this decision in my stead, and I no longer believed there was a better, kinder life awaiting me if I but shed a few more drops of blood. *No.*

All that lay down that path for me was more death, more ruin, more destruction.

His eyes were screwed shut, muscles braced, head bowed in surrender to fate.

"What is your name?" I said to him.

"Janus."

"Janus what?"

"Janus Metz, Your Supremacy."

My jaw clenched. *Your Supremacy.* I'd hoped never to hear that accursed honorific again. But since he'd used it, I seized his hair and tilted his face up to make him look at me. "You will not tell another soul you saw me."

"No," he said.

"Good, because I will remember your name, and if you are lying to me . . ." I ripped a handful of hair from his head, and held it up for him to see. "I have your scent, Janus Metz. Do you know Diabolics can track like bloodhounds?"

It was a lie. My sense of smell was as dull as a regular human's. He couldn't know that.

He nodded, wide-eyed. "I know I can't run."

"That's very wise of you. You will take care of these bodies for me."

"Of course!"

"And you will never do anything like this again: no victimizing people on the street."

"I didn't want to—"

"You were weak. You gave in to them. Never do that again. I will find out if you do."

I would not find out, but I let him think so. He looked upon me with a strange, slack-jawed expression. "You truly are what they say you are," he whispered. "You seek justice." His eyes were actually shimmering with tears. "I will prove myself. I will deserve your mercy!"

I sighed and knocked him back to the ground with my heel, then stepped past him. But something made me turn back.

He was still sprawled on the ground. But over his head, on the rude brick, a pair of painted eyes glared into mine, their look accusatory.

I glared back. Nemesis the icon, the galaxy's own hero—a legend who did not and never had truly existed.

The Excess had believed me dead. Not at my husband's hands, but supposedly at the hands of the Partisans years before, during their attack on the *Tigris*. . . . It had been *my* attack, but blame was laid to them, for all the truths of the Empire were cloaked in lies. Apparently, the Nemesis slain in full view of the galaxy in the ball dome was a Partisan imposter.

Yes, I'd been dead as far as everyone knew, and in retrospect, I'd been better off for it. I could have lived a life of obscurity, forgotten, a short-lived and tragic memory.

Instead I'd set out to show myself alive by assassinating Tyrus— and then I'd truly ruined everything.

2

TYRUS, *I can't imagine myself without you.*

No. But . . . I can.

Those were our last words before Tyrus drove a sword into my chest.

Gladdic von Aton had delivered me—a body in a coffin, lingering on the cusp of death—to Neveni onboard the *Arbiter*. She'd saved me from my coffin, which had been launched toward a star for my burial. Even with my heart beating and eyes wide open, I could not shake off that deathlike sleep in those early, hazy months onboard the *Arbiter*.

Neveni had joined forces with the Partisans, the Excess who formed an organized resistance to the rule of the Empire. There were more crew than use for them on the *Arbiter*, and I had no technical skills, so I had no purpose among them. . . .

Neveni at first meant to have me among them like a person of leisure, doing nothing, even having meals brought to me. It was unendurable enough to be on the *Arbiter* without endless empty time for my thoughts to swirl down and down, so I'd insisted on doing something. Anything. Cleaning was as tolerable as anything else.

The engine core of the *Arbiter* was my preferred sector of the ship, because it was remote and there were no windows to behold the stars. Tangles of wires and panels, stray equipment that had not been returned to their holding places, and crumpled food wrappers were always littered there.

It was something to do, to remove the trash. To find the cleaning spray meant for use by a service bot and scour that grated metal to gleaming.

The hours passed quickly that way. Mindlessly. That was the most important thing, after all: to detach from the great and cavernous hollow that had become existence.

I went through my new life in that manner, lingering over every task at no cost to anyone, to anything, since my actions made no difference with or without me. I remained in the lumpy bed each morning until my back throbbed. I undertook slow walks through the colorless corridors with legs that grew heavier with each step. Long hours I passed over whatever communal meal the Partisans had produced that day, usually a lump of synthetic bread and meatstock, with a different chemical condiment to glob wetly at the side of the plate.

All the while, the Partisans watched me, whispered about me— unaware that I could hear every word they spoke.

". . . not sure she's actually the Empress, whatever Sagnau says. That doesn't look like the same person."

"The nose is all wrong. There's something so eerie about the way she just looks right through you. . . ."

". . . still think we should just kill her . . ."

"Sagnau has to mean to do it eventually, right?"

They viscerally disliked me. I was very much the enemy come among them—the wife of the Domitrian, even if he had cast me away.

All about me, the world felt muted.

The colors were dim and edges sharp.

I tried never to gaze out the windows, for the sight of those distant and indifferent stars called to mind those memories of my life with Tyrus. Then questions poured through me. . . .

Did he ever truly love me?

Was it all my imagination?

I could have endured a thousand years of torture and I never would have done to Tyrus what he did to me. Everything I had done for him, all I'd felt and meant and imagined and dreamed up, it simply had meant nothing to him in the end. Even the Venalox could not account for his willingness to kill me.

It was intolerable to remember, and Tyrus's words beat through my mind over and over again:

The universe has no design, no meaning, no arc toward justice.

Was that simply the truth? Did dreams bloom to life in one's palm and then get crushed, and that was the end of them?

I loved Sidonia and she was gone.

I loved Tyrus and now he was gone.

Without Tyrus, without Donia, was there anything left of that Diabolic who'd been anointed a person, recognized as a being with a soul? For I felt empty. I felt like my soul was gone and wondered if I'd truly had one.

Sometimes, I grew angry.

Not at Tyrus. It was too painful to think of Tyrus.

No. I raged at someone who did not deserve my animosity.

At Donia.

In troubled dreams, she stood above me, always above me, and we were back in the Impyrean fortress. But I did not sit and watch her do art, or contemplate the gas giant out the window with her. Instead I screamed at her for what she had done to me, because the entire framework of my existence was a sham, a joke, a farce, and it was *her fault*. *She* was the one who told me I could be more, that I mattered, that I had a soul, and then she had died and left me to this hideous delusion, and in my dreams I made her suffer for it.

"You told me I was worthy," I'd scream at her. "You said I had a divine spark. You were a liar! I am empty, Donia! There is *nothing* in me now! Everything you said was a lie! I was strong before you. I was complete! You ruined me, Donia—*YOU RUINED ME!*"

And I would lash at her beautiful, tragic face with my fists and tear at her with my fingernails, and how exquisite that distress tasted, the pain she would never share with me, and the fury filled my despair with something dark and glorious. . . .

Then I would snap awake to the familiar gray lines of the *Arbiter*, sickened by myself. She was the purest soul I'd ever known. Why did some part of me blame *her* for this misery?

But some resentful voice deep within me beat in the back of my mind, *It was her fault. It was all her fault!* She'd taught me to love, and so she had given me this terrible pain. I never would have known what it was like to be this empty, had I never known what it was to feel so complete. I wished I'd never loved her, never loved Tyrus. Oh, how I longed to be but a cruel and unfeeling Diabolic killer, with no attachment to anyone, to anything, and she had robbed me of that forever. . . .

"Nightmare again?" Neveni asked me sometimes, when she was sleeping in the bunks at the same time as I was.

Early in my time on the *Arbiter*, Anguish shared the bunk with her, and I'd glimpse his powerful, dark arm twined about her waist, sometimes stroking through her hair. *He* had the grace not to pry, to whisper to her in a deep, rumbling voice, "Leave her be."

I missed that—after she grew sick of him and took to ordering him away from her. When it was just me and Neveni, I felt too exposed. I never missed that glint of satisfaction in her dark eyes when I awoke from nightmares. She was eager for proof that I would be just the weapon I'd promised, that I hated Tyrus enough to fulfill my vow to the Partisans and kill him.

I'll destroy anyone you wish, I'd told her. *Anyone.*

So when she pressed me about nightmares, I always told her, "I don't remember." Then I buried myself back under the covers, turned my back to her . . . and pretended to sleep until her breathing grew slow.

We both knew a day would come soon when I had to fulfill my promise.

I was the only one certain I would do it. I would kill Tyrus.

This emptiness would not abate, would not retreat. It also left no reason to stay my hand.

Five months after my demise, the day came.

Tyrus was taking advantage of his puppet Interdict by appearing with him on Corcyra, the closest planet outside the impact zone of the recent supernova.

The Partisans onboard the *Arbiter* became a frantic hive of activity, throwing themselves into planning an attack. They recognized the opportunity here for a spectacular show of destruction, an unparalleled blow to the Empire.

I was informed of the plan. I was to be its key.

We would kill them both: Tyrus and the false Interdict. *I* would strike the first blow, and if I was lucky, I'd kill both of them.

But I'd certainly kill Tyrus.

There was no more symbolic blow to the Empire than having *me* be the one to kill Tyrus. If I died in the aftermath, I cared not. Nor, I suspected, did the Partisans.

A martyr is always useful. And I would welcome death.

A handful of Partisans and I were smuggled down to the planet in an escape pod. I parted with them and donned a hood, slipping out unnoticed among the crowd on Corcyra while the Interdict's vessel descended into the atmosphere. Security machines swiveled to alertness all around us, primed to protect the two most important figures in the Empire.

"Are you in position?" came Neveni's voice in my ear.

"Nearly," I replied softly.

Every single person on this planet had been scanned for weaponry. It mattered not. One of the Partisans who'd come in the pod with me was a sniper, and each of us had carried a single fragment of a laser rifle for him to assemble with painstaking precision. As I wove through the crowd, I knew the sniper was concealed somewhere behind me, my backup, instructed to kill Tyrus or the Interdict—whichever one I did not reach, for I would certainly kill one of them first.

Music swelled in the air. Millions of voices rose in a thunderous cheer, so loud it seemed to vibrate through my bones.

The *Penumbra* glided in above us, a vessel that with its thrusters extended resembled a hollowed pyramid. A bay door opened and out floated a triumphal platform bearing two figures glowing in the carefully aimed lighting. I spotted Tyrus's broad-shouldered figure just behind the false Interdict.

At first the spotlight was all for the Interdict. He raised his arms to accept the swelling cheers of the crowd. Then Tyrus stepped up to his side, and the cheers somehow redoubled. Framed by the light of the *Penumbra*'s bay behind them, dressed in magnificent robes that amplified the light, the two appeared as radiant as gods.

How long had Tyrus pored over the plans for that visual effect?

I forced my way forward.

Soon I was so close to that floating platform, I could feel the heat of its propulsion jets rolling over my skin.

Neveni's only explicit instruction had been this: *Make sure they see your face. The power in this gesture comes from you, Nemesis. Everyone will see that you're alive, that you were never dead—and the Empire is founded on lies. Then you'll deal the final blow when you kill Tyrus for what he did to you.*

The Interdict's holographic image boomed to life in all corners of the square, looming over the crowds as Fustian's voice resounded: "How grand to see this vast crowd turned out today! I know what you seek: words from me to explain the recent supernova in the six-star system. I will speak plainly and directly: on occasion, our divine Cosmos chooses to bless certain among us above all others. . . ."

The crowd shifted and stirred, eager to hear why a young star had gone supernova well before its proper time.

"The truth is, malignant space is not merely an act of destruction. It can also be an act of great and sacred *holiness.*"

At the word "holiness," the crowd quieted under the weight of disbelief. I paid their reactions little mind and continued forward.

"Our Emperor, Tyrus von Domitrian," Fustian said, moving aside so that Tyrus could assume prominence of position, "has the ability to unleash this great power himself. Something magnificent has happened. A miracle . . ."

It was time.

I tore back my hood, then leaped up onto the shoulders of the man in front of me and hurtled the remaining distance up onto the levitating platform.

I landed behind the men, blocked from the sight of the crowd by the two exalted figures. And then, before I could pounce forward and finish this, Fustian made his declaration:

"OUR EMPEROR HAS BECOME A GOD!"

The words—so absurd, so irregular—awoke me out of the haze of resolve.

They seemed to rouse me from a trance, as though I'd jolted awake after an extended dream, for they were . . . they were ridiculous.

"How lucky we are to have a god among us!" Fustian almost sobbed with feeling. "Hail the Living Cosmos for such a gift! Hail to our Divine Emperor!" He threw himself down to his belly.

And smiling, Tyrus swept forward and said, "I thank you, my exalted friend, for recognizing my divine nature. And how honored those of you on Corcyra must feel—to be the first to hail your true God!"

I stood rooted in place with utter shock. Tyrus's face was earnest, his eyes blazing with total conviction on the vast holographic images of him in the corners of the square. He earnestly seemed to believe in his own words.

"Set the example today for the rest of the galaxy," Tyrus said. "Hail me as your God—and be rewarded."

Instead of cheers, his demand was met with confusion, with restive stirring in the crowd. Excess were looking one to the other, and some were heeding their instincts and retreating.

A few—a brave few, filled with conviction—cupped hands over their mouths and jeered.

Tyrus's cool-eyed gaze fell upon one such fellow, and his lips curved into a remote smile. "Today is the example for all the days to come," he said, almost softly, gently, his tone eminently reasonable. "Deny that I am your God, then. Reap the consequences."

Then he raised his hand.

Overhead, a vessel ripped through space and tore a skein of bright white malignant space into the void. The newly declared Divine Emperor stepped to the front of the platform, his arms spread wide. The building-size holographics showed his mad grin and elated face. His arms rose, as though he were embracing the entirety of the screaming crowd, even as they turned and fled. They rushed to escape what could not be escaped: a bright and vivid slash of malignant space tearing across their star system.

I hurled myself down onto my hands and knees beneath the brilliant plume seeming to split open the sky, my blood thundering in my veins, disbelief blazing through me at what he had done. Then Neveni's voice lashed in my ear, reminding me of where I was, what this was: *"You're in reach. KILL HIM, Nemesis!"*

Kill him.

Yes.

Kill him. I was here to kill him. My eyes rose up to look at that figure with his back to me, and beyond him to the holographic projections showing his ecstatic face smiling upon the screaming crowd. . . . And everything inside me abruptly contracted with horror and the shame of realization that Tyrus had gone *insane.*

He was *insane.*

His mind had been *broken.*

He had lost his mind!

This was the answer. This was the answer to every single question and doubt that had tormented me these last months. . . . For he had loved me. I *knew* that was not my imagination. He had *loved me* and then he had lost himself utterly, and . . . and it wasn't his own doing.

Pasus had done this to him.

I had done this to him.

Tyrus's star-shaped security bots swiveled around, noticing me. They must have flashed a warning straight into his mind, for he whipped about and froze at the sight of me, all expression dropping away from his face.

Yes, even that mad smile.

"Please, Nemesis!" Neveni's voice was hoarse, frantic. *"End this! Kill him!"*

It was the look on his face that undid me. A strange sort of unguarded wonder, something I had never expected to see from him again. "Nemesis . . . ?" he said tenderly, in disbelief himself now.

"KILL HIM!" screamed Neveni.

I loved this man. I loved him. And here I was before a ruin of him, because this was not Tyrus. This had never been Tyrus. He had been imprisoned and his mind had been mutilated, destroyed, *taken from him.* He'd never meant this to happen; he'd had such beautiful dreams and plans once, and now here I was, come like a monster to destroy someone I had reduced to this. . . .

You've been the joy of this sun-scorched existence. Every moment of unhappiness I've had, I'd relive a thousand times just for the heartbeats I've passed with you. Now by the light of the stars, save yourself!

Those were the last words the true Tyrus had spoken to me, that day on the *Tigris* when he'd accepted his imminent death and pleaded with me to let it happen. All he'd wished was to escape Pasus with his mind and his soul intact—and I had stolen that choice from him.

We both knew it.

I made my choice, he'd flung at me that final day, with our swords drawn in the ball dome. *I would free the woman I most loved and serve those people of my Empire, and it was all I wanted. I trusted you to let me decide, and you knocked me unconscious and left me with them. I chose and you took that from me.*

This wasn't who Tyrus truly was. This wasn't who he was supposed to be. A thousand moments flashed through my mind in an instant . . .

His lips meeting mine; his tongue tasting me; his hands firm and clever, drawing me to the heat of his body. I remembered the warmth of his voice as he spoke my name, as he called me "my love." And then it became "my wife." Tyrus standing in coronation garb, offering me his hand, for all the galaxy was meaningless without me by his side. . . .

I suffocated on the sweetness we had lost, and then a flash appeared in the periphery of my vision.

The sniper.

The sniper!

NO!

I threw myself at Tyrus, intent only on shielding him from the lethal ray. The shot blazed past me, sizzling the air, and I . . . I hurtled right through Tyrus.

For it was not Tyrus.

It was a figment of light.

As I crashed to the platform, winded, I realized that Tyrus had never truly been present. This was the Empire's most sophisticated holographic technology—so seamlessly real the eye could not pick out its fakery.

I stumbled to my feet and became abruptly aware of a change in the crowd. Even amid the panic of the malignant space aglow overhead, the crowd had seen me, and now they called for me, my name traded from mouth to mouth. "Nemesis. It's Nemesis!"

But all I saw was that holographic projection of Tyrus, standing before me with his haunted eyes upon mine, and I could not look away from his face. Then reality registered in the form of Neveni's bitter, poisonous voice in my ear: *"I knew you'd save him."*

The *Arbiter* rose over the buildings in the distance.

"If we can't use you alive, Nemesis, then at least I know exactly where you're standing!"

A bloom of light swelled from the *Arbiter*'s laser cannon.

I realized then that Neveni was going to fire on me. To *fire on me*, regardless of the massive crowd around me, all the people who would also be torn to shreds by her weaponry. Neveni was going to kill me.

Did Tyrus say something to me, in that last moment? I believed sometimes that he might have, but all I knew then was that there was no escaping this. There was no saving myself—but I could get as far from this crowd as possible. I hurled myself through the air, aiming for the fringes. The explosion blasted my ears as a wall of heat slammed into me. . . .

That was the last I remembered until Anguish found me.

The mind had a way of playing cruel tricks, for even now, two years later, as I walked away from the men in that alley, my thoughts sprang back to the look Tyrus sent me just before the blast. . . .

And I cursed myself for still wondering if that had been fear on his face. For it couldn't be fear for himself, not when he wasn't actually there.

Fear for me.

The curse of being involved with Tyrus was his visibility. The galactic Emperor was visible everywhere, reminders were *everywhere*. As I left the men behind in the alley, I passed a Tributary Image, one of the holographics liberally spread throughout the Empire. The current sovereign always had such depictions everywhere, and this one was a generic image of the Emperor Tyrus in full imperial finery. His hair was set in the halo style of his coronation, his body adorned in liquisilk and crystal.

I stared at it unwillingly, as miserably riveted as a fish speared on a hook. *Damn him.* When would the day come that I felt nothing at all when seeing his face? The worst part was that I could not even rage.

I would have welcomed anger, embraced it, for anger was simple—so much simpler than this hideous sorrow I felt at the sight of the broken, destroyed soul I'd once loved.

I remembered those cool blue eyes and that carefully controlled smile he wore in the weeks following the events on Corcyra. The Eurydicean media deemed it a "Partisan Terror Attack." They claimed rumors of my appearance were but a lie, and there was Tyrus filling the transmissions to give credibility to that lie.

The galactic rumor mill whispered another story entirely. Many decided the attack had been perpetrated by the mad Emperor himself. He'd opened malignant space so close to Corcyra, the planet had but a decade left of safety. He must have blown up the crowd as well. The rumors spoke of me, of those who had glimpsed my face in person— and many swore they had seen me on the public feeds before the blast. I was more beloved in death than ever in life, and the Excess had long cherished my memory.

Soon the public imagination seized upon the idea that I was alive. . . . That I had been dead, but now I lived, and a ludicrous notion grew that I had defied mortality, that I had returned to seek revenge upon the Emperor who presumed to declare himself a god. That the Emperor himself had been the one to blast the crowd and murder thousands to hide evidence of my return.

No planet dared to laugh at the self-declared Divine Emperor Tyrus after that fateful day. Wherever Tyrus went, he was met with full-throated cheers, and in return, he showered those who worshipped him with imperial largesse . . . He flooded the coffers of his most ardent believers, and the example of Corcyra silenced those who might have dared to doubt.

But the few, those restive few who stuck by their convictions— they'd learned a new hope that day.

Protests were few, but when they boiled up, the words "Nemesis Lives!" were screamed by the defiant. My image offered terrifying warnings on walls across the galaxy. The Excess called the words as their sacred images were desecrated, as they faced the threat of malignant space, as a tyrant who held total power over them demanded that they bend to him in worship.

These humans wielded my name as a threat against a man who had declared himself a god.

I could not stop what Neveni had set into motion that day on Corcyra.

My name was their invocation, their prayer of hope.

Nemesis Lives. I hated those words. I'd begun to loathe my own name. I hated the image glowering at me from the wall of that alley, for it was a *lie*. It promised them a savior, a legend, a myth—and I was but a defeated ruin of what I'd once imagined myself.

Everything I had loved, I had managed to destroy.

As I gazed at the holographic, another rumor swam up from the back of my mind. . . . That the "Divine Emperor" had implanted *his* Tributaries with surveillance cameras, ones he used his godlike ability with machines to peer through every so often. According to hearsay, Excess seen offering fealty and worship and gifts to his Tributary Images sometimes found themselves unexpectedly rewarded with largesse; those who defiled the Tributaries faced the strictest of punishments.

My burn scars concealed my features, but a skitter of anxiety passed up my spine. Not at the thought of his eyes peering back out at me through the empty holographic face before me . . .

But because—stars curse me—some part of me was tempted to march up to it and stare into them until I felt him looking back.

Instead, I turned on my heel and left the Tributary and the alley far behind me.

3

MORE THAN TWO YEARS AMONG the Excess had dimmed my memories of life among the Grandiloquy. The masses did not live in sleek and polished corridors that looked out upon the stars, nor did they have humming service bots ready to satisfy their every whim. Excess were bound to their planets, with varying gravital conditions, climates, and smells.

Devil's Shade was a mining colony. The rogue planetoid had been flung from its parent star by the great supernova five centuries ago, and solar sickness was almost as common as a cold. Most of the locals were trapped in a perpetual cycle of working in the mines to pay off medical debts incurred while . . . working in the mines.

I'd chosen Devil's Shade because so many were sickly. I'd meant to take advantage of the public medical bots.

I'd hoped they might help a Diabolic, even. Anguish grew frailer by the day.

The mercy in the alley imperiled not just myself.

Neither Anguish nor I had any reason to fear street violence. We *were* what should be feared on the street, and so we'd found dwellings on Harvester Row, the most dilapidated area of an already hopeless province. The entire colony was underground; the interior-most level was Sector 001. We lived closest to the surface, on level 203, the sector most exposed to cosmic radiation.

I passed through the familiar causeway where miners ambled home, drillers floating behind them. They traded quips and curses, as street-side vendors called out their wares. The scent of waste and sulfur and scorched rubber reached my nose.

As I drew closer to our apartment, I reached the most crowded areas of Harvester Row, where hollow-eyed beggars scrabbled for handouts, though there was no use in offering them anything but food. They spent offerings not on the necessities, but on the drugs that had already reduced them to penury. These people wore their misfortunes on their faces, their weeping sores left unattended, their children for-gotten, their minds consumed by chemical need.

The Grandiloquy had indulged in the same substances, then wiped away physical consequences with top-grade, private medical bots. They condemned and imprisoned the Excess for drug addiction. But in their own circles, a varied selection of chemicals was as necessary for a party as a fine gown and jewels.

Creating these chemicals was not so fashionable—especially those that could not be produced by a synthesizer, but had to be grown and harvested instead. The Grandiloquy looked down to the Excess for such manufacturing. They looked to places like Harvester Row, where I now walked. It was a scene of miseries that made the mines look pleasant. Desperation and urine perfumed the air. I passed a crunch of trembling bodies, all pressed close together, waiting in line for a turn at the Harvester's chair.

There were two different substances that Devil's Shade specialized in. One was Cosmic Ray, a popular psychedelic among the Grandiloquy. . . . It was a fungus that on Devil's Shade was known as "desiccating rose," and the optimal growth environment was within human subcutaneous tissue.

I passed first those people with dimpled skin, their faces twisted with a low, constant pain, waiting their turn at having the desiccating rose extracted from their flesh, and likely a new set of spores implanted there.

The other group of Harvesters were the more richly dressed ones—who used the Excess to produce Novashine.

"Hold him still. Help me," one Harvester called briskly to an associate as I passed the chair where a young man—strapped down—had broken his bindings in his panic and freed his arm.

His eyes were wild with terror, and guttural screams issued from his lips. His fear was potent, which meant the Novashine would be strong. It was prized when drawn directly from the veins of a terrified human being. Excess lined up to be stimulated by a diode that catapulted their brains into horror, terror, pain, and caused their bodies to dump adrenaline into their systems. Light-years away, Grandiloquy would receive genuine, human-produced Novashine to enhance their mental well-being . . . and the hapless Excess would earn a week's pay in five horrifying minutes.

The Harvesters pinned the man down, held his arm still with both their combined strength, and fixed their eyes on the blood funnel drawing a red stream from the man's veins. By the time I passed out of sight, the Excess no longer struggled, his draining complete.

Afterward, he'd be allowed a few minutes to rest up and would be given a mug of hot chocolate in consolation. He'd likely have nightmares until the next harvesting. Indeed, the terrors would last until his adrenal glands, exhausted, ceased to react to the stimuli of horror. The Harvesters would then deem him "tapped out," unable to supply quality product for the Grandes and Grandeés at the center of the Empire, whose evenings were so pleasantly spiced with the by-products of terror.

The universe was cruel. I didn't understand how anyone could live somewhere like this and think otherwise.

As I descended into our small corner of the Obsidian Tower Dwellings, I braced myself to tell Anguish what I had done. He would insist on relocating at the next transport window, although in his weakened state, such a journey might kill him.

But when I saw him, my words died on my lips.

Anguish dan Domitrian was out of bed. Standing without support, gazing out the faded window at the view: a causeway swarming with dirty crowds of workers. Some alert quality to his posture, the straightness of his back and the tilt of his head, made him appear both engaged and prepared for whatever he might see.

"You look well," I said in amazement.

He cast me a quick, slashing look. "Of course."

There was no "of course" to it. Not anymore . . . Yet even his voice sounded stronger. I swallowed my news and gently laid the morning's rations on the table. I would not ruin this small miracle by mentioning the skirmish. He would be alarmed that I'd left one of them alive, perhaps would insist on testing his strength by going to finish the job.

"Where have you been?" he demanded, peering suspiciously at the satchel slung over my shoulder.

"At the synthomat. I have to work, so I fetched our rations early. They're ready for the heater when you get—"

He swung fully around. "Wait. You're alone? But . . . Where is she? Is she still out there?"

The words pulled me up short.

"Who . . . ?"

"You should not have left her on her own," Anguish said gruffly, shoving back from the window. "Tell me where you left her!"

Her. Oh.

He meant Neveni.

After everything, his mind still lapsed back into thoughts of Neveni.

They'd argued often as their relationship decayed. At first she just disliked his well-meant interference, when Neveni tried to show me the latest transmissions of Tyrus's doings—the laws enforcing state-sanctioned faith in him, the brutal repressions of riots, the crackdowns on dissenters. They were all her not-so-subtle attempts to keep my wounds fresh, and revenge at the forefront of my mind.

"Leave her be," I'd heard Anguish advise her.

"Stop telling me what to do," Neveni would shoot back at him.

They'd found each other when they united against me to take the *Arbiter* and strand me in the Sacred City. Now, as Neveni grew on edge, almost manic in her desire to weaponize me, Anguish moved to shield me.

Their disagreements grew more heated. I neared my sleeping chamber on the *Arbiter* one evening to hear their voices inside, and my ears were keen enough to pick out the substance of what they were saying.

"You don't motivate her when you rub salt in her wounds," I heard Anguish chide her. "You merely hurt her."

"I don't need her sad and moping, Anguish. I need her to remember what he did to her."

"She does. She remembers."

"She can take care of herself."

"We are Diabolics. We are not invulnerable."

She gave a bitter laugh. "Her, or you? What is this really about?"

"I have told you—"

"Did I hurt your feelings and you don't have the guts to say it?"

"This is about Nemesis."

"Then leave it be," she snarled. "I know what I'm doing."

And then I'd stepped into the chamber with them and they both fell silent.

I had brought them together, and now I drove them apart. Her irritation with him swelled. All the small gestures Anguish made to show he loved her seemed to go awry. She was no longer charmed by the protective instinct behind his offers to beat the crewmen who challenged her authority.

It didn't help that her crew feared and distrusted him. They fell silent and shrank back when he strolled past them. None who saw him could have doubted his Diabolic nature—his vast size, his fierce demeanor, announced it plainly. He had never learned to blend in with humans as I had; he'd never had a master like Sidonia, who treated him as an equal, who might have taught him to be more human. As Neveni's hostility grew, Anguish's befuddlement did as well. He did not know how to fix what was going wrong.

And soon I no longer saw him in the bunk with her.

Anguish and I hadn't fit in with the Partisans, neither of us, and since he'd lost her, his loyalties shifted toward his fellow Diabolic. After Neveni blew me up on Corcyra, he stole a pod and took it down to the surface in search of me. In the chaos of the mass casualty event, Anguish forged through the destruction. Amid the carnage of thousands who had been killed and injured, he found me, and his were the arms that swept under me as hoarse screams erupted from my lips, my skin chafing where it touched him, and my brain was a tangle of terror and hopeless confusion.

He tended me in our hiding place in the Corcyra Field Museum and stayed long after the *Arbiter* had fled orbit. When I was well enough,

we didn't even need a discussion; we simply understood each other—
and we traveled away from the accursed planet together to leave them
all behind. Tyrus. Neveni. The Grandiloquy. The Partisans.

Everyone.

Now, on Devil's Shade, I was the one caring for him.

And I could not let him step out of here to seek Neveni.

He tugged on one arm of his coat—far too large for him now—and
aimed for the door. I hastily stepped in his path to block his way. The
feverish, dark eyes met mine, and that small flame of hope I'd felt upon
seeing him upright died away, for I perceived the murkiness in his face.

"Neveni should not be wandering on her own in this place—"

"Lie down, Anguish."

"It's dangerous."

"She is not here, Anguish. Remember?"

He would have shoved straight past me, had it been earlier days,
before his strength waned. As it was, I caught him easily and man-
handled him back toward his cot. There, Anguish collapsed—just
aware enough to register the irregularity of being overpowered by me.

I snared the arm of his coat to divest him of it, but he gripped more
tightly, his face twisted as he battled to understand this situation. . . .
And so I let him have the coat and clapped my palms over his heated
cheeks, forcing him to focus on me.

"Anguish: remember. Where are we?"

"Corcyra . . ." He fell silent, confusion washing over his face. "No.
We're . . ."

"We're on Devil's Shade. Neveni is not out there. It's just you and
me now. Two Diabolics. The last of our kind."

His face cleared somewhat. "Family."

"Yes. I am your family."

For that was what we'd become. Did we not share most of our DNA, with mere variations in exterior phenotype? We were closer to each other than all but identical siblings. At the core, he was fundamentally the same as I was, and so distinctly unlike any normal human. What was inhuman in me was inhuman in him; the brutality of my upbringing was matched by his.

It was why he did not blame me, when I tried to save Tyrus.

He was a Diabolic.

He understood devotion. Even when it was one-sided. Perhaps especially then.

He let me adjust his position on the bed, confusion still writ upon his face—as it always was now. "I have been ill," he murmured hazily.

"Very much so." I glanced at the clock on the wall. I was going to be late for the acid ponds. "Anguish, don't you recall why we're here?"

"Medical bots."

"Yes." The public medical bots. Even now, illness cast a gray pallor over his face. He was small enough that he could have passed for a regular human now.

Misfolded proteins. That was what had gone amiss with him. Somehow the proteins in his body were learning to contort themselves unnaturally, and an increasing number of them had acquired the same distortion.

A kindhearted healer had put it differently, more simply: "It's like malignant space for the body," she had told me. "The corrupted proteins can't nourish him. They also corrupt other, healthy proteins, causing them to assume the same distorted shape."

The healer could not have chosen more piercing words. I had not understood the damage a folded protein might do, but malignant space—*that*, I understood all too well.

Malignant space destroyed all it touched. It grew relentlessly, exponentially, and seemed to change the nature of matter to what *it* was:

a bright and vibrant and hideous death that devoured stars, planets, perhaps galaxies. As I had lain dying in the ball dome, Tyrus's blade in my chest, malignant space had been the last thing I saw. . . .

When the healer compared Anguish's illness to malignant space, I finally understood that he was dying.

Now, here on Devil's Shade, I moved through my days working to get funds for different procedures from the public medical bots, just hoping to find something—*anything*—that could heal Anguish at last.

I was but two hundred credits short for his next one, and . . . and nova blast me, for not thinking to rob those two men I'd killed. I lived like a cur but had not yet gained the instincts of one.

"Your rations are on the table," I told him, "and the heater is ready for you. Eat something even if you're not hungry."

But his eyelids were sagging down already, and my heart sank, for I knew he would not. And I could not stay here and wait.

As I stepped out of our apartment, the stale and sour air of Devil's Shade met my nostrils, and then it all seemed to crush down around me like something within me was splitting, breaking, splintering apart, creating sharp little pieces that raked me from within.

I could not lose him.

The air felt thin. Inside my head it felt as though a thousand horrifying futures were blaring at me, for I would be alone in this universe soon unless . . .

Stop this, I thought.

Stop this.

STOP THIS.

I slammed my fist against the wall, and the pain woke me from my spell.

I drew in a deep breath. *I. Will. Save. Him.* I could not save others, but I could still save him. So I forced myself forward to do just that.

4

THE SMALL, slippery eels swirled beneath the murky waters of the pond as I carefully sifted through the algae, waiting for the pH measurements to register on my sensor rod.

"Hi, Nym!" came a piping young voice from behind.

My fake name.

Clumsy footsteps thumped through the tangled flora toward me. I didn't turn, but raised a hand idly. "Atmas."

Atmas Forst was the seven-year-old daughter of the pond overseer, and far too fascinated with me for my liking. I blamed the burn scars on my face and body. She was on an endless quest to learn all about them. Since the child often strayed too close to these deep-cavern ponds about us, I told her, "I fell into an acid pond just like these."

I credited myself with the increased care she took near the ponds after that.

Grandiloquy did not bring children to court, so I had never had prolonged contact with one—not since Donia and I had been small ourselves. It was rather bewildering to have one fasten herself to me like this.

"I drew you a picture!" she declared, and presented her latest offering.

I pulled the pH rod out of the acid and carefully set it aside, then took the crinkled paper she thrust toward me. It was a scribble of round blackness, with bright yellow stars dotted all about it.

"It's a black hole," she told me helpfully.

I'd seen a black hole. Tyrus and I had flown toward one to frighten the Interdict Orthanion into cooperating with us—and in doing so, we'd ruined everything. We hadn't realized time slowed as one drew nearer to the black hole. We'd lost thirteen months and given Alectar von Pasus the time he needed to trap us upon our return.

The memories must have shown on my face, because Atmas frowned at me. "You don't like it?"

I could hardly tell her that. The silly girl constantly came to me with new offerings of her art. They were rudimentary, inaccurate things: figures with overlarge heads and very tiny arms. I let her give them to me, and for some reason, kept them hidden in a corner of my apartment. They were the silly scribblings of a child, and I truly meant to throw them away . . . at some point.

"You need something else in the drawing to illustrate the curvature of the black hole," I settled with saying, tracing my finger over the edge of the darkness. "You wouldn't see the black hole in the void unless there was matter being drawn into it. A star. Or a planet." Then, after a moment, "But it's very . . . good."

It was not good, but she grinned at me anyway. I'd noticed children simply took for granted that most anything you said was the truth, without questioning it.

"I have another one," she said proudly. "But this one's for school, so I can't give it to you."

"And I'm certain you wish to show me," I said, turning my attention back to the pond. The eels swirled beneath the surface of the acid. They were nutritious, an additive for the meatstock the miners subsisted on. The algae that grew at this pH carried the true value, for it generated a substance that was distilled into liners for most standard space-sheaths. I prepared myself to look impressed when Atmas showed me whatever her latest scribble was.

And indeed, that was what the next drawing she unrolled resembled: a scribble. Two giant heads with lopsided eyes, and slashing dark lines that were meant to be arms holding something. . . .

"It's the Emperor and Empress . . . I mean, the imposter."

My heart gave a curious jump. I snatched the drawing from her. Now I could decipher this scribble: the figure with the slash of bright yellow about its head was meant to be me. The red fizz about the other meant he was Tyrus. And they held blades.

"No blood," I murmured.

"It's at my favorite part. Before the Emperor killed the imposter."

"This is for school?" I released my grip on the paper, and let her take it back from me and hug it to her chest.

"We're talking about the Partisans," burbled the little girl. "Everyone thought the Empress died in a Partisan terror attack, but then she came back, and everyone was so happy. The Emperor even married her—but then he realized she was just a Partisan imposter. The Emperor killed her, but . . . but . . ."

She lowered her voice, for even a child had the sense to take care with such things.

"Some people say it really was Nemesis who returned," whispered Atmas. "And the Emperor killed her anyway."

I released a slow breath. "Don't believe everything you hear. If you want to live a long and honest life, do not repeat anything to strangers that can get you into trouble."

"But you're not a stranger."

I looked at her. I was the person she annoyed at least once a day. "Knowing my name does not make me less a stranger."

Atmas looked ready to argue, then caught sight of a lizard scuttling over a nearby rock and ran off to investigate. A brief commentary on the lizard followed, and then a new announcement: "I'm going to be a Grandeé one day."

"Impossible," I said, faintly exasperated. "You were not born to them."

She came back to my side, little fists planted on her hips. "I'll marry one. Like Nemesis. She was a Diabolic."

The scar over my chest seemed to pulse with the memory of pain. "And look where that marriage got her," I said coldly. "Gutted."

Atmas's face fell. Not for the first time, I felt an odd flicker of recognition: she reminded me of Deadly, my dog. . . . The same bounding energy, the naked and unconcealed enthusiasm. She liked me.

I cleared my throat, wishing her away.

"A fine drawing. Now take it from the ponds before you drop it in."

But Atmas's cheerful chatter lingered in her wake. I knew why her school was talking about the Empress Nemesis.

Today was the anniversary.

At the conclusion of my shift, I found myself wandering out into stone corridors transformed, for the usual shift schedules were not displayed on the screens. Just as I couldn't escape the lavish fanfare of Consecration Day, or Victory Week, today I was trapped beholding images of myself on every screen I passed—for the Excess were all fascinated by the most dramatic event in recent imperial history.

Waiting for my turn in the gravity shaft, I was stuck staring up at the screen showing this:

An Emperor and Empress twirled in fluid circles about each other in zero gravity, encircled by a vast diamond ball dome. There were swords in their hands. The Emperor was young, vital, handsome, with his reddish-brown hair and gentle blue eyes, and the Empress was ethereal in her silvery gown, white-blond hair haloing her as though in preview of the tragedy soon to come.

"I killed the Interdict Orthanion when I destroyed the Sacred City," declared the Empress, her voice ringing defiantly.

It was the last instance of truth in the transmission.

"That's absurd," replied the Emperor.

"It's the truth. That man up there is an imposter. The Sacred City is destroyed." The Empress seemed to be transforming, losing the bloom of beauty, her eyes narrowing and growing cold. "I destroyed the Sacred City and proved the Helionic faith is a lie."

"Why," breathed the Emperor, "you are not Nemesis. My love would never say such lies!"

At last it was my turn to enter the grav shaft. I slapped in 203 and vaulted into the dark. Up I shot through the air, my ears tightening, popping, and then I landed with a thump on my level and strode out into the stale stone corridor . . . only to pass another screen playing the ending of the same scene:

"The Partisans will destroy the Empire!" The Imposter Empress had now dropped all pretense of being the true Nemesis. The subtle editing of the transmission had rendered her features distinctly unlike the true ones by now. "We will drown this Empire in blood!"

"Never!" declared the brave Emperor, and he drove his sword through her.

I ground my teeth. This lie, this lie! They all believed this lie.

A mournful Eurydicean newscaster began to speak.

53

"We all remember the fateful day when the Partisan imposter attempted to assume the identity of the late Nemesis Impyrean, but our cunning Divine Emperor exposed the truth of her before our Empire. It was nevertheless a grievous tragedy for our benevolent Divine Emperor and marked a drastic turn in his policy of reconciliation toward the Partisan terrorists who have been ravaging the Empire for . . ."

I shoved my way past the line inching toward the grav shaft. It was impossible to escape my past.

As for my future . . .

I knew what awaited me when I returned to my dwelling. My last friend in this world was twisting, turning with his latest fever, and sometimes when he spoke I could not understand him anymore.

And how long would I have after he perished? What was there to live for, once it was just me?

An icy hand seemed to pull me to a stop. I could not go home just yet. Not until I scraped together the strength to look upon him again, to witness his suffering and bear the full weight of my failure to help.

I turned back toward the crowd. One of the less-frequented Harvesters was working on a woman whose arm was sheared open. As he extracted the desiccating rose, her face turned toward me. . . . Eyes glazed with anesthetic, creased with lines. The scar tissue on her neck, her cheek, indicated just how much of her skin had already been donated to growing the substance.

I could hear her low moans.

The first time I'd seen the Harvesters at work on this planet, I had tried to intervene. I tried to save a young girl I saw bound to the Harvester's chair. The Harvester had shouted at me for interfering. *She consented of her own free will!* All the Excess waiting in line had raged at me as well.

How foolish I had been, trying to save those who were doomed.

One of Tyrus's Tributary Images was stationed here, gazing with its sightless imperial eyes upon the Harvester's doings, and I wondered darkly how potent his power over machines truly was. Did he ever glimpse this faraway province and see the degradation of his subjects here?

How is this for tribute, Tyrus?

But suddenly the Tributary Image shifted—as did all the images on every nearby screen. In place of Tyrus and the Eurydicean newscasters, a frantic, harried-looking man peered out, asking us, *"Am I getting through? Can you hear me?"*

My heart dropped. Tingles of ice moved through my limbs at the sight of the man who had just hacked every transmission feed on the planet.

Nova blast me, I should have killed him!

"I have news," the man said, his voice shaky. He had not sounded so shaky when harassing a lone woman in an alley. But breaking into the transmission tower of Devil's Shade, hijacking its signal, apparently warranted his nerves. *"This is the most important news you'll ever hear! This day is a lie. I have to tell you the truth about the Empress Nemesis. . . ."*

The speaker, of course, was Janus Metz.

5

"YOU KNOW ME," Janus was saying frantically. *"I am not a liar. Many of you have worked side by side with me. We've had drinks, we've seen each other around."*

His voice trembled with excitement.

"You know I am not a madman when I tell you all there is hope. I tell you all, it's real what they say about Nemesis. It's true!" Janus sounded like he was going to weep. *"Nemesis is everything they say! She demands that we be good, and she will enforce justice against the wicked! She will destroy the Emperor for his misdeeds—"*

"Oh, don't say it," I moaned, but he could not hear me and in truth, it was already too late.

"Nemesis Lives! NEMESIS LIVES!"

With those two words, he was committing treason. He was throwing his life away, for that phrase declared the Emperor a liar.

With joy blazing on his face, he shouted these words to the world, to every immiserated creature on this misbegotten hellhole of a planet. Onscreen, the door behind him burst open, and silence fell around me. The crowd waited to witness his death at the hands of planetary security.

But Janus had anticipated this. He opened his coat to reveal the explosives strapped to his chest, and turned to greet his assailants with a triumphant laugh before he blew himself up with them.

The transmission tower was not so far away. Within a moment, the explosive blast sent a violent shudder through the stony passage in which I stood, causing dust and ash to billow into the air and blot out the glow of halogen lighting. As the dust thickened, the world grew dark, and an ominous rumble came from the walls. Shouts rang out as the chamber buckled and heaved.

I gagged and choked, pushing forward as panicked bodies buffeted me. Finding a pocket of fresher air, I paused, blinking to make sure it was not my imagination—the dust was settling, the darkness receding. But a sudden rockfall sparked renewed panic around me, and I fought for my footing amid the people rushing to escape.

As the air once again cleared, I spied survivors scrambling for safety, trampling bodies as they fought to exit. My ears were ringing from the blast, but through that din, I caught the shrill screams of the trapped.

I stepped on someone's arm and instinctively reached down to drag the person up . . . and found myself hauling up a child no older than Atmas.

A cold horror washed over me. Nemesis lived, did she? What marvels she brought to the people! How many more atrocities would be committed in her name?

Hot determination surged through me. The crowd still flowed toward us, and I thrust myself in the opposite direction, my sheer physical power keeping me upright against the tide of bodies. I reached down amid kicking legs and hauled out those who were trapped beneath the feet of others. Then I forged forward and sought those in greater peril, crushed beneath the displaced rock, crushed against the ground, suffocating.

There were cries of gratitude from those whom I liberated, but I ignored them, surging ahead to free the next, and the next.

After an immeasurable time, I emerged from my trance and found the skin of my hands scraped bloody, my lungs raw from the toxic, gritty air. Those still half-buried were blue and clearly dead. There was nobody else to save.

I rubbed my bloodied hands on my trousers, aware now of the heavy silence engulfing this chamber.

That silence was animate: it was the deliberate, hushed silence of a hundred observers or more, all of them watching me with charged expressions, stricken or reverent or wondering.

They had witnessed my strength. Watched me lift debris too heavy for a human to hoist.

With Janus's words ringing in their ears, and my image fresh in their minds, they knew exactly who I was.

Some broke into tears, then, and sagged to their knees. Others gawked, their lips forming words that their ragged breath could not carry.

And yet some still found the strength to speak them.

"Nemesis lives."

"Nemesis."

"Nemesis lives!"

I swallowed what tasted like blood. It would be *their* blood, soon enough, if they spread word of what they had seen today.

And they would. People could not hold their tongues.

At least I could be away from the sight of these kneeling people, the onrush of attention sure to follow.

"Stay away," I said unsteadily. "*All* of you." Then I whipped around and left them there, moving as quickly as I could through my aches and pains.

A clock had just begun ticking. Tyrus would learn I was alive, and he would come after me.

From now on, I would be hunted.

The Excess learned where Anguish and I lived. They thronged the corridor outside the Obsidian Tower Dwellings, eager for a glimpse of me.

It was a disaster.

I did not intend to speak to any of them. Not to the crowd of miners who gathered outside our dwelling to call for me to emerge, not even to the Viceroy who cleared her way through the crowd to officially seek an introduction. She tapped on the door until I shouted through it, "Begone or I will kill you!"

That sent her away.

I drew the window slats to block out the sight of the ever-growing crowd. By nightfall, it seemed that the entire population of Devil's Shade had pressed its way into the mine shaft to catch a glimpse of the one fabled to be Nemesis. *The* Nemesis.

Our intercom chimed relentlessly, disturbing Anguish from his restless slumber.

"What is happening?" Anguish said to me hazily. He tried to push himself upright but fell again, his sheet matted with sweat.

My gaze swept over his graying skin, his sunken cheeks, and the sickening yellow sheen now creeping into the whites of his eyes.

"Nothing, Anguish. Go back to sleep."

59

Then I turned to the intercom and smashed it with the butt of my blasting rifle.

When more hands began to knock, and then pound on the door, I lost patience, aimed my rifle toward it, and shot at the wall—too high for anyone's head.

The weapon's punctures did what my words could not.

No one knocked again for several hours.

I fell asleep facing the door, rifle in my arms, Anguish's deep breathing the only sound in the room with me. There was no moving him, and no hope of escape. Spaceworthy vessels would not arrive until the formal transport window three weeks from now.

It was just a matter of waiting here in our dwelling until Tyrus's forces reached us.

After a time, I crawled into the bed next to Anguish and rested my head on his shoulder, the way we'd sometimes done before his illness, back in those months after Corcyra. We'd taken his pod to a small moon and avoided humans altogether while I healed, roving abandoned wilderness areas, sleeping in the open with the stars above us, killing and devouring prey that we roasted over primitive, wood-fed fires.

Nostalgia was a strange emotion, not one I'd often felt before. But it filled me now, a sweet, gnawing, poisonous ache. That had been an easier time. We hadn't spoken much—speech had come to seem superfluous, a distinctly human affectation. With looks alone, we communicated everything necessary. Two Diabolics, in our very own wilderness far removed from the moon's human settlers, alone beneath a vast sky.

That the wilderness could feel like our proper place had taken me by surprise. We had both been born and raised in the sterile environs of space, and at first, the changing weather, the rain and humidity, had seemed like affronts. The sun tormented my unpigmented skin. Anguish loathed the biting insects.

But we adjusted. Anguish grew indifferent to the stings. I found a soothing soil that, mixed with water, protected me from the scorching blaze of the white dwarf star overhead.

What a luxury to smell the fragrance of flowers in the wind. To step on living ground, and watch the rain water it into green abundance.

One night, as a fire crackled between us, Anguish spoke my own thoughts.

"I understand the Excess at last. I see why the Partisans coveted their own planets. A ship does not compare."

No, it did not.

I had learned to sleep peacefully through evenings rattled by wind through trees. But Anguish did not rest so easily. Sometimes, at night, he'd murmured Neveni's name. When his dreams woke me, I'd watch his face and feel the stirring of empathy.

Diabolics were not supposed to be able to love. But Anguish and I had both learned differently, to our sorrow, with Neveni and Tyrus.

But now—to our joy, because we had become a family. Like a brother and sister, linked by blood and our shared nightmares, our shared heartbreak.

I closed my eyes now and listened to his breathing, shallow and rapid even in his sleep. My breathing wanted to match his. Had I had the power, I would have given my own life's blood to restore his health.

Instead my actions today had damned us both.

Oh, what did it matter? Really, what difference did it make that I had been exposed?

We were at the end of a road. We had been approaching it since he first began to lose his memory, to forget the details, to stumble and fall when walking.

I have done everything in my power to save you, Anguish. I swear it, I thought. *And now, if need be, I will die by your side.*

A tentative tap at the door sliced through my sleep, and my eyes snapped open. . . . The silence reverberated. The crowd had dispersed, it seemed.

"Nym? Empress Nemesis?"

I knew that small voice.

Oh no.

My gaze flew toward the door. It could be a trap. Maybe someone had ascertained that I knew this irritating child and had coerced her into coming here.

And yet . . . she *was* here, and if she was waiting with a weapon to her head, I could make certain it was removed. I drew my rifle and prowled over to the door, then slapped it open and aimed.

6

JUST THE TWO of them. Alone. Atmas gave a squeak and ducked behind her father.

"S-sorry. I'm sorry," stammered the nervous Stalis—the overseer of the acid ponds who'd paid me little mind until now.

Fool! "Why would you come here?" I glanced down the empty corridor. The hall was never empty. The rest of the Obsidian Tower Dwellings had been evacuated by the Viceroy, whether in fear of me or in deference to me, I knew not. "Who sent you?"

"We came on our own. My cousin does maintenance here." He took a deep breath. "My daughter was desperate to see you, Your Supremacy."

Nonsense. I did not believe for a moment that this man had risked dire consequences just to satisfy his child's stupid wish. But I lowered my weapon, nodded for them to enter, and closed the door behind them.

Stalis had brought my last week's wages, along with a satchel of dried eel. He darted a nervous glance toward the visibly ill Anguish, then offered to prepare a stew. Atmas, meanwhile, stood staring up at me with wide, awestruck eyes.

"What are you looking at?" I asked her, torn between irritation and that inexplicable, unwilling affection that she stirred in me. "Make yourself useful by helping your father. The heating unit's in the corner," I said to Stalis, pointing the way to our small kitchen. After all, Anguish could use the nourishment.

"Are you really the Empress Nemesis?" said Atmas. Her eyes took in my scarred face, seeing the truth of me now.

I touched it self-consciously. Strange how exposed I felt. "Yes."

"I knew it!" she cried. "I always knew!"

"Oh, certainly," I said, doubting her.

"Can I ask why you're here?" called Stalis abruptly, and clanged an empty pot into the sink, before turning on the water to fill it. "The rumors are—"

"All inaccurate," I bit out.

"Not all of them," he said. "You're alive."

"'Nemesis lives.'" My bitter tone startled him, which did nothing to help my temper. "That is the only fact that people have right. The Partisans blew me up, Stalis. It's why my face looks this way. My own husband tried to kill me. *Me*, not an imposter. If there were a single spaceworthy transport on this sun-scorned planet, I would already be gone. You're a fool to have come here. Leave now, and pretend you never knew me. Otherwise, you may die with me."

He'd finished depositing the eels and a collection of dried vegetables into the simmering water. Now he turned and stepped back from the convection plate. "Your Supremacy . . ." Visibly gathering his resolve, he said, "You can stop him."

A laugh scraped from me. "Is that so?"

"You must see the Emperor has gone mad," Stalis said, desperate. "He creates malignant space. He demands we worship him. . . ."

"I know." The words barely escaped my lips. I knew all too well.

"You're the only one who can speak against him. People will listen to you!"

The stew had begun simmering, casting the sulfurous scent of the eel into the air. "People will take up arms if *you* ask it of them."

"The Partisans have asked it of them for centuries."

"No one believes in the Partisans. They're terrorists. People believe in *you*."

"Oh, they *believe* in me, do they?" He flinched from my sneer, and I felt no pity for scaring him. "So you suggest I reward their faith by leading them to their deaths—is that it?"

"I—"

"You have no idea of the power you are up against! There is no glorious victory in a futile cause. There is no revolution possible against an Emperor with electronic eyes that watch your every move, machines that he can summon with a thought, a fleet of massive warships—"

"But *you are alive*," he cried. "You live. You have evaded him. Escaped him. *Survived* him!"

"Until now," I said flatly. "I have no weapons. Not even a ship. If you want to do something useful, Stalis, then tend to your daughter. Protect her. Hide with her far away from me, whatever happens."

His eyes fell upon the counter by the stove and halted there. It took me a moment to follow his gaze, to see what he was looking upon. . . .

The pile of drawings Atmas had given me over time.

I cursed inwardly at myself, for not throwing those away.

They seemed to give Stalis courage. He stepped around the stove, walked toward me with a square-shouldered courage that few men had ever shown a Diabolic. "What about Atmas? My daughter has no future in an Empire where we must call Tyrus von Domitrian our *God*. Don't you see? We are people of faith. We won't profane ourselves for a mere Emperor. How long do you think we will remain safe?"

I closed my eyes. Perhaps he was right: Devil's Shade would never have been safe forever. But my actions today had ensured that the danger would arrive sooner than even Stalis imagined.

"Stop this," he pleaded. "End this. You are our only chance."

Others had said similar things, once. They had called me their only hope, and they had sent me to Corcyra, to assassinate Tyrus.

And I had failed them utterly.

Even now, looking at these two members of the Excess who would live and die at his whims, I could feel no hatred for Tyrus, only a crushing remorse at his desecration.

We'd vowed to make this galaxy better.

He'd had such beautiful dreams.

How to salvage a dream, when the dreamer himself had been destroyed?

Stalis looked at me with exhausted, tearful, impassioned hope. But when I contemplated the size of this Empire, a helplessness washed over me. How arrogant we'd been to imagine that even an Emperor and Empress could reform something so vast.

Act to change things? I couldn't even bring myself to kill Tyrus after what he'd done to me.

"You need to leave," I said. "Now."

He gave a noise of objection, but I didn't let him voice it. I seized him, dragged him to the door, and hurled him out. Then I turned on Atmas and gave a single jab with my thumb.

"Out."

She stared at me, lip jutting mutinously. "Daddy said you would fix things."

"For Helios's sake," I cried. "Atmas, your father knows nothing. Everyone wishes someone would come and save them, and no one ever does."

"But you're Nemesis."

I approached and took hold of her shoulders, fighting the temptation to shake her until she let go of the ludicrous notions that adults had been pouring into her head. "Don't you understand that if you wait for a hero to come and solve your problems, nothing will ever change? Some problems are too large for a single person. Expect nothing of people—especially me."

Her eyes grew glassy with tears. I fought an odd, deranged need to apologize—to temper my tone and speak falsehoods to her. *I'm sorry. It will all be well, I promise. There's no need for you to worry.*

Instead I steered her to the door and nudged her out after her father. He refused to look at me, and so I grabbed his hand and stuffed the wage chips into his palm.

"I won't need them now," I said, then pulled the door shut.

The quiet sank around me. Anguish lay as still as a corpse at the center of a tomb.

Save him? Help *them*? Rescue the Empire? Absurd.

I couldn't even save myself.

Anguish and I did not have long to wait. We could not escape the planet, and his deteriorating condition would have made it nearly impossible to scout out a hiding place, had there even been one that could evade the Emperor's all-seeing machines. Instead I gathered our scant supply of weapons and waited for the attack to come. Tyrus, I assumed, would have received word of my reappearance within minutes of it occurring.

I was correct.

Days later, we awoke to an alarm ringing through the mining complex, and shouts outside. I swiped up my pulse rifle and rushed to the window. A single glimpse at the stone corridor outside showed security bots soaring through Harvester Row, headed our way.

My hand found Anguish's shoulder where he remained in his deep, fitful sleep. With grief knotting in my throat, I shook him awake. I helped him sit up, helped him rest against the wall behind him.

I gripped his face. "Anguish, they've come for us."

"Today?" He slurred the word, his eyes unable to maintain focus on my face.

My heart sank. He would be little help.

"Yes," I said, "today." I dug under the bed for the second pulse rifle and placed it into his uncertain grip.

Together we waited, listening to the mounting clamor outside, the shouts and heavy footsteps, the drone and hum of machinery. The noises grew louder and louder, closer and closer—

A laser sliced through the wall before us.

Anguish and I both tensed, weapons in hand. Blood surged through my veins, hot and eager. It was time.

More lasers seared through the wall, opening a fissure. The first of the star-shaped security bots erupted into the room. I raised my pulse rifle to unload fire into it.

Anguish collapsed.

He fell with a heavy thump, his pulse rifle sliding away from his limp, splayed hand.

My own hand froze around the trigger.

If I was alone, survival meant nothing. The fight ahead meant nothing.

I threw myself down over him to shield him with my last breath.

The bots veered toward us, their lasers locking onto me, and I did not care. What good was a fight without something to defend? Even Diabolics needed love to power our hate.

I held tight to Anguish, covering him with my body, and closed my eyes to await the end. I had faced worse deaths than this, in my past. I would be glad to go while shielding the last soul in this universe who meant anything to me.

But after a moment, as the bots continued to buzz overhead and I continued to breathe, puzzlement forced my eyes open. I peered up at the metal phalanx of dozens of machines humming overhead, their dark-mouthed barrels fixed on me, poised to discharge a murderous volley.

Still they did not fire.

Movement drew my gaze to the hole torn in the wall. Through it stepped a woman wearing robes blacker than night. Several men followed hard on her heels.

They wore the Inquisitor garb, called the Dark Star, dress for the ruthless sect of vicars who did violence in the name of the divine Cosmos. The robes' material absorbed all light, rendering it blacker than black. Within sheaths strapped high on their backs, an array of blades jutted out, like the rays of a sun.

And yet, though the machines pointed weapons at me and the Inquisitors assembled themselves like vicious shadows, only two drew their blades in readiness.

The first of them stepped toward me and took the lead.

"I come with a gift," she said in a low, deep voice. From her pocket, she withdrew a glinting black screenlet. With a flick of her finger, a tiny holographic image bloomed to life over the screenlet's gleaming surface.

Tyrus, in full imperial regalia, his hair formally arranged in a halo, his eyes like ice. *This is a message for the imposter.*

His voice was as cold as his face. I felt the Inquisitor's eyes, intent and malevolent.

"I demand your presence in person. You are ordered to accompany these Inquisitors. They will escort you to me. Resist, and there will be consequences."

"Consequences?" I said to the Inquisitors.

The female Inquisitor merely dropped her gaze to Anguish on the ground. "We take you by force. And leave your companion behind."

I clenched my fists.

"Or," she said, "we preserve his life."

"If I go with you, you'll treat him."

"If the Divine Emperor wills it," she said.

"You will treat him or I will not go."

"His life will be preserved. His fate belongs to the Divine Emperor. As does yours."

"You would obey the *Divine* Emperor in everything," I sneered, "you servant of the Living Cosmos. Are you a true vicar, or one of the mercenaries he used to mutilate them into granting him his scepter?"

Her face was like stone, not even a flinch of recognition at the odious way Tyrus had forced the vicars of the Empire to at last give him the Domitrian power over machines. He'd hunted them down one-by-one, and the mercenaries had taken either their hands—with the diode of a vicar's authority in them—or their heads.

"I am a subject of this Empire," she answered simply, "and my fate belongs to the Divine Emperor as well."

In other words, she knew he could choose to kill her if she did not secure me. There was only one person with power, and he was nowhere near this planet. The fight died away from me.

I sat up cautiously, never moving away from Anguish, who lay limply, breathing in ragged, choking gasps.

"I'll go with you," I said. "Just keep my friend breathing."

7

THE JAUNT through hyperspace was mere days, but it felt like weeks. I remained by Anguish's side, where the medical bots on the ship had placed him into stasis to put a halt to his degeneration.

I was sitting next to Anguish, dozing, when the Inquisitor's ship jostled and roused me awake. Out the window, I could see the *Alexandria* had arrived. It was Tyrus's own vessel, a jutting tip of a spear looming vast and sleek against the starscape, dwarfing the Inquisitor's vessel.

In mere minutes, the doors to the medical bay slid open to admit a half-dozen machines. I'd expected the star-shaped security machines, but in poured a mass of spherical beauty bots.

Following in their wake came Shaezar nan Domitrian, the lavishly self-decorated royal servant whose sole job was to beautify public figures for state occasions.

"I am to prepare you to meet the Divine—"

Shaezar jerked to a startled stop at the sight of me. His amazed survey cataloged each aspect of my altered appearance: the scars twisting over my face, the pink patches of scalp where my hair had been permanently burned away, the defined and bulging musculature that had replaced my once lean and wiry arms. He obviously had not been warned about the immensity of the task at hand.

I folded my arms and leaned back in my seat. "You intend to beautify me? I fear you'll be kept busy today."

"Stars, I see you've . . . been living roughly."

I just gazed at him flatly. "Get on with it, then."

Shaezar began to work on me. The medical bots swept over my scarring with lasers, stripping away the damaged skin with a stinging precision, and then running green, tingling beams over my face to stimulate the growth of pristine skin cells that would replace the scar tissue. Feeling prickled back into regenerated nerve endings.

I opened and closed my jaw, over and over, rubbing my fingers over my cheeks as Shaezar's bots turned their attention to the burn scars down my shoulders, arms, and back. Everything felt like it was tingling. It was strange to recover sensation where I'd grown used to the masklike numbness of scars.

Questions raged in the back of my mind about the intention behind restoring me to a pristine appearance. Did the Divine Emperor simply require everything that met his eyes to be beautiful? Or was this a signal that he did not intend to summarily execute me? He'd brought me here for some purpose. The Inquisitors could have swarmed me with bots and taken me by force, but instead they'd been specifically tasked with ensuring my cooperation. Why?

Tyrus wished to behold me, so security bots came not to escort me, but to array themselves with their lasers aimed at Anguish . . . Eight bots for a comatose Diabolic.

A pair of Domitrian servants, lavishly dressed in golden liquisilk, were there to bring me to him. They led me in silence to the boarding artery leading to the *Alexandria*.

"I know the way from here," I told them, but they tailed me all the way to the Emperor's private chambers.

I stepped through those familiar doors into Tyrus's private study onboard the *Alexandria*, with its crackling fireplace and blooms of vegetation. The smell struck me first, heady and intoxicating, a blend of fire-flowers and burning cedar, so intimately familiar that my treacherous heart flipped in my chest. This was the scent of memories I had tried to forget, the days and nights on this vessel when Tyrus and I had first discovered our feelings for each other, had first touched each other, had kissed as we lifted away from the vivid purple atmosphere of Lumina. . . .

I could not afford these memories.

I forced them down, away, to some hard, cold place deep inside me, where I hoped they would be crushed into dust.

As I surveyed the chamber, I could see signs of vandalism, only partially mended. After capturing Tyrus, Pasus had handed this vessel to supporters, who had scrawled lewd artworks across the walls that laser repair had not managed to fully efface. Elsewhere, the wall had been violently slashed and gouged.

This chamber had once been Tyrus's pride and joy, his retreat from a murderous family whose conspiracies imprisoned him as thoroughly as he now imprisoned me. It sank into me again, that temptation not to hate him, but to feel profound sadness for what he might have been.

I passed Tyrus's fireplace and indulged in the desperate thought of seizing a burning log and setting fire to this haunted place.

When I stepped into the adjoining chamber, the hush that met my ears was deceptive. At first my senses were fooled into believing the chamber empty.

And then my eyes adjusted to the sudden dimness and I made out his starlight-shrouded form, his back to me, where he stood before the window, utterly still but for a ring he turned in his finger over and over again.

My every muscle tensed, grew tight.

He did not turn.

Even as I stepped fully into the chamber and the air split with the hiss of the door sliding shut behind me, he did not stir. Instead he remained there, a tall, tense form, seemingly oblivious to me.

My awareness widened. Beside me gleamed an array of sharpened blades magnetically fixed to the wall.

No security bots hovered. No guards lurked to protect him.

He knew precisely what temptation he offered me here. I stood five meters away, within easy reach of weaponry, while he steadfastly ignored my presence, his vulnerable back exposed.

This had to be a test of some sort. There must be a force field between us, shielding him.

With my eyes locked on his back, I reached out and slid one of the blades out of its holster. The glinting metal threw shards of starlight across the walls.

Tyrus drew an audible breath, then tipped his head back to look at the ceiling. Had he caught sight of the blade's reflection?

In a low, husky voice, he said, "Go ahead."

My eyes narrowed. I raised the blade in readiness.

He turned as gracefully as a large cat, light on his feet, unhurried. His eyes were inscrutable. "Well? Why hesitate?"

I whipped the blade forward. He didn't flinch. It embedded itself in the wall between the windows, the handle vibrating musically. A few inches over, and I would have driven it through his skull.

Tyrus ripped it from the wall, considering it impassively. "You used to have better aim."

"There's no force field." I was stunned by the realization.

His lips twisted. He held the blade familiarly, casually, like an old friend. "I was certain I wouldn't need it."

Two years since I'd seen him last. The passage of time had left its mark on my husband's face. He looked hardened, older, in a way that no beauty bot could repair. He was dressed with meticulous elegance: a long oiled-leather coat over a liquisilk tunic, high boots, trousers tailored expertly to his narrow hips and muscular thighs.

"So," he said. "Nemesis lives."

I had once been able to read his moods, but now, even his voice sounded strange to me. Lower, rougher. A man's voice, a man's body. And a madman's mind.

"Don't blame yourself," I said. "You did your best to kill me."

"Your wounds are all healed, then. I am pleased I could do that for you." He scanned my face a long moment. "Though I miss your nose as it was. You straightened it."

"Why would you care?"

His slight smile either mocked me or pitied me. "Should a husband not care for his wife?"

"And here I thought I was an imposter."

"You're in my blood. We could be parted for centuries and I'll always recognize you. You were on Corcyra, of course. And since then . . . where else, besides Devil's Shade?"

"Nowhere notable." I spoke warily, unwilling to offer more information than necessary. If I were wise, I would not look at him at all. But a terrible curiosity had seized hold of me. Those shadows beneath his eyes—I had not imagined them. His jaw was squarer, sharper. He'd continued to subtly alter himself with beauty bots, lending his reddish hair more of a golden tint, smoothing his skin to a flawless mask.

But from the way he moved, I could verify that his musculature was genuine. He moved with a grace that spoke of intense physical discipline.

He'd resumed his rigorous physical training, then. My memories unwillingly rushed back to those many mornings we'd passed in sparring together. His enthusiasm had outstripped his skill in those days; it had been quite impossible for him to physically match me. But he'd laughed so good-naturedly when I bested him. He'd even seemed to admire my physical superiority.

A pang struck me. How had we come to this?

"It matters not where I've been," I said, shaking off the memories. "All that matters is that I am alive *despite* your best efforts. Unless you brought me here to change that."

"If I wanted you dead, you would already be dead. But you did not try to kill me on Corcyra, and after that happened, I began to . . . miss you. That's why you're here now. With me once more."

"I am not with you in anything but the purest physical sense."

"Would you like to be?" he said, arching his brows.

I sputtered incredulously, unable to muster a syllable.

"I have warranted your vengeance time and again, yet still you have not attempted to kill me when you've have the perfect opportunity. Just now—once again, you refrained. I think you still love me, Nemesis. Tell me I'm wrong."

"You're wrong."

He'd drawn close enough that I felt the heat of him, became unwillingly aware of the new breadth and muscled density of his body. There was nowhere safe to look. I lifted my eyes to his and found myself pinned by the intensity of his gaze.

"Hand me back the blade," I challenged him softly, "if you are so confident."

Tyrus smiled slowly, but did not take me up on the challenge. "It's touching. Whatever misdeeds I commit, what foul atrocities are put at my feet, you still feel a need to protect me. You speak to me right now as though you feel naught but hatred for me—but you only show me the sweetest devotion."

Heat burned through my face. How could I argue with him, how could I deny it?

"And now you blush," he said very softly, his hand reaching up—a calloused finger tracing down my cheek. I hated myself for the shudder it sent down my spine. "Just as a bashful lover might."

"I blush for shame." The words scraped out of me, the more painful for their truth. I loved him still, and it appalled me. I could hate him even as I loved him, for he was in my bones, in my soul. "I am ashamed that I cannot do the right thing and end your life."

He shrugged negligently. "You'll have other opportunities." Then he withdrew from me. "It's gratifying that you love me still. I see opportunities in this situation."

I fought the urge to step back from him, for my skin was crawling from his nearness. "Opportunities," I echoed flatly.

"Life without you is most tedious. It seems Gladdic von Aton did me a favor without realizing it, when he saved you. . . ."

Gladdic. He'd found out. My heart clenched. "Did you kill him for that?"

"On the contrary," said Tyrus. "I've given him a chance to win my favor back. Most lucrative chances."

"He serves you willingly after you tried to execute him?"

"He doesn't remember that. I gave him but a small dose of Scorpion's Breath after the ball dome. I could not abide him gibbering and quaking at the very sight of me."

He'd wiped Gladdic's memory of his near execution, then.

Of his own feat of heroism, saving me.

Tyrus caught the expression on my face. He missed nothing. "How concerned you are for your friends. Anguish as well." He tilted his head, his eyes growing very narrow and cold. "If he is your friend. Tell me, are you lovers?"

"Lovers? Are you asking if I love *Anguish*?" I forced out a laugh. "Yes, of course, two Diabolics in love—what could be more beautiful? Long romantic dinners after fighting each other bloody."

His eyes glinted. "I know you. That would be a riveting time."

"Don't be absurd. If you wanted him dead, you would not preserve him."

"Attachments are most inconvenient, are they not? Weaknesses so easily exploited. Misfolded proteins is a complicated, progressive ailment. There *are* a handful of medical bots in the Empire that could cure him, but . . ." He spread his hands.

My teeth ground together. "But the Divine Emperor does not have these bots."

"Oh, no," he said. "I have them securely in my possession. But I won't use them for free."

"What. Do. You. Want?"

All expression dropped from his face. "It's simple. I want you. You, Nemesis. Join me at my side once more. As my wife. As my Empress. Zeus needed Hera, and Caligula his Drusilla. I am now the God of this Empire. You will be its goddess."

"I would sooner die," I said with a harsh laugh.

"Naturally, but would you sooner Anguish died?"

That silenced me.

He studied me with a calculating glitter in his eyes. "Yes, I know you. A Diabolic to the marrow of your bones. You'll preserve what you love—at all costs. Even to dignity. Even to one's very soul."

"This is vengeance on me, isn't this?" I murmured darkly. "For the *Tigris*. You will never forgive me for that. Now you demand my integrity."

"More than that, my love. I want your soul. I've already lost mine. Join me in a beautiful, shared damnation—and this entire galaxy will fall prostrate at our feet."

8

THE FIRST TIME Tyrus and I kissed, it had awakened some-thing in me, a sign that there was more humanity within me than I'd realized. No technician would have thought to engineer passion into a Diabolic. But it had swept me like a fever.

I had been ill ever since, to this very day.

At the time, it had seemed more miracle than sickness. Finding something in myself that was born of nature, not engineering, seemed a sign that the vicars were wrong and Sidonia was correct: I was not some soulless creature but a person like any other.

I walked ahead of the servants and made a hasty retreat from the *Alexandria*, mindless steps aimed clumsily back toward Anguish. A despair the likes of which I had never felt seemed to be gripping me.

For he was truly lost. He was lost. There was some monster wear-ing Tyrus's face, speaking with his voice, existing in his body, and what he now demanded of me was intolerable.

And I had to obey him.

It felt as though a great abyss was yawning open below me, for I could see no choices before me. There was no escape. To refuse meant destroying Anguish.

To agree . . .

To agree meant destroying everything I valued in myself.

My throat felt like it was squeezing tighter and tighter, my chest constricting, my eyes beginning to sting. . . .

And then I felt it.

A slipping of moisture down my cheeks.

My steps jerked to a halt and my hand flew up to my cheek. I snatched my fingers away to see the redness, but all I could see on my fingers was a glistening of clear liquid. For a moment of dumb shock, I stared at my hand, trying to understand what I was seeing.

This was . . . These were tears.

Tears.

Shaezar nan Domitrian awaited me in the medical bay, ready to reclaim the gown he'd placed on me for the meeting. I greeted him by seizing his neck and ramming him back into the wall.

"What have you done to me?" I roared at him.

When his wide, uncomprehending eyes met mine, I pointed to my eyes accusingly. . . . For even now they blurred and welled with more liquid.

He choked out a garbled reply, and I remembered abruptly through the rage pounding in my temples that he required air. So I released him and thrust him to the ground, where he tumbled onto his hands and knees.

"I am sorry . . . I didn't intend to . . ."

His panicked explanation spilled out: It must have been a function of the medical bots. When they repaired my burned skin, my damaged nerves, they'd regenerated all that *should* have been there—were I but a normal person.

Including a capacity most humans had that the genetic engineers had intentionally removed from Diabolics: the ability to weep.

"I can remove it," he pleaded with me.

I tore off the gown and flung it to the floor. "Just begone from my sight."

This was the last thing I needed to deal with right now. Tears. Blasted tears. They continued to trickle down my cheeks after he was gone, after it was just me at the sleeping Anguish's side once more, listening to his breathing.

Tears. Such a strange sensation. They made me feel exposed, painfully raw—as though there were nowhere to hide, even when alone. I would pay any price to be but a Diabolic again rather than expose myself this way. It felt like I'd been perforated, cracked up, my very guts exposed to the air. However I wiped the tears away, they continued to streak down my cheeks.

And yet there was something . . . strangely satisfying about the feeling. Like some poison was seeping out of me.

My bitterness and despair were blunted, and I sagged down to rest my head against Anguish's shoulder, feeling drained of life.

I awoke to the medical bay doors opening. A coterie of bots floated through, trailed by a Domitrian servant.

"The Divine Emperor has ordered a preliminary treatment for your . . . companion."

I sat up warily. My fists clenched and unclenched. "You don't mean to cure him?"

"A sweeping of his system to remove . . . many of the damaged proteins."

"Not all?"

"The Divine Emperor does not wish—"

Of course he didn't wish Anguish cured. He wouldn't forfeit his leverage, but I hugged my arms over my chest and stepped back from the bedside, glad for whatever treatment I could get for my last friend—for my brother.

The tears ceased entirely as I watched the bots hover over Anguish, small injectors pricking his skin, funneling out the blood through his veins and purifying it, before injecting it once more.

And then, at last, Anguish stirred.

It had been months since I'd glimpsed such clarity in his eyes. I hastened to his bedside as his lashes fluttered open. His gaze found mine—then widened in alarm.

He snapped upright, his muscles tense beneath his rich brown skin. "Where . . . ?" He seized my arm, and I inwardly rejoiced at his speed and the strength of his grip. "Are you all right?"

"We're onboard the *Alexandria*." I covered his hand with mine. "There are security bots in the corners with lasers locked on you, so do not move too quickly."

His dark gaze scanned overhead, finding each of those star-shaped metal bots where they hovered throughout the medical chamber.

Calculating intelligence glittered in his eyes. Here was the Anguish of old: I knew he'd already ascertained the best means of evading their beams, of destroying them before they could harm us.

I squeezed his hand, noting how quickly his pulse raced. "It's fine. We're safe. There's a . . . a deal for your restored health."

"A deal?" He eased away from me but did not lie back. "What kind of deal?"

"How are you feeling?"

In answer, he flexed his muscles, testing limbs that had betrayed him in recent months. What he felt must have pleased him, for he surged off the bed and rose to his full height.

"I feel . . . that I could kill a ship full of Domitrian lackeys."

I restrained my answering grin. In those words was a suggestion, an invitation. If I gave the gesture, he was primed and ready to seize this vessel.

Not yet. I gave a subtle shake of my head. "Your system was swept, the defective proteins removed in great numbers. . . . But not all of them. They'll spread and multiply again."

His eyes narrowed. "Unless . . . ?"

"The Emperor decides." I could not speak his name. "He expects something of me."

He nodded once, his jaw tight. He'd been treated, but not cured. "What?"

This would be harder to explain. I turned to stare out at the stars, so many that one might imagine them ungovernable—unless one had the hubris of a god. "You won't believe it," I said. And then I told him of Tyrus's demand.

As I spoke the words, those accursed new tear ducts welled once more, and Anguish stared, aghast, as my eyes overflowed. He interrupted me by catching my arms, drawing me closer to him. "Your face is healed, but . . . you weep. What has been done to you?"

"They're merely tears," I snapped, impatient with myself. "The bots that fixed my face gave me the capacity. I suppose I should get it removed again."

In fact, a powerful urge gripped me to use these medical bots right now to remove these glands, but . . .

But I could not issue the order.

Instead I prowled away from Anguish and searched for something, anything, to vent my anger upon. I drove my fist into the nearest thing I found—a ceramic statue of Tyrus's great-grandmother, the Empress Acindra.

Her fine nose shattered at my blow, and the answering pain that slammed up my arm did little to assist with the weeping, but it at least gave more reason for my damnable eyes to tear up than the agony twisting in my chest.

It also caused the Domitrian servant to scurry out, the medical bots trailing him. I waited until the doors slid closed to speak again.

"I should be able to stop them on my own," I told Anguish, "without removing the capacity altogether. Humans can do it." I'd seen Tyrus fight them back many times—especially in those early days we were in Pasus's control.

"Distract yourself," Anguish suggested.

"I have tried," I said through my teeth, my throbbing fist clenching and unclenching as I paced the narrow confines of the secured medical bay.

Trying to be helpful, perhaps, Anguish approached me, and then dealt me a backhand.

In a flash, I punched him back, and then for a moment we both froze, staring at each other, gasping raggedly for breath.

He broke into a slow, broad smile, and a savage grin came to my lips, for a sudden burst of happiness surged in my chest. He had received my blow—and kept upright. He was healthy enough to endure it!

I stepped forward to throw my arms around him, and then I remembered the look on Tyrus's face, demanding to know whether we were lovers. . . . Anguish's arms had risen, and now I quickly evaded them, alarm for him driving away the impulse.

"How long will this treatment last?" Anguish said.

"I don't know," I admitted.

Tyrus had not removed all the corrupted proteins. They remained like a cancer, ready to spread once more and overtake his system, in case I changed my mind and ceased to cooperate. Fail to play a goddess, and Anguish would succumb and relapse into that listless, delirious state if his illness took its course. All the rage and frustration ripping through me blazed hotter, for the very sight of his health in bloom once more warned me to do exactly what Tyrus commanded. What alternative did I have?

"There they go again," marveled Anguish, and indeed, the sun-scorned blurriness of moisture had welled in my eyes once more.

"This is infuriating!" I snarled, dashing my sleeve across my eyes. The angrier and more helpless I felt, the more the tears overflowed. "Humans don't weep at every hint of dismay. Why can't I stop this?"

"The Grandeé Devineé's child used to weep often," Anguish remarked. "The child would weep too much. She shouted at it oftentimes. Sometimes slapped it. Sometimes the child would stop crying."

"Sometimes."

"It rarely worked," Anguish admitted. "The child just as often wept harder."

"I didn't realize Devinee and Salivar had any heirs." I shook my head, and the distraction had slowed the flow of moisture once more. "Perhaps the child realized their parents were perverse rapists. I understand why they wept."

"By the time you were at court, they did not have an heir anymore."

Of course. Another murdered Domitrian. "Was it Cygna or Devineé herself?"

He shifted his gaze away from mine. "It was me. The Grandeé Cygna wished it."

The breath seemed stolen from me. "She ordered you to kill a child."

His jaw tensed. He averted his gaze. "I made it quick. Painless. She did not order that."

I stopped myself from saying another word. I almost asked him: *What threat does a child pose? Didn't you question the order?*

But I knew the answer: no, we were Diabolics.

Just as Tyrus said, we were engineered to save those we loved. And that was all.

I'd been luckier than Anguish in the choices I had to make to do that. At least until now. The nightmare of my childhood in the corrals had ended with Sidonia, the most beautiful and gentle of souls, who would have taken a blade to herself before harming some innocent creature. She would never have asked something so profane of me. She would never have tainted me with such a cruel task.

Tyrus's grandmother, Cygna . . . She had not cared to keep her Diabolics stainless. She would not have given a second thought to such a profanity. Anguish had fallen into her possession and she used him as she used any weapon, for the infliction of violence upon others, for he'd been nothing more than another tool to her.

A child Domitrian was easier to kill than a grown adult.

Anguish may have done this for her gladly.

It was the curse of a Diabolic—to love others more than ourselves. To serve the interests of a master and sacrifice whatever they required, for after all, we were nothing outside of the service we rendered. Since finding me again, Tyrus had reminded me at every turn of my failure to act on my grievances against him, all the while exploiting the reason for this.

This curse was the reason Tyrus felt so confident I would never harm him. A Diabolic's love was not something sweet, something gentle. It was possessive, ferocious, all-consuming. I found myself thinking of that nameless child, long dead because of a Diabolic's love for his master. Our love was crafted for violence, for the infliction of evil.

And I still loved Tyrus. Not who he was now, but who he had been, and all I could think about was the evil of its power over me. Perhaps I would never be free of it.

9

WE WERE PARTING within hours, to reunite publicly at his Imperial Triumph. He summoned me to his study.

I found him once again staring out at the stars. His hands were planted on the sill of the window, and he leaned forward that way, his head centimeters from the clear diamond. For a moment, I just waited for him to register my presence.

And then I asked, "What is it out there that transfixes you so?"

He straightened up without turning. "It's not what's out there, but what's in here." He gestured vaguely to his temples. "Since I claimed the scepter, at all hours of the day, there is a buzzing in my mind. A sea of machines across this Empire are linked to a central network that feeds directly into my thoughts."

"You hear them all at once?"

"But the noise, not the substance." He slanted me back a long, searching look—as though inwardly debating what to tell me. After a moment, a shrug. "I receive intelligible information only from those directly before my sight, or sometimes in the same star system, if I focus upon them intently. There are other factors at play. A nebula, an active star, the like, can all distort the information." After a pause, his face cleared, and he said, "I have a gift for you."

He swung back around to gaze out the window, and then—responding to his thoughts—a starship swerved into sight and gracefully arced toward us, coming to a halt just outside the window so we might look upon it.

It looked fast and sleek, with a jutting triangular shape, like the tip of a spear.

"Consider it yours," Tyrus told me. "I constructed it out of the remains of the *Colossus*."

Pasus's vessel. The one I had destroyed with the *Hera*. I drew toward the window, and despite my wariness and mistrust of my benefactor, his gift pleased me. It was all that remained of our mutual enemy, who had tried so hard to kill us both.

"It's called the *Retribution*," Tyrus murmured.

An unwilling smile curled my lips. "A fine name."

As it turned out, Tyrus meant me to arrive in this ship to the Imperial Triumph on the *Halcyon*—the setting for my public return. Tyrus had invented the holiday. The entire event was a tribute to himself, and he'd imposed the first of the festivities last year.

It was a celebration of the Divine Emperor's ascent to godhood.

"And I have full command over it?" I said.

"You're keyed in as the ship's master."

I slid him a mistrustful look.

"I've told you, Nemesis, I want your cooperation. Our reunion needn't be painful."

"Heal Anguish and release him. Then I will be a perfect friend to you."

He cast me a mocking look. "Ah, yes, forfeit my leverage. Very wise."

I stepped closer to him. So close, his muscles tensed as though in anticipation of attack. So close, I could feel the heat of his body in the air between us.

"I don't think you even believe yourself a god, Tyrus," I whispered to him, though none were here but us. "I think you are playing a game for your enjoyment, forcing this galaxy to grovel to you like one. You're a con man."

He leaned down toward me, his eyes dancing with a cruel sort of glee. "In that case, I'd be more than a con man. I'd be a propagandist. A tyrant. A dictator."

"And sickeningly unashamed."

"Oh, I feel quite clever," he said cruelly. "My reforms were foiled by religion. So I have reformed the religion itself. *I* am now the divine authority. It's a remarkably powerful tool, divine authority. I have believers now. Actual believers who cling to every word I say. Don't you see why we failed, Nemesis, when we dreamed of creating a better galaxy?"

"We failed," I said through my teeth, "because we *did not know* the theory of relativity. That was *it*. Tyrus, it all would have happened differently but for *that*."

A wistful look passed over him. "No. We would have failed, either way. Every institution and tradition resists change for a reason: their very survival *depends* on things remaining as they are. If we had overcome the Grandiloquy, do you think we would have triumphed? No. We would have had to face all their co-conspirators among the Excess who helped them reinforce the status quo."

"You impose a falsehood upon this galaxy," I said. "Reality itself will undermine you."

"Reality has no power against a collective delusion," he said. "Every system is essentially a vast, shared delusion that exists merely because everyone has agreed to believe in it. The whole reason there's power in such a thing is because most people *want* to believe in the same thing all those about them seem to believe. And sometimes those delusions are blatant mistruths, but it doesn't change matters. Some will be outright fooled by their own brains into genuinely embracing a collective mistruth. As long as they are fashionable, and they are in fashion by believing it, people will uphold any falsehood proudly, for doing so makes them *belong*."

He swung around and began pacing. "*This* is what we missed before, Nemesis. You and I tried to do away with falsehoods altogether. We wished the body of this Empire to swallow unpalatable truths when the vast majority of human beings crave conformity to shared lies. We should have been crafting a falsehood that suited us as I have now done."

"You cannot fool everyone. There are Excess who see through you."

"I know. They invoke your name." Tyrus's grin was malicious. "You are the hope of the dissidents. They long for *you* to rise up and speak for them. They pray for your voice to speak the questions they cannot make heard, for you to put doubts in those who otherwise would simply believe. And this is why, tomorrow, you will shatter their hopes—when you publicly cast your lot with me. Imagine what it will do to these restive few, this irate and tireless minority, when they see *you* playing goddess at my side. I cannot silence them, Nemesis. But *you* can."

My heart gave a curious twist, though I could not say why. I *wanted* them to stop revering me. I *wanted* them to stop placing their hopes in me. I knew I could never fulfill those hopes.

Yet suddenly I understood what I would be doing to them. This was worse than ignoring them, than disavowing them entirely.

I would be crushing them.

Despite myself, I thought of Stalis begging me to help the Excess.

And then I thought of Atmas.

What would it do to her, when she'd had such an attachment to me, to see me playing God at Tyrus's side?

She knew who I was. She had believed in me, in a way. . . . Not in Nemesis the legend, but in the Nym who'd looked at her drawings and talked to her about the stars by the acid pools.

What would it do to her to see me as a Tributary Statue beside Tyrus's, proclaimed as a false goddess, playing the same cruel joke as he? What would it cost her to see a woman she had considered a friend turned into the face of her own oppression?

The years of her life seemed to rush before my eyes.

I could see her growing up walking past Harvester Row, growing into a teenager who was too accustomed to the horrors of that place to be properly afraid of them. They paid a premium for the blood of the young. Perhaps the prospect of credits would tempt her to donate her blood or body. Her father would surely warn her off, but what if she did not listen to him? What if she grew up amid those stone confines, gazing up at the vast and glowing image of that Divine Emperor and Empress she was compelled to revere, and knew at so young an age that no one could be trusted, that the foundation of everything was a lie. . . .

Would she begin to notice how narrow her world was, how little hope there was to travel beyond it? In such a mind-set, all the unwholesome opportunities of Devil's Shade could appear like the only chance she had.

Stop, I commanded myself. *Stop thinking of this!* But I could not shut out the thought of her, the image of Atmas strapped into the Harvester's chair as I glowed above her, the false goddess in the skies. . . .

"Do take comfort," crooned Tyrus, eyes fixed on my face, reading my turmoil. "Don't you see what this means? My love, you needn't bother shutting your ears to the despair of the Excess after tomorrow. Those voices screaming, 'Nemesis lives' will at last go silent forevermore."

10

THE *RETRIBUTION* slid into the docks of the *Halcyon* without drawing notice. The *Halcyon* was a massive cityship, an artificial structure in space that could not propel itself or make anything but small changes to its position, yet served as a habitat for hundreds of thousands of people. I would reappear amid the Imperial Triumph.

Anguish had been released into my keeping on the *Retribution*, and he followed me to the disembarkation deck. Tyrus had crewed the ship for me—stationing several armed Inquisitors onboard. They tailed our every step now, but by tacit agreement, we ignored them.

"You need not do this," Anguish said, not for the first time.

I was growing tired of this argument. "Do you want to live? Then, yes. I must do this."

He caught my arm as I tried to push past him. "There must be other ways." Leaning close, he spoke into my ear. "We can find a medical bot somewhere, steal one. . . ."

I shook off his grip. "I will not risk your life on stupid gambles."

"Nemesis. Surely that is *my* choice. And I say—"

"Enough." Whatever cost I had to pay, it would be well worth his survival. "I will be back as soon as I can. Be ready for me—I don't want to stay a moment longer than I must."

Then I arranged the sweeping liquisilk hood over my head to conceal my face and stepped into the boarding artery that connected my vessel to the cityship. The masses had already gathered for the celebration, and as I strode down the featureless passageway, I could hear the growing din that awaited me.

In normal times, the cityship *Halcyon* was a vast floating museum. It contained artworks and antiquities, including those of Ancient Earth, too valuable to risk storing in planetary atmospheres. The curators took vows before entering service: they would never leave the ship again, never marry or have children. Their sole calling was to protect and maintain the collections. Until recently, no others but the Emperor and a very few Grandiloquy had ever visited the *Halcyon*.

As I stepped onto the ship proper, I saw that times had changed.

Tyrus had not told me many details of the planned celebrations, but he'd mentioned that every soul on the *Halcyon* today had earned their invitation by dint of their eager and impassioned belief in their Emperor's sacred nature.

What he had not mentioned was that he had invited *thousands*.

Tributary Statues lined the corridor as well as giant busts of Tyrus's proud face, before which everyone made a great show of bowing as they passed.

I continued toward the arena where the celebration was due to take place; the sheer number of people made me feel nauseated. I knew that assembling this congregation had entailed an Empire-wide search. Only the most ardently outspoken believers had been summoned—those Grandiloquy and Excess who had publicly proven their zeal in the new faith, either by informing on skeptics who questioned Tyrus's divinity, or by actively rooting out the older faiths and punishing the practitioners.

But there were so many!

Tyrus's new sigil was everywhere. Six stars being devoured by a black hole. People displayed the sigil on armbands and necklaces, on embroidered silk sashes. Some had even tattooed it on their cheeks and hands. Others had adopted Tyrus's facial features or hair color—an unnerving effect, as though Tyrus were everywhere around me.

I picked my way around a pile of flowers mounded beneath a portrait of the new God. The faithful here were competitive. As one man knelt before this portrait, the next man fell to his belly. A woman had started to sing the praises of the Divine Emperor, and another, joining her, shouted her praise, drowning out the singer.

Right and left, the stilted praise spoken solely so others could overhear it:

"How lucky we are, to be led by a living god!"

"What times these are, when a Divine Emperor can command the stars!"

"He has no more devoted subject than me!"

I passed next through a chamber lined with tanks some thirty meters tall. Within these tanks, dancers wearing artificial gills twisted sinuously amid fluid-rendered holographics that depicted the glories of Tyrus von Domitrian's reign. Some dancers reenacted these scenes; others mimed acts of worship and prostration. In the domed cupola above, performers in antigravity boots flipped and dived, messages flashing from their robes when the light struck them:

Hail to our Divine Emperor!

Hail to the Domitrians!

Sidonia had always wanted to come visit the archives here, but she'd never had the chance. Tyrus, too, had entertained grand plans for the ship. He'd meant to open access to the Excess, to share the heritage of Earth with those who had been robbed of knowledge of it.

How wonderingly he had spoken of it. *Artwork is the very expression of the human soul. That is the power of it, Nemesis. That's the reason every petty tyrant seeks to censor, control, shame, or dictate to artists. If you can control them, you can control ideas of the human soul.*

As I stepped into the main exhibition corridor, I saw that he'd learned that lesson well.

For the vessel had been desecrated.

A bronze plaque spoke of a rare series of stone columns from a human civilization called Greece. What stood in the artifact's place was a marble statue of the Emperor Melchoir von Domitrian, gazing down upon all who passed. The plaque denoting a line of terra-cotta statues also stood above something decidedly altered—statues of other Domitrians.

An empty, aching sorrow filled my heart. There was something of a curse in dreams that came true in the wrong form, long after their meaning had been extinguished. Tyrus should have had a chance to be the idealist he'd once been. He would have treasured the artwork that belonged in this place. He should have had a chance to exhibit them across the Empire. He *would* have done something magnificent here, had he been given the chance before his corruption.

Even this place meant nothing to Tyrus now.

The walkway took me directly toward the gaming arena, where yet another of Tyrus's statues loomed outside the entrance, its arms spread wide. From some other person, that posture would look like a warm invitation, an embrace. But Tyrus opened his arms only to destruction. Thus had he posed on the day he'd unleashed malignant space above the skies of Corcyra.

I gazed up at the statue, feeling ill. And then something beneath it caught my eye.

A tinier image stood at the feet of Tyrus's statue. Someone had placed an active holographic disc there . . . of me.

The hairs rose at the nape of my neck. This was not Tyrus's doing. He would never have chosen *that* image—the Nemesis I'd seen on the alley walls on Devil's Shade, crowned by a halo of white fire. This was the Nemesis I was supposed to destroy today—the threat I would defuse by disavowing all who invoked her.

Whoever had placed that holographic disc had done so not in praise, but in challenge.

The Excess who passed pretended not to see the holographic. They trained their gazes steadfastly on the bronze Emperor's feet, which they rubbed for good luck.

As I watched, one brave devotee of Tyrus's decided to take action. He smashed the holographic, and a brief, restive murmur passed over the crowd. But the general cheerful hubbub soon resumed.

I took a deep breath, and for the first time in hours, my lungs felt clear and full. Somewhere amid these deluded masses, some lonely, defiant soul had risked everything to place that holographic. *Here*, in the den of Tyrus's most loyal—even here, some brave human refused to bend to that which was unworthy of reverence. They chose not to conform.

Somewhere nearby was a fine example of true humanity.

And now I turned into the arena—to betray them.

11

THE ENTRYWAY to the arena was a pathway of thunder. Actual thunder—raw and furious, vibrating the floor underfoot. I froze in place as bodies shoved past me. Six great columns led the way forward, floor-to-ceiling security fields containing the swirling, churning atmospheres planted there for aesthetics.

The thunder, I realized, was the sound of "gods"—the gods being the six heads of Tyrus projected in flashes overhead, appearing and disappearing from within six bright gaseous clouds. Had I known nothing of science, I might well have imagined this the threshold to the divine. Or to hell.

The first time I had stepped into the sky dome of the Chrysanthemum, I had felt just so: overawed and disconcerted by the great expanse of atmosphere overhead—blue and cloud-strewn.

I had imagined then that I would never again see its like. But then I'd visited Lumina and had learned that illusions, no matter how magnificent, could not compare to a true planetary atmosphere.

A mournful ache spread through me. I wanted to be back roving in a wilderness with Anguish, breathing natural air, feeling marvelously and perfectly suited to the demands of my surroundings.

Nature, *true* nature, was raw and fierce, created by no man. What it required was strength and quickness and wary respect. *This* place, with its false thunder and phony gods, wanted only awe—gaping, vapid, unthinking.

This was a show designed for the Excess. Tyrus had invited primarily the planet-bound to this event to better spread his propaganda to the street level of the Empire. Now I felt a softening within me. The average Excess had never seen such technology, so how could I expect them to see through it? They had been trapped inside a net they were not even aware existed.

At last the arena proper yawned wide about me. The stands rose upward so high that their uppermost walls faded into the thickness of the chamber's atmosphere. In the lowermost stands, a current of bodies flowed toward what a holographic placard proclaimed a Tributary Fount. It appeared to be a standard matter incinerator with a gaping maw. Into that wide metallic mouth, they cast gifts of varying value as tributes to their Divine Emperor.

One enthusiastic young girl shouted, "For the Divine Emperor!" and slashed away her impressive braid of scarlet hair.

Not to be outdone, the woman behind her—whose hair was short— hastily tossed in the holographics she'd brought, then took a knife to her hand to contribute her own blood.

"For the Divine Emp . . . Emp . . ." She had sliced deeper than intended in her enthusiasm, for when she beheld her gushing hand, she paled and swayed. Someone caught her and shoved her aside, to make room for the next supplicant.

Looming above it all stood the largest statue of Tyrus yet, its palms extended toward the center of the arena as though he were offering some great gift to his subjects.

"You will follow me."

The woman's voice broke through my concentration, but I was not startled. I'd expected Tyrus to send handlers to instruct me. Of the two figures that materialized by my side, I recognized only one: the Inquisitor Synestia, who'd found me on Devil's Shade. She wore plain civilian garb today.

Without the Dark Star garb, she appeared but an unremarkable figure who would blend in with any crowd. She sported a Domitrian armband, and her gaze dropped to my bare arm—where I had refused to don the one that had been waiting with this hooded disguise.

I held her gaze defiantly.

The crowd began screaming. The dancers had cleared away, and a large low-gravity plate had been slid into the center of the arena. There, a pair of massive scorpions had been unleashed for a face-off.

The two graceful predators circled each other, and for a moment, as their poisonous tails wavered in the air, dripping venom, it seemed as if they would not strike, as though they might come to some accord.

Then one lanced forward and they became a tangle of gleaming red-and-black limbs, contorting about, tails driving forward in desperate jabs to penetrate each other's armor. One drove its venom through a crack in the other's shell, and its tail turned into a stabbing, vicious prong, injecting its toxin again and again.

"You will be cooperative, will you not?" Synestia said as we threaded through the crowd.

"I will cooperate. I have told Tyrus as much."

"The Divine Emperor," she corrected me.

I narrowed my eyes, then spoke the words that seemed to choke me: "The Divine . . ." I could not finish it. My gaze had become riveted beyond her to the scorpions, where the victor stalked forward for the kill.

At that moment, the poisoned one surged forward and I glimpsed a flash of sharp teeth that had been engineered into the creature. A moment later, the teeth sank into the skull of the other, ripping it away in a gush of fluids. The screaming of the crowd filled the air as the victor gave an unearthly shriek.

"The Divine Emperor," I forced out.

The scorpion's legs folded beneath it as the poison tore through its veins. Just like that, it was all over. And both scorpions were dead.

Even as I followed the Inquisitor Synestia, I hated every step, every heartbeat. I hated that I was reduced to this. Better to have never been found; to have lived out life on Devil's Shade.

No.

No.

Better to have let Tyrus die that day on the *Tigris*. Better to have mourned him—the one I loved more than myself—than grow to hate the ruination of him that I knew now.

In a sumptuous, velvet-walled antechamber in the interior of the arena, Inquisitor Synestia put the beauty bots to work. When at last they retreated, I looked into the mirror and beheld a ghost.

The ghost wore the sign of divine blessing: her black leather suit parted in a deep V over her chest to expose the Interdict's concentric sun sigil. It was the mark of blessing the Interdict had given me to mark my humanity, my personhood, to proclaim me more than a mere Diabolic. The girl's hair was long and a gleaming white-blond.

Thus had I looked, the day the *Hera* had struck the *Tigris*. The last day I had truly loved my husband. The day I had refused to let him die, when I had forced him back into Pasus's captivity.

Something felt stuck in my throat. I could not swallow it down. If I could go back in time to warn this girl . . . to do everything over . . .

"So everything that has taken place since," I said dully, "the wedding, my execution, Corcyra—"

"Never happened," said Synestia. "You have been dead. Those appearances were made by imposters. Today, the Divine Emperor summons you back to life."

My laugh felt rusty. "Did you ever truly believe in your faith? Or was it always just a path to power, even before he decided to play God?"

Synestia did not answer me.

Outside, the roaring of the crowd mounted into a new crescendo. My gut tightened.

The Inquisitor gestured me onto a steel platform. The platform jolted and began to carry me upward. Overhead, a square patch of ceiling retracted, and the crowd's shouts redoubled.

I braced myself and emerged onto the floor of the arena to find myself circled by the six columns of storm clouds. They'd been moved to this spot, and now they twisted and roiled with lightning, shielding me from the arena's view.

Then the source of the new cheers reached my ears over the pounding roar of the storms.

"My subjects. Behold! I have animated stone to be among you! How glorious I find your tribute to me. . . ."

Through the gale of flashing lightning, I saw that the massive statue of Tyrus no longer extended its hands. Instead it spoke, and Tyrus's words issued from its mouth.

It had also been a hologram. Of course. What fools he took these onlookers for, to suggest this was true stone and he was animating it! Weariness seeped through me, for he was entirely a falsehood now, it seemed. Falsehoods upon falsehoods, and how foolish of me to still hope for something of substance beneath the illusions.

"... I commend you for the fine example you set for the entirety of this galaxy this day," Tyrus's voice carried on. "You were summoned because you have proven yourselves prepared to give all to our holy crusade! You have sacrificed to me, sometimes neighbors, friends, even family—all to please your God and spread our truth! You have been rewarded for it, I trust, and today you will be rewarded further still!"

The crowd was reaching forward, palms extended to him as though to grab at his distant image and draw some of his divinity unto themselves.

The Inquisitor was right. Tyrant, God, what matter? The crowd would worship him regardless. And now, suddenly, I realized the full extent of what it would mean to stand beside him.

Would they shout such things to me? Would they reach for me as they did him?

Would I learn to enjoy it?

Would I come to relish it?

Would I even learn to *endure* it?

My heart roared my answer: *NO.*

In the meanwhile, discordant shouts bubbled up from amid the crowd as he spoke, always along the lines of, "Hail to the Divine Emperor!"

"Hail to our God Tyrus! Everything we have is yours!"

"Have my life, Divine Emperor! Have everything I own!" rang one particularly booming voice.

Tyrus's image swiveled its head toward that voice, and a reptile-cold smile crossed his lips. "Are you certain you wish to speak such words? Let him come forward. Let him make public his testament of faith!"

With a flourish, a short, balding man emerged from the crowd, which eagerly shuffled him forward. He was lovingly clutching a stone bust of Tyrus, like a cherished icon.

"Everything I have is yours, Most Ascendant Divine Emperor! My family, my love, even my life! For you, I give anything!" And with that, he threw himself down to his stomach.

The crowd swelled with applause for this noble man, and a broad grin blazed over Tyrus's lips. His holographic held out its arms in welcome.

"Oh, do stand. Such bravery! Such conviction! What is your name, you glorious soul?"

"I am Tavistock Strafe, Your Divine Supremacy."

"A good, solid name. I hail you, Tavistock! Everyone show Tavistock the reverence you would show me! Your God commands it of you."

The audience did. They reached for him, hailing him. Tavistock visibly teared up, drinking in the praise and acclaim of the crowd that broke into shouts of his name.

My eyes remained locked on Tyrus's face, on that grin that only grew wider.

"Now, Tavistock, follow through on your pledge," Tyrus said softly. "One mustn't scorn vows made to a god."

I knew those words. I knew where this was leading. I *knew* it.

Tavistock did not. The balding fellow blinked up at Tyrus, thrown by an expectation he was eager to fulfill, but did not yet understand.

Tyrus gestured with a magnanimous smile to the matter incinerator.

"Sacrifice yourself to me."

12

FOR A MOMENT, the man, Tavistock, stood there with his face oddly slack and expressionless, like he could not quite understand what was being asked of him.

"How brave you are, Tavistock," proclaimed Tyrus. To the audience: "Give him your adulation for this noble act!"

There'd been a dimming in the voices of the onlookers, just for a brief time, as though they, too, could not believe what their Divine Emperor required of one of his followers. Yet some of them immediately raised their voices in wild cheering—the true believers. Some of them had to truly believe the mass delusion they all shared, that their Emperor was indeed a god. Some were not bribed or threatened into obedience, but internalized what the people around them only pretended to believe.

They would celebrate anything their Divine Emperor asked of them, wouldn't they? Even something so terrible as this.

Once the true believers gave voice to their cheers, the others followed suit. How could they do otherwise? They had no choice, in their minds, but to obey the group lest it turn on them. They would forfeit all the riches and acclaim they'd earned from subscribing to the delusion of Tyrus's godhood. Even that lone soul who'd placed my image at the foot of the statue had done so in stealth. There were no heroes to be found here.

And the hapless Tavistock, standing in the same public place where he'd so proudly drunk in their praise just moments before, had gone waxen with realization.

A wicked sort of malevolence filled me at the sight, for he was not so gleeful now.

"M-may I . . . ," he stuttered, as his Divine Emperor, looming above him, raised his vast granite palms to beckon for silence so Tavistock's voice might be heard. "Might I not serve my Divine Emperor in . . . in some other manner?"

The reaction was immediate, a firestorm of boos erupting from the crowd, but Tyrus silenced these as well.

"You have pledged me devotion in any form I deem fit, Tavistock, and this is what I now require of you. Do not jeer at him for seeking to please me in another way. He is in his rights to wish for some other way to please me, but Tavistock—there is no other way. This is what your Divine Emperor demands. Sacrifice yourself to me."

Tavistock was visibly shaking now, his gaze crawling to the matter incinerator, and the encouraging cries of the crowd seemed to electrify the air around him.

Go ahead, show the substance of your faith, I raged at the fool of a man, waiting for him to turn tail and run. Perhaps when he fled this demand, he would awaken some of the others.

Yet the man did not turn to flee.

Instead he lurched forward one step, two, then paused to send a dismayed, almost childlike look about at the crowd cheering him on, applauding him for his obedience to something that was certain to destroy him.

Is he mad? I thought disbelievingly. What *was* this power Tyrus had seized, to compel his faithful to act against their very survival instincts?

I had assumed his control over the Excess stemmed solely from his combination of bribes and threats, and yet this was something more. This was a human instinct: conformity. All the pressure of the humans around Tavistock forced his steps forward.

The thunderous roars of approval from the crowd felt like an energy on the air, and Tavistock kept looking about as though to imbibe sips of public approval. His resolve visibly strengthened with each moment of adulation, even as my own thoughts thundered at him, *You FOOL. They are lauding you for self-destruction!*

With a sudden courage, his jerky steps drew him to the incinerator, his doom.

That was the moment I glimpsed it: the slight gap between the funnels of storms walling me off from the audience. Perhaps in his preoccupation with the spectacle he'd created, Tyrus was unaware that there was enough space through the gauntlet of swirling, raging winds and security fields for me to penetrate if I wished.

I looked at Tavistock once more. This man was entirely unworthy of my intervention. I saw Anguish in my mind again and my heart gave a hideous twist of pain, because I knew what this would lead to with him, with the last Diabolic. The only brother I would ever have . . .

Yet the alternative was to support this debacle: a human being killing himself for a false deity, all for Tyrus's gratification. I had always been a monster, but I was not this sort of monster. My evils had been thrust on me, engineered into me, but this was the sort of wrong that one chose for oneself, that one thirsted for. Power and influence were the intoxicants the Domitrian monsters of Tyrus's family craved.

If this was a scene I would witness again and again in my future, I could not accept it. The falsehood and cruelty of it would choke me.

I *could not* tolerate this bargain. I *could not* endure it.

So I would not.

I dashed forward and sprinted through the gap in the storm columns, the roaring of the storms thundering about me. . . .

And then I had broken through to the floor of the arena proper, with the stands expanding up and on all sides of me, thousands upon thousands of watching faces gazing down, and a hush fell as a new person appeared in the arena. . . .

I did not think. I did not have to.

"Tavistock!" I bellowed at that pathetic man, now clutching the lip of the matter incinerator, trying to work up the courage to fling himself inside it. . . .

The pathetic wretch turned, and his eyes widened in dumb shock as he registered just who I was. The crowd reacted with a similar swell of shocked cries, for there was no mistaking me. Everyone knew precisely who I was.

I stalked over to Tavistock and seized the bust of Tyrus right from his arms. Then I whipped around and hurled the bust right at the "granite statue" with all my might, sending the rock careening directly into the holographic projector. The massive granite illusion of animated stone vanished in a snap as sparks surged from the unit, and in the thick silence, my voice was thunderously loud:

"Don't you see. It's but a hologram? *HE IS NO GOD!*"

13

FOR A MOMENT, all I could see was the total amazement washing over the sea of faces at the sight of me, and I knew it would be but a moment before Tyrus reasserted control over this situation somehow. It astonished me that he hadn't already reappeared in some form or other, but I took advantage of my captive audience to spread my arms and turn about so all could see me, could see the Interdict's mark over my chest, and those facial features Tyrus had healed and restored down to the crooked nose, to the state they'd been the day I first vanished.

"It is me," I told them. "I am Nemesis. I am *the* Nemesis. I am alive."

And then a bloom of another holographic projector, and Tyrus reappeared in standard human size just at the end of the arena, laughter lurking on his lips. "Come now, can it be another Partisan imposter? At this gathering of the devoted?"

He'd given his cue to his devout, and those most slavishly

obedient to him among the crowd rose from their seats, screaming,

"*Partisan!*"

"*It's an imposter!*"

But I was the real thing. I was reality. Let the gullible among them deny the evidence of their eyes all they wanted—I would show them something undeniable about me.

So I forged across the distance to Tavistock, still hovering uncertainly by the incinerator. I seized the machine, ripping it from the floor with the brute strength no ordinary human being could ever hope to match.

"You want a sacrifice, Tyrus? Take mine!"

Then I hurled it with all my strength toward the metal plates containing the wall of storms. The incinerator clanged to the floor with its gaping mouth suctioning, and the storm generators began to crinkle with a piercing shrieking noise, before being funneled down into their destruction.

The containment field vanished, and the boiling dark clouds surged outward in a ferocious howl of gases, upending the containment plates of the others, unleashing the angry multihued clouds within the closed atmosphere of the arena.

Like that, I had unleashed Tyrus's storms.

Screams arose as the bright torrents of storm lashed outward, the gases intermingling into explosive bolts of bright lightning. The sudden onslaught of new vapors destabilized the atmosphere in the chamber, triggering a hideous suction noise. Even Tyrus's holographic image registered a flicker of genuine alarm.

As the winds began to swirl and tear around me, I gave a mad laugh. I was free, *free* of Tyrus's choke hold over me. There was no going back, no undoing this.

"Prove you're a god!" I jeered. "End your own storms!"

The winds knocked me off my feet, but I clawed my way back up, intoxicated by my liberation. All around, faithful followers surged for the exits. Their exalted Divine Emperor shouted for calm, but his voice was lost amid the thunder of the storm.

Nearer to me, the fearful cried out for Tyrus, some dropping to their knees to pray for salvation. Those fleeing trampled those on the ground. As this human tide reached me, some hurled themselves at *my* feet to beg for aid. But the crush of the crowd did not spare them or me. I was pushed and carried toward the doors, and even I could not combat the combined force of so many panicked bodies.

I was forced straight out of the arena into the entryway. The storms did not follow, but panic still reigned. I found myself wedged between frantic, shoving masses. At first I fought to free myself, but there were too many people in too little space. The press was too powerful. I wheezed for air, and spots began to cloud my vision, the sea of heads fading as darkness overwhelmed me. . . .

Instinct took over.

My fists clamped onto the body in front of mine. I launched myself forward, vaulting up from over his shoulders. Hands reached up, clawing at me—trying to seize on my momentum or to halt it, I knew not. I leaped from one set of shoulders to the next, aiming for the door, where the bodies had jammed into an impassable barrier. With one great, final, bounding leap, I kicked through the wedge of bodies that clogged the entryway.

As soon as I broke into the next chamber, I dragged a great gasping lungful of air. A clamor of people immediately swarmed in behind me, and for a moment I was overwhelmed by the memory of the fire in the Great Heliosphere, the bodies blue from lack of oxygen that Tyrus and I had hauled out of the jammed entrance. . . .

But there was no fire this time. The storms had remained confined to the arena. I had the time and chance to help. I clasped the hands scrabbling for mine, pulling people free of the dangerous pile. "Help me," I cried to each person I liberated. "Help me save the others!"

But few listened. Some, still powered by panic, ran from me. Others stumbled away like drunkards, then fell to their knees even now to loudly acclaim their Divine Emperor. When I finally freed enough people to clear the doorway entirely, the liberated crowd trampled one another without remorse, ignoring my shouted instructions:

"Walk, don't run!"

"For Helios's sake, be patient! I will free you all!"

The mob knew no reason. They tore forward like wild animals, heedless of who suffered. I found myself backing away, my heart jerking wildly in my chest. Human terror was cruel and careless. And those who had not lost their wits, who had recovered their breath and then moved stalwartly onward, ignoring my pleas to help . . .

They were the worst. For they did not seek to allay the panic, or to aid their fellow humans. Instead some made a show of loudly praising their Divine Emperor for their survival, and others . . .

Others saw me and called for my blood.

"Imposter! Imposter!" screamed one crazed young woman. Her raving drew the notice of others, who swarmed about me as the young woman yelled, "She did this! This was her fault!"

And they descended upon me in their rage.

I had fought multiple opponents before, but never so many. Even so, I might have leaped clear and evaded them—had something solid and heavy not crashed into the back of my head.

I reeled as my own blood splattered the floor. At the sight of that blood the mob howled, like a pack of hunting dogs loosed on prey. They had discovered that I was mortal. That I, too, could bleed.

A man armed with a stone bust hurled himself at me. I didn't see his face, just the granite block that flew into my vision. I swung up my arm to divert the blow, drove my foot into the man's torso. I tore his arm out of its socket—and a heavy blow smashed me from behind.

A man had tackled me—his weight heavy, cumbersome. I stumbled forward, and my heart lurched in terror. If I fell now, I would die. I would be ripped apart, limb from limb.

I found enough footing to push myself into a flip. The man clinging to my back took the brunt of our shared impact. I drove my elbows into his ribs and heard the gratifying crack of his bones. His strangled shout fed some new fire within me—bright, hot, dangerous.

They wanted to fight? Very well.

As I rose, so too did the nature I had long restrained—for a Diabolic was bred to fight and knew no fear in it. Others surged toward me, thinking they were safe in their superior numbers. I laughed. Crouching to duck a blow, I caught an assailant's fist and twisted it into splinters, then drove my fist into his jaw. His neck snapped like a twig. I clutched his body and turned so the corpse could absorb the bright slash of a blade that flashed my way. Then I hurled the body into the crowd before me.

Arms grabbed both of mine. I wrenched back and drove the two grapplers together, their heads knocking into each other's. Another rushed at me, and I propelled my boot into his head, felt his skull yield and shatter.

My heart was pounding now as though from a drug, some glorious elixir. *This* was what I was built to do. A blade flashed. . . . I dodged and delivered it back into the gut of its holder. A throat bared itself before me: my arms were occupied, so I sank my teeth into the cartilage and ripped. The iron taste of blood bloomed between my lips. I spat it out as I straightened and wrenched free of the entanglement of bodies. Another blade presented itself, stabbing toward my eyes: in thanks, I took it and drew it across its wielder's throat.

Now armed, I slashed through everything that neared me, cutting a swath through the hostility, ignoring the panicked shrieking all about me. At last I found myself standing in a clearing over the mass of fallen. A short distance away, Tyrus's faithful huddled tearfully, shrinking into themselves as I looked them over.

The horror in their faces awakened something rational and human in me. I grew aware of the blood cooling on my hands, my clothes. Of the corpses littered about me.

"They attacked me." My voice was hoarse, breathless. Why did they look at me so, as if *I* were the monster? "*They* attacked *ME*. I was defending myself!"

A small group leaped to their feet and raced away. I recognized two of them as women I had saved from the crush. Yet they were running—from *me*.

For a brief, awful second I felt betrayed. Wounded and scorned.

And then those feelings twisted into anger. Would I be judged for defending myself when attacked? What of my attackers? Was their violence not to be reviled? Was it only I who was expected to lie down and submit myself like a lamb to slaughter?

I had protected myself. I had been *able* to protect myself. And this made me monstrous to them.

My gaze sharpened as it swept over this collection of people, a sampling of the most repugnant of the Empire. The enforcers of false decrees; those corrupt or deluded enough to show themselves willing to police the virtues of their fellow Excess.

These people deserve him.

The thought scorched through my mind, hot and poisonous. The whole lot of these enforcers of Tyrus's delusions were pathetic and revolting followers—and such people *deserved* a god like Tyrus.

So let them have their Divine Emperor.

I whipped around to leave them to their chosen fate.

None dared step forward to stop me.

I passed out of the room, stalking onward along the causeway. Right and left, groups huddled, bedraggled escapees from the arena, entertainers, and vendors scouring the area for news—all fell silent at the sight of me. Many of the Excess fell to their knees, either in fear or disbelief. My hair was askew, my leather finery splashed with blood. None dared address me. For a short while, it seemed I might walk all the way back to the *Retribution* with no interference.

I had reached the boarding artery to the *Retribution* when the security bots surrounded me. A gleaming phalanx of metallic stars, they aimed their lasers directly at my head.

I stopped and looked up at them wearily, fixing my gaze on one of the pinpoint cameras that was feeding surveillance images directly to Tyrus.

"Go ahead." I spread my arms. "Shoot me."

The machines hovered noiselessly. It would take but a thought from Tyrus to direct their destruction of me, or for that matter, to make a nearby intercom broadcast his verbal response.

Instead he let the silence extend, let it thicken.

I was sick of his talent for drama. "I won't be your goddess. That's impossible now, anyway. As for your flock—you have collected the most despicable sort of humans to your banner. Most Excess are good, but I see the worst among them here, so eager to enforce your lie upon others, to punish those who dare to believe other than they do. They are repugnant, and they suit you well now—for you are not the Tyrus I knew. You're a sick, desecrated shadow of the Tyrus I loved. So just shoot me, Emperor Tyrus—and be sure to kill Anguish, while you're at it. You own my fate, but you will never own my will."

As my words hung on the air, my body began to ache—and not simply from the blows I'd taken at the hands of the mob. My heart felt like a great, clanging hollow. There was nothing left to believe in. Not in this universe or any other.

I was so tired. I was ready for this to end.

The security bots parted silently, clearing my way onto *Retribution*.

For an incredulous moment, I hesitated, expecting some treachery. Then, cautiously, I backed away from them into the boarding artery.

They hung in the air, watching.

I turned around and began to walk.

A dreadful premonition seized me.

I burst into a sprint, flying down the boarding artery, convinced now that something dreadful awaited within the *Retribution*—some hideous vengeance for the decision I'd made today.

But as I reached the ship, I spotted Anguish dragging the last of the dead Inquisitors toward the exit. His pulse rifle whipped up—then lowered at the sight of me. He looked over my bloodied state and grinned approvingly.

"I saw the feed from the arena," he said. "I thought I'd help."

I stared at him. "You're well."

"Better once we take this vessel and leave. Or try," Anguish said.

"Anguish, the only reason you're alive is because I promised to cooperate with him. I broke that bargain today. Do not help me, *condemn* me. I've betrayed you."

He scoffed, then dropped the dead Inquisitor and strode over to me. Taking my shoulders in his large hands, he looked directly into my eyes.

"If I live, I live. If I die, so be it. It will be on *our* terms. Not his. You never betrayed me. And now, you have not betrayed yourself."

My throat closed. I did not deserve his forgiveness. But how easily and wholeheartedly he gave it.

I flung myself against his chest. He hugged me so hard that he knocked the wind from me. But I welcomed his grip. The weight of today's decision left me unsteady, and his embrace kept me upright, firmly on my feet.

"We'll find a way out of this," I said.

The *Retribution* shuddered suddenly around us. We pulled apart, exchanging a wordless look before sprinting together to the command nexus.

A curious sight waited out the windowed wall before us.

Our boarding artery was retracting all on its own; we were drifting back from the dock.

"You . . . ?" I said to Anguish.

Jaw tense, he shook his head.

A cold feeling ghosted over me. Whatever was happening here, it was not on our terms, but Tyrus's.

"What is going on?" I demanded to the air. He was certainly eaves-dropping on us even now. "Tyrus! What do you have planned?"

"A truce."

His calm voice floated on the air behind me, and Anguish and I both spun to see the holographic projectors alight with his image. After an hour of bloodshed and chaos, it felt jarring, surreal, to view his serene visage—the smile on his lips beneficent, even secretly amused.

"You refuse to be my goddess. Very well." His gaze flicked from me to Anguish, then back. "If we can't reach an agreement, you'll go your own way."

My hands balled into fists. "What a marvelous change of heart," I said flatly. I would not believe it at sword point.

"Take the *Retribution*. It's yours." He gestured about us with a single wave of his finger. "Anguish dan Domitrian? Live."

I caught my breath, not willing to believe. . . .

"There's a bot in the medical bay," Tyrus said. "I've unlocked its full functions. It awaits you with your cure."

None of this made sense. I crossed my arms. "Why?"

"Cannot a god be merciful?" Tyrus gave a one-shouldered shrug. "My condition of your survival is exile. Go to the most obscure reaches of imperial territory—and then keep going. I never wish to see you again."

"No. I'm sick of these games." After what I had just done, he could not mean to let me go. "Whatever you mean to do, *do* it. I won't run just so you can find amusement in chasing me."

His eyes were like ice. "I am not setting you free, Nemesis. I am *exiling* you. You caused me a public humiliation, and so I want you gone. Leave my territories. Never return."

Anguish made a low, contemptuous noise in his throat. "He deceives us."

"Test me," Tyrus said icily. "If you wish to die today, then by all means, refuse to leave."

"Anguish," I said in an undertone. "Get us out of here."

As Anguish turned to the navigation console, Tyrus went on. "As for those followers of mine who witnessed that debacle—"

His despicable faithful.

"You are right. I tried to be most gracious and magnanimous, spreading financial favors and largesse to those who hailed me most readily, but I comprehend that doing so has but attracted the worst sorts of opportunists and fools to my cause. Such cannot be trusted to remain silent about the events of today."

"Like with like: you deserve each other."

"Look out the window. Call this a . . . a *divine* act to delight your senses. Consider it my parting gift."

Outside the window, a lone vessel streaked toward the *Halcyon*. I caught my breath in horror as I realized what Tyrus intended.

I'd despised those people. I'd felt nothing but contempt for them.

But a cry escaped my lips as the ship erupted into a bright white flare and tore a skein of malignant space into the darkness. Within moments, it reached out and began to rip through the great cityship's hull.

Almost instantly, the vessel began to crumple into the bright ribbon of white and purple light. Flames erupted from all the ships tethered to the *Halcyon*, flames that bloomed like flowers before they, too, were swallowed into the malignancy, contracting into nothing.

Nausea churned through me. Bile clogged my throat. I turned back, ready to spit it at Tyrus.

He was already gone.

14

HE PLANNED it in advance, I thought.

My eyes flew open, staring at the ceiling of the silent bunk, the realization sinking into me.

I'd been twisting back and forth all night in a restless sleep, images of malignant space and the crumpling *Halcyon* tormenting my mind, and the faces of those pathetic, accursed Excess flashing before my eyes.

But somewhere between wakefulness and sleep, my brain had latched upon one fact that revealed everything:

He had moved all the art off the Halcyon.

All those priceless artifacts of human history had been displaced, and instead there'd been Domitrian tributes everywhere. I'd believed it an act of pure egotism, but I knew Tyrus. I knew him. I knew how many contingencies he planned for, how far ahead he thought—and a sudden dreadful understanding set in:

He moved the priceless art to protect it in case his plan went awry and he had to destroy those who witnessed my return.

Oh stars, as soon as I realized it, I knew it was true. Of course he preserved the art.

The malignant space hadn't been a spontaneous act. *That* was the true reason he had not come in person, but rather appeared by hologram. He *hadn't* decided on a rash impulse to kill the Excess, to obliterate the cityship.

No, he'd planned it all in advance just in case I would not prove a willing tool in his hands. Then he'd executed it without a shred of remorse. The bastard. The *bastard*.

A gift to me, he called it. That meant those deaths were laid directly at my feet—a response to my actions. Those deaths were my doing.

I sat up in bed with my heart roiling in torment, hearing Anguish's peaceful breathing from across the chamber. He'd long since dropped off to sleep. I rubbed my throbbing temples and just listened to his steady breathing. The sole blessing of this situation was Tyrus's unexpected mercy with Anguish.

Tyrus's medical bot had performed as promised. Anguish was fully healed now. We could safely retreat into obscurity, as I'd wished.

Yet with this terrible understanding unfurling in my mind, how could I? How could I run?

I *had* been hiding. Most shamefully, I had been doing so all this time, ever since Corcyra. I had disavowed my power to change this galaxy's situation. Now there were . . . only the stars knew how many dead, because of me. And how many more would follow?

Tyrus had committed a premeditated act of mass murder.

I had walked right into his chamber with no security field before us; I had thrown a knife awry. If I had but aimed it at his heart, *this would not have happened.*

My chest and throat felt tight. This was not the first mass murder he'd committed. I'd seen him slay thousands—or had it been hundreds of thousands?—of Grandiloquy in that final day in the Chrysanthemum. But those had been enemies, who'd pushed our backs to the wall. They would have destroyed us.

His ruthlessness had stunned me, regardless. Convinced that he was no longer fit to hold power, I had put myself between Tyrus and Gladdic and thrown my life away on Tyrus's blade.

This was worse.

Infinitely worse.

And this was all my responsibility.

On a deep breath, I looked out the window, seeking solace in the pitch blackness of hyperspace—the one place Tyrus could never track us, no matter the tech he'd implanted in the *Retribution.*

But the darkness did nothing to soothe my troubled thoughts. I rose and slipped out of the room.

Perhaps it was the Interdict's mark of blessing over my heart, but something compelled me to search out the vessel's heliosphere. I found it tucked beneath the command nexus.

I stepped into the great shroud of darkness and found myself gazing once again into the depthless expanse of hyperspace. We were flying at unimaginable speed, yet we might have been standing still, hanging in an abyss. My own shadowy reflection was all that moved against this void as I grappled for an understanding that still eluded me.

Tyrus, where are you?

I knew where his body was. It was living, animated flesh, ruling his Empire. His mind as well.

But . . .

But what of *Tyrus*? What of his true essence?

For there had been a different Tyrus once. The real one, whom I'd loved before the Venalox destroyed him. Now someone with his face and name and memories ruled this universe—and sought to enslave it.

I accepted at last, without doubt, that it all came back to the *Tigris*. To the day I should have let Tyrus die.

Go into exile and live.

Exile.

I had spent the last years in a self-imposed exile, as though removing myself from the galaxy would somehow prove a salve to its wounds. Yet all I had done was let the evils I'd left behind fester and grow.

Perhaps there was no fleeing reality.

Perhaps there was a fundamental evil in turning your back to a situation when you still had the power to change it. And what would the Tyrus I'd loved—the true Tyrus, the lost Tyrus—think of me, running away into exile and allowing him to do this? I had to think his soul existed somewhere, intact, if no longer present behind those eyes I'd glimpsed on the *Alexandria*.

If I fled again, how could I ever live with myself?

The answer was this: I could not.

Not everything could be undone. But some things *could* be mended.

I would go to find the Tyrus who remained—this Emperor with his name and his face, who never would have existed but for one fateful decision I'd made. I should have let him die, but I had forced him to live.

My mistake. I would mend it now. Nothing would stop me this time.

This was not the first time I'd made this decision, but it was certainly the first time I knew in my very soul that I would do it. And it was the last time I would have need to make such a resolve.

I stood in the darkened heliosphere before the sprawling windows and I swore on the Living Cosmos, on my very soul, that I would hunt Tyrus down.

Then I would kill him.

15

ANGUISH DID NOT object to my new resolve. I did not expect him to.

"He killed Enmity. He killed my master. He killed those Excess," Anguish told me. "I am glad to rupture any agreement with him."

Before we acted against Tyrus, Anguish and I needed weapons and a ship that was not likely to be tracked. The *Retribution* was Tyrus's gift to me, which meant it could not be trusted. Though Anguish and I had combed the vessel for surveillance tech, we would have had to physically dismantle the vessel before we could feel certain we had caught all the Emperor's traps.

So we set out to seize another ship. Anguish and I roved the outskirts of a highly trafficked system that supplied luxuries to the Chrysanthemum, waiting until a transport appeared on the edge of our sensors.

"This one," said Anguish, eyes gleaming with anticipation.

"This one," I agreed.

We greeted the ship by filling every transmission frequency range with static, so they could not send a distress beacon.

At that move, the freighter's crew was on alert. Their sensors had to tell them we were unarmed, so they likely found our move a laughably empty threat. Weapons turrets rose from the steel flanks of their triangular vessel. The blasting laser's depths bloomed red as they charged and readied to fire.

"What now?" Anguish said to me.

I might have no tactical understanding, but I knew what I'd do if I were fighting face-to-face. Like a Diabolic, the *Retribution* was tough: heavily armored, a defensive citadel that could endure far more punishment than the freighter could.

"Just ram them," I told Anguish.

"This may be a fatal error. We could both explode on impact."

"Then we won't have very long to lament our mistake. Do it."

He blasted the thrusters and propelled us straight into the other vessel. Though we both gripped for support, the impact sent us careening across the floor of the command nexus. I scrabbled back to my feet and over to the central console. With a flick of a control, I jammed our tethers into the other vessel's.

Anguish was still clambering to his feet when the other vessel jerked hard against our tethers, knocking us both down again. The lights flickered ominously, and our ship continued to rock. Anguish crawled over to a nearby security console and retrieved the emergency rifles we'd need for our invasion. I clawed my way back to the central console and jammed our boarding artery against theirs.

When we emerged onto their ship through the boarding artery, the mere sight of Anguish sent the crewmen fleeing. Pulse rifles in hand, we stalked through the corridors, waiting for resistance they did not mount.

At last we came upon a small group that hurled down its pistols at the sight of us. I'd donned a hood, not needing the questions about who I truly was.

"Who's in charge?" I demanded.

"I'm the captain. Please," said an older man. "We're just transporting medicines to Eurydice—"

"I don't care about your cargo," I snapped. "Is this vessel still functional? Can it enter hyperspace?"

"Yes, but—"

"Then we're trading ships. Get off."

My words silenced them.

"Go," I said, pointing toward the boarding artery. "Take the *Retribution*."

The captain opened and closed his mouth, sending an astonished look out the nearest window at the imposing Grandiloquy vessel. He had to think I was mad.

"Take your goods with you," I added. And then, because the whole lot of them seemed dumbstruck and bewildered, I raised my voice: "Do as I say or I will shoot you all and give you nothing!"

The captain hastened into action, barking orders for his crew to move their cargo. He kept his eyes on me warily as his crew began to file past.

"All . . . all respect intended, uh, Grandeé . . ."

He settled on the title with obvious uncertainty, guided no doubt by our Grandiloquy accents and the magnificence of the *Retribution*.

"Yes?" I prompted.

"This . . . this is not exactly an equitable trade—"

"I am forcing you at weapon's point. It isn't meant to be equitable."

"For . . . for you," he said. "That vessel is surely worth hundreds of this one. Is there some defect I need to know about in advance? Just for the safety of my people—"

"I assure you, the vessel is every bit as fine as it appears, and . . ." My voice faded as I spied the first crate of goods being levitated past me.

I whipped forward and halted its momentum with my palm. The diagram on its surface depicted elegant phials tucked within. I seized the lid and shoved it open, and within were portions of dark red liquid. They were unmistakable, but still my mind insisted that my eyes were mistaken. I lifted one of the crystalline containers. No label indicated the nature of its contents. These could be simple blood products—but how many times had I seen such things displayed on the luxury shelves across the Empire?

And how many times had I seen Excess strapped down beneath blood funnels on Devil's Shade, screaming in terror as they created this product?

"Novashine," I murmured. "Isn't it?"

The captain grew rigid, perhaps fearing I would covet this valuable substance for myself and renege on our agreement.

"Poor quality," he assured me. "It's watered-down stuff—"

"Helios Devoured, I don't give a damn what quality it is." My voice came out as a low growl, dark anger barely leashed. All I could imagine was that some of this blood was Atmas's. Certainly this evil trade had ruined a million girls just like her. I turned on the captain, my pulse rifle aimed directly at his head. "What else are you carrying?"

Some were legitimate medicines, rare antibiotics and the like. Others were the sort of chemical products that required factory-size synthesizers to produce in significant quantity. Those, I let him keep.

The Novashine and the other human-grown products—with so many variants of desiccating rose—I blasted apart crate by crate. The captain and his crew winced and cringed at the sight of their profits being blown away, but they dared not intervene, especially after Anguish took up position just behind me to monitor them while I worked.

But destroying this supply wouldn't be enough. This captain and crew could take the *Retribution* and sell it for more funds to sink into more distribution of these evil narcotics.

I could simply kill all of them—send the *Retribution* into a star . . . The temptation pulled at me until I'd transformed the last crate of desiccating rose into a smoking pile of rubble.

Then I turned on the kneeling crew of the vessel and saw their hollow-eyed faces, pale and waxen with fear—and in some cases, shame. My hatred shifted, becoming contempt. They knew what they did was wrong, yet they did it regardless.

I stepped toward the captain as I tore off my hood.

His jaw dropped, his eyes growing wide with confusion, disbelief.

"Do you recognize me?" I said.

"You're . . . you're Nemesis!"

"Yes," I said softly. "And so you know I have returned from death, more than once. You know I am a Diabolic. I have ripped hearts from living chests. I have killed so many with my bare hands, I have lost track of their names."

He was visibly shaking now; he dared not take his eyes from my face.

"Don't sell those products again. If you do, I will hunt you down. I will hurt you. And you will wish you were dead long before I put you from your misery. Do you understand?"

He threw himself down to the floor. "I swear, I swear—I won't."

I looked down on him where he prostrated himself in terror. Here was the abject submission that Tyrus called "worship." This was the sight his Venalox-warped brain had grown to relish.

Perhaps I had a use for it, after all.

"There is one more service I require of you. In exchange for your life. For the lives of your crew. For the vessel I am giving you."

"I will never breathe a word of this encounter!" he vowed, anticipating me. "Nor will my crew!"

I doubted he would hold his tongue for long. But if fear kept him silent for a few days, it would delay Tyrus's realization that the *Retribution* no longer offered a way to track me. "Good. And you will take the *Retribution* to the Paradox star system. Listen to me carefully: the second planet from the star. That is where you will go."

Anguish slid me an amused glance. He knew what I was doing.

"I . . . yes, the second planet. What shall we do there?" The captain was pitifully eager to take instruction now. "Tell me exactly."

"Why, what but sell your cargo." I shrugged. "It's a wealthy province on the frontier. Plenty of buyers waiting. You will sell there— *not* on Eurydice."

"That's what you require?" the captain said, confused.

"Precisely that," I said. "Send and receive no transmissions until your task is done. I'll know if you do not obey me."

And he swore again to do so. I did not know if he'd keep his word, but it mattered not. Anguish and I watched as his crew gathered their belongings and departed, leaving us their freighter, the *Phoenix*.

"The Paradox system," Anguish said after they were gone, a laugh twitching at his lips. "That's nearly two months in hyperspace, is it not?"

I offered a brief, satisfied smile in reply. Two months was enough time for Tyrus's tracking sensors to mislead him, to persuade him I was heading in one direction while our new ship went in the other. He would assume I was limping off to exile. By the time he realized I was not onboard the *Retribution*, well . . .

There was a great deal of havoc one could wreak in eight weeks. I intended to make the most of them.

16

THE OFFICIAL GALACTIC news broadcasts began covering the woe and tragedy of the *Halcyon*'s destruction. From the command nexus of our new freighter, the *Phoenix*, Anguish and I beheld the transmissions by the Eurydicean media.

These were the state-sanctioned lies: Malignant space was not mentioned as a cause of the tragedy. Rather, the cityship's power core had "overloaded."

"Hiding their Divine Emperor's crime," I muttered to Anguish.

The transmissions claimed that the bulk of the Excess had escaped before the shocking tragedy. Anguish and I exchanged a glance at that, for we'd witnessed it happen—there was no chance a wide-scale evacuation had preceded the disaster.

The media also claimed that the catastrophe took place a full hour after the disruption of the ceremony.

Another lie.

But Tyrus now controlled the collective perception of reality. The actual number of dead would never be widely known.

"How do they lie so unflinchingly?" I wondered aloud.

Anguish shrugged his massive shoulders. "If all still operates as it did under my master and Randevald, then those on Eurydice are supplied with truth from the Chrysanthemum. They are well-practiced in repeating what they are told."

Of course. Tyrus had once sworn to purge corruption from the Empire. Now he exploited it just as his predecessors had.

As for rumors of my reappearance . . .

"It's clearly become a favorite Partisan tactic, using a beauty bot to adopt the late Empress's appearance," said one newscaster dismissively. *"One cannot lend any credence to the claims that she was there. We all know she perished years ago."*

They were going to dismiss me. *Again.* This time, with most of the witnesses conveniently dead, it would be easy.

If any had even survived, they'd still hail from Tyrus's most devoted followers, for only the devout had been invited aboard the *Halcyon.* They'd believe any explanation for the disaster he furnished. They'd spread his new public narrative uncritically. Anyone who could believe Tyrus a god could fool themselves into believing anything.

It was easy to convince oneself of a lie you wished to believe. Hadn't I done just that when I'd decided that Tyrus was insane rather than irredeemable?

And then a familiar face appeared on the transmissions, and my every muscle grew rigid.

"Nemesis. Ah, yes, Nemesis . . ."

It was someone I knew well.

Gladdic von Aton.

Dressed in the rich, flamboyant manner of a Grande, he smiled pleasantly for the galactic news cameras.

"What can I say about Nemesis?" He paused, thinking it over. *"She was remarkable. Nemesis was . . . Oh, forgive me."* A polite chuckle. *"The Empress. I know it was an imposter who claimed the title, but I haven't forgotten that our Divine Emperor invested her with it posthumously. Please understand, I don't mean to be disrespectful to Her Late Supremacy, but we were friends before her engagement to our Divine Emperor—"*

In my shock I could hardly focus on what he said. He looked flushed and well-fed, practically glowing with health. What a contrast he cut to the pitiful figure I'd glimpsed on the last, bloody day in the ball dome.

"No," I said aloud.

"It's him," Anguish said.

Gladdic's interviewer asked some question that amused him. He threw back his head in laughter, displaying a flawless set of straight white teeth. He did not look like a man who had ever known beatings or fear.

Tyrus had told me he gave Gladdic lucrative opportunities to earn his forgiveness. Perhaps I had secluded myself away on Devil's Shade too thoroughly, shut my ears too completely to news of the galaxy. . . . For I had not realized Gladdic had become a propagandist.

"As a close friend of Her Late Supremacy," Gladdic was saying, *"I know Nemesis would be appalled by these Partisans acting in her name. She loved our Divine Emperor to the last. I watched the imposter die. It wasn't Nemesis, I assure you. Believe me, she is dead."*

"Liar," I rasped.

"Forgive me," Gladdic said, blinking rapidly as he clutched his heart. *"It's still hard to speak of her—she was such a dear friend. I assure you, though, that these rumors of her 'return' are an insult to those who have*

mourned her for years. If you see anyone wearing her face, know that they profane her. It's not Nemesis."

I'd always protected Gladdic! And now, he lied about me.

I glared at the image. "You coward."

"Are you surprised?" said Anguish darkly.

I caught my fist before it could slam into the screen. Instead I clenched my jaw as I glared at the image. "You coward," I muttered.

"This surprises you?" Anguish said to me. "He has always protected his own life over his integrity."

No. No, it didn't surprise me. A cold malice crept through me, and I looked at Anguish with a wicked plan in mind. "We need more information about targets to determine where to strike first. We have to start somewhere. Perhaps by striking at a member of the Grandiloquy."

Anguish arched his brow. "Him?"

"Oh yes. Him."

We both looked at Gladdic as he rattled off more lies about me, but no longer was pure anger beating through my veins. . . . For there was a giddiness inside me, knowing we had our first target.

17

THE *PHOENIX* had been equipped with sufficient weaponry to scare away pirates. But it was no match for Gladdic's ship, the *Atlas*. Nor could I repeat the trick I'd used to acquire this vessel. If we slammed into the *Atlas*, we wouldn't survive.

Of course, neither would the *Atlas*.

Gladdic's movements were highly publicized, now that he was a propagandist for Tyrus. Anguish and I headed to the planet Daedalus in time to meet him on the way back from a public event with the system's Viceroy. We watched on our sensors as his vessel rose from the surface of Daedalus, and then we began to stalk his ship, staying just at the edge of our sensor range.

We bided our time until the *Atlas* reached that patch of space known as a chaotic gale, where certain electromagnetic properties wreaked havoc on the technology of passing vessels.

Special protocols had to be followed to pass safely through these patches of space. Wise captains approached at high speeds, building momentum so they could shut down their ships' engines and all non-essential tech and coast through the gale. To do otherwise was to risk catastrophic system failure—equipment, security bots, and computer systems would short out, and engine parts would fail.

We carefully navigated through the vast asteroid belt encircling the vivid pink-and-blue dust of the chaotic gale, monitoring Gladdic's vessel as it flirted with the edge of our sensor range. We waited until the *Atlas*'s lights dimmed, signaling the withdrawal of its security bots into its bays and a downshift to minimal power mode to limit the exposure of equipment to the electromagnetism.

"Go," I said to the *Phoenix*, and the autonavigation propelled us on a course that exactly matched that of the *Atlas*.

Then a burn of the engines propelled us to a reckless speed.

"Turn all noncritical systems off," I told the *Phoenix*'s computer.

The vessel cut its power and stranded us adrift, propelled by our momentum on a collision course directly with Gladdic's vessel. We threaded through the bright nebular dust, and then Gladdic's vessel appeared through the haze.

Neither of our vessels had full communications powered on, but a coded message swiftly blinked from the windows of his vessel to ours. Anguish had learned to interpret these signals while with the Partisans. He translated for me.

"'Change course,' they say," Anguish said. "'A collision will kill us both.'"

"Return this message: 'I know.'"

A grim smile tugged at his lips as he flicked our own lights to convey the message.

We veered closer and closer. The next message blinked faster and faster: "'Stop,'" Anguish translated. "'You will kill us both. Stop. You will kill us both. Stop. You will kill us both.'"

I smiled. "Tell them: 'Yes, I will.'"

The *Phoenix* drifted closer and closer to the *Atlas*, our momentum barreling us through skeins of pink and purple stardust. My clenched fists squeezed so tightly they throbbed.

"Turn on your engines, Gladdic," I whispered to the distant Grande. "You don't want to die."

Gladdic's obedience to Tyrus told me he was desperate to survive. He had to be far, far more afraid of death than I was.

Soon we were close enough to the spherical vessel to perceive the windows speckling its hull. The occupants within had a fine view of their impending doom.

Anguish rose to his full height as we veered dangerously close. "Nemesis, I think we—"

"Wait for it." I could not be wrong. Gladdic was too much a coward—

The *Atlas* abruptly lit up, engines firing. The thrusters blasted the *Atlas* clear of our ship, and its lasers fired a rebuke toward us that sliced apart the gale of pink and purple clouds.

The *Phoenix* jolted violently, then rocked and bucked as though trying to shake off the blow. Anguish barked out a laugh, and I grinned as I pressed my palms flat against the vibrating command nexus, its panels sparking and sizzling from laser damage.

Gladdic had just lost.

We listed forward through space, end over end, still coasting on momentum, and I found a window from which I watched the *Atlas* founder through the clouds, veins of bright plasma discharge dancing over its hull. In powering up, the vessel had damaged itself.

Anguish came to my side. I took his hand and gripped it hard as we watched the receding vessel succumb to the strangely lovely bouts of internal power surges. Small pieces of its hull began to peel away like rotten skin. The large windows near the forward bow showed the dancing brightness of flames.

"Now what?" said Anguish.

"Guard the ship," I said. "I will have a talk with Gladdic."

We caught up to the *Atlas* as she limped out of the chaotic gale. There were no defensive shields in working order, nothing to stop our landing tethers from snaring it in our grasp. I extended our boarding artery and then stalked onto the ship, a pulse rifle in hand.

The Grandiloquy relied on security bots for the same reason they had once depended on Diabolics: it was easier to engineer a guard than to find a lackey willing to die for the Empire's elite. The Aton servants who saw us simply raised their hands in surrender.

"Where is Aton?" I asked one. His shaking hand pointed toward the command nexus.

Inside, Gladdic von Aton whipped around to face me. He was still dressed up for his appearance on Daedalus—he wore a headdress resembling a haloed sunburst, and a metal half-shirt that bared his machine-sculpted abdomen. His surprise at seeing me was lent a comical touch by his makeup; his green eyes were darkly lined and framed by extravagantly long, thick lashes. Propagandists had to keep up appearances.

"It's been years, Gladdic. Miss me?" I asked.

His gaze dropped to the rifle in my hand. "Nice touch," he said, his voice cracking. "You sound just like her."

I tossed the rifle aside and drew a blade, letting the metal catch the light. Then I hurled it toward him. He shrieked and dropped to the floor as it plunged through his ridiculous headdress, pinning it to the wall behind him.

"Next time I aim between your eyes," I snarled. "You despicable worm."

Gladdic shoved himself up on his elbows, still gaping at me. The shock seemed to have eroded his wits. He closed his mouth, but it immediately fell open again.

Not for the first time, he reminded me of a stricken animal. *Poor Gladdic*, I'd often thought. That memory stirred an accompanying sensation. . . . I'd often felt protective of him.

Not again. In shielding this weakling, I'd enabled his pathetic feebleness to be weaponized by Tyrus and used against me.

I was all out of pity.

"To your feet," I said.

"It can't be you!"

"I said *to your feet!*" I reached down and dragged him up by the collar. Metal flashed—a small energy weapon he'd hidden until now. It was aimed right at me.

Mockingly, I smiled. I spread my arms. "Go ahead, then."

His hand trembled. "Don't move," he quavered. "Don't move a centimeter."

"Why did you lie about me, Gladdic?"

"You can't be Nemesis. She's dead. The real Nemesis is dead—"

"Pathetic," I said flatly. "Obeying Tyrus like his little lapdog. I should have let him kill you."

"You're not Nemesis."

I seized the barrel of his energy weapon and pressed it to my forehead. "Shoot me. Go ahead!"

His eyes glistened with tears.

He would weep? How dare he? I seized hold of the energy

141

weapon, yanked it to the side, and then kicked his knees out from under him. He landed with a heavy thud, and I caught him by the hair, wrenching his head back before I jammed the weapon into his mouth.

He gagged.

"Shall I show you how murder is done?" I asked him.

"P-puhhh!"

"Please? Is that what you mean to say?"

Tears streamed freely down his face as he nodded gingerly. A mixture of contempt and guilt coiled in my stomach, sickening me. To see a grown man reduced to this sniveling and helpless pile—alas, I had use for him. I tore the weapon out of his mouth, then laid my hand to his forehead and shoved him backward.

"You had no need to lie for him," I said coldly. "No need to be his mouthpiece. All you had to do was stay *silent*, Gladdic. To say nothing rather than lie . . . Oh, but then I suppose you wouldn't have been given your ship back. Was this a gift from the Emperor?"

At his silence, I roared, "ANSWER ME!"

Gladdic bowed his head. "Yes," he whispered.

"Ah." I nodded and looked around the command nexus. "So the *Atlas* was more valuable than your integrity. Well, it's a fine ship, to be sure. Do you know what I mean to do with it? I am *taking* it. Where is that bust of Cygna? That was to be my wedding present. It's rightfully mine as well."

His tears had stopped, leaving his eyes wide and dry. He remembered well that bust Tyrus had used to beat his father to death, the one Tyrus had cruelly forced him to display. I'd ordered him to give it to me—as a mercy, so he would no longer need to look upon it. Now it told him everything.

"It . . . it is you. How is it possible?"

"Because *you* sent me to the Partisans!" I roared at him. "You did, Gladdic! You injected me with oxygen pellets and contacted Neveni to seize my tomb before it burned up in a star. It was *you*. You don't remember because Tyrus dosed you with Scorpion's Breath afterward so you'd forget your near-execution and play a better propagandist for him. *You* are the reason for my survival! Yet now you play propagandist for the man who tried to murder me!"

He grew deathly pale. "I saved you?"

He seemed horror-struck. He didn't realize Tyrus already knew. He likely was thinking of what Tyrus would do to him if he ever learned the truth.

I could use that.

"Yes," I said with malevolent relish. "You. You saved me. And you are going to help me once again. Because I mean to kill Tyrus."

"Oh please, no. Please leave me out of this," he whispered. "I've only just crept back into his good graces. Nemesis, please—"

I stepped forward and cuffed him. It was a light blow, but it still knocked him back against the wall. I seized his collar and wrenched him off the ground, slamming him into the wall so hard I heard him wheeze.

"What do you fear, that Tyrus will kill you? Believe me: he won't get the chance if you refuse me. You'll figure out a way to help me destroy him, or I swear on all the stars, I'll give you good reason to be afraid."

18

ANGUISH AND I boarded the *Atlas* and set Gladdic's crew to salvaging engine parts from the *Phoenix* to replace what had been destroyed by the chaotic gale. Then we used the *Atlas*'s blasting lasers to shear the *Phoenix* into shreds. Sooner or later, Tyrus would learn that we'd stolen that vessel. Let him find another dead end when he tracked it down.

Once we'd taken the *Atlas* into the enveloping darkness of hyperspace, I began scouring the vessel's databases for our next target.

We needed resources, and I found a dozen sites of interest: major armories, hidden arsenals, vaults of imperial riches.

We hadn't bothered to lock up Gladdic. He was our prisoner all the same, trapped on this ship with a small contingent of servants who would not risk themselves to help him. Nor would Gladdic dare ask them for help—I had explained that he would be held accountable for any acts of sabotage they committed. As for the man himself, physical bravery was not among his notable qualities.

One might have expected him to keep to his quarters, but Gladdic had never been circumspect. He came into the conference chamber now, wearing another absurd headdress—this one a holographic image of a galaxy swirling about his temple. He was eager, he said, to be helpful. Fear had total power over him.

He told me about each of the targets I'd selected, offering whatever important or insignificant details he could dredge up.

Nothing truly lit my interest until we reached one of the lesser targets.

I'd found it in the *Atlas*'s flight logs. This ship had been among a coterie that accompanied the *Alexandria* to an obscure location: an asteroid within the Jubilee Belt.

"That's the Clandestine Repository," Gladdic said. "But we can't go there."

And *that* caught my attention.

"Why? What is it?"

"It's like a central bank, you could say."

A bank. "Wealth?" I said sharply.

"And information. All the greater Grandiloquy families have vaults there. They store family records. The Divine Emp—the Emperor used to visit often."

I leaned forward. "When?"

"Not for years," said Gladdic. "I . . . I guess he wished to peruse the histories. Family records, mostly. Surveillance footage or senatorial holographics from early in the Empire."

All I could think of was the pitiful weapons bay of the *Atlas*. Like most every vessel, Gladdic's ship carried basic blasting lasers and a handful of sophisticated missiles, but only the smallest number and not nearly sufficient for a proper attack against a juggernaut like the

Alexandria, much less the fleet of thousands of security drones Tyrus could deploy at will now. With a store of wealth, we could provision ourselves for a proper onslaught.

And if we funded our actions against this Empire with wealth stolen from the great Grandiloquy families, all the better. Let them feel the vulnerability of having their most secured vaults plundered.

"That's where we'll start," I said.

"No," said Gladdic sharply. "Trust me, it's too difficult to raid."

"Is it?" I said. "If only the Grandiloquy and their most trusted servants know of this place, they've likely grown complacent—too assured of its security."

"Only the Emperor can grant access."

I smiled. "That's why we have you, Gladdic. You've crawled into his good graces. You'll want to see your vault."

"It doesn't work that way." Agitated, Gladdic began to pace. "Even if the *Atlas* were allowed to dock with the Repository, they'd bring the Aton vault to *me*—and then they'd make sure we left. We can't just dock and walk inside."

"We won't walk," I said calmly. "We'll dock and then shoot our way in."

"But . . ." He saw the look on my face and visibly wilted. "I suppose I have no chance of talking you out of it."

"None whatsoever." I grabbed a mobile computer console and plopped it before him, along with a stylus. "Now draw."

"Draw . . . ?"

"Everything you remember about the layout. The defenses. Everything."

Gladdic's memory was patchy at best, his drawing skills little better than a child's. But he gave me a fair idea of what lay ahead. The *Atlas*

146

shot out of hyperspace into the Jubilee Belt, where the Clandestine Repository was located, and our long-range sensors confirmed at once the scant details that Gladdic had provided.

An enormous asteroid with indications of activity beneath its surface. Kilometers of solid iron walls guarding it . . .

A single exterior bay.

"I told you," Gladdic repeated as Anguish and I looked over the bleak tactical situation. "There's just one entrance, and a thousand armed personnel within, *minimum*. You can't penetrate it with machines; the walls are lined with power dampeners. Even if you force your way in through the bay, they'll know exactly where you are. They can seal off the exterior chambers and vent you to space."

I stared at the distant asteroid belt, thinking. If there were power dampeners seeded into the walls, then the defenders of the Repository must have no automated machines for their own defense. Since I had none for offense, that was an advantage in my favor.

"We should leave before we're detected," said Gladdic.

"Quiet." A manipulation of the sensors and I had the scan of the interior. The greatest defense of the Repository was the shape of its structure: a single exterior bay, leading to a long chain of rooms, one after another, the innermost of them containing the vaults. The place was built to be defensible, for there was only that single way in, and no other. To travel through, one would face the entirety of the defensive force, with no possibility of avoiding them.

My eyes traced across the schematics over and over and then fixed on the very interior most of those chambers. They gave way to narrow waste tubules and energy ducts.

Those could be used as an entrance. If someone dared.

"They expect us to invade here," I said to Anguish, pointing to the bay. "They count on sealing the exterior chambers and venting any invaders back into space. So you won't leave the *Atlas*. You'll raise the ship's shields to protect you from impact, and then fire straight through these chambers—impacting the Repository from inside it. They'll concentrate their defensive forces on you. In the meantime, I come at them from the other direction."

"What other direction?"

I tapped the diagram, indicating the waste tubules.

"Those are too narrow," he said.

"The primary waste vent should be large enough for one person. For me," I clarified.

"Unacceptable," he said tersely. "You've no idea what you're facing."

"There's only one way to find out." I shrugged. The plan was not optimal, but it was all we had. "They're not prepared for a dual assault."

There'd been so many times I'd felt helpless. I could do nothing while Tyrus murdered the Excess on the *Halcyon*, while Pasus forced the Venalox on Tyrus, while Donia suffocated in my arms.

But at long last, a path had opened before me, bright and clear and vivid—a path to redeeming my former failures. For in that Repository were secrets, technologies, and stars knew what else.

This could be the first real step toward victory.

19

ANGUISH DEVOTED HIMSELF to helping me with grim resignation rather than enthusiasm. There was one launching system the *Atlas* could deploy undetected by those in the Repository: the funereal launcher within its heliosphere. I would travel crammed inside a coffin.

While Anguish programmed the trajectory of the launching chute, I injected oxygen pellets into my blood. There were breathing gills on the *Atlas*, but I couldn't trust them to survive the impact. I could only hold my breath during strenuous exertion for twelve minutes. The oxygen pellets would buy me time beyond that—but I could not guess how long.

There was no space in the coffin for weaponry, only a med bot that Anguish carefully packed inside a small impact capsule. "That does it," he said, stepping back.

As I studied the cramped box, unease snaked through me, and my chest tightened. I would have felt better with even a small energy weapon, but we couldn't risk the g-forces leading to a power discharge while I was trapped in a small space with it.

There was no choice but to rely on myself alone.

I swept past Anguish and leaped into the coffin. He strapped me in, then gazed down at me, his pinched brow betraying his agitation. "Nemesis . . . if something goes wrong—"

"We are Diabolics," I said. "We can pull this off."

A muscle twitched in his jaw. Then he leaned down to kiss my forehead. "You can do it," he said gruffly. "You *will*." Then, with one swift move, he slammed shut the lid of the coffin.

Pitch darkness surrounded me. Nerves writhed in my stomach, pointless, stupid. There was no going back now. No need to panic. All I needed to do at this moment was wait.

The darkness heaved as Anguish loaded the coffin into the launching tube. The coffin rumbled toward the exit slot. Time slowed, seconds stretching unbearably.

I distracted myself by reciting what I knew: the *Atlas* was even now veering toward the Repository. Gladdic would be able to get us no farther than the dock, but we needed to go no farther. By the time Anguish began battering his way in, I would be climbing out of the waste tube to assault the Repository from the interior . . .

. . . if the plan worked.

If it did not, I was already in my tomb.

Stop it.

I turned my hands palms out, to trace my fingers over the cold crystalline glass of this enclosure. It was not designed to withstand an impact. When it lodged into the waste vent, it would shatter, almost certainly breaking or dislocating my limbs. Our chances of success depended on the med bot tucked beside me, and its ability to heal the damage done to me.

What if it didn't work?

The frantic thought sliced through my mind, vivid as a blast of lightning cutting through dark clouds.

What if I'd miscalculated? What if this plan was a mistake? What if—

My ears ruptured with the explosion of sound blasting the tube about me, propelling me out of the *Atlas*.

All I could do now was await my fate.

Impact.

Agony.

The crystalline coffin shattered, shards slicing my skin as they flew away. A tearing, ripping, blinding light engulfed me. My limbs were dislocated, the bones within them separating and my organs being battered. My supersonic helmet protected my skull but could not protect my neck from whiplash; my own blood choked my lungs. I was dying. Or maybe I was already dead. . . .

From a great distance came the ludicrous thought: the Diabolic Nemesis, smashed apart by her own idiotic ideas!

I heard the wheeze of my own broken laugh and became aware that the impact capsule had popped open. The med bot was already at work on me.

Pain receded from my burning chest and arms. Relief spread in a tide of fire down my waist, my hips and legs. My vision dimmed, the light subsiding into darkness. The rancid stench of sewage stung in my nose.

I had survived the impact.

Breathing hard, I tried to keep still while the healing process sent searing lashes of pain through me. *Think.* By now, the Repository's defensive systems would have erected a force field to seal the breach. With luck, the staff would attribute it to a minor asteroid impact.

A jostling rocked the world around me. That would be the *Atlas* docking—or so I hoped. Soon Anguish would begin to open fire, to engage the defenders and draw them away from my position.

I had to move *now.* Slip in behind them, be in position for the opening assault.

I clenched my fingers, which tingled from the rapid repair of my nerve endings. My grip strengthened. I flexed my feet and felt them respond.

I rolled over in the pitch darkness.

The med bot wouldn't survive the sewage, so I left it behind. It had done its job well, for I felt no pain whatsoever as I stood and shoved my way forward through the waste tube. No doubt my adrenaline helped—I sped through the viscous weight of the sewage, barely registering its resistance. The tube began to slant downward, and the foul stuff climbed to my chest, then my armpits.

At last I reached a low point in the tube where the passageway descended fully into the muck. I drew in a deep lungful of air and thrust myself forward. I swam—pumping my legs and arms hard, until they burned, until my lungs grew hot and panicked for oxygen, and only my will kept me from inhaling.

Red panic bubbled through me. How much farther must I swim? I could not safely turn back now. Only the oxygen pellets in my bloodstream kept me alive, and as I battled forward, I knew they must be rapidly expiring. Escape could be meters ahead or kilometers. It would have been better to die in the coffin. I would drown in waste.

No choice. I grappled with hands along walls, until I reached one that dead-ended.

I kicked up to the surface, gasping frantically as I found scant inches of clean air. With my head craned back so my neck burned from the effort, I breathed, deep lungfuls of stinking soiled air, as I groped overhead for a break in the tube. I swept my hands out wider and wider, desperate now.

A break in the tubing made me gasp with relief. I extended myself to my full height and braced my hands on either side of the overhead pipe; then with a roar I leaped upward. The thick sucking weight of the sewage pulled me back down. Bracing myself again, I leaped once more—and this time managed to catch myself, spread-eagled, my feet and hands planted on opposite sides of the overhead tube.

My limbs trembled from the force of the pressure required to keep me suspended. But I could not afford to pause. With another grunt, I climbed.

The tube narrowed steadily, so that I began to fear being trapped here. No choice but to find out. I kept clawing upward, until the smooth surface of the tube suddenly yielded to something rougher. Giddy relief flooded me. A maintenance hatch! With all the leverage I could muster, I slammed it open and shoved myself through.

I hit the ground at the feet of a startled young mechanic and slammed my fist into his face.

As he fell, he was already gagging at the smell. I hauled him up by the collar and clamped my hand over his mouth to cut off his noises. He vomited against it. I lifted it away so he would not choke while I hissed at him, "How many in the next rooms? Quietly."

He looked at me and screamed, *"INTRUDER!"*

Fine. I enjoyed surprises.

I seized his head and rammed it against the wall. A door slid open, and the men who'd responded to the cry lifted their pulse rifles. I hurled the unconscious guard at the nearest of them. They averted their weapons to avoiding hitting their colleague. I lowered my head and charged into them, knocking them backward.

I ripped away one of their rifles and shot two rapidly.

The last shrieked as his colleagues fell.

I aimed the pulse rifle between his eyes. "How many guards ahead, and what is the layout of the chamber? Talk or die."

20

I HAD THE GUARD speak into his transmitter and issue his colleagues a firm warning: "Throw down your weapons and surrender, or you will die today."

Then I knocked him unconscious.

My route through the Repository led me past a door with a great sigil etched upon it.

Specifically, the Pasus family's supernova sigil.

Anger sparked within me. This family, this family! For a moment my mind catapulted back to Elantra's spiteful smile as Sidonia suffocated from her poison, Alectar von Pasus's taunts as his servants carried a limp and unconscious Tyrus into his ship.

Though Elantra died, her heart pulsing in my hand, and Alectar had followed—sliced apart by Tyrus's security bots—it struck me now that they had effectively won. They'd destroyed Tyrus, they'd murdered Sidonia, they'd taken all I loved, and now I was setting out to kill the boy I'd loved to end what *they* had started.

As much as I wished to destroy everything in that vault, I had to preserve it for looting after we conquered this place. Everything we did from here depended upon what we could steal from these vaults. I continued onward.

". . . an intruder somewhere in this sector . . ." came a voice from down the corridor.

Since they were heading toward me, I sprinted as fast as I could to face them on my terms. The Domitrian servants didn't know my location, so they were startled when I burst into the next hall, my pulse rifle blasting.

They barely managed to get off a shot before all six of them fell. As I charged into the next chamber, an ambush awaited.

I glimpsed the four men before a flamethrower blasted through the air. The wall of fire boiled up between us, but still, I did not hesitate. I squeezed my eyes shut, fixed my mind on the image of where I'd seen them standing. I had already survived fire once, and I could do so again.

Pain screamed through me as I hurtled through the flames and seized the first attacker. There was a lot of flesh and sinew to char away before the flames could truly damage me, so I forged forward, reaching, seizing, tearing. They were all dead by the time I hit the coarse carpet beyond and rolled out the fire.

One of my eyes was blinded, stinging, perhaps ruptured. As I quickly looked myself over, my one good eye showed the extent of my burns, my curdled skin as pale as egg white where it was sloughing away from subcutaneous tissue. My hair was gone. My nostrils felt scorched but I had not inhaled, so my lungs still functioned, though they itched and seized against the smoke that lingered in them. I coughed, then struggled not to vomit as I staggered onward.

Forward. Keep going forward.

I barrel-rolled into the next chamber, where several sharpshooters awaited. A sting lanced my shoulder, but the pain barely registered. I lunged forward to seize the nearest shooter, then held him before me as a shield while I picked off his brethren. In the next room, I repeated the technique.

As I moved onward, I encountered a group of frantic, terrified medics who skidded to a stop when they spotted me. A med bot hovered over their heads.

They did not seem to be armed. "Heal me and live," I told them.

They complied. The bot sterilized my wounds, then knitted together the torn and melted scraps of my skin. The oozing, putrid flesh turned into hard scar tissue. I required no mirror to know that I was hideously disfigured once more. It would take a half-dozen beauty bots, all working in tandem, to restore me this time.

No matter. What need had I of beauty? I would overcome Tyrus. I would save the Empire from him if I had to maraud to the ends of the universe, under fire the whole way.

The medics' work was nearly completed, with only my damaged eye remaining, when a rustling came from behind. I ducked a sudden spray of laser blasts. Two medics collapsed beside me, sightless eyes fixed wide. I twisted and rolled to dodge blasts, then lifted my rifle and shot both attackers in the chest. Springing to my feet, I charged forward again.

Diabolics are engineered to thrive on violence. The frenzy that overcame me then felt sweet and hot and exhilarating. I lanced through the next section, then the next, dispensing no mercy: I could afford none. Half-blinded and outnumbered, I shot only to kill.

When I encountered windows, I blasted them out and counted on my strength to hold me to the wall until the wind stopped tearing at me, until I could force open the next door. Incendiary pipes I blasted, then threw myself to the floor until the angry flames abated enough to allow me passage. When I met water mains, I ruptured them and knocked electrical equipment into the liquid. I leaped clear of the talons of bright light that forked over the water and sent my assailants into fatal seizures. On those occasions when my scrabbling hands found no safe grip, I plunged back into the electrified water, trusting that my Diabolic's heart, designed to withstand combat and torture, would continue to beat as the rest of my muscles locked and froze.

And always, always, I eventually staggered back to my feet and continued onward.

A little farther, just a little more . . . I kept moving, shooting anyone who tried to kill me, operating on sheer instinct now. Humans had designed those instincts. Humans now died by them.

As I progressed, the med bot's restoration was quickly ruined. My left arm was shredded, bone and subcutaneous tissue visible. I left bodies like litter in my wake. Each step felt as though a burning-hot poker had been jammed up my thighs. Stiffened scar tissue tore as I leaped, nerves raw and screaming. I had to claw away blood that seeped and stung blindingly into my good eye.

Then, through the haze of violence, I spotted something fixed to the wall before me.

Another sigil of a great family, the sun rising from behind the curvature of a gas giant.

This was the vault of the Impyreans.

21

MY LEGS went weak. My burning fury collapsed into cinders, my vision blurring as I stared at the sigil of the Impyreans. Hands numb, fingers tingling, I limped toward the door and laid my palm against it, not daring to hope. . . .

My breath caught as I heard a telltale chime.

The door slid open.

For a moment, I stood stunned on the threshold, transfixed by an ache far worse than the physical agony of my wounds. Donia, my beloved Donia, must have snuck my DNA into the authorization database. The system recognized me as Impyrean.

How long ago had she done this? She had been dead for so many years. How had she guessed that one day, I would need her help?

Grief made my throat tighten, clench. My grip loosened so the rifle slipped from my hand, clattering to the floor.

I stepped past the array of empty shelves. Once, no doubt, they had held antiques and other valuables, which had been seized after the family was wiped away. I stepped past empty pedestals that had once lovingly displayed data crystals and personal effects.

And beyond these, at the end of the vault, were the smaller personal vaults, more priceless to me than a tower full of ancient gold. For one of them belonged to the heiress of the Impyrean family, long perished.

My hand shook as this one, too, opened for me. Within it, I found one remaining trinket, something priceless to Sidonia, and yes, now priceless to me—but useless to any thief.

It was a precious child's toy. A thing of our shared childhood.

It was Sidonia's cloud sphere.

I withdrew it and sank down to the floor. I'd had nightmares about her where I screamed at her, where I punished her for making me learn to *feel*, to experience the pain that came with love. Now it was pain that rushed through me, and yet my anger at her was gone, a disgraceful, shameful memory, for I still loved her. I still loved Donia, and oh stars, I missed her.

If only she were alive. If only she were here with me. If only I could hear her sweet voice one last time, and tell her how I loved her, how sorry I was for everything that had happened. . . .

In the distance, muffled explosions continued, the destruction I'd wrought now taking on a life of its own. In this room, a strange silence descended, a hush that felt thick and sacred. My hands shook a little around the crystalline sphere, the bright glowing gases swirling and dancing.

Donia had liked to play a game when we were small. The Impyrean fortress orbited a gas giant planet, and she would point out all the shapes she saw in the swirls of red, yellow, and orange clouds. A bunny. A frog. If we were on the dark side of the planet, she would use this cloud sphere instead, pressing her eye close to it, trying to find shapes in the gases.

She always tried to convince me to play.

I refused.

I told her I saw nothing in the clouds, that such games were a waste of time.

But I'd lied. I had indeed seen shapes in the cloud sphere:

An injured man dragging himself along, one leg a stump.

A face contorted by terror, mouth wrenched wide in agony.

Pools of blood splotching a trail across the clouds.

I would sooner have died than tell Donia that truth.

She'd loved that game, and when she'd outgrown it, she'd kept this toy. She must have slipped it in here unnoticed. The Matriarch would never have tolerated the preservation of something so silly.

My legs felt weak with gratitude that she'd preserved it. Now, as I stared into this little orb cupped in my scarred and shaking hands, I found myself remembering something else: the sight from the window on the *Hera* as Tyrus and I departed the Sacred City. That day, after we'd made love for the first time, he'd fallen asleep in my arms, and I had found myself tracing the Interdict's mark over my heart, that mark of blessing that deemed me a person, as strings of dust and starlight unfurled out the window. And for the first time, staring at that view, I had seen beauty in shapes: not hideous and violent things, but two hands interlinked, a current passing between them. . . .

A pair of humans wrapped in an embrace . . .

Trees, mountains, shooting stars. So many wonders. My eyes had been opened to them.

Donia, I had thought. *Donia, I see them now.*

A great thundering boom ripped me out of my reverie just as the floor rocked beneath me. The asteroid shuddered violently as—I guessed, I hoped—Anguish's onslaught began. If all was going according to our plan, then the *Atlas* had just jammed itself into the docking bay and was picking off the security personnel who hastened to attack it.

Anguish would not leave the ship until the way was cleared, or until he saw me. I needed to leave this place, to fight onward to meet him.

I took a deep breath and slipped the cloud sphere into my pocket. Then I touched the Interdict's mark on my chest. But it was no longer there. Scar tissue met my touch.

I looked down to see the mutilation of that concentric sun mark. It had been lost amid the twisted, contorted scars of my skin.

Feeling oddly numb, I stepped back out into the main chamber.

My victims littered the room, their blood swirling in the ankle-deep water. As I stepped through the bodies, the mutilated mark of personhood seemed to burn. The butchery around me made a mockery of my claims to humanity. I didn't know how many people I'd killed to get this far. I hadn't kept count. I did not want to know.

I stepped back into the previous chamber I'd torn through, and the corpses there floated and bobbed as though on an unseen tide. My stomach felt acidic and unsteady. In the whisper of the water along the walls, I heard echoes of names that others had called me, names that had angered Donia. *You are no monster*, she had told me. *You are as human as I.*

Something nudged my leg: the foot of a corpse, which had drifted toward me.

I turned away and vomited.

When I straightened, wiping my mouth, I made myself stare through the open doorway into the room before that, to the bodies that waited there as well. I could count all the corpses on this asteroid, and all the others I had killed in my lifetime, and still they would not make up a thousandth of the total murdered by Tyrus. And he would not stop now. In his pursuit of absolute power, he would kill anyone who offered him an excuse.

A thundering of footsteps approached. I took a deep breath, then made myself bend to pick up an energy pistol floating beside the nearest body.

I had never claimed to be good. But I was better than Tyrus. I had been engineered with a thirst for murder, but I had leashed it. Now I would use it only to end his murderous reign, to rectify the mistake I'd made forcing him back into Pasus's hands.

And maybe it took a monster to fight a monster.

I lifted my energy weapon and turned.

A pair of Excess men skidded to a stop in the doorway, their hands on their weapon holsters. They looked young, untried, their horror plain as they surveyed the carnage. And then one of them raised his eyes to me, his hand tightening over his weapon as he studied me.

"Don't," I said. "Let me spare you."

He aimed the pulse rifle—

And dropped to the floor, dead from a shot at point-blank range. I hadn't fired my weapon.

His companion had. He lowered his own energy pistol and looked at me with awe.

"Nemesis lives," he whispered, his face aglow with wonder. He plunged to his knees beside his victim, in this flooded chamber strewn with my victims. "It's a miracle!"

22

THE SURVIVORS of the Clandestine Repository surrendered rapidly, with several more of them hastening to declare, "Nemesis lives!" I'd killed so many of their colleagues. I searched their faces for terror and saw only wonder and devotion.

I was no Tyrus, to accept this as my due. I told them to get off their knees when they tried to bow to me. But I was grateful for the surrender that put an end to the bloodshed. An enterprising female engineer offered to jam all subspace communications, and I followed her to the transmission array to watch this be done.

Plyno, the Excess man who'd shot his own colleague before hailing me, had disappeared to contact Anguish and signal the Repository's surrender. By the time he returned with Anguish, I was battling dizziness, my vision fading in and out.

Anguish wore a ferocious smile as he joined me. "An entire battalion could not have done what you did here today."

My head pulsed with a stabbing headache. "Not without cost. I am injured, I think. . . . At least the workers here are feeling cooperative." Then my legs buckled.

Anguish and Plyno both caught me. Whatever they said was lost to the haze in my head, but I was dimly aware of being gripped by the waist and steered forward.

My consciousness slipped in and out as I staggered under someone else's direction. Arms steadied me, catching me when I stumbled. Our slow progression felt like hours, but at last I registered familiar surroundings: I was being guided aboard the *Atlas*.

Relief drained the last of my strength. As I dropped to the floor, someone caught and lifted me.

The world lurched and my shredded arm bashed into the wall, yanking me awake on a wave of pain.

"Oh, I'm sorry!" cried Gladdic.

Before I could reply, all went dim again. I roused once more in the medical bay as Gladdic summoned one of his servants. "Doctor nan Aton, attend to her."

He made to withdraw, but I snared his arm.

"Wait," I managed, my voice a threadbare whisper.

Gladdic eyed me nervously.

"Thank you," I managed. Then the med bot was hovering just above me and the world faded once more.

Gladdic was there when I awoke, a glass of water in his hand.

My mouth was bone dry, and my skin was raw and tingling where the med bots had debrided and healed it once more. With his hand supporting the back of my neck, he helped me sit up, and then offered me the water. As soon as the cool liquid touched my lips, I realized I was desperate for it.

After several voracious swallows, my head cleared enough for my vision to focus. His brow was knitted over his troubled green eyes, his handsome face soft with kindness.

He would have been a fine healer, in another life.

I at last turned my head, and he withdrew the cup. If I'd had the strength to shove myself upright, I would have slung my legs over the side of the medical bed and left straightaway. My thoughts were already returning to my surreal, horrific triumph at the Repository.

I had killed people. I'd had to do it, if I meant to stop Tyrus, but that made it no less a crime. They had merely defended themselves from me. Done their duty to their Emperor, their Empire. How much blood would need to be shed to reach Tyrus? How much more would I have to defile my hard-won humanity, to strip him of his power over this galaxy?

My arm buckled under my weight, and I collapsed to the mattress, gasping for air, my body a vast, throbbing wound.

"It's all right," Gladdic told me, straightening the sheet over me. "Anguish is working with the . . . the survivors in the Repository. He has everything in hand. He told me to keep you here."

I snorted. As though Gladdic could stop me if I meant to leave!

Then again, right now, he likely could.

"Do you need anything? I know medications don't tend to work with crea—with you."

"With creatures. You can speak that word."

He looked unhappy, folding his arms over his chest and shifting his weight as though frustrated by something.

"What is it?" I asked.

"I wish to be of help."

"The Repository is secured now," I said.

"Not that kind of help. Help to *you*, Nemesis. You're in pain."

Bewilderment washed over me. "Why?"

He blinked, as though it were a bizarre question. "Why what?"

"Why help me? Why do you care if I'm in pain?" He must have seen the interior of the Repository. The hallways riddled with corpses. Did he not understand what I was?

He still looked uncertain, and also—was it my imagination?—hurt. "I won't blame you for doubting me. After what you went through during the last years, to hear me speaking so—"

What was he talking about? "Gladdic. Are you *sympathizing* with me? You cannot be this . . . idiotically compassionate. It will be your undoing."

He gave a small smile. "This is who I am."

"It doesn't serve you well."

"No," he said, looking off into space. "The last person I tended like this was . . . not kind to me afterward."

This caught my attention. The haze cleared from my mind, leaving in its wake a crystalline sharpness. "Was it Tyrus?"

The question seemed to startle him. He opened his mouth but uttered no sound—then finally nodded. "Yes."

My eyes drooped closed, the chamber a swaying, tilting thing around me. "Tell me."

"Tell you . . . about what?"

"He became a monster when I was away." *And now I've become one, to fight him.* "I want to hear about that." I wanted the certainty of understanding. I wanted to know why I *had* to do this.

So Gladdic told me.

After the *Tigris* was destroyed, and I was off with Neveni, Tyrus's erosion under Venalox had proceeded gradually and then rapidly.

"The Grandiloquy were furious with him after you left," said

Gladdic. "Most everyone had lost someone on the *Tigris*. Family. Friends. They blamed you, but they thought you were dead. They also blamed Pasus, but they were too afraid to say so to him. But the Emperor . . ."

I could guess.

"He was glad to be blamed," Gladdic said. "He gloated over it."

I could imagine it. . . . Tyrus had been totally in the thrall of Venalox, surrounded by enemies with reason to hate us, and they were totally unleashed, once I was not around any longer. They had no reason to fear what I'd do to them—for there was no one else but me to protect Tyrus.

They must have made him suffer for the *Tigris*.

And Gladdic told me of that first month after my escape. . . . The hysterical meetings of the privy council, where Grandes and Grandeés demanded reparations for the lives lost in the collision. He told me of Tyrus's unvarnished satisfaction listening to them, however much Pasus rebuked or punished him for it.

"You all want compensation? Truly?" Tyrus had said. "Well, let me assure you, if I had but a nugget of gold, I would piss on it and throw it in the waste reclaimer before I'd give any of you a flake."

Pasus had ordered him to cease such talk, for he helped nothing by it.

"Excellent, for I don't intend to help," Tyrus had replied, causing the Grandiloquy to erupt with cries of anger. "If I could have killed the entire lot of you in that arena, I would have! It was the mercy of my wife—yes, the Diabolic you despise—that ensured any of you survived! I wanted you all dead. She won't be here to save you the next time it happens."

And though Pasus seized his hair—disrespecting the Emperor in front of all of them—and whispered some threat in his ear, Tyrus had only laughed.

"Do your worst, Alectar," he'd said.

"I didn't see much of him for a while," Gladdic told me. "Pasus confined him to his chambers. He'd only allow him out at ceremonial occasions, and then he'd be drugged, but . . ."

But that had not been the end of Tyrus's defiance of the Grandiloquy. They had committed the mass murder of the Luminars, then had taken him prisoner—of course he had not cooperated.

But Pasus had set out to force him into submission. And in my absence, no one had defended him.

I clenched my jaw as Gladdic recounted the myriad indignities through which Tyrus remained strong.

"I was the only person he would speak to civilly," Gladdic told me. "He passed days staring out at the stars, waiting."

Waiting for *me.*

I must have made some noise, for Gladdic paused, looking at me questioningly.

My throat was too tight to speak. I shook my head, and he went on.

"He claimed to be indifferent to the mistreatment, but as the months passed—"

I was only supposed to be gone for a month, at best, but we'd known it could be longer. Neither of us had realized it would be years.

"He took on a hunted look," Gladdic was saying. "His hands developed a tremor. And I began to suspect . . ." He paused. "Nemesis, I really only saw some of it. What Pasus permitted the court to see."

I tried to tell myself these were the travails of another Tyrus. The real Tyrus. Not the one I'd seen murder those Excess on the *Halcyon.* Not the one who could create malignant space.

"If I were to say one day changed things," Gladdic told me, "it was about five months after you left when they found some of the debris from the *Tigris.* Pasus had been searching for the scepter, or for your body, because really, it would quash all the Emperor's hopes if they just found you dead. One day they found a body . . . It was Hazard dan Domitrian."

Hazard had been a Diabolic. He had not survived like Anguish and I had.

"The Grandiloquy celebrated. They actually celebrated," Gladdic muttered, looking abashed. He had likely been there, playing along with them. "They threw a great gala, and Pasus did not inform the Emperor of the reason for it. It was in the ball dome, and the Emperor was suspicious that something was in the works, but he had no choice but to attend. Pasus insisted he take the first dance, as per custom, and it was ghastly, Nemesis. They . . ."

"What?"

"They propelled Hazard's body out of the Empress's box. I suppose they all thought that if one Diabolic couldn't survive the vacuum, then . . . Well, everyone thought it meant you had died."

I looked at him, at his carefully averted eyes, my heart heavy in my chest. "And what did he do?"

"The body floated down to him and he . . . I don't know. He didn't move. He did nothing, he just stared. I think he assumed the same as the rest of us—that it meant you were dead too. He stopped fighting after that, Nemesis. He stopped eating, speaking. He became catatonic."

I closed my eyes. *Enough*, I wanted to say. I could bear to hear no more.

But I felt deserving of punishment. Of pain. So I did not stop him from continuing.

"It went on for . . . well, long enough that Pasus was afraid. They knew I was the only one Tyrus would speak to—I'd always been the one sent in to reason with him. But he would not acknowledge me. I'm not sure he even knew I was there. Mostly I passed the time by reading to him. He'd stare at the wall. For a while, I think Pasus even skipped the Venalox. There was no need for it anymore, maybe. He'd already won."

It felt like a solid stone was jammed in my throat. Tyrus, my Tyrus, the Tyrus I had known, lost and hopeless among endless enemies, utterly broken . . .

Broken by my death.

I rubbed my pulsing temples. "And then?" I made myself ask.

"They tried everything to rouse him," Gladdic said. "Nothing worked. But I . . . I helped him, I think."

My eyes flew open. "How?"

He gave me a tentative smile. "I told him a secret. Pasus's people found the casing of the scepter on sale on the black market. Everyone knew what that meant."

Neveni must have sold it when she realized it was not the actual scepter.

The scepter had been with me.

So if it had escaped from the *Tigris*? Then so had I.

"That restored him?" I realized I was rubbing my chest. It hurt, and not from any physical wound.

"Yes. It was proof you'd survived, wasn't it? Pasus wanted it kept quiet, but I told the Emperor. I wasn't supposed to, but I knew of no other way to help him."

My heart thudded wildly. "And . . . ?"

"And then he looked at me. He *saw* me. For the first time in months, he was there. He asked if I was sure, and I said yes. Then he got up, he showered and dressed and . . ."

I leaned forward. "And what?"

"He began to ingratiate himself to Pasus."

I narrowed my eyes. "What? You mean, he pretended to obey?"

171

Gladdic shrugged helplessly. "At first I thought it was an act too. The Emperor would sometimes send me a look, like we were in on some joke together. But then . . . well, he came *here.*" He gestured about us, indicating the Repository we were docked with. "And he brought Pasus with him. He'd offered Pasus access to the Domitrian stores and treasures. I don't know what happened here, but when he came back, he . . . he *turned* on me, is the best way I can put it."

I knew from Tyrus's own account what had happened from there. He had resolved to liberate himself from the Venalox. He'd brutalized and terrorized Gladdic into using Venalox with him, so Gladdic might serve as his test subject for neutralizers.

Yet I had not known it was a visit to this Repository that started him down that path.

Gladdic's eyes were shimmering with tears. "I grew to fear him. I often wondered if he hated me for having seen him so weak, or maybe . . . maybe he hated himself because he'd needed me. I can't remember the day he sentenced me to death, or—anything, really, from that time. I just remember waking up and . . ." He loosed a shuddering sigh. "The Emperor was sitting at my bedside, watching me. He said he wanted a 'fresh start.' I didn't realize until others told me that I'd nearly died at his hand. That *you* died intervening for me."

"And you don't remember saving me," I said hoarsely. How cruel of Tyrus, to rob Gladdic of that single memory of heroism.

Although, to be fair, Tyrus likely hadn't known until Corcyra that I'd been saved at all.

At the bleak shake of his head, I snared his hand. "But you did. *You* saved me. *You,* Gladdic."

Gladdic's hand briefly tightened around mine before he pulled free. "And what have I done since?" he said in a soft, miserable voice. "I've spoken lie upon lie—whatever he wanted me to say. I said I'd seen him transform into a god. I did it all with a straight face. You're right: I'm despicable."

"Oh, Gladdic." The last remnants of my anger with him now crumbled away. I reached up, wiped the tears from his cheek. "It's over. It's done now."

Tenderness did not come naturally to me, but receiving it came easily to him. He closed his eyes to my touch. "I am not brave," he said very quietly. "Not like you."

My mind returned to those Excess who'd tried to fight me off in the Repository, the ones I'd slain so easily. That was not bravery. It was not noble, either. "Bravery is not the same as battle skill," I said slowly. "I was bred to fight. It's not born of courage. In truth, I think I lack the strength to be like you."

He snorted. "Timid, you mean?"

"Gentle. The Grandiloquy are vipers, and you live in their snake pit—yet you have never been one yourself. You seek to understand others, to understand me, to understand Tyrus, even though none of us has ever repaid that kindness to you."

My words were slowing under the weight of my fatigue. My hand, still damp from Gladdic's tears, dropped like a lead weight back to my side.

"I don't understand you," I said honestly. "Just as I never understood Donia. But I know enough to wish I could be more like you."

Yet it was an impossible ambition. When I was hated, I replied with hate. After Tyrus had stabbed me, I'd tried to inoculate myself with hatred; I'd finally succeeded after the *Halcyon*. And in hating, I had become hateful. . . .

It takes a monster to kill a monster.

But was that so? For I had forgotten the fundamental truth that I was more than a Diabolic. I did not want to be this way. Merely because I was *created* to be a monster did not mean that was my destiny. For I had also been invested with a mind and a will, and my fate was my own to decide.

That Gladdic could look at me so kindly, even after beholding the slaughter I had wrought, was a gift indeed. It showed me that I was more than my worst mistakes.

I *wanted* to be more.

Perhaps that was the true difference between me and the Tyrus that now existed.

I would find a way to stop Tyrus, but I would not sacrifice my own soul to do it. There had to be a better way.

After a long minute, Gladdic spoke again. "What do you think the Emperor found in this Repository, to return from here so changed?"

"I don't know," I said. "But I mean to find out."

23

"I MUST FIND something while we're here," I said to Plyno. "Do you recall the Emperor visiting this place in the company of Senator von Pasus?" At his nod, I pressed, "Do you know what they were looking for?"

Plyno nodded. "Pasus spent his time poking through the Domitrian vaults. But the Emperor only wanted a tour of the facility."

"Do you know where he visited, what he looked at?"

"It could have been anything. Anywhere. It's the royal prerogative to see all the contents stored in the Repository."

"I need to know anything he examined, Plyno."

Plyno took me to the Repository's data archives, where we discovered that Tyrus had covered his tracks well. He'd deleted all surveillance records of his visit and had taken efforts to erase his digital footprints in the system too.

But clever as he was, Tyrus had no technical training. "Give me a moment and I can find out if he looked at anything in the Repository databases," Plyno said.

I nodded. With Pasus distracted by a greedy inventory of the Domitrian vaults, Tyrus certainly would have stolen the opportunity to ransack the data files.

"Here." Plyno tapped the console and the large screen before us lit up. Together we studied the backed-up logs from the archives, which showed every ancient record that Tyrus had accessed.

Most of them he'd perused only for seconds. Old proceedings of the Imperial Senate, scraps of surveillance collected by the late Emperor Randevald, footage of traitors long since executed . . . As I began to flip through the files, I gained a sense of what Tyrus had been searching for.

He'd been hunting for proof of Pasus's culpability in the mass purges of political adversaries under Randevald. What had Tyrus intended? To use these records as blackmail? Expose them to the public? Or . . .

My breath caught. *This* was what I'd been searching for.

Tyrus had watched two holographic records repeatedly—five times and twenty-two times, respectively. He'd copied them both to a data crystal.

"Play these," I said to Plyno.

My heart thudded with anticipation as Plyno cued the nearby holographic projector for the first record. An image bloomed to life between us.

For a fleeting moment, I thought it was a younger Tyrus that I gazed upon, standing in the center of the Grand Sanctum of the Chrysanthemum.

But a slight shift of the angle revealed this boy to be much smaller, with hollowed cheeks and a sulky demeanor that Tyrus had never exhibited.

Stars, they looked so similar. The same hair, the same eyes . . .

"Who is this?" I said to Plyno.

Plyno did not even have to consult the data log. "That's Emperor Tarantis von Domitrian."

Tarantis had reigned nearly five hundred years ago. What would Tyrus possibly learn from some old record of Tarantis the Great?

The holographic image abruptly panned back. My eyes narrowed as I studied the decoration of the Grand Sanctum. Bright banners and multihued flags covered the walls, but none of them showed the six-star sigil of the Domitrians. Strange.

Were these Senators? They sat where our current Senators sat, and held themselves as our Senators did, yet I glimpsed no family sigils on their garb as they discussed legislation. The representatives were wearing a variety of odd fashions, some of the same palladium and metal fashions preferred by the Grandiloquy as formal wear now, some wearing garbs of cloth. . . . Strange fashions. Hair, makeup, jewelry, clothing—so many different styles, and no two alike. Everyone wore a translator node, clipped to ears or throat or collar.

"Volume," I said.

Plyno touched the projector. A babble of voices spilled over us.

"What language are they speaking?" I asked him.

"I don't know," Plyno said.

It took me a moment to realize they were all speaking *different* languages. From *one another*. I could make out several distinct tongues.

"They didn't all speak the same language," I said, astonished. The Empire did not tolerate use of old Earth languages outside of academic study. The use of other tongues was considered subversive.

As the recording proceeded, Tarantis raised his hand and said, *"I humbly seek the honor of service to the United Republics. I ask you to accept my pledge of loyalty to the people of this galaxy."*

A voice called, *"Is this appointment ratified?"*

The image panned from one representative to the next.

"On behalf of the electorate of Lumina, I approve."

Electorate? What in the name of Helios?

"On behalf of the electorate of Atarys, I approve."

Were Senators *elected* back then?

"On behalf of the electorate of Gorgon's Arm, I approve."

My head whirled. I was watching the proceedings of a Senate—an *elected* Senate—representing *self-governing* provinces of humans from a vast swath of the galaxy.

It resembled no history I'd ever read or heard about. And yet, here it was.

"I don't understand," Plyno murmured. "The Domitrians have ruled for over two thousand years. It is the law. So what . . . why would he . . ."

He trailed off as a member of the Senate rose and pronounced Tarantis to have been ratified by the power of the electorates of the Empire.

"Go back," I said rapidly. "Let us hear that again."

Yes, Tarantis had been ratified by a body of *electorates*. And in response to this news, he bowed low—like a servant to his masters!—and *thanked* the provinces for the honor.

"They granted *him* the power," Plyno said wonderingly.

I had to play it again just to make sure of it, but to my mounting disbelief, my suspicions were true.

Tarantis was not being treated as an imperial royal, but as a servant. A servant granted power by this multitude of people.

A vicar drew forward, holding the imperial scepter high over his head. *"Do you, Tarantis von Domitrian, swear to protect and defend the United Republics, and preserve the independence and liberty of all inhabitants to the best of your ability?"*

Tarantis dropped to his knees, kneeling before all the chamber. *"As Grand Spymaster I vow to serve this galaxy to the best of my ability."*

Plyno made a noise of amazed disbelief at that word "serve." Service was something a Domitrian demanded of others—but never had we heard of an Emperor applying it to himself.

"I vow to use the powers granted me only for the public good, and to uphold the constitution to the best of my ability, so help me Helios."

A prickle moved over my skin; I barely dared blink. I watched the vicar hand Tarantis a knife, with which the young man sliced his palm. As the blood welled, he brushed his palm across the scepter—a ceremony not unfamiliar to me. This was how new Domitrian Emperors officially claimed the power invested in their bloodline.

But it was not his Domitrian ancestry that legitimized Tarantis.

Nor was he an Emperor.

The chamber applauded as the vicar raised the anointed scepter for all to see. But that scepter was not *imperial*. It wasn't even royal. This took place only five hundred years ago, just before the great supernova had destroyed half of civilization, and yet no one knelt to Tarantis or treated him as royalty. He must not have been an *Emperor* at all.

As the group of representatives proceeded to discuss their business—laws, the interests of their provinces—it dawned on me that these weren't even Grandiloquy. These people held power over Tarantis, but they hailed from individual planets. When they used titles, it was "Representative," not "Senator."

"There was no Empire," I said to Plyno.

"So it seems," he murmured.

No Empire. Just this governing body at the center of what they called the United Republics.

When the first hologram winked out, Plyno muttered, "I don't understand how this could be."

All the lies of Tyrus's reign swirled through my head, and more besides. . . . The mistruths and propaganda the Grandiloquy used to control the Excess . . .

What if there were lies even greater than we knew, long used to bury the truth? Why, this was the past. The true past of this galaxy.

"I think I know what this is." The smile that curved my mouth felt dangerous. "Our entire history is a lie."

24

ON LEAVING the data archives, I hastened my people onto the *Atlas*, anxious to depart though we'd plundered only a fraction of the wealth we'd hoped to gain. The supporters I left behind swore to conceal, deny, and lie about what had happened after our onslaught, but I knew it was inevitable that someone would leak the news. The Chrysanthemum would soon learn that we had used the *Atlas* to attack the Repository, after which we would be hunted in truth.

There was no time to waste. Only once we were safely into the pitch darkness of hyperspace did I unveil the data chip containing the holographics. Then I showed the first one to Anguish and Gladdic.

After the conclusion, Anguish began to pace. "It's a forgery," he said. "It must be. There is no possibility the Grandiloquy could have concealed such a truth. Everyone would know the Empire was but five hundred years old—"

"How?" I asked. "It was half a millennium ago."

"Word would have been passed down through the—"

"Half a millennium, Anguish. And in all that time since, the Grandiloquy have had total control over the provinces, the educational system, the media. Even the galactic forums are censored by the Chrysanthemum's automated network! How would the truth have been 'passed down'? By word of mouth? How many would dare to speak, if it got them killed?" I caught his arm to draw him to a standstill. "How many dare, even now, to say aloud that Tyrus is no god, only a man?"

Anguish, scowling, looked mutinous. With a sharp shake of his head, he stepped out of my grasp.

"What's the second holographic?"

Gladdic's quiet voice startled me. I'd almost forgotten he was there. I looked into his pale, grave face and saw that he understood the implications. "You believe this. You know it's true."

He glanced past me. Whatever he saw in Anguish's face caused him to avert his gaze to the floor. "I don't *know* it's true. But I know there were many secrets that I was not trusted with, even after I became Senator. And we both know that Domitrians are skilled at conspiracy." He offered me a wan smile. "Skilled enough to rewrite histories, even. Does the next holographic show more of these . . . United Republics?"

"The next one," I said, "is why we had to flee. The next one is what we need to protect and share."

Then I played it for them—this transmission Tyrus had watched twenty-two times at the Repository before copying.

The one that had changed his whole life, and might yet destroy the galaxy.

In this holographic, the Grand Sanctum again was crowded with representatives of various territories. The Spymaster Tarantis looked a good twenty years older, heavier through the shoulders and waist, with ruddy cheeks and hair grown long.

His demeanor had also transformed. Two decades of power over the Empire's security and surveillance machines had invested him with an insouciant confidence. Rather than standing at respectful attention before the galaxy's greatest leaders, he lounged in his floating central chair, his legs kicked out and crossed at the ankles.

"As instructed, I present myself today before this noble assembly, after two decades of faithful service, so the duly elected representatives of our United Republics might vote on whether to strip me of office." As he glanced over the crowd, the recorder caught the gleam of contempt in his pale blue eyes. His tone was lilting, sardonic. *"However, I invite you to spare yourselves the effort of making a case about my incompetence. Rather, I intend to make a case for* your *collective incompetence to* you.*"*

Cries of outrage sounded around him. Tarantis's lips twisted in amusement.

"I used to wonder why my predecessors aged so quickly once in this exalted position. Now I understand. You granted me the eyes to monitor every surveillance machine in the United Republics, and the power to collect all your secrets. I've come to know the entire lot of you better than many of you know yourselves. I've never been a spiritual sort, but the more I learn of you, the more I understand that hell is real—because I see so many of you busily creating it."

He sat back in his chair—supremely relaxed, conspicuously indifferent to the shouts of objection. Fixing his eyes on some distant point, he continued casually, *"Power has sickened you. You have become so inured to your excesses that you seek ever more lurid depravities to stimulate you. I am the eyes gazing through your surveillance cameras. I am the ears listening to your furtive messages. It is my mind reading your texts—and, yes, your discreet-sheets, which you never expected me to glimpse. So you see—I am not just a man. I am a network of interlinked machines with a human interface. I am your surveillance state. I am your security state. I am the bulwark between you and those whom you represent—your 'subjects,' as you call them."*

His voice grew cutting. *"'Tarantis,' you say, 'it is your job to ensure our security. It is your job to neutralize the radicals on my planet! Silence those who speak against me. Imprison them, destroy them, for if you do not, we will replace you with a Domitrian who will!'"*

He shook his head in disgust.

"It's no accident that a revolutionary spirit now burgeons across the provinces. You've been clumsy in your crimes—the stealing, the murders, the perversions. One man can be silenced—or a hundred, or a thousand. But you cannot silence an entire galaxy. Your collective perfidy has grown too obvious. The people will no longer abide it. And so—what is your solution? To blame me. I, *who have kept your secrets just as my ancestors did, as my entire family has done since you enslaved us fifteen hundred years ago."*

A stirring passed through the crowd of representatives. Having studied this holographic repeatedly, I knew why. Throughout the Grand Spymaster Tarantis's speech, his security bots had been stealthily infiltrating the Grand Sanctum. Only now did the representatives notice their increased presence overhead and all around.

"Yes, I said 'enslaved,'" Tarantis bit out, as the security bots assembled into a gleaming metal formation above him. *"For I am not my ancestor, Melchoir, your first 'Grand Spymaster.' You enslaved the first Domitrians for the crime of what we are. You used us as your tools, and over time, you chose to please Melchoir and offer him an official title, as though that legitimized our slavery. He was appeased by this. I have never been deceived. Involuntary servitude was our sole family inheritance."*

A few of the representatives—too uneasy to remain—made for the doors of the Grand Sanctum.

Tarantis's gaze cut toward them.

One of his machines, weapons extended, zipped down and blocked their exit.

A hush fell over the chamber as they finally realized they were in peril.

"Yet was not the crime of we Domitrians convenient for you? For fifteen hundred years, you have used it as an excuse to force Domitrians to be your puppets. You've interbred us to keep the power in our blood, and bound the most powerful of us in each generation to slave for these"—his lips twisted sarcastically—*"great republics of freedom! Now you call me here, who never asked to serve you, and demand that I account for my failure to protect you from the consequences of your own actions."*

Gasps and shrieks went up as Tarantis's bots, now fully encircling the representatives, deployed their weapons. He threaded his fingers together and smiled down on the scene.

"Naturally, I know what you've been plotting. You wish for a unified galactic government. You wish your powers to be permanent, not subject to the whims of voters. You wish your corruption to go unpunished. And you are correct in one regard: we have reached a turning point in history. Either you will succeed, or there will be a vast, sweeping revolution across this entire galaxy, ending only with your deaths. Why should I protect you? Give me but one reason."

Uneasy stirring and murmuring across the chamber.

"Tongue-tied? All of you?" Tarantis sighed, impatient as a tutor with disappointing pupils. *"Very well, I will supply it: Domitrian machines were what enabled your corruption. The galaxy will see me not as your tool, but as your co-conspirator—for without all my work, your subjects would have overthrown you long ago. Even if I disavowed your actions and killed you where you stand, the people would not spare me for long. Liberated from your tyranny, they would turn on the Domitrians who'd guarded you. They would seek to destroy us along with you."*

A pause ensued, in which the mood of the room shifted tentatively toward hope. Shoulders loosened; a few people coughed; others leaned toward one another, relief and speculation fueling their whispers.

"There's an alternative to all our deaths . . . one only I can effect. The

masses of the United Republics agitate against you, but they might be shocked into total submission, if I but lifted a finger and acted. I have the means of unleashing malignant space at will. I could weaponize it to create a disaster unprecedented in our history, one from which all in this chamber and their loved ones will remain totally immune—but the masses will bear the brunt in full. In the aftermath, they would crawl on their knees to us for safety. They would beg for the yoke they now decry as oppression. Of course, you know I will have a price for this."

A security bot floated near Tarantis's shoulder. Theatrically, he cupped one ear, as though to hear its message. *"Ah,"* he said after a moment. *"Indeed. You are all growing willing to pay my price. How good of you. Here it is, then: I require a permanent investiture of my own. For me, and for all my descendants. We will have an Empire. You will be its nobility. And I? I am no longer your slave. You will instead become mine. Today, you will declare me your Emperor."*

The holographic went dark.

"What happened next?" Anguish said.

"Ten days later," I said to him, "there was a supernova. You saw Tyrus cause a supernova with malignant space. He learned of the possibility from somewhere, and I think it was *here*. I suspect Tarantis did it first. Tyrus figured that out, and he replicated it."

Silence fell as the implications registered.

That other supernova, in Tarantis's time, had enabled a new galactic order. The supernova had wiped away all electronic databases, all records of contemporary society. To replace them, the powerful had concocted a new version of "history" in which Domitrians had always ruled. And they had persuaded the Interdict to declare scientific education to be blasphemy, ostensibly to prevent another mass disaster, but now I suspected another motive: a scientifically educated people might one day figure out what Tarantis had done.

No doubt some people passed the truth on to their children. But fear must have constrained most to whispers—and over time, whispers faded. And so the truth of the pre-supernova galaxy had been eradicated from the collective memory.

"So," Anguish said, "the Grandiloquy are thieves and liars." He glanced stonily toward Gladdic, who cleared his throat and crossed his arms defensively.

"To lie," said Gladdic sheepishly, "one must first know the truth."

"It's not just the Grandiloquy," I said. "'Tarantis the Great' saved civilization from the aftermath of a supernova—so we are told. But that was the disaster he promised the Grandiloquy, the one that ended all the rebellions brewing on their planets, the one that made them all the new nobility. . . . He *caused* the supernova. Just as Tyrus did. With malignant space."

Gladdic flinched. From Anguish's throat came a low, deep growl. "That's mad," he said. "Billions died in the great supernova."

"Hundreds of billions," I corrected. "Perhaps more. You say he changed after the Repository, Gladdic, and I think this was why. He discovered the destructive potential in his hands. Who is to say he wasn't doing just as Tarantis did—following his actions?"

I glanced again toward the data chip holding the holographics of Tarantis. A chill slipped down my spine as I belatedly realized what Tyrus had been doing with beauty bots.

Lightening his hair, resculpting his jaw, hollowing out his cheeks . . .

He'd been slowly but steadily emphasizing his resemblance to Tarantis.

It dawned on me that he was not merely emulating Tarantis's looks. He was copying Tarantis's strategies. Like his ancestor, he was deploying malignant space in order to consolidate his power.

What if he chose to cause another supernova? He had the means on hand, and he clearly had no care for the cost. A billion lives—what would that matter to a mind poisoned beyond repair?

We needed to kill him—quickly, before he found some new reason for murder. But how did one vanquish an enemy whose weapon could annihilate whole solar systems?

There was no other choice. "Anguish," I said. "We need to make contact with Neveni."

25

GLADDIC had no memory of saving my life, but learning himself capable of such a feat had given him the courage to do what I asked. He was nervous, though. I had promised him that Anguish and I would follow a half block behind, ready at any moment to assist. But as he promenaded down a street in the city of Tribulation, capital of Atarys, the only threat he faced was a surfeit of public adoration.

This was an Aton province, after all, and Gladdic was one of the few Grandiloquy who could claim in full truth to be beloved of the Excess in his domain. Especially now that Tyrus had raised his profile by appointing him chief propagandist.

"Grande von Aton!"

"That was him, I swear it!"

"That was Gladdic von Aton who just passed! Come on, let's catch up to him!"

While I was no stranger to fame, I'd been an inaccessible and distant figure, as those of true power often are. I wasn't accustomed to being swarmed by admirers. At imperial events requiring my appearance, I had been kept at a controlled remove from the crowds.

But today, on Tribulation's high street, Gladdic's devotees surrounded him. Another man might have been cowed by their wild enthusiasm, but Gladdic was all smiles. He hugged babies, slapped backs, and dispensed kisses with charm and ease.

At the top of the high street, with hundreds of people trailing in his wake, he mounted the steps of the capitol building and then lifted his hand for silence. Into the ensuing hush, he spoke—his words captured by countless recorders held aloft.

"Some of you have asked me: What am I doing on Atarys? I confess, it's a complicated story." Gladdic paused, his sigh tragic. "It goes back to an incident that happened several years ago. Back before Lumina was destroyed."

Lumina. That single word silenced the remaining chatterers gathered below him. All waited raptly now for him to continue. The recorders remained aloft. His words would be circulated across the galaxy by nightfall. They would draw attention.

And Neveni Sagnau would hear them.

Anguish and I had parted with Neveni on ill terms, to say the least. Her fellow Partisans would know that we were no longer trusted allies. Our old contacts would not help us find her.

So somehow, we had to lure her to us.

And Gladdic was the way.

"You see," Gladdic went on, "I was staying as a guest at . . . ah, I can hardly bear to speak his name; I've tried so hard to forget it. But I will tell you now: it was the husband of *Viceroy* Sagnau. A proper ruffian he was! Sometimes, at the oddest moments, I'm reminded of that dark time, of how *disgracefully* I was treated. There was some trifling dispute between my father and the Emperor, and I was ordered to stay in the residence of the Sagnaus. They *quite* mistreated me. There were . . ." He cleared his throat, finding my eye through the crowd. I nodded encouragingly. "There were beatings," he said—not very persuasively, although the adoring crowd offered up a sympathetic hiss, which seemed to hearten him. "Yes, beatings," Gladdic repeated more firmly. "And cruel words! And—and—oh, force-feeding of spoiled meals!"

The crowd gasped and booed. "Curse Sagnau!" an older man yelled. "Curse the Viceroy!"

Too late for that. The Viceroy, along with the rest of Neveni's family, was dead—victims of the Grandiloquy who'd deployed Resolvent Mist on Lumina.

Neveni had rage she could never hope to satisfy.

I was counting on it. Nothing would enrage or agitate Neveni more than hearing her late loved ones unjustly smeared. To fend off Grandiloquy retaliation over the technology Tyrus had offered Lumina, the Sagnaus had indeed kept Gladdic as a hostage at their home—but they had treated him like visiting royalty.

"In fact, I'm thinking of writing a book about my ordeal while I'm here on Atarys enjoying your beautiful binary stars." Gladdic was speaking fluently now, and his flush actually worked to his advantage, suggesting a wealth of repressed emotion. "Then, once I've returned to Eurydice, I'll speak further about my victimization at the hands of Luminars. No doubt it is right to mourn the loss of that planet—I don't mean to discount anyone's grief. But I think history must reckon with the full truth, the *dark* truth, of those who dwelled on Lumina—above all, the Sagnaus." He cleared his throat, squared his shoulders, nodded smartly. "I welcome any inquiries from journalists who'd like to compose a holographic exposé for me."

Anguish and I exchanged a look. There was not a chance that Neveni would let Gladdic carry out that plan.

It was only a matter of time now before she struck back.

We'd chosen Atarys for its close proximity to the last sighting of the rogue Partisan vessel, the *Arbiter*. Neveni likely wouldn't strike in person—she might suspect a trap and deploy someone else—but someone connected to her certainly would. We would use *that* person to track her down.

Gladdic's family owned a great swath of property here, so he'd secured us a small manor house just outside the capital. Hidden from the main road by a stand of lavender-leafed trees, the building was practically indefensible: it boasted four entrances, uncurtained skylights and windows that offered a clear view of the interior, and a chimney large enough to accommodate the entry of a dozen security bots.

We'd chosen this property for its relative seclusion—and the ease with which it could be surrounded and attacked. At this remove from the populace, there should be little collateral damage if a true battle began.

Gladdic was the bait.

Waiting was not a skill that came naturally to me. I was picking irritably at a mediocre stew from a nearby tavern when Gladdic's transmitter chimed.

I pushed away from the table as Anguish grabbed his weapon. "Answer it," I said to Gladdic.

Gladdic looked up from his transmitter. All the blood had drained from his face. "It's not her," he said. "It's the Emperor."

Anguish and I exchanged a sharp look. Tyrus must have noticed the irregularity of Gladdic's public announcement. Perhaps he'd also learned the truth of what had transpired in the Clandestine Repository. If he knew Gladdic was with us, our situation had just gotten much more complicated.

"I don't know what to say to him." Gladdic was panting rapidly. If he kept it up, he'd pass out.

I stepped forward to the holographic transmitter and rapidly jabbed in an avatar sequence to lend me Gladdic's face and voice. "I'll answer. Leave the room."

He seemed to collapse into himself with relief. Anguish, taking his arm, hauled him to his feet and out the door. I waited another moment, took a bracing breath, then answered Tyrus's transmission.

"Your Divine Reverence," I said, dipping to my knees and drawing my hands to my heart, ice water in my veins.

Tyrus's image bloomed to life before me in explicit and painful familiarity—arms folded, fingers drumming an impatient rhythm against his bicep. He was no longer accustomed to being kept waiting.

How like Tarantis he looked now!

"What in the name of Helios do you think you are doing, Gladdic?"

I straightened to my full height. "Showing Your Divine Reverence the respect you are due."

"Don't be cheeky. Why are you on Atarys fawning before the recorders? I ordered you to Eurydice to represent me at the Media Divinity Summit."

I wanted to snarl that he could find someone else to lie for him. But Gladdic would never be so impudent. "Forgive me, Your Divine

Supremacy. I'm very tired—and anxious. The crowds expect so much of me, I fear to disappoint them, to represent you poorly, due to my own exhaustion." That sounded like a plausible excuse from Gladdic. "I just craved a brief respite, to recover my strength."

"Yes. Yes, and apparently to mull over your trauma at the hands of the Luminars." Tyrus's voice was dry. "Tell me, isn't it enough that they're dead? Why profane their memories by inventing stories of abuse?"

I opened my mouth but was too surprised to manage a reply. Was he actually attempting to take the high ground here?

"Well?" he prompted.

"I . . ." I imitated Gladdic's anxious demeanor. "I felt moved to speak of my—my feelings about the past. Perhaps it was ill done of me. I am sorry."

"For a man so anxious about his public performances, you nevertheless seem remarkably eager to draw attention." Tyrus's voice was harsh. "There are consequences. I intercepted Partisan chatter of a plot to hunt you down."

My heart gave a strange, skittering beat. That was exactly what we'd meant to engineer.

"I'm going to have you evacuated from that planet before they act on that plot," said Tyrus. "I've contacted the Viceroy and have an armed guard mobilized for—"

"No," I cut in.

"No?" His brows arched.

I could see Tyrus's mind at work, speculation sharpening his study of me. I cursed my carelessness.

"I'm leaving shortly, Your Divine Reverence," I said. "I need no escort."

"I've never known you to refuse security, Gladdic." Tyrus's voice grew soft. "Surely you remember what happened on Eurydice two months ago."

"Yes. Of course."

"What happened?"

I stared at him.

He drew closer to the transmitter on his end. "Tell me in your own words what happened on Eurydice two months ago."

Heart drumming, I said nothing.

"You don't recall, do you?" Tyrus tipped his head just a fraction. In someone else, it would have signaled polite interest. From him, it was tantamount to a predator baring its teeth. "The microgravity dancer and the incident with the wine?"

"Oh, of course. That dancer."

His smile was slow and humorless. "In truth, you weren't on Eurydice two months ago. Gladdic would know that. But you aren't Gladdic, are you?"

Gladdic would look, feel, horrified—panicked—wounded by such an accusation.

Panic was not difficult to fake. I felt something like it. "Your Divine Reverence! I—it is true that I haven't felt like myself of late, but I am not sure—"

"Who are you?" He spoke coldly, all expression evacuated from his voice, his face. "Is Gladdic alive?"

My stomach sank. There was little point to carrying on this pretense. But admitting the truth would be even more unwise. I took a breath, preparing to compose another nervous, Gladdic-like reply—but I was interrupted by the shrill of the perimeter alarms, even as a great shadow blotted out the sunlight overhead.

"Never mind that." Tyrus's eyes gleamed. "I know your exact position, and I already have forces in orbit. You'll answer all my questions shortly—whoever you are."

I slapped off the transmitter and charged to the window. A starship was descending through the atmosphere. Footsteps pounded behind me: Anguish and Gladdic rushed up to my side, Anguish shoving a weapon into my waiting hands.

"We need to leave," I said.

The *Atlas* was docked on the far side of the city. We would never make it.

The imperial vessel was a massive silhouette descending toward us.

Anguish and I both lifted our weapons, aiming them at the ship. Running was useless. So we would fight.

A flare of light caught my attention. It came from *above* the imperial vessel. As I squinted up, the light pierced the hull of Tyrus's ship, burning straight through it. Below, trees exploded into flames, and a shower of purple leaves hit our window.

The imperial vessel bucked beneath the assault, then twisted in an attempt to target its new foe.

But it was no match for the *Arbiter.*

It had been the Interdict's vessel, and it was heavily armed. It blasted at the imperial ship again and again, causing molten steel to erupt on all sides. Anguish seized my arm and Gladdic's, too, then hurled us away as a tumbling fragment roared toward us.

I hit the floor on my belly just as the wall behind us exploded. A wave of fire rolled down the far wall, sucking the oxygen from my lungs as it went. Windows shattered, glittering shards slicing down all around me. For a moment—less than a heartbeat—silence fell. And then the house groaned all around us, beams snapping and cracking—and collapsing.

Darkness. I reached out blindly, trying but failing to find my companions. Each breath made me retch and gag—dust and powdered concrete choked me, and the thick, bitter taste of ash coated my tongue. Through the ringing in my ears, I could make out explosions and weapon fire. Loud and then louder, so loud that the explosions seemed to come from within my aching skull. My hands over my ears did not help; I could not drown out the roar of it. A war was being waged overhead.

Never before had I felt so small, so helpless. Unable to breathe, to see, or to think. I tried to crawl to cleaner air, but in the darkness, I did not know which way to turn, and found my path blocked again and again by rubble. Even a superhumanly strong Diabolic was nothing, matched against a pair of interstellar killing machines.

The air was clearing. I could breathe again, choked and heaving breaths. A hand grasped my wrist—Anguish hauled me to my feet. Under his other arm, he held up a swaying Gladdic. We stood together amid the burning wreckage of the house, inside a forest on fire, with the remnants of fractured, scorched security machines littered all about us. Sirens pealed in the distance. As the air continued to clear, I spotted a bright inferno, green flames fed by some chemical from an injured starship, that marred the distant vista of Atarys.

And overhead, the other starship, still intact, descended steadily, its lethal rings spinning. As the *Arbiter* settled on the ground, it raised another choking cloud of ash. I was still coughing, my eyes watering, when armed Partisans appeared through the haze, respirators masking their faces, weapons aimed at us.

Anguish looked at me with a question in his eyes. I'd intended to reunite with Neveni on my own terms—to ambush one of her people, learn her location, and then surprise her.

Instead I would be at her mercy. *Again.*

With gritted teeth, I tossed down my weapon. After a stubborn hesitation, Anguish did the same.

The Partisans spoke not a word. They jerked their weapons to indicate that we should precede them onto the *Arbiter*. And thus—as prisoners—we did.

26

THE PARTISANS fastened treatise bands about our necks, set to detonate if we stepped out of line. Then they brought us to the command nexus of the *Arbiter*.

I barely recognized the Neveni Sagnau who awaited me there. Once upon a time—so long ago it felt more like a dream than a memory—we had been friends. But that lively, irrepressible girl was as dead as my affection for her. The Neveni who turned to acknowledge me wore her dark hair sheared close to her scalp, the better to show off the scar that slashed across her cheek and ran into her hairline, and her eyes were hard and cold.

The scar had been gifted to her by the very Partisans she now commanded. *I offered them my loyalty, and in reply, they tried to kill me and take the* Arbiter, she'd told me once. *They didn't succeed.*

"So Nemesis does live," she said. "You look like hell. Was that my doing?"

"Don't flatter yourself." I stepped forward and was halted immediately by Partisan weapons leveled in my direction. "We need to talk."

"You agreed to kill the Emperor, then went back on your word. There is nothing left to say." As her gaze found Anguish, her voice soured. "But you? You surprised me."

He folded his arms and lifted his chin, broadcasting defiance. "I valued her."

"More than you did me, clearly. You betrayed me for her. Well." She gave a one-shouldered shrug. "It doesn't matter now. My mistake for trusting either of you."

She started to turn away—then paused, a laugh scraping out of her as she noticed Gladdic.

"And Grande von Aton . . . of course. Your little speech was far from subtle. Bait, was it? It worked. I was really hoping the Emperor had put you up to it—that, at least, would have been interesting. But I suppose you'll crawl for anyone, provided they toss you a bone now and then."

Gladdic grew rigid at her contempt. "I am not with the Emperor," he said. "And neither is Nemesis!"

I stepped between Neveni and Gladdic. "I knew no other way to contact you," I said tersely. "I need you to see this. There are two holographic recordings." I withdrew the data chip I'd saved from within my glove. "Watch them."

She gave it a brief, dismissive glance. "What is it? Some poorly designed piece of malware?"

"Forgotten history," I said flatly. "I could tell you, but you must see it to believe it."

Neveni eyed me without trust but nodded for one of her Partisans to take the chip from me. A tense silence hung in the command nexus as their holographic transmitter bloomed with the same images we'd watched in the Repository.

"What is this?" demanded Neveni when young Tarantis appeared.

"That's Tarantis—"

"Tarantis von Domitrian. Yes, I went to school. But why . . ." Her voice trailed into silence as Tarantis bowed to the assembly and she realized what I had: Tarantis had not been Emperor when this recording was made.

In rigid silence, she watched the second of the scenes play out. . . . Tarantis deciding to create a mass catastrophe so he might build his Empire, giving the provinces of free people over to the custody of the Grandiloquy. Her fellow Partisans were not so restrained: they swore and murmured among themselves as the drama unfolded.

Only once the images had faded did I speak again.

"Did you catch the date of the recording?"

She gave me an opaque look, then turned away to speak with a crewman.

Did she not understand? I started toward her, but a wall of weapons forced me back. "This was made ten days *prior* to the supernova," I said to Neveni's back. "Don't you see? He spoke of causing a catastrophe, and then he did. The Interdict always believed that supernova had an artificial cause. He was *right*, but he misplaced the blame. It was Tarantis's doing. Tarantis conspired with the Grandiloquy—"

"Stop."

She whirled on me, thunderous anger contorting her face. Her searing glare passed onward to Anguish. "Do you think I'm a *fool?*" she demanded to him. Her gaze swung back to me. "Do you think I am stupid enough to believe this nonsense?"

"Nonsense?" I echoed. "You saw with your own two eyes—"

"Vent them all from the air lock," she snapped. Two of her Partisans started toward us.

Calculations unfolded instantly in my brain. If we did not resist, we'd die.

If we resisted, our treatise bands would detonate, blowing our heads away.

I was on Neveni before any of her Partisans could shoot. She gave a howl of indignation as I hooked my arms around her. Her teeth sank into my arm, drawing a grunt from me, but I hauled her closer yet, so that her feet dangled off the ground and our cheeks pressed together.

"My dear old friend," I snarled in her ear. "What a quandary. Blow me up and you die too."

She fought my grip, clawing and kicking desperately, but she was no match for a Diabolic. "Detonate it!" she shouted at her Partisans. They traded uncertain looks, briefly hesitating. "*Detonate* it," Neveni screamed.

One young man moved toward a nearby panel to obey her. But Anguish had seen his opportunity. In one great lunge, he seized the man and immobilized him.

Now we had two human shields.

"Stop this!" Gladdic raised his arms as though in surrender. "All of you, stop!"

Now, *that* was nonsense. "Grab a weapon!" I roared at him.

"This is ridiculous," Gladdic said. "Neveni, you two are on the same side."

She sank her teeth into my arm again and I hissed in annoyance. "Do you really think you can hurt me?" I bit out.

"Nemesis, stop that, too!" said Gladdic. "Loosen your grip—she can't breathe."

The note of command in his voice was so foreign and unexpected that I heeded it, easing the pressure of my near stranglehold on Neveni. "You have a better plan?" I snarled. "How delightful. Share it, if you please." For all about us in the command nexus, the Partisans aimed weapons at our heads, and Neveni still struggled in my grip.

But Gladdic had no interest in answering me. His attention was on Neveni. "Why do you want us dead?" he asked, a certain helpless befuddlement in his face. "Don't you want these holographics of Tarantis?"

"They are *fake*!" Neveni shot back. "Stars, did you really think I'd be such an easy mark? That you would march in here after all this time and happen to bring *exactly* what I'd want most to see?" She made a choked noise, scorn and disbelief combined. "And then you'd discredit us, no doubt, by having us spread it everywhere."

"It's no fake, you little fool!" I would have shaken her until her teeth rattled if I didn't need to keep her head pressed close to mine. We would die together, here and now, if that was how she insisted it go.

"No. No. Neveni, listen to me." Gladdic raised his hands even higher over his head, his fingers trembling, and slowly approached Neveni. "It's real," he said, his green eyes wide and guileless. "We found that in a place called the Clandestine Repository—a vault for the Grandiloquy. I tell you, it's *real*."

"Oh, Gladdic," whispered Neveni, then mumbled something.

His brow knit and he inched closer to us to hear.

Don't do that, I thought, exasperated by his naivete. But I didn't warn him. He was fool enough to deserve the lesson.

Neveni's leg lashed up and rammed his face, throwing him to the ground.

I'd had enough. Snaring her even more tightly in my arms, I twisted to keep her between me and the weapons of the Partisans. "Let's talk," I rasped in her ear.

I hauled her step by step with me out of the command nexus, into a short corridor, and at last—to a dead end.

An air lock.

I hurled Neveni into it and then followed her, sealing the door behind us.

A swift inspection of the metal alloy around us heartened me. Neveni couldn't order her crew to detonate the treatise band in here. Any explosion would reverberate and most certainly kill her as well.

Then I looked back at her and realized my mistake: She was angry enough at me not to care. She would kill us both out of pure spite.

27

AS NEVENI and I squared off, she fell into a fighting stance, her face ablaze with hatred.

I felt suddenly exasperated. "You betrayed *me*," I reminded her. "You blew me up. I should tear your heart out for that. Instead I am offering you my hand as an ally."

"And why should I believe you?" she demanded. "You're the tyrant's stooge. You've sabotaged every chance you had to kill him—if he crooked his finger now, you'd go crawling back to him like a whipped dog!"

My arm flew back and I nearly struck her. Nearly. Only the knowledge of how easily I could kill her stayed my hand. I needed her alive.

Instead, I seized her jaw, not flinching when she spat on my cheek. "Maybe I should have let Pasus execute you that day on the Chrysanthemum. It would have spared me this drama."

Why, that seemed to be the constant in my life. Both Neveni and

Tyrus had welcomed death and I'd clawed them back from it—with their lasting animosity as my only reward.

"I could do it now," I said grimly. "Vent you straight into space."

Her jaw flexed. "Is that supposed to scare me? You're trapped in here too."

"Then I'll go with you." The thought made me feel weary. "Will that satisfy you? Let's both choke on vacuum. We might as well— you're my only hope of ending Tyrus, and if all you want is to stew on past wounds—"

An animal sound broke from her. "If it weren't for you and Tyrus, Lumina would still be there."

I could not ignore the desolation in her face. "I know."

"If I hadn't agreed to be your go-between with Pasus," she whispered, "I would still have a planet."

My grip eased. She did not seem to notice; her gaze was unfocused, as though she was looking through me at some distant, unchangeable nightmare.

I let go of her and took a step back. "So that's it. You blame me for Lumina."

"Of course," she said dully.

I took a deep breath. She was right, in a way. Lumina's destruction had been Pasus's doing. But had I never entered Neveni's life, he never would have destroyed the planet to gain power over Tyrus.

"I cannot make it right," I said raggedly. "I cannot ask you to forgive me for it. It isn't forgivable—I understand that, Neveni. But I have to—I *must*—ask you to look forward now. Without your help, I can't touch Tyrus."

A strange, strangled laugh came from her. She sat down onto the floor, laid her head in her hands.

Her voice was muffled as she spoke again. "You took Anguish."

I hesitated, then sat down across from her. "He left," I said gently. "You didn't value him, Neveni. And he knew it."

She raised her head. "He acted like a Diabolic with a master. Always protecting me—"

"It's the love he's learned. We are both that way."

"I didn't want a Diabolic. I wanted *him*. I thought he . . ." Her eyes narrowed. "What are you to him?"

Was that a hint of jealousy? "Not lovers, I assure you."

"Then what? Best of friends with a shared interest in screwing me over?"

I ignored the sneer in her voice. "Something more important than friends, Neveni. We're equals."

She blinked, then looked away from me, absorbing herself in a study of the stars.

I watched her with unwilling sympathy. Anguish certainly still had feelings for her. The more I interacted with her, the more I suspected she felt the same. Each nursed a bitterness that concealed something more tender, and thoroughly unwanted by either of them.

"I loved him." She looked at me, her dark eyes wide and stricken. "We were fighting . . . over you, of course, but I *did* love him. He knew that, he *must* have known."

"That is a conversation you have to have with him."

Her mouth tightened, disbelief falling back over her like armor.

I grew impatient. "What is it you imagine—that we've gone to the trouble of returning merely to seek revenge on you?" I folded my arms, trained my gaze out the window at the star-pierced void. "I ruled that out long ago. Vengeance is a never-ending abyss. There is always a new grievance to redress. I won't fall into that."

She was silent. She knew that well. Then, "But you say you want to strike at Tyrus—"

"It's not revenge," I said quietly. "It's . . . what I owe him. Maybe this will comfort you. I invented endless excuses, endless reasons not to harm Tyrus. The day I forced him back to Pasus, you told me that I was a fool. That I'd betrayed him by saving his life. And you were right."

She looked at me silently.

"He died that day." My voice was thickening; I cleared my throat before I continued. "And a great many others have died since. And all of it was my doing." I met her gaze squarely, letting her see what a Diabolic was not designed to show: the pain I felt. The grief and the guilt. "I have to fix my mistakes, Neveni. I *will* fix them. But I can't do it alone."

"And so you come to me," she said softly. "One of your first victims."

We'd been each other's victims. But my lingering anger and resentment toward her was evaporating, for I saw that my sorrows were but a fraction of hers, my struggle no match to one she'd faced. "You have resources I do not. You know how to wage campaigns against vast, overwhelming odds. There must be a way to get to him. If we don't stop him . . . he may do what Tarantis did."

Her eyes sharpened. "Is that his plan?"

"He's deluded the Empire into believing that he's a god. A god can do as he wishes—can remake the galaxy or the entire universe, for that matter. But if he encounters opposition? *Yes*, I think he'll resort to something far worse. He *created malignant space*, Neveni. I loved him more than myself, but when I think of what he's become . . ." My voice caught; it felt strangled in my throat. "I betray the Tyrus I loved by allowing this one to live."

She stared at me for a moment longer, then slowly rose—one hand braced against the wall to aid her balance, her movements as slow and clumsy as an elderly woman's. "I left you in the Sacred City," she said, "because I meant to ruin him. I didn't care that it was Tyrus. I cared that he was a Domitrian. I thought I was saving your life."

"I know. Now."

"You made me a party to his survival. I will never forgive you for that, either."

"I don't need forgiveness, Neveni. I need us to reach an understanding. If we stand together now, there is nothing that can stop us. Not even Tyrus. Don't you see how we can use this information? It's dangerous. If the truth of Tarantis spread, it would threaten the integrity of the Empire. Tyrus knows a few voices shouting a cold, hard truth can rupture a galaxy of lies. If he learns we have this, he'll seek to destroy us. We can use this as bait to trap him."

"How?"

I hesitated, sighing. "Well, that's where I need you," I said. "I have no idea."

I deserved her snort of contempt. "You came here expecting *me* to figure out how to kill an Emperor?"

"I can think of no one better qualified."

After a moment, Neveni's jaw hardened. "Betray me again," she said softly, "and I will end you."

You will try, I thought, but I offered her my hand. "Same to you, Neveni."

Her lips twitched grimly as she clasped my hand. For a moment, her grip tightened, her eyes fixed on me. Then she released my hand and turned away.

"As for your bait idea: that could work. But I think we have better bait on hand than a couple of holographics. . . ."

28

"WAKE UP!"

My shout jolted Gladdic out of sleep. I tore the sheet from his body and dragged him off the bed.

"QUICKLY!" I bellowed, waving with my pulse rifle. "Get up and run!"

Bleary-eyed and confused, he reached for his robe—and froze as he belatedly noticed the two unconscious Partisans sprawled on the floor nearby.

"What—what's going on?" His voice was thready with fear.

I took his arm again and hauled him with me into the corridor. Overhead, the track lighting pulsed red, issuing a silent alarm. "The Partisans have turned on us. We have to flee."

"What? Wait." He came to a stop, shoving hair out of his face. "Why?"

"Neveni doesn't trust me. She's turned on us!" I shoved him back into motion down the hallway. "Anguish is waiting by the escape pods—"

A pair of Partisans tore about the corridor, shouting at the sight of us. I yanked Gladdic behind me and took them both down with shots to their legs. "Run!" I screamed to Gladdic, and burst into a sprint.

His footsteps pounded behind me as we ran. "But I don't understand," came his ragged protest. "What happened? What did you say?"

"*Me?* Neveni is mad, that's what happened!" I roared back at him.

I nearly collided with Anguish as he barreled around a turn. He quickly lowered his weapon. "Come," he snarled, breathing hard. But his eyes danced with enjoyment. "This way is clear."

"Can't we talk to them?" Gladdic panted as we raced onward.

"Shut up and run!"

At the turn in the hallway leading to the escape pods, Anguish abruptly drew up short, showing us his palm. I caught hold of Gladdic just as a half-dozen Partisans appeared. Laser pistols sliced the air, and Anguish gave a shout as he charged at them, heedless of the deadly rays.

I shoved Gladdic behind me to put the corner between the Partisans and ourselves. I gave Anguish a few moments to battle and then shot forward to deliver weapon's fire that strayed over the heads of the Partisans. A glimpse of Anguish told me he was handling the battle well enough, exchanging a vigorous series of blows. I retreated and turned back to Gladdic, huddling against the wall, out of sight of them. Harshly I told him, "We can't work with these people. They're bent on revenge against Tyrus, against me—though stars know we've tried! She's irrational. She blames me for Lumina—"

"That's absurd," gasped Gladdic, shrinking into himself as the weapon fire briefly intensified.

Anguish's sudden, guttural bellow was my cue to step away from Gladdic and bolt back around the corner—to find myself face-to-face with Neveni, my weapon aimed between her eyes, her laser pistol aimed at Anguish's head, the floor around her littered with Partisans.

"Put down your weapon," she said icily. "I swear to you, I will blast his head open."

Anguish's weapon lay across the corridor. His muscles were bunched with tension.

I became aware of Gladdic creeping out behind me, and silently cursed his inability to stay put. "Neveni, please. You've misunderstood. We—"

"Oh, I understood from the first," Neveni cut in, her vindictive gaze glittering. "The Partisans have bled for this Empire. For centuries, we have fought and died for the liberation of the people. And you, who never lifted a *finger* to help them—who *saved* the tyrant who slaughters them en masse—for *you*, the Excess scream." Mockingly, she chanted, "'Nemesis lives, Nemesis lives!' Well, I'll show them the truth of it— Nemesis lives, but not for long. I'm going to flood every transmission with your execution. Every eye in the Empire is going to watch you die."

"Gladdic," I breathed, my weapon still trained on Neveni, hers on me. "Whatever happens, get out of here. The truth of Tarantis must be known."

"Whatever happens?" he blurted. "Nemesis, wait." Louder, "Neveni, please—"

Baring her teeth in a wordless, animal snarl, Neveni swung her weapon down and blasted at Anguish . . .

Point-blank.

I screamed and fired, again and again. But a tremendous battering now assaulted my back: Partisans charging me from behind, pummeling me to my knees and then flat onto the floor.

"Go!" I managed to gasp at Gladdic as I fought off my attackers and made it back to my hands and knees. "RUN!"

Then, gaining my footing, I charged toward Neveni. Her Partisans scrambled to defend her, giving Gladdic the chance he needed to make a break for the escape pods.

Hands choked my throat, seized my elbows and waist, but I was stronger. I tackled Neveni to the ground as her Partisans descended on me. . . .

And the *Arbiter* jostled as the escape pod sealed and ejected itself.

Neveni and I froze. The hands that had been clawing at me now slipped away.

I shoved myself off her. She slowly sat up.

"Think he bought it?" I said.

Neveni shrugged and raised her transmitter glove to her lips, speaking to her crewmen: "Fire some shots toward him. Don't hit him. Just close enough that it seems like we tried before he made it into hyperspace."

I leaped to my feet and reached out to help her up. Meanwhile, Gladdic's escape pod hurtled into the dark tapestry of stars, chased by blinding flashes of weapon fire.

Anguish gave a low groan as he shoved himself up to a squat. "Low power?" Scowling, he rubbed his forehead, then reached for Neveni's weapon. "Show me those settings."

Snickering, she held it out of his reach. "You'll survive." And then, smiling, she offered him a hand—and though he hardly needed it, he let her pull him to his feet.

Throughout the corridor, fallen Partisans resurrected themselves, leaping or staggering to their feet—and some, who had fared a bit more poorly than others, tumbled right back down. I helped several of them up in my walk to the window, where I watched Gladdic's escape pod disappear at last into hyperspace, the misdirected weapon fire ceasing immediately thereafter.

I let out a slow breath. Perhaps Neveni mistook the cause of it, for as she joined me, she said, "Don't relax just yet. This is Gladdic we're talking about. Odds are, he gets lost or blunders into pirates."

From across the room, Anguish called indignantly, "I programmed the course myself. Unless you doubt *my* navigation skills—"

"And if he tries to hide away somewhere?" Neveni cut in.

"Tyrus will find him." I was reassuring myself as much as her, for space looked vast and limitless from this window, and Gladdic's escape pod was very, very small. But he would not be alone for long. "As soon as he's away from us, Tyrus will hunt him down. He'll know by now that Gladdic was with me."

"But if Gladdic escapes him—"

"He won't. Tyrus will find him." There was no question of it in my mind.

And once he found Gladdic, he would hear the story we'd staged here—that a calamity had befallen me at the hands of the Partisans. That I had sought them as allies, and they had turned on me . . . That they had murdered Anguish, and intended to torture and kill me next.

Gladdic was afraid of Tyrus. We could never expect him to lie convincingly. So we had made sure he would believe what he said.

And Tyrus would not like this story. For it hit on his true flaw—not his lust for power, or his taste for petty cruelties. No, I had aimed for the single weakness that had survived his transformation into perfect villainy.

He thought I was his. His to keep or dispose of. His to love or to kill. And no one else's.

I was his weakness. *I* was the bait in this trap.

Tyrus would learn that the Partisans meant to kill me. He would not permit that to happen. He would come for me—trusting no other with my life but himself.

And then he would die at my hands.

29

THE PARTISANS had no single leader. They were a decentralized network of cells operating across the Empire. Each was headed by a subleader, who made decisions for the group. Each knew a handful of fellow subleaders. No one knew every person in the vast network.

Neveni, in possession of the *Arbiter*, had become one of them—but only after she'd proven herself to the others by thwarting their attempts to kill her and take her ship for their own.

From there, she'd recruited followers to man the vessel. Some were Partisans on loan from other cells, who had the technical expertise required to run a vessel; others were Luminars who'd been off-world during the destruction of their planet, or Excess from provinces like Devil's Shade who had never reaped the benefits of the Empire, only the burdens.

The galaxy-wide network of Partisans also depended on sympathizers, people who were embedded throughout the Empire in places of strategic value. Some served as the Partisans' eyes and ears in Grandiloquy households or aboard Grandiloquy vessels. Others helped not by choice but by necessity, having been coerced or blackmailed into feeding intelligence to the network.

The identities of these informants were known only to subleaders, who held the key to an elaborate system of codes and identifying signals. When Neveni had at last been accepted into their ranks, she became privy to these codes, which she had kept a secret even from Anguish.

It fell to her, then, to assemble the forces necessary to withstand an onslaught by Tyrus. Neveni sent coded transmissions to a series of messengers throughout the Empire, who then contacted subleaders whom Neveni did not know herself.

All of them, however, knew Neveni, the infamous terrorist who possessed the vessel of the Interdict. In the entire vast organization of Partisan rebels, only she approached the status of a public figure.

Now her reputation would grow even more fearsome, for she had captured me. It was crucial, we agreed, that visiting Partisans believed me an unwilling participant in the plot. Otherwise, some might refuse to trust or cooperate with me, for despite my rebellions, I remained the Domitrian Emperor's wife. Also, should Domitrian spies have infiltrated the Partisan ranks, they would at least carry back the same story that Gladdic had already told.

And so weeks passed as we waited for the network to mobilize. I spent my time pacing the corridors of the *Arbiter*, undertaking any menial task that needed to be done, trying to master patience—and failing. We had no way of knowing when the first Partisan co-conspirators would arrive, and I fretted that Neveni's crew, if challenged, would reveal that I was no hostage.

"We need to make it convincing," I told her one day, as we sat in her chamber playing that silly card game she liked. "Beat me."

Neveni threw down her cards, exhibiting with a flourish her quintuplet of kings. "Trust me," she said with a grin. "You're beaten."

I threw down my pair of fours. "I mean *physically* beat me. As you would a hostage."

"I don't beat hostages," she said mildly. "If they annoy me, I just kill them."

I snorted. A fine time to develop morals! "I'll ask Anguish to do it, then."

"Nemesis." Sweeping up the cards, she shot me an exasperated look. "You are literally disfigured. Scarred and burned. Trust me, you already look like I've brutalized you."

A fair point, but I still needed fresh bruises. "Just think of the Resolvent Mist on Lumina."

Neveni hurled aside her cards and did just as I asked: she delivered punches in earnest at full strength. When she finished, she studied the effect, and said, by way of apology, "You can hit me back once if you want."

"No," I said, gingerly feeling my face for bruises.

She bared her teeth in a smile. "Just think of me stranding you in the Sacred City."

And in a flash, I'd backhanded her. Harder than I'd intended.

Neveni caught her balance and swung around on me. For a moment we glared at each other with mutual, unvarnished hatred. Then . . . a change. Her lips twitched, and so did mine, and we were both smiling. . . .

Two mad, crazed dissidents with an ugly history and very little to lose.

I realized with some surprise that I had missed her.

Fresh bruises still littered my face when Galahan, the first of the Partisan subleaders, arrived to verify the truth of Neveni's story. The leader, a burly man with pockmarked cheeks, looked me over. His gaze lingered on my wrists, which had been bound in cabled steel.

"Yes," Neveni said, "as you see, *the* Nemesis. And yes, of course I verified her DNA."

"Rumor had it she was too smart to catch," the man said.

"I told you, she trusted me. She fell right into my hands."

The grizzled subleader's suspicion was no doubt part of the reason he had survived into middle age. But with the clock rapidly ticking down, Tyrus already hunting me, I found myself resentful of how long this man had taken to arrange a rendezvous with the *Arbiter*. I returned his close scrutiny with a glare.

"You'll understand," Galahan told Neveni, "if I must test her for myself." He stabbed me in the side with a syringe, then jammed my blood into a DNA analyzer.

But even once my distinctly inhuman results glowed on his hand-held screen, he doubted them. "How can this be?" he muttered.

Neveni was not concealing her annoyance now. "How many times must I explain it? Let me make it as simple as I can: the Emperor tried to kill her. He failed. Now she's ours."

The man's lip curled. "A fine story. But there's a trick here. I can smell it."

The scar down Neveni's face flushed a livid red, lending her a threatening air she had never possessed before the loss of Lumina.

"Come on," she said, "what else must I do to convince you? You have her DNA—"

"She is a Diabolic, yes. A creature," Galahan said, meeting my glare with his own. "But there were many iterations of that creature back when the Empire produced them—"

"I *am* Nemesis," I interrupted. "I've been on Devil's Shade for the last few years—"

"*It* looks nothing like her," Galahan said to Neveni, as though I'd never spoken. "It will be difficult showcasing her when you've mutilated her."

"*Difficult?*" Neveni, touching her own scarred cheek, laughed bitterly. "You'll find a way to get over it. Besides, who captures a Diabolic without leaving a few marks?"

The man weighed her words a long moment. "You suggest using her to lure the Emperor to us. But why would he care to come for her? You say he tried to kill her. Why wouldn't he be glad to let her die?"

"You can't be this thick," she said flatly. "People across the Empire are rallying to her name. 'Nemesis lives,' they cry. He can't *afford* to leave her fate in our hands."

Galahan sucked on his teeth, then shook his head. "We would expose ourselves. Our only advantage is that we're scattered, hard to find. Uniting in one place, for one battle, might destroy us. In a single day, you would hand the Domitrian his victory over our entire network."

"Or this works, and we will *kill him*," Neveni said, her eyes flashing. "There is no scepter. There is no heir. The Domitrians will die with Tyrus. Think what possibilities that will open!"

He was silent.

"At least listen to the rest of my plan," Neveni said. "I know a way to nullify any advantage he has over us."

"Not likely," Galahan scoffed. "He commands all the machines of this Empire. He'd dispatch drones in the thousands, seize control of our ships from us—"

"I got this information out of Nemesis," Neveni said. "His powers have limits. He can command ships within the same system, yes—"

"And you propose putting all our forces in reach of him—"

"But *not* if we face him under the right conditions." With a jab of her finger, she called up a map of the galaxy. *"Here,"* she said, pointing at the spot I'd suggested. "We meet him where there will be subspace disruption. He won't be able to sense our ships and command them with his mind. Not only that, but any automated machines he sends after us won't be able to function. He'll need to rely on manpower—human direction, human skills, human *errors*. We take the hostage to the chaotic gale, and we face him there."

The chaotic gale was where I'd captured Gladdic. The subleader knew of it. I could tell by the spark of possibility that suddenly kindled in his eyes. He understood that the gale would neutralize Tyrus's technological advantages.

When Galahan's gaze found me again, I made sure to slouch like a beaten captive, though my heart was soaring.

"Your plan," he said to Neveni, "has potential."

With Galahan to vouch for her, Neveni began to gather forces. We convened near the asteroid belt that ringed the chaotic gale. Day by day, I looked out the window to discover new ships, new fighters and supplies, sent from all across the galaxy. There were repurposed freighters, some civilian transports, and ancient battle vessels that had fallen into disrepair before being salvaged and patched up by the Partisans. Most were armed with stolen weapons, converted piecemeal to an attack force.

It was more than I had expected. It was far less than I might have hoped. I found myself mentally comparing this paltry lot to the vast armada that constituted the Chrysanthemum—thousands of inter-linked vessels designed to the most lethal specifications. In ordinary conditions, I would not wager this ramshackle armada—large as it was, and growing by the day—against a single great ship like the *Hera*, or Tyrus's *Alexandria*.

But the chaotic gale changed the odds. I just prayed it was as devastating to Tyrus's machinery as it had been to Gladdic's.

As for Gladdic himself, news of his apprehension finally reached us from Partisan spies in the Chrysanthemum. A follow-up trans-mission spoke of the Emperor's sudden departure into hyperspace, followed by the bulk of his ships. Rumors flew across the galaxy that he was building up his forces for an assault on some target—but which, the rumor mill could not say. Embedded imperial spies could be counted upon to do the rest, and point Tyrus to the chaotic gale.

One by one, the Partisan vessels departed the asteroid belt. Each ship's lights brightened, its engines powering to maximum—then, having launched itself into the chaotic gale, it dimmed and dis-appeared into the thickly massed clouds.

Soon the *Arbiter* was alone, stationed here until the Emperor's fleet arrived. We would not depart until Tyrus's forces had detected us. We needed him to know exactly where we'd gone, exactly where he should follow. Once we joined the other Partisans in the chaotic gale, they would know the battle was upon us.

Happily, we did not have to wait long. I was in the heliosphere, staring into that opaque tangle of clouds, when Neveni's footsteps whispered behind me. "We've detected imperial signatures at the edge of the system. They're emerging from hyperspace now."

A shiver passed through me. It had come.

Neveni joined me, her gaze also drawn toward the gale that awaited us. For a moment, she looked fragile and very young. The breath that slipped from her sounded shaky. "God, I hope this works."

"I thought you didn't believe in God anymore," I murmured.

"After Lumina? No. It's just an expression, Nemesis."

Together we watched Tyrus's armada enter the other end of the vast field of asteroids. From such a distance, it should not have been visible to the naked eye. But such was its size—a vast gleaming retinue of metal, catching and reflecting the light of the nearby star.

"Or maybe it's just today," Neveni whispered. "Maybe today, I have to believe in something more."

In the window's reflection, I met her eyes. She looked as tense as I was, alert and prepared for imminent victory—or disaster.

A strange, tremulous feeling opened within me, a mix of emotions that it took me a moment to recognize: gratitude and hope, affection and fear. We'd shared some of the greatest moments of our lives, and many of the worst as well. We'd inflicted so much pain upon each other. Perhaps there would always be too much mistrust to ever again call each other friends.

Despite that, I could have asked for no greater comfort than her presence beside me as we once again faced our fates—even if she later despised me for what would happen next. This was the eye in the storm of our friendship, a precarious calm before the winds swept us up again.

I reached out and clasped her hand, hard. Her fingers went limp in surprise, then tightened around mine. Her pulse was racing.

Our eyes met, and it seemed that a current flowed between us, each drawing strength from the other.

I smiled at her. After a moment, she flashed me a fierce, jubilant grin.

I laughed and let go of her hand. She raised her transmitter glove to her lips to speak to her distant helmsman. "It's time," she said. "Take us in."

30

THE *ARBITER* shot straight into the clouds, an arrow flying along a course planned days in advance. Soon the haze began to thin, revealing the other Partisan vessels.

We'd chosen a lifeless planetoid as our rendezvous point. Its gravity caught the *Arbiter* and disrupted our darting momentum, first arcing us toward the rocky hulk and then looping us pendulously around it. Out the windows, I caught sight of the other orbiting vessels as we swerved past. The Partisans were already in formation, ready for the incoming onslaught.

Our force had advantages that the imperial armada would not anticipate. Because the Partisans relied upon whatever they could loot, steal, and extort, they had grown skilled at improvisation. Many of their weapons were crude mass projectiles constructed in the style of ancient human weapons. Their missiles often lacked internal guidance and navigation, or any sort of independent targeting system. They had to be packed into tubes and powered by shipboard combustibles that thrust them forward in a straight line. Their own internal explosives would detonate only upon impact.

In other words, they were powerful enough to blast apart an asteroid, or put craters in soil. They were haphazard enough that poor aim or rebound blasts could damage allies as easily as enemies. And they were utterly useless against any form of energy shielding. The Partisans stood no chance in open combat.

But all changed inside the chaotic gale.

Within the destructive electromagnetic influence of the gale, functional energy shielding was not possible. Sophisticated weaponry would be rendered useless. This was as close as the Partisans would ever come to a fair fight against imperial forces.

Thus when the first of Tyrus's vessels breached the sector ringing the Partisan defensive perimeter, Neveni flashed a grin of anticipation and ordered, "Hold fire."

This hesitation was critical. The Partisans relayed the command from one vessel to the next by a series of coded flashes through their windows. Meanwhile, more Grandiloquy vessels emerged through the layers of clouds. Among the half dozen, I recognized the *Apogee*, the *Ouranos*, and Credenza von Fordyce's *Eternity*. These behemoths filled our windows and view screens, blocking out the clouds.

Anxiety electrified the command nexus. Neveni stood braced against her console, her grip white-knuckled. "Hold," she murmured. Tremors visibly racked her frame. "Hold . . ."

It was critical that we wait until the bulk of Grandiloquy vessels were in range before we commenced to fire. We'd have only one chance to surprise them with our advantage. We needed to use that chance to destroy the majority of Tyrus's fleet.

But the commander of another Partisan vessel lacked Neveni's self-discipline.

As gravity carried us around the curve of the dead planetoid, we saw a Partisan vessel unleashing its weapons on an approaching Grandiloquy vessel.

"Damn it!" roared Neveni. "I told them to wait!" Now she had no choice but to attack. "Tell the rest to open fire!"

The message was flashed. In a matter of moments, every Partisan ship unleashed their crude projectiles on the incoming Grandiloquy vessels.

Too soon. I counted no more than a dozen of Tyrus's vessels in firing range. But these were vast imperial starships, undefeated in their lifetimes. Knowing no cause for fear, they sailed straight into our onslaught, likely planning to grapple us with their tethers and simply haul us, helpless, out of the gale.

Our missiles scorched through the clouds of gas and rammed straight into the oncoming vessels. Explosions swelled across their metallic surfaces. Hulls bubbled like burning skin.

For a moment, everyone around me was silent, maybe stunned. The Partisans were accustomed to covert attacks and sabotage in the shadows. These vessels, which had never been scraped by so much as an asteroid, represented the might of the most powerful man in the galaxy, who had killed countless thousands and had the temerity to declare himself a god.

And we'd fired on them openly.

"Come *on*," Neveni yelled at the view screen—and as though in reply, the Grandiloquy commanders panicked and committed their fatal mistake. These were not battle-hardened commanders, but rather spoiled aristocrats who'd just discovered their vulnerability to us.

Almost in unison, they directed power to their sophisticated lasers and attempted to return fire—and instead sent prongs of bright energy spidering over their own hulls, as the energy of the gale shorted out their weaponry.

The Partisans around me whooped as the deadly energy currents built on themselves, gaining force, mauling the ships' structural integrity. Fires bloomed, then died as they met the vacuum of space. The vessels began to shed fragments as trees shed rotting fruit.

Their lights went out. They floated, dark and dead, defenseless.

"Fire," Neveni said grimly, and the order was flashed out through the windows.

Adrift and helpless, the imperial vessels endured multiple blasts of firepower, until one by one they ruptured into bright fragments, the detritus rattling past our hull.

"Eight down," someone crowed.

"I counted eleven!" someone else shot back.

Neveni spun toward me, her face jubilant. "It worked! What's wrong? Didn't you see? Your plan worked!"

I opened my mouth, but nothing came out. Neveni was pulled away into the jubilant embrace of a fellow Partisan, while I found myself staring at the view screen, empty now but for the spinning ruins of the ships that had briefly confronted us.

As the celebration continued, some strange cone of silence enveloped me, as empty and cold as space itself.

Eight ships? Or eleven? I had not seen more than six, had identified only three. What if the *Alexandria* been among those eight or eleven? He might be dead. *Dead.* He was dead.

"Nemesis." Neveni grabbed my chin. "What is it? Are you all right?"

I yanked free. "Fine," I bit out. What a lie. I was *a fool.* I should *pray* that the *Alexandria* had been destroyed. Killing him was the whole point of this madness! If he was dead, then we had just won, and it was as bloodless a victory as I could have hoped for.

But he wasn't dead. Not yet.

My agitation faded. I knew Tyrus too well. He never would have accompanied his first wave into an unscouted battlefield. He was not that brand of rash. He'd likely chosen those first ships from a bevy of Grandiloquy eagerly vying for the honor of eradicating Partisans. Even now, he would be digesting news of the defeat and preparing his next tactic.

The soundness of my own reasoning should have made me despair. I should not have felt calmed by it.

"Here comes the next wave," Neveni yelled, and the revelry died instantly as the Partisans returned to their mission.

Stars. If Neveni could divine my feelings, she would be right to kill me where I stood. I stepped up beside her, fists clenched so tightly that my knuckles throbbed. Given privacy, I would have smashed them against something unbreakable, the better to punish myself for my idiocy.

Feel what you like, I told myself. *It makes no difference. You will do what you must, regardless of what you* feel.

The Partisan vessel that had fired early, prematurely revealing our advantage, ended up costing us dearly in this second wave. The new round of Grandiloquy starships had witnessed the fate of their predecessors and did not repeat the mistake of trying to fire on us. Instead their engines flared—and though the gale's discharge forked over their surfaces, the thrust of their engines catapulted them out of range of us.

"Damn it," Neveni snarled, smacking a nearby wall. "Think how many more we could have had!"

Instead of making a devastating dent into Tyrus's forces, we'd obliterated only a fraction of his starships. We swerved in our orbit past the debris of shattered hulls, glittering as their internal fires ruptured into space.

A few Partisan vessels expended their weaponry trying to catch those enemy ships who were fleeing, but Neveni growled, "Flash a message at them: cease fire! They're too far away. Don't waste the ammo."

That was a significant downside to relying on projectiles rather than energy weapons.

You could run out of them.

She turned to me as that second wave receded, the light of the scorched and ruptured Grandiloquy vessels playing across her face. "We should have gotten more," she said hoarsely.

"But you got a great many," I soothed her.

Her teeth flashed in a vicious grin. "Oh, yes."

My gaze fixed on the windows overlooking the field of Partisan vessels, this crude fleet coasting on the momentum they'd built outside the gale, now swinging in orbit around a dead planet, circling like sharks, awaiting the next reckless approach of the Grandiloquy.

"Once they limp out of here," I warned her, "he won't send another wave without synthesizing projectiles of his own."

But even Tyrus, with his army of synthesizers, could not match the Partisan stores, amassed over years on end.

"The wisest course for him would be retreat," I said. "I wouldn't be surprised if—"

"Oh, he won't." Neveni gave a heady laugh. "I didn't tell you—I prepared an incentive to keep him close."

The incentive, I discovered quickly, was a series of fabricated holographic images of me. Since they'd been crafted with equipment we could not activate within the gale, I couldn't watch them, but Neveni described them in enough detail to give me an idea of what Tyrus would see.

They showed my torture and mutilation at the hands of the Partisans. After a few hours passed without a new attack, Neveni ordered the holographics to be encased in a probe and launched out of the gale.

The images also carried a demand from the Partisans: that the Emperor himself come in person to discuss their terms.

"He'll never risk himself like that," I told Neveni.

"He'll risk others, though," she said with contempt. "He won't be able to stop himself. And I've readied other probes with even less pleasant images. Every hour he delays, they'll get worse."

The probe required time to travel through space, propelled as it was by a crude launcher. We waited in a strange atmosphere of elation mixed with tension. Some played card games to pass the time, as their sophisticated gaming devices could not be activated here; others tried to doze. For my part, I paced the corridors restlessly, then sparred with Anguish until both of us were too battered to continue. We ended in a draw, much to the disappointment of the small audience of Partisans who had gathered to watch while placing furtive bets on the outcome.

At last the *Arbiter*'s alarms blared, sending Anguish and me sprinting back to the command nexus, where Neveni impatiently waited. She directed my attention toward the view screen, asking urgently, "Can they fire on us?"

I saw that the next wave had arrived, and this time Tyrus had launched his own security drones . . . thousands of them. The Partisan vessels were taking the offense, blasting missiles through the rain of drones.

"I don't know," I said honestly. It was possible that the drones could each get off one shot before shorting themselves out.

Possible.

But Tyrus did not bank on mere possibilities.

"Wait," I said, divining his strategy. "Neveni—he wants you to waste your firepower. He knows you'll run out of projectiles. Don't fire!"

Her wide eyes flitted back to the view screen. She surveyed the incoming thousands and then roared, "Flash the message: 'CEASE FIRE!'"

The decision seemed to drain her of strength. She staggered back a pace, wringing her hands as she anxiously watched the window.

Meanwhile, the Partisan vessels flashed their windows, one to the other, the message spreading through the fleet. But some disobeyed it. Here and there, vessels continued to fire on the bots.

"Idiots!" Neveni roared. "Flash it again!"

And sure enough, when Tyrus's drones reached us, a few dozen attempted to power up weapons—only to succumb to the forked electrical discharge caused by their own systems rupturing. The others coasted past, and the only hazard they posed was as floating debris.

Neveni, bathed in sweat, gave a giddy laugh. "Keep flashing that message," she told her Partisans. "Make sure everyone got it. The bots can't do anything but drain us dry firing on them."

I followed her from the command nexus to the adjoining chamber, designed for a commander's respite. She waited until the doors closed behind us to collapse against a wall, sagging with relief.

"God," she said. "God, I thought we were done there." She slid down the wall, laid her head in her hands. "If they'd been able to shoot," she said in a muffled voice, "I would've gotten us all killed."

I reached out and gripped her shoulders, pulling her back to her feet.

"But we're alive," I said. "You outmaneuvered him." I felt a flicker of venomous satisfaction as I pictured Tyrus's face now that his oh-so-clever ploy had backfired.

Yes, I knew whose side I was on. My earlier bout of weakness now seemed like a distant dream. I would not allow myself to feel pity again for a monster who deserved none.

"Well done," I told Neveni fiercely.

She gave me a bloodthirsty smile. "Think this merits the next probe?"

I grinned at her. "I trust it's a horrifying one."

"Thoroughly appalling. It would make you proud."

31

THE CREW slept in shifts. When my turn came, I lay restlessly on a cot, listening to the snores and sighs of a half-dozen Partisans sleeping around me. My brain felt swollen, overheated by racing thoughts. No position felt comfortable. That anyone could sleep amazed me.

This entire plan hinged on Tyrus's continued devotion to me. If he decided that preserving me was not worth the effort, we'd lose. He and the remainder of his well-supplied armada could simply wait outside the chaotic gale until our stores ran out—until we starved or tried to flee.

I thought of the exhausted faces I'd passed in the corridors today. I felt the weight of every soul aboard this vessel, and across the Partisan fleet. Whether or not they knew it, all their hopes were pinned on a singular thing: the obsession of a madman for a creature made in a lab.

If Tyrus abandoned me, their blood would be on my hands.

Stop.

The Partisans had chosen this. With their eyes wide open, they'd decided to wage a violent resistance. They knew that the stakes were life and death.

But we would win, because he would not abandon me. I *knew* it.

I twisted in the sheets, then shoved them off, breathing deeply of the stale air. How could I feel so certain of his continued fixation? Why did that certainty feel just as painful as the fear that he might let go? The idea that he still loved me despite everything that had passed between us—despite the fact that I'd arranged this plot only to kill him—made my stomach lurch. But I refused to name this sick, shrinking feeling. It could not be guilt.

Instead I forced myself to remember the agonies he had inflicted: his sword through my chest. His malignant space ripping through the *Halcyon.* His taunting smile as he arranged so many deaths.

Perhaps he loved me. But what did "love" mean from someone like that? What kind of "love" could promote such abuse? None that I wanted. None worth valuing.

The door slid open. I recognized that oversize silhouette. Glad of the excuse to abandon the cot, I rose to my feet and followed Anguish out of the room.

The auxiliary lighting cast a greenish pall over the pale, curving corridor, and the smooth white floor. Anguish settled against the wall, folding his massive arms as he gazed down at me.

"Why aren't you asleep?" I asked.

"Why aren't you?"

I hesitated. Anguish would not be able to dispel my fears. And I was no child, to want false comfort.

Anguish spoke first. "You're afraid he won't come."

I was startled. "When did you come to know me so well?"

"When I started to call you my family." He left no pause for me to digest this remark. "He'll come, Nemesis. He cured me, didn't he? Why would he have done that, but to please you?"

I leaned back against the wall beside him, our shoulders brushing. In friendship, one took comfort from such proximity. It showed one was not alone. "Perhaps he wished us to feel reassured, lulled into complacency—so it would have more impact watching him murder all those people on the *Halcyon*."

"Perhaps," he said neutrally. "But I don't think so."

"No?" Bitterness crept into my voice. "He healed you just in time for us to watch the lies spread across the media about an evacuation. He guaranteed we would feel strong, restored, capable—and then, all at once, thoroughly powerless. From one perspective, healing you was just a new way to hurt me."

"More evidence that he will come," Anguish said evenly. "For why should he wish to hurt you if he did not care?"

"Hatred?"

Nodding, he turned toward me. "Possible. Love and hatred are not always inseparable. Certainly I hated my . . . Cygna."

I blinked. He rarely spoke of her. And never so personally.

"I hated her with every breath," he said. "I cursed my fate that I loved her—that I lived and breathed for such an unworthy, despicable creature. I prayed that a day might come when I would awaken to feel only revulsion. But the entirety of my being, the *entirety*, pulsed with need for her."

Tears pricked my eyes. I pressed a hand over my brow to disguise them. "It's cruel what we are." Held hostage to our own genetic design, destroyed by our inbuilt capacity for unwavering devotion. We had been created to love villains—to gladly offer our throats to their knives.

"No," he said softly. "No, Nemesis." He pulled my hand away and looked on my wet cheeks with a small, fleeting smile. "I begin to think we are not so different than they are. Our bonding process is artificially induced—but the result is no different from what they feel toward one another." He raised a palm. "Sometimes, toward us."

I hesitated, then spoke carefully. "I think Neveni didn't understand how she made you feel."

His jaw tightened. "It is the past."

"Not for you." I'd heard him murmur her name in his sleep. I saw his face when we spoke of her.

"We may all die soon. It will be irrelevant."

I laughed. "Don't be so optimistic, my friend. You may still survive to hash it out with her at some point."

His lips curled. "If we survive, and the young Emperor lies dead at your feet, then I vow on all the stars, she and I will have a discussion."

A sudden blare of alarms sobered us. Wordlessly we turned and sprinted toward the command nexus. My passing glance at a chronometer showed that just over six hours had passed since the last assault. More than enough time for Tyrus to receive and review Neveni's latest holographic image, as well as its reiteration of the Partisans' only demand: that the Emperor come in person.

He would not do it. I'd spent a great deal of time convincing Neveni that he would, that he could be driven to do so. But Tyrus would be deliberate. . . . If I were truly a hostage, as he believed, then he had to suspect we would both end up dead if he made the error of surrendering himself.

In the *Arbiter*'s command nexus, Anguish and I discovered the eight gathered Partisans looking visibly perplexed by a strange sight on the windowed screen.

There were a series of laser beams cutting through the gale, directed straight into the planetoid we orbited.

"What is he doing?" Neveni asked me, as though I'd know.

I shook my head.

"They're coming from too far away—they can't be strong enough to harm us," she reasoned. "Or the planet."

We soon lost sight of the beams as the *Arbiter* arced around the curve of the planetary body. In the forty minutes it took us to orbit back around, everyone in the command nexus debated the possible purpose of the lasers. Other passing vessels communicated their theories with flashing lights. The act of speculating gave the crew license to voice fears they'd been trying to suppress. The fear, once voiced, provoked wilder and wilder suggestions.

By the time we rounded the curve of the planet once more, the atmosphere was unsettled and tense. The vessels directly before us, with a view we did not yet have, flashed a message back to us.

"'Hologram,'" Neveni interpreted, her brow furrowing. "What? How could it be . . ." She fell silent as we glided into view and saw the holographic projection.

The lasers, positioned outside the chaotic gale, projected inward like a makeshift holographic emitter, forming words that unfurled across the clouds.

"'Discuss terms. Radio frequency 101.1,'" Neveni read.

Her gaze darted between the message and the lasers still directed at the planet below us. The intersecting beams of light stirred a bright cloud of auroras in the planetoid's scant atmosphere.

"I know what he's doing with the lasers," she exclaimed. "He's manipulating the planet's electromagnetic field to generate radio waves. Someone—quick, help me tune our transmitter to that radio frequency."

I felt a lurch of alarm, fearing this might be a trick to lure the

Arbiter into powering up and exposing itself to the ferocity of the gale. I didn't know what this radio technology was, but Neveni's Partisans were familiar. Using components scavenged from the ship itself, they swiftly constructed a rudimentary radio. The inelegant snarl of wires lacked even a computer interface but would function within the gale without risk to our vessel.

The Partisans activated the device. A harsh, static buzzing resolved into the sound of a man's voice: *". . . reading me?"*

"We read you," Neveni said in return.

After a few moments' delay, the man's voice came again: *"Stand by for the honor of addressing our Divine Emperor."*

Neveni rolled her eyes. "Lucky me."

After another brief delay, Tyrus's voice lashed into the air. *"Partisans. I contact you to discuss terms. First, I demand proof of life."*

Neveni cast me a calculating look. "What proof?" she replied.

Another long beat. *"Sagnau."* Tyrus spoke her name as though it were something distasteful. *"You will ask my wife—"*

He used that word. He still used it.

"—exactly what she asked for herself before we returned from the Transaturnine System."

Pain stabbed through my heart. I remembered that day—a glorious, haunted day. We'd made love for the first time. We'd known we were on the cusp of disaster. Tyrus had made a suggestion.

We'd just lost a year in the Sacred City. We understood that Pasus had probably seized control of the Empire in our absence. Tyrus had suggested we fly toward the black hole and wait decades, or maybe centuries, before returning into a future in which no one would know us. In which we could be *free*.

I'd felt so tempted. Had I but given in to my impulse, how much suffering might have been avoided! Instead I'd believed Tyrus would never be at peace if we ran from the responsibility. I believed it would be the best thing for him if we returned to the Chrysanthemum to face Pasus.

I'd chosen wrong. In some parallel universe, we were still together right now, caught in the pull of the black hole. In that other timeline, there was no Venalox, no keying into the scepter. No confrontation in the ball dome, no sword through my breast. Only an Empire we'd abandoned to its fate, and the two of us, happy and hopeful together, eternally in love.

Stop.

"I asked him to ban Servitors," I told Neveni.

Neveni sent the answer over the radio. My attention shifted to the auroras dancing on the surface of the planetoid below. Our radio transmissions were being sent there, reinterpreted by those lights, relayed onward. Such an elaborate system of communication to bridge the distance between us.

"I thank you," said Tyrus at last. *"For assuring me she is alive—and revealing that she's onboard the* Arbiter *with you."*

Neveni cursed. Our eyes met, and I shook my head—*let it go*—the only consolation I could offer. It was the speed of her reply to him that had exposed my location. Had I been onboard another Partisan vessel, they would have needed to use their light system to pass my answer along to Neveni, causing a delay of several more seconds.

Tyrus continued. *"Your holographics made your terms explicitly clear, Sagnau: I offer you my death to prevent hers. But I have no reason to believe she'll be alive after my blood has been shed."*

"You'll just have to trust me," Neveni said venomously.

A delay as the signal reached him, and then his reply: *"As Nemesis trusted you before you betrayed her? I'll make no such mistake. I've already erred in tolerating the existence of the Partisans."*

Neveni gave an incredulous laugh, one that would not reach him in time to interrupt.

"You did serve a useful function, for a time." The new malice in Tyrus's voice put me on edge, had me instinctively shifting my weight in preparation for attack. *"The Partisan assaults on your fellow Excess were a large part of why my family stayed in power."*

"Liar," muttered Neveni.

"Imagine how many resources we would have wasted, had we needed to deal with every resistance against us. But my family never feared protests— not even the most civilized and compelling. Because we knew the Partisans would destroy them for us."

Neveni looked at me incredulously. "Does he seriously imagine he can shake me with this nonsense?" she whispered.

I opened my mouth, then thought better of answering. Neveni would not like to hear it, but Tyrus was no longer taunting her. I recognized that new note in his voice. He believed he was speaking the truth.

"Your Partisans join peaceful movements—and subvert them," he said. *"As the people call for justice, you set the city alight around them. Your violence becomes the only story, the only protest that others remember. And the silent Excess who might have joined the calls for justice . . . they look at the destruction and decide they want no part of it."* His laughter was soft, laced with acid. *"You* kill *revolutions, you Partisans. And yet you call yourselves champions of the people!"*

Neveni took a deep breath and said into the radio: "If you're done—"

"Do you have any idea how many you killed that day on Corcyra? Do you know the death toll at the Sacred City?"

Neveni stared mutely at the view screen.

"Your victims were not playing our games of power. They were innocent people. Have you dared ask yourself if anyone deserved your brand of 'justice'?

I've no doubt you've rationalized all that collateral damage somehow."

Neveni's silence began to alarm me. I stepped up to her. "Don't let him get to you. He has no right to talk." Tyrus had committed more than his share of atrocities.

Neveni seemed to gather herself. Again, she activated the radio. "Get to the point."

"The point: I have no interest in negotiating with an irrational idiot blinded by hatred. I would say this even had I not seen your vile cruelties to Nemesis. These are my terms: return Nemesis to me. Alive. Immediately. You will all surrender. In return, I give you your lives. If you fail to comply, I will destroy every single ship in your fleet but the Arbiter.*"*

Neveni laughed with disbelief. The Partisans were smiling at his audacity as well. She crowed back into the radio, "You don't have the firepower for that! Unless you plan to lay siege to us for weeks while you build up your projectiles—while we continue to do as we like with Nemesis. Don't you get it, *Your Supreme Reverence?"* She spat that title, pointedly leaving out the "Divine." "We *outgun* you!"

But before he could have had a chance to receive those words, he spoke again:

"You no doubt think I lack projectile weapons."

"Of course he does. He needs time to synthesize more, and what else does he have? He can't use malignant space," Neveni said, half to herself. "He'd destroy the *Arbiter,* too."

"Happily, my drones told me the orbit of every single vessel in your fleet. I can calculate their positions to a fraction of a millisecond. I can hit every last one of you."

"With what?" snarled Neveni. She turned to face her crew. "He doesn't have any firepower that can reach us here." The mounting unease on their faces made her swear. "I tell you, *he's bluffing.*"

"Rest assured, Sagnau, I can reach you. Let me demonstrate."

And then a Partisan cried out, calling our attention to the view screen just as an asteroid tore out of the gale of vivid clouds. At first its path seemed random—but as it careened past us, its trajectory became plain. Gasps split the air.

The asteroid slammed into a small Partisan vessel, ramming through its hull. Debris spilled into space.

"Stars. He's weaponized the asteroid field," Anguish breathed.

"No," Neveni said. "No, it's not possib—"

She choked off her words as two more asteroids flew past. As though steered by the hand of the Living Cosmos, they slammed directly into the wounded flank of the Partisan vessel.

A moan passed through the command nexus.

The vessel exploded.

"As you see, I have my own projectiles to propel your way. Those are but three of them," Tyrus said coldly. *"And I have five-hundred million more. Surrender Nemesis to me now, or I swear on all the stars, I'll slaughter every last one of you."*

32

"SURRENDER to him."

Neveni snapped out of her stupor and whirled on me. "What?"

"Surrender," I said in a low voice. "You can't win this."

"Are you *insane*?"

"Evacuate the *Arbiter*. Let me go to him. I have a plan."

She tore across the distance between us, suspicion flaring in her eyes. "You have a plan? *This* was your plan!"

I had not looked forward to this moment. But I refused to show my regret. It would not matter to her. "This was the first part of my plan," I said impassively. "And so far, it has gone exactly as I hoped."

Realization flashed over her face—followed instantly by rage. With a bloodcurdling howl, she threw herself at me.

I twisted to unbalance her, and threw her to the ground behind me. Her hand flashed up with a weapon, but I'd already drawn mine. I aimed at her head.

For a moment, we froze in a strange tableau, her eyes wild with anger and betrayal, our weapons drawn—mutual destruction a single finger's twitch away.

"You knew," Neveni said in a guttural voice. "You meant this to happen!"

"For him to overcome you?" I kept her trained in my sights. "Yes. It had to seem convincing."

"Convincing? You liar, you soulless sun-scorned *traitor*!" Her gaze flicked past me to her fellow Partisans. "*Shoot* her!"

"Wait!" Anguish stepped up behind Neveni, his weapon pressed to her skull. "Anyone shoots, and she dies," he said to the Partisans.

Startled gratitude coursed through me. I had not told Anguish of my true plan. But he trusted me, regardless. He trusted me enough to take my side, blindly, against the woman he'd loved.

I gave him a brief look of gratitude. He nodded curtly in reply.

I leaned down, and Neveni adjusted her weapon so it shoved into the tender underside of my chin. I jammed mine into her belly and leaned forward to speak into her ear. "He was always going to win," I told her. "He'd outwit us, outgun us. Would you have agreed to come here if you'd known that was the only possible outcome? But this way, we still have a chance. He will think that he's truly rescued me—"

"This is his victory! You sold us all out—"

"I AM GOING TO *KILL* HIM!"

A nervous twitch from Anguish suggested that the Partisans at my back were losing patience. But she *had* to be made to understand.

"I've done the *very same thing* that you and I did to Gladdic," I said. "And it will work. I swear to you, Neveni, it will work. I swear on my soul that by the time this is over, he will be *dead*!"

Panting, Neveni pulled away to search my face, her study frantic, as though with enough effort, she might uncover some hidden mark, some sign that belied my words. Her weapon still pressed into my chin. Mine dug into her abdomen.

"What?" she said roughly. "What's next in this plan?"

On a deep breath, I took the greatest risk of my life.

I pulled my weapon away from her and threw it away to one side. She had the upper hand at last. "I'll tell you," I said. "And you'll help me make it happen."

"Have you lost your wits?" roared one of the Partisan subleaders.

The other vessels had not reacted favorably to Neveni's flashed order: to power up engines and escape the chaotic gale. They knew that meant they'd be flushed out of hiding and emerge crippled before Tyrus's waiting armada.

Several of the other subleaders had seen the hologram and cobbled together radios to rage at Neveni directly.

"I need you to listen to me, Galahan," Neveni spoke tonelessly, her face ashen.

She'd accepted that my plan was our only hope now. She didn't like it—or me. She could barely meet my eyes, and her tightly knotted fists betrayed the rage she was holding in as she addressed the other ship.

"Don't use my name, you little idiot," raged Galahan. *"You think the Empire can't hear us?"*

"I've no doubt the Emperor hears every word." Neveni cast a bitter glare my way.

"You're going to send us all to our deaths!"

"We have to surrender," she said. "We'll stand a chance of surviving if we cooperate. If we don't, he'll kill us all." She couldn't share what we had planned, not without Tyrus overhearing. I knew it was maddening for her.

"Like hell I'm going to stand down. You've led us to our doom!"

Galahan cut off communication. At my urging, Neveni contacted other commanders in the fleet. But they were torn. We watched on the view screen as other ships flashed messages to one another, debating what to do. An hour passed, then another.

Time ran out.

More asteroids blasted through the clouds—a shower of them, more than two hundred. Cries erupted through our command nexus as we watched the asteroids barrel toward Galahan's vessel. Tyrus had indeed been listening. He knew precisely whom to target.

Galahan's crew vented plasma to give themselves a push, but it did not work. "You fool, you fool," Neveni was muttering, her eyes bright with unshed tears, when at last they fired up their engines—too late.

Galahan's vessel coasted directly into the path of a smaller asteroid that tore straight through its hull. A larger asteroid followed, and the next impact dealt a fatal blow. The vessel ruptured into a bright flower of fire and debris before arcing down to burn in the planet's atmosphere.

Neveni's jaw hardened. In a lifeless voice, she said, "Flash the message again: 'Power up and escape.' The smart ones will obey."

Just outside the main power core, I curled into a crumpled ball to wait. My breath heaved against my upper arm, which was sticky with blood.

Tyrus would expect to see a torture victim. This time, Neveni had required no persuasion to make sure I looked the part. Knowing that I'd sacrificed her ship, her entire cause, for a plan that might not work, she'd enlisted her Partisans' assistance in beating me to a pulp.

She'd enjoyed it, and I could not blame her. Her rage at me must have felt boundless.

As I waited now, swallowing moans against the pain, I kept my eyes fixed on the single, narrow window above me. Through it, I saw the glint of the Partisan escape pods streaming out of the *Arbiter*'s bay, carrying all the crew but me.

They would not make it far. Only a half hour ago, the *Arbiter* had been towed by two other Partisan vessels to the very edge of the gale. Both of those ships had damaged themselves by igniting their engines in the gale, but they'd preserved the *Arbiter* from enduring the same power discharge. Through the window, I'd glimpsed the fate of that portion of the fleet that had exited before us. . . . Tyrus's remaining security drones, those not wasted on the bait charge he'd sent into the gale, had converged around the crippled Partisan ships and trapped them in virtual cages of metal, hundreds of weapons aimed at each.

Now I watched as the escape pods were also surrounded and trapped by these drones.

How Neveni must be cursing me. She'd spoken no words of farewell as she personally delivered the last blow, but tears had been running freely down her face.

"It will work," I'd managed to gasp.

With a snarl, she'd turned and stalked away.

It will work, I told myself now. But the sight of those bots encircling the Partisan fleet sent a chill through me.

What a coup for Tyrus, to apprehend the bulk of the Partisan firepower in a single day.

The victory will blind him. It will make him careless.

So I told myself.

My eyes blurred, cheeks throbbing from the impact of Partisan boot heels. I blinked hard and saw a new shape cutting through the thin sheen of clouds at the edge of the chaotic gale.

The *Alexandria* had entered the outermost reach of the gale.

The *Arbiter* jostled as tethers clamped into place. Now came a long pause as the vessel rumbled with the contact. . . . Tyrus would be scanning for traps.

He would detect none. There were no explosives primed to erupt, no engine core powering up to self-destruct. Nothing waited to kill him.

Nothing but me.

I heard distant footsteps, the first of his servants entering the ship, their boots thudding down the hallway. A low hum droned through the air as his security bots buzzed down the corridor. I finally permitted myself to moan. Between the scarring and my new beating, I not only looked the part, I felt it.

When the first bots swerved into sight, I stared wildly into their lenses. They could only glimpse me, could only steer about here within the chaotic gale. They could not fire stunners without destroying themselves, so I could afford to give Tyrus, on the *Alexandria*, a long look at me through their recorders.

With a bestial shriek, I staggered to my feet. "Get away. Get away from me!"

Gripping the wall for support, I limped through a doorway into the power core's antechamber. A pair of the security bots followed. When they came to hover over me, I hurled myself down to the floor, throwing my hands over my head, wailing like a terrified child.

"Get away, GET AWAY!"

Curiously, as though I were truly afraid, my eyes welled up. It was adrenaline that made me begin to shake, I was certain.

This had to work. It had to.

When the servants found me, I escaped once more with a panicked cry. I passed into the next room, where the power core throbbed and pulsed, and found a new spot beneath it to huddle into myself. With each breath, I choked on what I hoped seemed to be sobs—not difficult, when the Partisans had cracked my ribs.

If I was shaking even harder now—if the shaking was not entirely within my control—all the better. Tyrus thought I'd spent the last month being tortured. Anyone would shake, in such circumstances.

Make a show. Keep him focused on you. Otherwise he might think to destroy the Partisan vessels before he came to deal with me.

The servants did not follow me into this innermost chamber. Two security bots quietly slipped through the doorway, but they kept their distance.

Then I heard footsteps in the doorway.

He'd come at last.

It was Tyrus.

33

"NEMESIS."

I ducked my head and didn't look at him. "Stay away from me." My voice wavered. It sounded weak, beaten.

His voice was soft. "Nemesis, it's all right. You're safe now."

I chanced a glimpse at him from beneath my arm and saw that he held no weapons. His bare hands were outstretched toward me. And his face . . .

Shock jolted through me. He no longer looked like Tarantis. He looked like *himself* again . . . that cleft in his chin, the faint dusting of freckles, the coppery hair disordered over his fine-boned face. His pale blue eyes looked shadowed by exhaustion and stress, as though it devastated him to see me in this state.

"Don't touch me." The alarm in my voice was real. I took a sharp, pained breath. How clever he was, what a diabolical monster, to approach me unmasked, unarmed. "Stay back."

"I won't hurt you. I swear, I . . ." Hands still upraised, fingers spread, he took one cautious step toward me, then another, never taking his gaze from me.

But I saw the swift calculations behind that gaze. The security bots overhead rocked slightly, wavering in response to his internal debate.

Our eyes met.

His face crumpled. "Oh, my love . . . don't weep."

I touched my cheek—felt the tears trickling there once more.

Grief suddenly coursed through me—grief too deep to be born of this moment. It felt endless, bruising, raw.

I realized I had been grieving for days now. Weeks and months.

This was the only way it could end.

He wore a face I had loved so well.

He misunderstood my tears. "It will be all right now," he said tenderly. "Nemesis, I am here to save you from them. Look, let me help you. . . ."

"Stay back." My raw, quiet voice halted his forward advance.

"I cannot imagine what's been done to you." His words came out thickly, strangled. "Let me help you. I have doctors, medical bots. . . ."

Any way but this. Open battle, hurled curses, his sword again through my chest—I would have preferred fury and open hatred, I would have chosen any other ending than this one. The tears shimmering in his eyes were teaching me a lesson I did not want to learn. I had wondered if what he felt for me was love or obsession, but I saw now that the two were not as different as I'd wanted to believe.

I saw love on his face. It was real. A villain could love. He loved *me*.

But love was no reason, no justification, no excuse.

"STAY BACK!" I shrieked, and cringed into the computer panel below the power core.

I saw some new resolution clarify in him, firming his mouth, clearing the frown from his brow.

"I can help you. Nemesis, I . . ." He paused again. "I hate to do this, but . . . I've been assured this will not harm you, even within the gale. So I must."

The neural suppressor hummed back to life in me.

I loosed a shuddering sigh. "Don't," I said. *Thank you*, I thought. This face he wore now, his original face, was only another kind of mask. I could have asked for no better reminder than the weakness flooding through me, the sapping of my will and agency. A villain's love was no love worth having.

"I'm sorry," he said raggedly. "I know how I've hurt you, Nemesis. I abhor all I have done to you. I abhor that I must do this now."

But activating the neural suppressor gave him the confidence to cross the last few steps to me. His security bots had scanned me and detected no weapons, nothing that could be used to kill him. The weakness in my muscles now was the final moment of disarmament.

I'd been counting on it.

"I swear, I will protect you. Let me heal you." He knelt before me, gathering me up in his arms.

I closed my eyes, taking a deep breath. Once upon a time, I had found such wonder in this embrace. His touch had been my own proof that a kind god existed, that the universe bent toward justice.

"You're safe now," he whispered.

My heart spiked in my chest. I opened my eyes and looked into his. I looked past the monster he'd become. I looked deeper; I looked into the soul of the boy I'd loved, and I smiled. *This is for you*, I told him.

"I've been so afraid for you," Tyrus told me, tears in his eyes.

"Shh . . . I'm safe now."

Did Tyrus lean toward me, or I toward him? Somehow our lips met, a kiss so gentle that it roused an echo of the old wonder, raising goose bumps as his hands closed softly around mine. He kissed me deeply as he drew me to my feet, his fingers twining through mine, the marriage electrode in my palm meeting his.

I was shaking, but so was he. I drew our conjoined hands to his tear-streaked cheek.

This was right. Fated. He was everything, all to me—even after the horrors that had passed between us. Fingers twined with his, I stroked the faint stubble covering his lean jaw. I brushed soft coppery hair away from his temple.

His mistake was simple. "You never stopped loving me," I murmured.

The tears shone in his eyes. "I could never stop. Not until the final stars burn out."

And my mistake was the same. "Nor could I. Till the very universe ends." I turned my hand in his, so my palm pressed against his temple. With my free hand, I cupped his head, my fingers tightening in his hair as I spoke that single word: *"Now."*

And before he could understand, before his eyes could even widen or his machines react—the engine behind me shot to full power within the chaotic gale, and the massive discharge of power erupted.

It spiked toward us, and in that last moment, I looked into his eyes. *I love you.*

The bright blast of light flooded the air, its lethal path boiling toward us from the engine core, and there was no escaping the force of it. . . .

And then Tyrus shoved me away from him.

Hard enough to send me toppling over to the ground, but he did not move from where he stood.

It struck him in full, and then the remaining bright tendrils of electricity spiking out of him hit me, and bright white talons of purest pain arced through me. Screams erupted from our lips, our muscles locking. Security bots clanged to the ground, released by Tyrus's mind.

I love you, Tyrus.

The floor slammed into me and then he toppled down beside me, his eyes wide open and fixed, his mouth still open, arms extended where he'd given me that push.

I love

34

WHEN MY EYES opened, I found myself in the finest chamber on the *Arbiter*. Overhead, through the ceiling window, the chaotic gale's purple clouds swirled into the shape of a scorpion. Its lethal tail curled in victory as it hovered over a crumpled opponent.

I blinked, and all I could see was a twisting cloud.

"You're awake."

I twisted to find Neveni beaming down at me. She looked . . . different.

"Your hair." My voice came out scratchy. I felt sluggish. Had I been ill?

Neveni reached up self-consciously, tracing the vivid blue streak in her dark, shaggy hair. Her scar was gone. She looked glowing, rested and content.

Unease itched through me. There was something I needed to do, something I had forgotten. . . .

"We found a bunch of beauty bots," Neveni was telling me. "Probably not the time, but I felt like celebrating. Speaking of which . . ."

Eyes dancing, she leaned over to the bedside table and lifted a mirror up to show me . . . myself.

My skin was smooth and unblemished. The disfigurement had been erased. "His med bots worked wonders," Neveni said. "No surprise, he had enough of them. They didn't shut down with the other Domitrian machines."

Memory slammed through me like concrete.

I killed him.

I leaped to my feet. Neveni said something, but I could not hear her through the roar in my ears.

The window in the wall looked directly onto the boarding artery linked the *Arbiter* to the *Alexandria*, Tyrus's prized starship.

Tyrus was dead.

His lifeless eyes. His slack cheeks, still damp from his tears. He was dead, and I had killed him.

My vision darkened. The softness of the bed caught me as my knees gave way.

The overload should have killed me. How was I alive, when he was dead?

"You won the day."

I looked blindly toward the sound of Anguish's voice. He stepped in from the doorway, his expression somber. He wore none of Neveni's jubilant glow.

"Anguish," I whispered. What a fitting name he had been given. *Anguish.*

Tyrus was dead.

And the image of him filled my mind.

Along with the memory of what Tyrus had done at that last moment, with his last act, the very last impulse firing in his brain . . .

He had . . .

He had pushed me away from the blast.

"It had to be done." Anguish stopped a few paces away, his tone gentle as he said, "You saved us. You nearly perished yourself. . . ."

"I was farther from it than he," I said, my head reeling. I hadn't been farther, not at first. Not until he'd pushed me from the blast.

He'd had time to react, and he'd reacted . . . by shoving me away. He'd made no move to escape it. If he'd but leaped forward, I would have received the full force of the discharge along with him, but instead . . .

Instead . . .

He'd absorbed it all himself. Now I was alive and he was dead.

"His drones went dead as soon as his heart stopped." Neveni looked gleeful, as though fighting back the need to whoop and dance about the chamber. "It was a complete . . ." She trailed off as Anguish touched her arm, then cleared her throat. "It's over, is what I mean."

A dim chord of recognition made me stare at her. Here was the old Neveni, the one I'd known before the loss of Lumina. Enlivened by hope.

And yet I could feel no joy in response.

The overload should have killed me. I'd been as close to it as he had. His body blocked it from hitting mine.

Neveni seemed to mistake my silence for disbelief. "It's over," she repeated. "Truly. The Grandiloquy panicked—once the drones died, they fled. We fired our remaining missiles at the *Alexandria*, then invaded. The resistance was—"

"Why am I alive?" I murmured, thinking of what Tyrus had done.

"You were still breathing." She glanced at Anguish. "Well, you weren't the only one with a secret plan. When the others left the *Arbiter*, Anguish and I stayed behind. There's a cargo box that blocks sensors, just big enough for the two of us. We waited in there. When we felt the power discharge, we got out and went looking for you, hoping—"

"You were very close to death," Anguish cut in. "But still alive."

Of course I had been. Tyrus had stayed right in place, planted between me and the explosion.

He hadn't tried to escape it.

Why hadn't he *tried*?

"But we found you in time." Neveni laughed exultantly. "Oh, Nemesis—" She clapped. "When I saw you there beside him—when I saw *him*, when I realized you'd actually done it . . ."

My mouth felt bone dry. I stood up on legs I could not feel. "And . . . him?" I could not speak his name.

They exchanged a swift, unreadable look.

"You did it," Neveni said again, as though this were an answer.

Except—it *was* an answer.

I turned away, staring at the boarding artery connected to the *Alexandria*.

I was certain I should feel something. Grief. Triumph. Yet I was numb. My thoughts felt like clay, thick and unwieldy.

"All the machines linked to him are disabled?" I heard myself ask, thinking of those security bots I'd watched clang to the ground about us.

"Yes. We've walked through the *Alexandria* and they're all disabled. Waiting for another Domitrian with the scepter to take command." Satisfaction filled her voice, for there were no more Domitrians and the scepter was destroyed. "And we get his ship."

"How?" I said. "You can't take command unless—"

"Oh of course I know the ship is useless without his authorization codes," she said hastily. "But we'll find a way around it."

I just stared at her.

"Don't you see? This is the time!" Neveni came to my side, eagerness radiating from her. "We'll take his ship to the Chrysanthemum. They'll think it's the Emperor, returned from the disaster—alive and well. We can fake his image in a holographic. The entire Chrysanthemum is in orbit around Eurydice right now. Once we're close enough, we can *destroy* it."

"How is that possible?"

"We've run the calculations. If we move quickly, if we use the element of surprise, the ships won't be able to unlink in time. We'll just need enough explosive force to deorbit the whole thing. Without a Domitrian mind to synchronize the systems and tell the linked vessels where to navigate, they'll—"

"Burn up in Eurydice's atmosphere," I finished for her. How curiously calm I sounded. Should I not be jubilant, as she was? I remembered his eyes, the moment before he died. I remembered our lips, pressed together.

I had learned to weep. But my eyes now were dry. All I could think of was Tyrus before the power core, awaiting the blast. . . .

Was I not so human as I'd thought? Was I truly just a creature? For there was no feeling left in me. The explosion of the power core had killed it.

Anguish, I saw, was frowning at me. But Neveni's bright mood did not flag. "You have to come with us," she said, grasping my arm and pulling me toward the door. "Once we pull it off, we'll land right on Eurydice. The galactic media will all be there. They'll be in shock, of course, but if you—"

"Neveni. Let her rest," said Anguish abruptly.

She started to object, then looked between us. Smile fading, she let go of my arm.

"Of course," she said hastily. "Rest, yes—you nearly died, after all. And got a makeover. And killed the Galactic Emperor." A quick, uneasy laugh. "Not in that order, of course."

She hesitated, as though awaiting my agreement. "Of course not," I said. "No use making over a corpse."

Wrong reply. She looked stricken, suddenly. Then her eyes flooded with tears.

"Oh, Nemesis." Abruptly, she surged forward and threw her arms around me. "Thank you. Thank you!"

I did not move as she pulled away, as they left me alone in the room. In the silence after their departure, I turned to stare again at the clouds.

I could no longer see any shapes. The clouds blurred, but not because of my tears. My eyes remained dry, and the clouds continued to blur and resolve as I waited for something to clarify.

I had killed Tyrus.

He was dead.

I turned that strange thought around in my head.

I'd killed him. It was done. I had finally done it.

I had ended the threat to this galaxy.

He was dead, the person whom I'd loved more than anything.

He would never breathe again. I would never see him again.

I had done that.

And yet he had to know what I'd done. He must have understood it in those final moments.

Still—he had not moved, as though he *meant* to shield me from the blast. He had saved me. He had forfeited any chance at saving himself to save me. Though I killed him.

And the tears would never return—I understood that suddenly. The explosion of the power core had killed Tyrus.

Yet something in me had perished as well.

35

TIME HAD GONE awry, as though we were close to a black hole. Each second felt unnaturally extended. I would look at the chronometer, convinced that hours must have passed, only to find it had been mere minutes, sometimes seconds.

I wandered the swarming corridors of the *Arbiter* with the odd sense that I had left some crucial task undone. The ship was crowded with Partisans transferred from vessels too crippled by the gale to function. Their conversations reached me in fevered snippets. Many had decided to defect from other subleaders to follow Neveni. They toasted to her, they roared her name.

They spoke my name too—but softly and reverentially, bowing their heads as I passed. They all now knew that I'd been a co-conspirator rather than a captive. Yet their awe only increased my detachment. When they pressed their hands to their hearts in tribute to me, I could not manage to return the salute. I found myself studying my own hand, rubbing my thumb over my fingers, amazed that I could still feel. Tyrus was dead, but *I* was the ghost—stranded among the living, untouched by their elation and untouchable.

Why had Neveni and Anguish revived me? A person who believed in fate, in the Living Cosmos, would wonder what possible purpose she might have now. I felt . . . extinguished.

My mind wandered again and again to Tyrus standing tall before the swelling light of the engine core, and then Tyrus as I'd last seen him, his eyes fixed wide. He would have had only a moment—long enough to understand that I had killed him. Long enough to feel surprise. Long enough to register that the blast would kill us both. Long enough to calculate the way to preserve one of us.

I wanted to see him. To close his eyes. To ensure they were not open anymore.

When I asked Neveni over the transmitter if I could view his body, a few moments' silence passed. Then, voice soft, she said, "Nemesis, we delivered his body into the star."

Out the window, my eyes found that star, gleaming through the thin bands of the chaotic gale—far beyond the asteroids and the scattered Partisan vessels, beyond even the dead drones that drifted through space, untethered from the Domitrian mind that had once given them purpose.

"Already? Why?" I whispered.

"If we'd kept it on the ship . . . ," she said with a hint of vexation in her voice.

It, I thought.

"Someone could have grabbed it. They might've used it to make him into a martyr. Or one of our people might have desecrated it. You wouldn't want that."

The star burned fiercely, and when I closed my eyes, a bright spot lingered. "You gave him a Helionic burial."

"Anguish said you would prefer that. Since I don't believe in the Living Cosmos, I don't care one way or another if the body burns in a star."

A Helionic burial. My mind at last sharpened into focus. Perhaps the old rituals would grant me some understanding, a measure of peace or comfort.

I made my way swiftly back through the crowds. I was grateful when I saw the sign posted on the outer door, forbidding newcomers from entering the sanctum for purposes other than quiet reflection. On this day of wild celebration, the chamber stood empty.

For a moment, I lingered on the periphery, oddly hesitant. Once, in this very place, I had been officially declared a person by the faith.

And once, in a very similar place, I had bidden farewell to Donia. It was the only Helionic funeral I had ever attended.

Only Tyrus and I had realized the significance of the ceremony, of course. It had followed shortly after his coronation, when the time had come to launch the remains of Emperor Randevald von Domitrian into the sacred hypergiant Hephaestus. The corpse had been preserved in stasis for a month awaiting the fanfare of its trip into a star.

Tyrus had not considered his uncle worthy of the honor of an Emperor's funerary rites. He'd told me—and only me—that he'd had Sidonia's body placed in the coffin instead. We'd stood amid the crowd in the Great Heliosphere, donning gems that linked mourners together into a great current that symbolized the pulse of the Living Cosmos, and we'd watched as Sidonia's black crystalline coffin was launched into the star.

I reached down now into my pocket, where Sidonia's cloud sphere still resided. It had survived the blast too.

I could think of no more precious substitute for Tyrus's body. My mind dwelled upon that supernova, for Donia had gone into that star.

Once the star erupted, it sent all of itself soaring across the galaxy.

"You are everywhere now," I whispered to Donia, my heart crushing in my chest. "And with me always." My lips traced the cold contours of the sphere, and then I placed it lovingly into the launcher tube.

A mechanical roar as the crystalline chute drew the device toward the lip of space.

I never took my eyes from it. Without Donia, I would not have learned to love. Not truly. For I'd loved her beyond a Diabolic's artificial bond. I'd loved her for being the human being who showed me that I had a soul. I had blamed her for this in my dreams, after what Tyrus did to me—for I would never have loved him if not for her.

But I also might never have stopped him if not for her. She was the reason I knew of my own humanity—and that was what awoke me to the humanity of others, the sacredness of their lives. I owed her an immeasurable debt.

This orb was the only physical token that remained of Donia. But today belonged as much to her as to anyone. And my love for her, and my love for Tyrus—these two were inextricable, for without one, I would not have had the other. She had been reunited with the pulse of the divine Cosmos and now he was there with her, and so perhaps this was a way to commemorate both of them.

I launched her into the star with a whispered, "Good-bye, Donia. Look after him, if you can. I will love you both until I join you."

Then the sphere receded into the blackness of space until it was too tiny to see, and utter silence fell about me, thick and unbreakable.

It dawned upon me that nothing remained to be done.

There was nothing else to commemorate, and no action left to take. It was all finished.

Hopelessness swirled through me. I stared at the launching tube.

Death was empty. There were no answers to be had, no one I could ask who could answer for Tyrus: *Why had he saved me?*

"Nemesis."

Anguish's low voice startled me. I turned to face him, this friend who had supported me when no one else could.

My brother.

"I launched Donia's cloud sphere," I said.

"I watched you."

He nodded toward the doorway, where he must have been lurking.

I realized I *did* feel something: the mildest, most muted anger. "You should have insisted that Neveni wait for me before she incinerated him. Why didn't you tell her to wait?"

His gaze shied away, and my anger strengthened.

"Why, Anguish?" I said. "I killed him. Was that not enough?" My voice cracked. "Now I have nothing else to send. Scorn me if you wish. I know what he became. But—but I know what he was before, too. Before the Venalox. And *that* Tyrus deserved—"

"I know." He sounded defeated, too tired to argue. "But it seemed best to act quickly, Nemesis. I'm sorry."

"Did anyone close his eyes? Tell me they did that, at least."

He frowned at me.

"Anguish, did someone at least close his eyes before the launch?" I could hear my own voice rising, but I couldn't help myself. The thought that he'd been sent into the star like that—eyes wide, mouth hanging open, shocked by my betrayal—

"I am certain someone did."

"Do you know or don't you? Weren't you there?"

His jaw firmed. "Nemesis, I have something you'll want." He reached into his pocket to withdraw something. Metal glinted as he held it out. "I didn't think to give this to you sooner, but this is the best time."

My breath caught at the sight of that familiar bejeweled metal hair clip, crusted with my blood. I'd used it to break my own nose.

I grabbed it, and some animal noise erupted from me. I sank to my knees.

This was the first gift Tyrus had ever given me, and given me again that evening in the oubliette after our wedding. Within it, he'd concealed the means of blocking Pasus's ability to eavesdrop on us.

At the time, it had meant everything. It had meant *hope*: that he hadn't been damaged by Venalox, that he'd saved himself from its ravages, that he still loved me.

I hugged it against my chest, and suddenly I was weeping—great, ugly, hoarse, gasping sobs.

A child's sobs. A child's grief, racking and bottomless, inconsolable. But not a child's, for this was ancient, crushing, it would kill me. I could not bear it. I wailed and I could not stop.

Distantly I felt Anguish's arms wrapping about me, crushing me against his chest. But what point? What comfort? For it was over, it was all over. I'd killed Tyrus, and I'd had no choice, I'd had to kill him, but it was done, there was no recovering what had been lost. He was dead. There would be no redemption. The nightmare of the last years was over, but a new nightmare was upon me, and it would last until I died.

I had lost him—and all possibilities I could yet save him from himself—and I would have to live with this forever.

In that moment, it didn't matter why I'd had to do this. All that conviction that drove me to end him faded away beneath the reality of losing him forever. The universe contracted about me. A black hole opened at the very depths of my being, crushing all of me inward, into something empty and gaping and eternal. I could not endure this, I could not. I'd had to do this. I'd had to—and yet now I could not live with it.

Gradually I understood this. Gradually my sobs diminished, for they helped nothing. This was reality. This hell was the reality in which I now lived.

Anguish still held me, offering comfort in a way that no Diabolic should rightly be able to do. And I accepted it, turning my face into his chest, miserable and wordless as the tears died away and exhaustion seeped through me.

Anguish stroked my back amid the silence of the empty heliosphere, the dim light of the distant star gilding the floor.

"How?" I asked at last, my voice threadbare. "Where did you find this?"

"You'd left it on the floor of the washroom—shortly after we retrieved your tomb from space," Anguish said. "I knew one of the Partisans would steal it, hawk it, but they had no right. I stashed it in one of the ducts here."

"Thank you. Anguish, thank you."

"Do you wish me to place it into the launcher?"

"I . . ." The magnitude of my loss opened again, directly within my chest. I put my fist there, unable to speak.

He reached up, brushing tears from my face. "Wait. Just wait. There's no reason to do anything right now."

His kindness was undeserved. "You hated him. Even before the Venalox."

"You are my family. It does not matter that I hated who you loved."

Gratitude mixed with my sorrow. I buried myself in his arms again, breathing deeply. It was my great good fortune that I was not the only Diabolic who had learned of love.

An intuition came to me then, strengthening as it clarified. I remembered how, after I had awoken, he had joined Neveni in the bedroom. The looks they had traded. His touch on her arm, causing her to pause, to speak more carefully.

I pulled back, scrubbing my face with my palm. "You and Neveni seemed . . . different when I awoke. Have you two . . . ?"

He gave a quick, abashed tug of his lips. "We had the talk you suggested. Trapped together in the cargo container—wasn't much else to do."

But some emotion wanted to break through his carefully schooled expression. As I watched, it briefly lightened his features, like the sun breaking through clouds.

They'd resolved something. He was restraining his joy out of respect for my own grief. I leaned forward and placed a kiss on the salty skin of his forehead.

"I'm glad for you," I said softly. Then I sat back, clutching the clip tightly in my lap. "Go to Neveni. Cherish what you have, Anguish. I want you to be happy."

"But you—"

"I would like to be alone."

After a moment of studying my face, he nodded and rose, leaving me to the company of my thoughts.

I turned the clip over and over in my hands, thinking of the future. Anguish would want to stay with Neveni. But I would not.

Nor would I join the Partisans in their bloodbath at the Chrysanthemum.

I would not be paraded before the galactic media, a puppet tasked to herald some new order of things.

I'd had enough of meddling in the fate of galaxies. Let others do it.

I rose, intending to place the clip into the launching chute. But my hand tightened, refusing to relinquish it.

He had touched this clip that I touched now. Had retrieved it barehanded from a nitrogen fountain for me. Touching it was as close as I would ever again come to touching him.

I could still see his clever fingers brushing over this piece to withdraw the small device that jammed Pasus's surveillance. A hundred times after he'd killed me, I'd tried to replicate that trick. Now I did so once more, tracing amid the jewels as Tyrus had once done, not in the hopes of uncovering some hidden weapon, but for the simple sake of touching the exact place he'd once touched.

And this time, something revealed itself.

One of the jewels suddenly ruptured into splinters to reveal a cube of metal, no bigger than the tip of my finger.

My heart lurched.

This was a data cube.

My heart began to hammer against my rib cage. Trembling, I carefully extracted the data cube with my fingernails, then held it up on the flat of my palm to study in the dim glow of the star.

Impossible. This was *impossible.* It had been waiting here all along. Waiting for . . .

For what?

I flew from the heliosphere to my chamber, shoving past Partisans, blind to their salutes and reverent addresses. Locking the door to my chamber, I placed the chip in the holographic projector.

Light bloomed into an image, painfully precise. I swallowed a noise, made fists to stop myself from reaching out to touch his face.

A dead man spoke to me.

"Nemesis," he said, *"I hope you never have cause to see this. I mean this transmission to erase itself if all goes to plan, but if you are seeing this, it's because my heart has stopped and sent the trigger signal to activate it. So. I am dead. In that case, I'm profoundly fortunate you kept this hair clip."*

I looked down at the hair clip, shaking in my hand. A tear fell, drawing a rusty trail through the old blood.

"I owe you an explanation for everything I have done."

I looked up again, seeing new details through the blur in my eyes. He wore his own face—that faint cleft in his chin, a scattering of freckles across his sharp cheekbones. The silvery coat that covered his shoulders was stained with fresh blood.

Stars.

He'd recorded this holographic the day he killed me in the ball dome.

I could not breathe. My head swam as the holographic showed Tyrus holding up the very hair clip that had been fastened into my hair when my corpse had been launched into space.

"I am placing this with you," he said, *"in a few short moments. The oxygen pellets will keep you alive long enough for the Partisans to find you."*

No.

"No." My hands flew up to grip my head. "No, *no.*"

"Gladdic will have to take credit for this," he continued. Some noise offscreen diverted his attention briefly, and when he looked back into the lens, his face was grimmer, his mouth tight. Yet he managed a brief, wry smile, regardless. *"I'm going to dose him with Scorpion's Breath so he never argues with his heroism. I can use his avatar to contact the* Arbiter. *I just hope on all the stars that Sagnau will take the risk of saving you. . . ."*

A moan broke from me.

Tyrus had killed me. And then he had saved me.

It had been Tyrus all along.

36

"*YOU ARE* lying in blood-loss-induced stasis at this very moment," Tyrus continued, "*from a wound that I inflicted on you. I set this up intending to send Gladdic away from here—to free him of me—but instead, it will have to be you. I mean the* Arbiter *to retrieve you.*"

My mouth was moving in a silent refusal, *No no no no.* I put one hand over my lips, forcibly stilling them. I watched from somewhere outside my body, my senses all dimmed as though I were at the end of a vast, dark tunnel. All I could do was stare at Tyrus's ghostly image, the ashen smudges of sleeplessness beneath his eyes. He stroked the hair clip like some precious thing, like his most treasured possession, as he spoke grimly of saving me.

"*You* will *survive,*" he said harshly, his clothes still saturated with my blood. "*This was the only way I could devise to ensure it.*"

As he fumbled with the clip, he paused and took a breath that audibly shook.

"I'm sending you away sooner than I planned," he said. *"I owed it to Gladdic, after what I've put him through, to set him at liberty. I thought if I sent him to the Partisans, I could use him later, somehow, but . . . Oh, I knew you'd react to his execution, but I hadn't realized you'd force me to do this in his place. I thought it would happen later, the day I drove you from me, after I'd had time to . . ."* He grimaced, shook his head. *"No, perhaps I meant to keep you as long as I could. Selfish of me—I knew I should let you go, that it would be safer that way. But—"* His throat jerked as he swallowed. *"Even now, a part of me wishes to walk over and revive you and tell you the truth of all this. But I can't."*

He stepped closer to the camera. A flush colored his cheeks, but otherwise, his face was deathly pale. *"If you're watching this, I failed somehow. I've died, and stars know where you find yourself. But you need all the information now, so know this: I spoke the truth to you in the oubliette. I overcame the Venalox. It did not destroy my mind. I am not mad."*

I put the clip to my lips, dug it hard into the tender seam of my lips. "Impossible," I whispered. *Impossible.*

Tyrus clawed a hand through his hair, setting it into wilder disorder. *"I broke Alectar's control over me, and then I faked the symptoms for years. I was waiting for you—waiting for a chance to free us both, to break this Empire from its chains. And then I saw . . ."* He blew out a breath. *"I found something in the Grandiloquy vaults at the Clandestine Repository. I talked Alectar into taking us there. He wanted the Domitrian treasure stores. But I saw a chance to find information, something, anything I could use to blackmail the other Grandiloquy. To force them from his side to mine. Instead I found . . ."*

He shook his head, his gaze briefly unfocused, as though to behold something far in the distance. *"I found out that everything is a lie, Nemesis. The legitimacy of the Empire, the power of my family, the hold of the Grandiloquy—it was all born from a lie. I've included here a transmission from my family databases: the truth of Tarantis von Domitrian."*

"I know." I spoke raggedly, to a man who would never hear it. "I know, Tyrus."

An option screen blinked up before me, asking whether I wished to access the auxiliary file. I waved it away, desperate to see Tyrus's face once more.

He looked so tired. So burdened. His voice grew raw with frustrated despair.

"The worst of it is, we've known the mechanisms of malignant space all along. We knew centuries ago, millennia—since the ancient migration itself! My ancestor Tarantis used that knowledge to weaponize malignant space. He caused the supernova that almost destroyed civilization—and then he used the chaos that followed to secure his hold over the Empire. I think he even deceived the Interdict about the cause of it. He buried it all afterward to conceal the truth of what he'd done—the cause of malignant space, and how to cure it."

Cure it.

Tarantis had known how to *cure* it? There was a cure?

"Once I realized all this, I knew I'd been battling the wrong enemy, using the wrong approach." He began to pace now, back and forth to the edges of the screen. *"Malignant space isn't the disease, it's only a symptom. The Empire—my Empire—should never have existed. My ancestors stole this galaxy for themselves and divided up the spoils among the Grandiloquy, and we've been living with that injustice ever since. Learning this taught me what my true task must be."*

He stopped, staring fixedly at the imager, as though desperate to see right into my eyes—into the soul of the future Nemesis who, if watching this, had also witnessed his destruction.

"I was never supposed to save this Empire. I'm the one meant to destroy it."

"Tyrus," I whispered. The pain in his face caused me to ache.

He had tried to save me.

He was addressing his own murderer.

"Hephaestus will go supernova," Tyrus said. *"And once it does, I'll put my plan into motion. I haven't"*—he gestured vaguely in the air— *"entirely figured out the particulars yet, but I intend to avoid the trap we ran into when we openly attacked the order of the galaxy. The Grandiloquy stopped us because we were trying to reform that which resists reformation. It was my fault. I underestimated how deeply rooted the institutions of power are."*

He resumed pacing, tension gripping his tall, muscular frame.

"I can't count on allies. Not even among the Excess. We're all too deeply entrenched in this system. The indoctrination goes too deep. Our media, our educational system, the very myths we use to understand ourselves—there's no story, no institution, no "truth" that hasn't been corrupted by Tarantis's propaganda. And when someone, somewhere, has thought to question all we take for granted—they've been shouted down by the crowd, bullied into silence, into ignoring their own instincts, their own reasoning, their own sense of right and wrong. It's a collective mass delusion, one that persuades us to ignore reality in favor of what we are told *is true. No one is allowed to question, and so, critical thinking is made impossible. It's that shared, societal delusion that I need to break, if there's any hope of creating something better."*

My legs sank out from under me.

So *this* had been on his mind as he spoke about conformity and belonging. I drew my knees up to my chest, locking my arms around them, holding myself tight as his words hammered the air between us.

"But how does one smash a centuries-old delusion? I can think of only one way: I need to corrupt the delusion, remold the lie into a narrative so absurd that it strains the ability to believe in it. Cognitive dissonance, that

is what the philosophers once called it. I want to break that instinct to subscribe to the dictates of a reality that does not exist, by creating a false reality so ludicrous that belief in it cannot be sustained."

He halted, staring for a moment at the clip, then looking back to the imager. *"So. Instead of fighting the system, I will use it. All the poisons that lurk in the mud will hatch out—because I myself will hatch them. I will become the lie, embody all the corruption of this Empire and make the problems we've buried burn so intolerably bright, none can avert their eyes."* He gave a faint, hopeless laugh. *"It's always been fashionable to repeat the lies of the elite, but I will create a lie so ludicrous, every fashionable person discredits themselves by retelling it. They will forfeit their power by merely believing in me—and with any luck, many of them will come to question their own obedience to the Empire as well."*

It hit me like a blast: this was the reason he declared himself a god.

"Oh, Tyrus." I did not know whether to laugh or to weep again.

He had declared himself a god, knowing it was a lie too ludicrous to believe, even by those who most desperately craved the belonging that came from a fashionable, shared delusion.

I knew he'd already succeeded in one sense, for those who had enforced and repeated the lies that held together this Empire had, indeed, conformed. They'd been rewarded with Tyrus's bribes, and approval from the other fashionable liars of the Empire, and they'd repeated the most ludicrous of lies as readily as they'd repeated all the Domitrian propaganda before it. They had hailed Tyrus as their God.

The galactic media had fallen over themselves to praise their Divine Emperor. The spiritual leader of the Empire had proclaimed him a deity far and wide. The Grandiloquy had competed to worship him most extravagantly. Those followers on the *Halcyon*—how eagerly they had fought among themselves to more reverently hail him for what *he could not possibly be*!

His believers were the very men and women who formed the backbone of this Empire. They were its enforcers, and now they enforced his false divinity. Tyrus had hoped that this lie—bald, brazen, and self-evidently wrong to those who used their minds rather than relying on others for their opinions—would undermine the authority of anyone who repeated it.

It would. It had. No one looking at these people from the outside could believe in anything they said anymore. They'd spent their credibility.

My misery would crush me. "You fool," I muttered. Anger, fury, was so much easier than grief. "You sun-scorned *fool*." Why hadn't he trusted me? Why hadn't he found a way to tell me?

I had killed him. He had saved me, and I had murdered him.

"There will be a reaction, of course. It will take time for the backlash against this lie—and all who repeat it—to grow, to take shape and gain power," he was saying, but I could no longer watch him. I felt as though I were being flayed from within, coming apart in bloodied shreds. I laid my forehead on my knees, but the darkness offered no comfort. His voice was still addressing me.

"If you are watching this, I don't know how far I progressed into the charade. But that is where you come in."

My every muscle tensed.

I had wondered what my purpose might be.

He was about to suggest one.

"I wanted more time with you, so I could lead you into a better understanding of this Empire before making you my enemy. But once you declared that you'd destroyed the Sacred City, that you'd killed the Interdict, I had to act. I had to sever your faith in me with a single violent act. Nemesis, please believe me . . ."

The pause went on so long that I finally, against my will, looked up.

He made no effort to conceal his agony. He looked like a man beholding his own grave.

"That was the hardest thing I've done in my life," he said quietly. *"I would sooner die than do it again."*

Pain rocked through me, my eyes blurring.

This could not be true. This could not be. I wouldn't accept it.

But even as I rejected his claims, my mind was piecing together his actions.

He'd driven his sword through me.

He'd ensured that I survived and was delivered to Neveni's vessel.

He'd saved my life on Corcyra. Then he hunted me down, in order to . . .

To taunt me for not rising up to fight him. For I had not played my part, and so he had tried to goad me into it: *My love, you needn't bother shutting your ears to the despair of the Excess after tomorrow. Those voices screaming, "Nemesis lives" will at last go silent forevermore.*

And now, all at once, I could imagine a different interpretation of our every interaction. He'd captured me and then ensured that cooperating with him would seem intolerable.

He'd intended for me to be his enemy.

And now, from beyond the grave, he was asking me to become his ally once more.

"When people begin to question this lie," he was saying, *"several things will probably happen: those who believe it—or claim to—will become increasingly frenzied and irrational in their defense of it. They will see an attack upon their belief as an attack upon their stature, their influence, their credibility. To admit they were wrong will seem unthinkable. The more glaringly obvious the lie becomes, the more desperate their conviction will become—and they will go to intolerable lengths to prove themselves right."*

I could barely focus on his words. This holographic might be the last true view of him—Tyrus in all his honesty, stripped of the Divine Emperor persona—that I ever had. I studied the curve of his mouth, the straight, bold line of his nose. I imagined touching him. What I would say, if we met again.

You should have told me, Tyrus. You should have told me!

"The backlash against the lie will swell entirely on its own, but here's the difficult part: even if doubts stir, most will not dare to voice them."

His conviction, the sober intensity of his explanation, broke my heart. How carefully he'd laid this plan. But I'd been right. His one mistake had been to love me too well.

"Even as the people of this Empire learn to doubt me, to doubt every established institution that supports me, and every prominent figure that follows me, there will be consequences to pointing out that the Emperor has no clothes. For that reason, few will dare. Someone must step forward to inspire the doubters to act and speak their thoughts aloud, rather than remain silent and complicit."

"A fine point." I spoke roughly, unshed tears in my voice. This was the last time I'd have a chance to speak to the real Tyrus. What matter if he could not reply?

"That is the most monumental task," Tyrus told the imager. *"It requires rejecting half a millennium of complacency and obedience. The first voices to question my lie will be silenced and punished. What happens to them will terrify others into silence . . . unless there is a figurehead too strong to destroy, and prominent enough to weather the consequences of speaking the truth. There must be a symbol of strength to serve as an example to others. Nemesis, it has to be you."*

"Me," I whispered.

"You," he repeated, as though he'd heard me, and my heart gave a quick stab of surprise. *"I would not have chosen to send you to Sagnau,*

but everything moved too quickly—I have no alternative. If all goes to plan, this will succeed and you will never see this holographic and you will never need to know this."

He paused, and his expression gentled, his mouth softening. *"My love. I would ask no one else—would trust no one else. But if anyone can overthrow this Empire, it is you. I am dead, but this can still be done: lead an uprising. The Empire will be primed and ready to fall to your onslaught. Whatever has happened between now"*—he gestured to himself and then to me—*"and the time you finally watch this, I can assure you: the Empire is weaker. I'll spend the time ahead ruinously depleting the treasury, empowering the most venal of public officials and removing the most competent of them. I'll cripple any social or structural support that keeps this Empire intact and powerful, so it should be ready to fall. I beg of you: finish this, or it will all be for nothing. Free this galaxy, Nemesis, and let the Excess reclaim the liberty my ancestors stole from them."*

I stared numbly at his face. From the very start, he'd been manipulating me, positioning me to become his opponent.

But it had gone wrong. I had been a deadlier enemy than he anticipated, and so Tyrus was dead.

"I know you must be furious with me. You've every right to be."

"Yes," I said softly.

"Nemesis, I could not share the truth of this with you. If you'd known, you would never have cooperated. You would never have risen against me—and that's what I most need of you. I need an enemy."

A hard fist of anger contracted in my chest. He'd used me. He'd been using me all this time.

"Time runs short," Tyrus said, *"so I must tell you that there's another element to this plan: I mean to create malignant space, to spread it openly. With the cure to it in hand, I feel this is a calculated risk, one that will hasten the backlash against me. If I am dead . . ."* He hesitated. *"If I am*

dead," he repeated deliberately, *"then that malignant space needs to be fixed. On this data chip, I give you the cure. I've left it in many other locations, just in case, but this is for you. Enclosed you'll find schematics for the creation of a synthesizer that will heal whatever damage I've inflicted. You can use this to your advantage: it can be wielded to gather support from the Excess. Spread it. Share it. Don't let it be lost."*

As if his life meant nothing. As if the greater game were all that mattered. As if my grief meant nothing—as if, so long as I saw his scheme to fruition, all the loss would be worth the reward.

"Damn you, Tyrus!" I shouted at his image.

He rubbed his palms over his face, like he was trying to fight back a migraine. *"And Nemesis,"* he said wearily, *"I obviously do not know how I perished, but I need you to know that if I died by your hand—"*

I flinched.

His hands dropped, and his earnest eyes seemed to bore into mine across space and time.

"You did the right thing," he said. *"The timing is not what I planned—but you did exactly the right thing. I know I must have been cruel to you. Perhaps I convinced you that I hated you, but Nemesis, know this: I loved you to my final breath."* Tears shimmered in his eyes. *"I would have desired nothing more than a life with you, but we were not fated to be."*

The words knifed me, and my eyes blurred with tears, for I was seeing him once again before that blast of light, shoving me back so he might take it all himself, and, oh . . .

"I hate you," I snarled at him.

I slapped my hand out and cut off the holographic projector, a scream of blind fury tearing from my throat.

"I *HATE* YOU!"

How could he do this to me? How could he put me in this position, of knowing *I had killed him* and it was *him* all along? It was the real Tyrus all along!

Those eyes, those fixed and staring eyes, they had been *his*. The concern he'd shown, his tears, the love he'd confessed—all real.

I screamed again. I slammed my fist against the window and felt my knuckles split open. I kicked the wall and the bones in my foot cracked and split.

Wounded, gasping, I sank once more to the floor.

And now what? Now *what?*

"Damn you," I whispered. "My love. *Damn* you."

Now I would save the galaxy for him.

37

I CHARGED down the boarding artery leading to the *Alexandria*, restored by med bots, powered by an anger that rivaled the power of a supernova.

I loved you to my final breath, he'd said.

But he hadn't needed to die. He could have been here right now, beside me. All he'd needed to do was tell me the truth. We could have made this happen together.

If I died by your hand, please know that it was the right thing to do.

How generous of him! What gifts he had left behind for me! The guilt of his death, the useless weight of my love, his sun-scorned *forgiveness* for it! And a plan that only *I* could carry out.

Or maybe, even from the grave, he was lying.

Both possibilities enraged me, and rage made a better medicine than any bot could administer. It burned out my grief, roared too loudly to accommodate thoughts.

I passed into the *Alexandria*, ignoring the startled Partisans who saluted me, heading directly toward the first computer console I could find.

There was an easy way to determine whether he'd lied on that holographic. No would-be liberator would have killed all those people on the *Halcyon* just to remind me he needed to die.

I activated the computer console in the *Alexandria*'s launch bay. Though the major systems would permit no access without Tyrus's authorization code, I easily accessed the vessel's surveillance archives.

Yet when I watched the footage of the destruction of the *Halcyon*, I could not make sense of it. I could not.

Because the *Alexandria*'s own surveillance showed nothing of the destruction Anguish and I had witnessed immediately after we'd escaped, and before anyone could evacuate. Rather, it depicted an evacuation, slow and carefully orchestrated.

I forwarded the footage. The evacuation continued. Hours passed.

The record captured the power core overloading and blasting open the cityship—but not until after the last passengers had disembarked.

I recognized this version from galactic media broadcasts. We'd dismissed it as manufactured propaganda.

"Lies," I whispered, watching the footage again at low speed, looking for any signs of editing or splicing.

But there were none.

My hand slackened on the console as I suddenly understood.

Anguish and I watched the *Halcyon* destroyed through the screen on the *Retribution*—a vessel that Tyrus had given to me, with systems he'd controlled completely.

He'd rigged the footage, all right—the footage he'd shown *us*.

I gritted my teeth hard as I turned away from the console. Another lie! And I'd swallowed it wholesale, falling enthusiastically into the role Tyrus had crafted for me.

He'd been telling the truth. His thinking had not been clouded by Venalox. His every action had been guided by a greater aim—the liberation of the Empire. It was the same sun-scorned goal he'd had the day I met him.

And he was dead by my hand.

He'd manipulated me. Deceived me. Used me. I would not let myself think about anything but that. If he were still alive, I'd kill him all over again! The cruel, despicable, evil bastard—

"Hey! What are you doing here?"

Neveni's startled voice called me back to the moment.

Whatever she saw in my face put wariness into hers. Her hand drifted toward the weapon in her belt, and then she thought better of it, and her palm drifted to her side.

I saw no need to explain. Let her put my odd manner down to grief. "It's not your concern."

"Were you looking for me? I was just heading back to the *Arbiter*." She took my arm to lead me away. When I yanked free of her guiding hand, she said, "You shouldn't be here."

"I'll go when I damn well please."

Her face hardened. "Nemesis, we are working on this ship. You need to leave. If I must, I'll have an escort take you back."

Gone, her jubilation at our victory. Whatever had occupied her on this vessel did not agree with her. "What are *you* doing here?"

A muscle flexed in her jaw. "Supervising repairs."

"What repairs? Did one of your Partisans decide to fire up the engine inside the gale?"

She shrugged. "Stupid. He's been demoted."

"Why waste time on repairing it?" I asked. "You won't be flying this vessel without the command codes."

She opened her mouth, then shut it. An odd reaction. As my eyes narrowed, she spoke abruptly: "We have hackers. We'll get those codes."

"The *command* codes?" I barked a laugh. "Are you joking? You can't hack your way into the system. Without Tyrus, you'll never . . ." A bizarre thought stopped my voice.

She had found me in time for me to be healed. But I hadn't been alone in that room.

She cocked her head, eyeing me. "Go on," she said sharply.

She'd had time to heal me. She'd had medical bots on hand . . . for me.

But . . .

But she hadn't used them on Tyrus? The medical bots could have started his heart, could have healed him just enough so he was still helpless—and at her mercy, with all the important intelligence in his mind there for the taking. . . . She hadn't bothered to do that?

How wouldn't Neveni think of that?

She had to have realized straightaway the power of holding the *Alexandria*. She had to have realized the only way to seize it was to force those command codes out of Tyrus.

Yet she didn't spare a medical bot for him?

As she waited for my reply, her hand drifted again toward her weapon.

"Without Tyrus, you'll never manage it." Somehow I sounded indifferent. Calm.

Neveni wished me to believe she'd disposed of Tyrus's body so hastily. That she'd given him the privilege of a Helionic burial rather than just casting the corpse out an airlock.

And Anguish had let her do it.

He wouldn't have let her do that. Anguish knew me better than that. He knew what it would mean to me, to see the body. He cared too much for me to do that, unless . . .

Unless . . .

"Our hackers are excellent," Neveni was saying with a shrug. "Given time, they can crack anything. Now, come, let's get back to the *Arbiter*."

She desperately wanted me off this ship. She was hiding something here—from *me*.

My heart was racing now, sweat prickling over my skin. What if . . .

I dared not believe it. I dared not ask her, either. She was lying about something, but confronting her would yield no answers: Neveni never backed down.

"All right," I said with deathly calm. I turned as if to leave, and Neveni fell into step behind me.

My elbow slammed her face. She staggered backward. My follow-up punch knocked her out cold.

Whatever the plot, I had to assume that Anguish was part of it.

I leaned down and slid her weapon out of her belt. Then I seized her wrist and spoke into her transmitter.

"Anguish: come meet me in Tyrus's study on the *Alexandria*. I'd like to talk to you."

Anguish reached me within minutes.

When he stepped into the study, his eyes drifted first to the antique hearth, which crackled with the flames set to flare to life whenever someone was in this chamber. Then he looked back to me—and the weapon I aimed squarely at Neveni's forehead. She lay sprawled over the desk, unconscious.

"No," he said.

"Yes. You *will* tell me," I said ferociously. "Where is Tyrus?"

"Dead."

"Try again," I snarled. "You need his authorization codes to gain control of this ship! He's alive somewhere on this ship. Tell me his location, or I kill her."

"Nemesis," he said, drawing toward me.

"Not a step," I hissed at him. "You healed me. But I'll wager you healed him first. Or *she* did. You—you might have chosen me. But she—*she* knew whose brain would prove more valuable."

"You are distressed. You are grieving."

A wild laugh escaped me. "Last chance, Anguish. And I promise you, there'll be no time for healing bots."

His dark eyes narrowed. "You will not kill her. That's absurd."

"I killed Tyrus!" I roared. "You think this won't be easier?"

Frustration contorted his features. "Why? Why do you demand to see him? Nothing has changed. He is an enemy!"

Is. Not *was.*

His face slackened as he realized his own error. "Nemesis," he said in a defeated voice. "Please. Don't do this."

"Last chance," I said very softly. "Where is he?"

Anguish slammed his fist into the nearby shelf, knocking over an antique bust of the Roman Emperor Claudius. "His mind is intact, Nemesis! Undamaged! We scanned it with the medical bots—the Venalox did nothing!"

Some complex, unnameable emotion blasted through me. I heard myself as though from a great distance, cool and flat: "Yes," I said. "I know."

"He did everything!" Anguish glared at me. "He's not some victim, some tragic figure—he chose this course of his own volition!" His eyes

spat fire. "You loved a tyrant! And now—what, you mean to *save* him? There's nothing to save! Don't you understand? The rot is *inborn!*"

"Brother," I said. For I had looked on him so. I had imagined us alike, united by nature, honed in the same cruel forge, tested by the same strange human tribulations.

But Tyrus's mind had not been damaged by Venalox. He'd not been destroyed by Pasus. He was alive. And he was *mine*. Mine to kill all over again if I still felt in this thunderous mood when I beheld him.

He was not *theirs* to torture.

"Brother," I said, "our paths diverge here. Tell me where he is. Or she is dead."

"Nemesis, see reason! He chose every evil you saw him commit! You are better than him. And he's dying, I tell you. The second we control the ship, he'll be—"

"Time's up," I said as I raised my weapon.

At the same moment, his hand flashed forward, hurling the stone bust at my head.

My shot burst it apart midair, but Anguish was already springing forward, leaping over the desk in a mass of muscle. His feet slammed into my chest, knocking me back against the wall. My hand plunged into the fire. I tore out a flaming log and swung it into his temple.

He seized me with an unbreakable grip, throwing me into the desk. It toppled beneath the impact, spilling me and Neveni to the floor.

She moaned weakly. I rolled out of the way of Anguish's stomping foot, then dragged her limp body up and took her neck in my hands.

Anguish froze, crouched on the floor, his chest heaving with exertion.

"Don't," he panted.

"Humans are fragile," I said. "Save her or don't. Decide *now*."

"Nemesis, please—"

"Slam your head into the wall. Knock yourself unconscious. Or watch me break her neck."

"This is a mistake," he panted. "The gravest mistake you'll ever make. Whatever you think you're planning, it won't—"

"Decide."

"Nemesis, please," he said. "I am your brother."

"Yes. So stop begging." I met and held his eyes. "Remember: we are Diabolics."

I hurled Neveni at him.

A Diabolic would have let her fall. But Anguish did not.

As he rushed forward to catch her, I whipped the weapon up from the floor and shot him in the shoulder. Then I hurtled forward and delivered a roundhouse to his head.

He slumped to the floor beside her, unconscious.

Thrumming with adrenaline, I stepped outside the chamber. "Seal the door," I said breathlessly to the air, before remembering I could give no such order: the ship was not under my command.

Nevertheless, I knew where to go. *He's dying*, my brother had told me.

I lifted up my weapon and sprinted toward the one place that would best support the interrogation of a dying man: the medical bay.

Bored Partisans were stationed along the approach. For a moment, I earnestly considered fighting my way through them. But direct combat would draw reinforcements, most of which I'd likely end up killing. There had to be a better way.

I tore off a strip of garment and set fire to it with my weapon, then ducked into an empty chamber to wait.

As the smoke curled up, an alarm went off. Partisans rushed past the door to quell it.

I waited until their footsteps receded, then dashed out. One Partisan, a slower runner than the others, rounded the corner just as I appeared. My fist collided with his face before he could make a sound.

I dragged him into the nearest empty chamber, then charged back toward the medical bay.

I'd anticipated needing to barrel through locked doors. Instead the doors sensed my approach and slid open, causing me to skid to a startled stop.

And there, sprawled out on a medical bed, ringed by med bots, his arms and legs bound to the cot, was Tyrus—unconscious.

But alive.

38

"NO. NO, wait!" cried a man's voice.

I wheeled on him, weapon raised.

But he was not armed. In fact, he positioned himself between me and Tyrus, his arms outstretched, as though to protect his prisoner from me.

"It's not what it looks like," he said desperately. "We're only keeping him alive for the command authorizations—I swear it!"

Why, he believed I'd come here to kill Tyrus. Again.

A laugh boiled up in my throat, but I managed to restrain it.

"How is he?" I demanded.

"Alive, but not for long. I have the kill dose on hand." He jabbed his thumb over his shoulder to indicate its location. "Once he's strong enough to answer questions, he's done for, I swear it. Please . . ."

I realized I still stood in the doorway. One step forward allowed the doors to slide closed behind me. "Have you tried to wake him recently?"

"No." He hesitated. "It's really not a good idea for you to be here—"

"I won't kill him."

I'd already done that. Now I needed answers.

The man relaxed a touch, eyeing me uncertainly. After a moment, he eased back toward his worktable, which was encircled by computers, the screens dark for want of access codes to activate them.

"He has no control over the machines anymore," he assured me. "Look. All the security bots are like this." He kicked something beneath his desk, and a security bot skidded across the floor, rolling over with a clatter.

"Fascinating." I fixed my gaze on Tyrus again, watching the slow rise and fall of his chest. His cheeks looked sunken, his skin clammy and pale. I wanted to inspect him from head to toe, to run my hands over his skin and make sure all was intact. To kiss his brow, to draw his breath into my lungs and bury my face in his throat, to smell his skin and—

No.

The rage was safer. The rage was the only thing I could trust.

"So the shock neutralized his power," I murmured.

"It seems so."

My thoughts traveled back to the holographic of Tarantis, and that reference to being stripped of power. The Interdict had mentioned the same thing to me. Electrical shocks to stop the heart had stripped Amon von Domitrian of his power. It had done the trick with this Emperor as well.

"What do you intend to do?" I asked.

"We have Liar's Bane ready." The healer, if that was his calling—for all I knew, his specialty was interrogation—lifted up a phial of reddish liquid. "It requires dilution, of course. Once he's strong enough, we'll figure out the proper dose. He'll spill the authorization codes, and we'll put him down."

Put him down. I would put this medic down, before I left this room. "Give it to him now," I said.

He looked startled. "But we have to wait for—"

"Now," I said. "Or should I?"

The healer still hesitated, his glance shifting toward the communications port on the wall. "I don't think—"

I lifted my weapon. *"Now."*

The healer shrank into himself, then nodded. He carried the phial to his workstation, where a dropper and a flask waited. "But this . . . it could kill him if it's too soon."

I had no choice. The fire would be put out soon enough. Then the guards would return. I was stronger than a human, but not a ship full of them, well-armed.

"I have killed him once already," I said.

My voice sounded indifferent. But inside me, a turmoil was stirring, unsettling my anger and causing my throat to tighten. I looked away from the healer, who was busy titrating the first dose.

Tyrus looked peaceful where he lay, the sheet draped high over his chest, his palms limp and loose at his sides. His lips parted slightly on his indrawn breath. He looked very young, and thoroughly helpless.

The sight of him arrested me. How many times had I watched him sleep? I required much less sleep than a normal human, yet I had been content to lie awake watching him, just as with Donia in my youth.

Donia had slept like a child, sprawling with an abandoned sort of innocence, as though no evil existed in the world. Not so with Tyrus. Even before the Venalox, he'd been tormented routinely by nightmares. I never saw him sleep for a decent stretch without tossing violently and then gasping awake, usually in reaction to some tiny noise: a shift of the pressure from the air ventilators, a purr of distant engines.

I'd understood the difference. In her childhood, Donia had been protected—by me.

In his childhood, Tyrus had been hunted—by everyone.

I had wished, as his wife, to turn back time. To meet him as a small child, and to persuade him of his safety, so he might sleep as Donia had. With Donia, I had lain awake out of pleasant boredom. With Tyrus, I had lain awake on duty. When he tossed and turned, my hand found his forehead and smoothed back his hair. Sometimes that was enough to sweeten his dreams. Sometimes he would clumsily seize my hand and graze his lips over my palm, or catch me by the waist and draw me nearer. . . .

Regardless, he'd never slept as he did now—peacefully, without a single flicker of his lashes or some contortion of limbs.

As for noise, I found myself listening to the *Alexandria*'s sounds. I heard the distant ruckus of the Partisans putting out the fire I'd set, the purring of the atmospheric vents, the humming of the lights.

This was not a quiet ship.

My eyes narrowed.

The healer stepped up to the bedside, the injection in his hand.

Tyrus's eyes snapped open. Somehow he'd freed his arm. It lashed up, snaring the man about the neck and dragging him down into the sheets.

"Release the restraints!" bellowed Tyrus.

I could have stepped forward. Instead I laid down my weapon and watched as the healer, frantic for lack of air, slapped his hand out to release the other three bindings.

With a roar, Tyrus flipped them both off the bed, onto the floor.

When he rose again, he held the healer in a headlock, a laser scalpel pressed to the man's throat. Tyrus's wild, bloodshot eyes found mine.

I had not thought it possible for him to grow paler. His freckles stood out lividly against his bluish skin. For the length of a heartbeat, his eyes softened. "Nemesis," he breathed.

And then his jaw tensed, his forearm flexing as he strengthened his grip on the medic.

"No closer," he warned me, "or he dies."

I stared at him disbelievingly. "Tyrus, I don't even know the man's name."

The healer moaned. "Ciprian! It's Ciprian!"

My eyes remained locked on Tyrus's. "Kill him or let him go. We have business, you and I."

Tyrus's bloodless lips quirked into a fleeting smile. "True enough." Then, baring his teeth, he shoved the man hard toward me.

Ciprian thought, perhaps, that he was stumbling to safety. Before he could bolt past me to the doors, my fist lashed forward and knocked him out cold.

Put down, indeed.

I stepped back to the doors and sealed them shut, then rounded back on Tyrus. He straightened to his full height—then sagged back against the wall, panting. The panting sharpened, turned into a ragged, hitching laugh.

"Try, try again." He opened his arms—and then, when I hesitated, straightened with visible effort, saying, "Come, now—no weapon? Use your fists instead."

I understood suddenly. He, too, thought I'd come to finish the job I'd begun by the power core.

I picked up my weapon from the floor and watched his laughter die. "Don't tempt me," I said softly.

But my hands were trembling, causing the weapon to shake. He noticed. The tight line of his mouth loosened, and he looked back into my eyes, a question on his face.

"So," he murmured.

How strong was he? Could he walk on his own power? How thoroughly had they healed him? Did he require med bots' attention?

"I *should* kill you," I said through my teeth.

"All those images that Neveni sent me—the tortures I watched you endure . . ." He took a hard breath. "Those were lies. Fine acting, Nemesis. You know how to dagger the heart."

I drove my hand into my pocket and unsheathed my own accusation: the hair clip. "Nothing I did to you was as cruel as *this*."

Tyrus recoiled, then caught his balance by grabbing the bed frame. It was taking him a great effort to remain upright, I realized. "You saw it?"

The answer was obvious. I did not respond.

He remained staring at the hair clip. "I was dead?" He sounded dazed.

All of a sudden, rage overwhelmed me. *"Yes."* Had he imagined himself immortal, untouchable? Did he not remember that his divinity was a *lie*? "Your heart stopped. As any fragile human's might. *I* killed you." But I no longer needed to feel guilty—for he was alive, and in his beautiful, accursed eyes, I saw the resumption of that calculating intelligence that had deceived me, manipulated me, reduced me to a grieving, sobbing heap. "Is that not what you wanted—an enemy? Is that not what your secret plan was all about?"

His face, when he lifted it, was hollow and ashen. "I never *wanted* any of this."

"Nova blast you, Tyrus!" I hurled the clip at his head. Dodging it, he staggered to his knees.

I lunged forward, looming over him. He hurled himself back against the wall, his shoulders drawing up as he prepared to defend himself from me.

But it would be a futile effort. We both knew that in his weakened state, I could kill him easily.

"Why did you do this to me?" I demanded.

He had never lacked courage. He showed it now by returning my look with determination—making an effort to conceal his weakness, his labored breathing. A bead of sweat snaked down his temple, and I curled my hand into a fist, fighting the urge to brush it away.

"You know the reason," he said raggedly. "If you have seen what you say."

"But why lie to me, Tyrus? Hadn't I proved myself trustworthy?"

"A thousand times," he said steadily.

"You deceived me. You manipulated and used me. You made me think—"

"I made you think I was a monster." His jaw squared mutinously. "I know exactly what I did. I sent you away when you put me in an impossible position. I ensured your survival when you tried to force me to leave this Empire or take your life."

Slowly, painfully, he began to shove himself back to his feet.

"You—" He panted with effort. "You were the only one who mattered to me, and I couldn't have you near me for this. And I—" He blinked, then visibly startled. Looking up and around, as though in search of something, he muttered, "They're gone. I can't—I don't feel the machines."

"No." My satisfaction felt bitter. "The discharge stopped your heart and disabled the machines in your blood. Even if you escape, you'll find it quite difficult to play the Divine Emperor now."

A bleakness passed over his face. "Nemesis." With new urgency, he stepped away from the wall. "Listen to me." He took hold of my arms, stepped close enough that I felt the warmth of his body. "The time for lies is past."

I wanted to lay my face in the crook of his neck and breathe him in, and I scorned myself for it. "How convenient for you" was all I said.

He caught hold of my face with urgency. Surprise twisted through my belly. His expression was vulnerable, naked of defenses.

"I *know* I have wronged you."

"Beyond the speaking of it," I said hoarsely.

"But I cannot undo what I have done. It's too late. You know what I mean to do. I have to finish this."

I gritted my teeth and held myself rigid as his hand slipped across my throat and down my arm, as light as a caress. His fingers entwined with mine, and the stroke of his thumb over my palm loosened something—the weight of my grief, the nightmare of my guilt, breaking away and dissipating.

And I could not lie to him. "I love you," I murmured. But even as he drew a sharp breath, his grip tightening, I added, "I'm not sure it makes a difference." My love for him did not outweigh my anger. "I can't trust you, Tyrus."

He exhaled. "I've given you no cause to trust me. And this"—he glanced quickly around—"is no place to persuade you differently. I'm powerless. Trapped. And I need to get out of here. I need your help."

"You need me now."

"Yes."

But anger was wiser than love. "You may need me," I said. "But you don't deserve me."

He laughed—a startled, swift, delighted laugh. "You finally realized that." And then, brows arching, he looked toward the unconscious medic.

Stiffly, like an elder, he knelt to retrieve the injector filled with Liar's Bane. "Here," he grunted. "A truth serum." He pressed the device into my hand. "Use it on me. Later. Give me the dose. Ask me anything you care to know then. But first—first, we need to escape."

Abruptly, the doors to the medical bay shook. Voices rang through the *Alexandria*'s corridors, and my urgent gaze remained locked with Tyrus's.

We were trapped in here.

A scorching smell pervaded the air. The Partisans were using a cutting laser.

"Up," Tyrus said, his gaze flying toward the ceiling. "We have to go *up*. I'll show you."

He heaved himself clumsily up onto the medical bed, stopping to draw in ragged breaths. Then he unsteadily swayed upright and pawed open a door in the ceiling, unveiling a darkened crawl shaft. Then, another pause to gasp for air.

He was too weak. This would be easy for Tyrus normally, but he could barely hold his balance right now as he groped for the frame of the vent.

I should knock him down. Restrain him. Open the door for the Partisans and let them have him. Anger boiled low in my chest, tempting me.

Instead I jumped up onto the bed next to him. "For Helios's sake, I'll lift you," I snarled, seizing his waist and hurling him none too gently into the vent. I steadied him from below until he'd pulled himself fully inside. In one bounding leap, I snared the edges of the shaft and yanked myself up into the crawl-tube after him.

Stars help me, I was a fool for doing this—but I would have answers from him.

Then I would decide whether I wished him to die for good.

39

THE AIR was icy in the crawl-tube. I crouched beside Tyrus, hemmed in on all sides by slick metal sheathing, while he studied the string of numbers that flashed across a rudimentary monitor.

In ancient times, the *Alexandria* had been retrofitted, upgraded, and rebuilt many times. These crawl-tubes had been built to access parts of the ship that now did not exist. Our search for a computer interface had been painfully slow. Already we'd turned back from a dead end and nearly died when another tube truncated abruptly, opening into a hundred-foot drop into darkness.

The screen cast a sickly greenish light over Tyrus's grim expression. "All right," he said finally. "This interface has some limitations—"

"What sort?" I said.

"Be mindful of our volume," Tyrus murmured. "These tubes are the oldest parts of the ship. I am not sure how far the sound carries."

And if the Partisans could hear us, they could find us.

"I can't access the newer systems," he whispered. "Security, weapons, the like . . . But I can interface manually with the launch bay."

"No point," I said curtly. "We're surrounded by the Partisan fleet. An escape pod would never slip by them—even if we could reach one."

I could certainly fight my way over to one, if Anguish was still unconscious and in no position to face me. But Tyrus could not make it that far. Even kneeling here, crawling along as we were doing, winded him. He was in poor shape.

He sighed and pressed his forehead against the grating, eyes closed. I could see his mind working swiftly. "I'll launch a pod. No, all the pods. It will keep them busy, tracking them down, and then we may seize the *Alexandria* itself."

We. I hoped he was not taking it for granted I would help him. The truth serum pressed against my leg and I found myself surveying him, contemplating whether he was strong enough to survive it if I simply forced it on him now and extracted every answer I wanted from him. Then . . . Then . . .

In truth, I didn't know what I would do. My head pounded.

His fingers flashed over the keypad. I focused on the sounds of the *Alexandria*. The muffled din of frantic activity rose from a nearby corridor—hurried footsteps, words I could not make out.

"There." Tyrus blew out a breath and leaned back as far as the tube would allow. "All set. I'll order the pods to launch just before we exit the tube."

"Exit?" I choked down a sharp laugh, lest it carry too clearly. "And what will we do once we're out of hiding? You no longer control the machines. Not like Tarantis after all. *He* managed to avoid having his power stripped."

"Nemesis . . ."

He reached for me, but I recoiled and wrapped my arms around myself, my fingers digging into my own flesh. He was alive, and we were safe for now. I did not understand myself—why I should ache for him so fiercely even as anger made me want to throttle him.

Tyrus sighed and sagged back against the wall of the crawl-tube. "I made Anguish sick," he confessed.

I froze. "What?"

"You were living off the grid, in the wilderness of the moon of Aramis. It seemed like you meant to stay there indefinitely, so I had him poisoned to flush you out, to force you somewhere more public, so word would spread of your survival. To give myself an opportunity to . . . goad you into action. But"—he shrugged—"you didn't respond as I'd hoped. You disappeared again—to Devil's Shade, I suppose."

I felt dizzy. "You despicable bastard. Would you have let him die?"

"I never meant him to decline that much. You cared about him, and that made him useful to me."

I could not draw a full breath. "Why are you admitting this?"

"Because you want honesty," he said roughly. "So here it is: I poisoned Anguish. It allowed me to set up the entire scenario around the *Halcyon*. I meant to push you into the realization you wanted to destroy me. I knew if my evils outweighed the value of Anguish's life in your mind, then you would understand, at last, that I needed to be killed as well. I convinced you that I'd murdered all onboard the *Halcyon* to cement your enmity. I wanted you to seek my destruction. I needed you to hate me."

"You succeeded," I whispered venomously. "I do hate you, Tyrus. I hate you more than you can understand."

"And now you know all my reasons for this."

"*Your* reasons. You didn't trust me after the *Tigris*. You didn't trust me to let you destroy yourself on this insane, mad course—"

"No." His voice was flat. "I didn't." He looked at me. "How could I?"

And there, I had no reply—for had I not proved to him on the *Tigris* that I would not let him die, even for the best possible reasons? My hands curled into fists, for the truth seared me that in this, he was correct.

He looked away again and released a long breath. "But there's more than that. I also didn't want you near me."

Apparently I did not need the truth serum to tear brutal truths out of him.

"If you were at my side, united with me in this . . . tyranny." His voice sounded scraped raw from his throat, his hand gesturing vaguely in the air. "Then that would have ended only one way: a tyrant's wife shares his fate."

These words, I hadn't expected.

"I could face the entire galaxy while they howled their hatred for me, and it would not make me flinch," Tyrus said. "They could scream for my blood and it would mean nothing if I knew I was doing something right. It would have been another matter if you were with me. If they wished the same for you. I couldn't endure that. It would break my resolve."

His hand reached toward me, and then he thought the better of it and dropped it back to his side.

"Neither of us has been willing to do this . . . to sacrifice the other. Allow me some human weakness. I would pay any price for the future I want to create, but a single one. For the sake of my very sanity, I had to preserve just one thing that remained sacred to me, one person I could not endure to see destroyed. You, Nemesis. Always you."

"You should have told me." The whisper scraped over my lips. "I had a right to know."

He leaned toward me. "And if you'd known the entire truth, would you have willingly led the opposition, knowing the endgame was my inevitable disgrace and destruction? Would you have?"

I did not answer that.

"You *had* to be my enemy for this," Tyrus said. "And you couldn't just be a member of the opposition. *You* had to spearhead it—because that was the *only possible way* you would be above suspicion. We are husband and wife. You would never escape my taint once I became an anathema. . . ."

I slapped my hand over his mouth. I stopped his lying tongue before his words could take effect, could persuade me once again to put love over anger, to prize hope over the lessons of experience.

The anger churned back through me, burning away all else. "You're a fool, Tyrus—far less clever than you think. Look at your grand design now! You are powerless. You are trapped. You think to play us all as puppets but here you are, and I can't even devise a means of saving your life from the Partisans. They want your blood and they'll have it. But you know everything, do you not? How else would you dare—*dare*, Tyrus—to turn me into your puppet? This grand plan of yours—*you gave me no choice in it!*"

My voice rang too loudly in my anger. I knew it, but I could not stop the words from firing from my lips. "You engineered me like one of your machines, engineered me to do your bidding, never once explaining why, and you dare to say you *love* me? That you *protected* me by lying to me? By letting me mourn for you, to revile *myself* for the role you engineered me to play? Yes, you set me afire with anger, with hate! And do you know how many I went on to kill in the Clandestine Repository? And then afterward, I killed *you*, Tyrus—because of *you*! I mourned for you—because of *you*! What kind of love is that? Perhaps you do love me—and perhaps I love you, too. But it means *nothing*! Do you hear?"

His lips moved against my palm. I snatched it away, shook off the feeling of his mouth.

"I hear," he said softly.

"I saved your life today," I snarled, "because the cost of taking it would have destroyed me. Now I'll likely die fighting to save you when they figure out where we are, and it will all be for naught."

His body grew very still as he thought it over.

"No," he said calmly. "There is another way."

I laughed hopelessly. "Yes, you have another scheme. Another plan. Always, another plan! Oh stars, I hate you so. I despise myself, that I cannot rip you from my heart. If we survive this, I will be *done* with you. Done with your lies, done with your schemes, and done with thoughts of you too. If we escape this place, I will never think of you again. Do you understand?"

"I understand, Nemesis." His palm covered my cheek, his touch gentle, and I realized that my face was wet.

I knocked away his hand. "The tears mean nothing," I said bitterly. "The ducts are malfunctioning. I'll have them removed."

His hand caught my jaw again, pulled me around to face him. "I don't know *how* to love you."

I yanked free. "Don't touch me."

"I was never taught to love. Nemesis—Domitrians do not love. I never *wanted* to love. But stars save me," he said roughly, "I love you beyond myself and everything else in this universe. And so I made you think me a monster. *Yes.* I sent you away when I could not protect you. *Yes.* And when you all but doomed yourself, I did what I must to ensure that you survived!"

"Deceit and manipulation," I snapped. "But go ahead, call it love."

"*Yes*, love." His voice hardened. "It was not pretty love, Nemesis. Not noble, not admirable. But it was love that kept you *alive*. And I will never regret it, even if it costs me everything. I love you more than myself, and more than this sun-scorned galaxy, and more than any ideal I've *ever* been guided by. I have only ever had two aims: to free this Empire, and to keep you alive."

My head was suddenly pounding. I lowered it into my hands, gripping my temples.

"I had a plan," he said. "A grand design to right the crime of my ancestors. But there is one price I will not pay for it. Nemesis, you mean more to me than anything else. I'd let this galaxy burn if your life is the cost of saving it."

I tensed against his words. Such words! How expertly he crafted them and speared them into me!

Deliberately, I curled my lip into a sneer. "Am I meant to find that moving? Your hypocrisy? After all the misery you created—am I meant to applaud you for abandoning your aims, for saying that your ideals mean nothing after all?"

"They mean almost everything." The defeat in his voice made my throat tighten. "Almost everything," he said raggedly. "But not as much as you. You are all I love."

"Stop it. Just stop." Oh, and stars, the tears were taking a new form. I curled in on myself, trying to fight them down, but they were jerking from me, those pathetic, hideous sobs as though I were back in the heliosphere, mourning a death. All the misery of the last years seemed to be crushing in on me, alive and fresh in my mind as though every bad memory had just happened to me, and I realized in that moment that the wounds had never scarred, never healed. They'd remained there fresh and tormenting me, and I had but ignored them until this moment, when the pain grew too great to ignore.

In the half-light of the nearby monitor, I saw that he was in tears now as well, his face hollow, ashen, haunted. A sudden rush of vindictive pleasure went through me, for at least he felt my pain! Perhaps this was one positive result of these damnable tears, of my inability to conceal my emotions from him—he could not escape them either! Let him drink in the hurt he'd caused me, let him suffer from it as well! I hoped he drank his fill, so he could no more escape it than I could!

At last, he spoke, his voice low, calm, and resolved. "I know what to do now."

"Of course you do."

"Nemesis, turn toward the monitor."

"Why?"

"Turn. I beg you."

I forced myself to look at the monitor, and a beam shot out to take a scan of me. Tyrus typed in a short sequence, then reached out carefully to take my hand in his. He placed my palm against the screen.

"Repeat the line before you," he bade me.

With a cold rush of understanding, I looked at him sharply. I knew what he was offering.

"Do it," he urged me gently.

I read the string of numbers aloud.

COMMAND AUTHORIZATION GRANTED, flashed the screen.

Astonishment prickled through me. But still I did not believe.

Hands shaking, I logged out, then pressed my hand to the screen again.

COMMAND AUTHORIZATION RECOGNIZED.

"Here it is," he said. "Your offering to Sagnau. The *Alexandria* is yours. It will save your life."

And with that spoken, he balled up his fist and slammed it into his own face.

For a moment, I just stared, wondering if he'd gone utterly insane. But Tyrus punched himself again. Then he bashed his head against the wall behind him. At last I reached forward to stop him, but he raised a hand and flashed me a smile with bloody teeth.

"Don't worry. This will work."

He dealt himself one last blow that made his nose crunch, and then kicked out behind him. . . . The side panel of the crawl-tube burst open and sudden light flooded in with us. A dozen voices of searching men roared out below us, and Tyrus managed a ragged whisper: "Trust me."

Then he flung himself down to the Partisans hunting him.

40

MY HEART gave a lurch as the Partisans shouted out below us, their footsteps beating against the ground. I did not think. I leaped down after Tyrus, only to find him stumbling gladly toward the armed Partisans, his hands up.

"Oh, thank the stars, thank the stars!" he sobbed, throwing himself to his hands and knees before them as they shouted threats, weapons raised. He crawled toward them pitifully as they aimed their rifles at his head, and practically pawed at the legs of the first one he reached. "Please help me. Please. She's insane!"

A few weapons swiveled toward me, and frightened young Partisans shouted for me to put my hands up, but I just stared at Tyrus as he sobbed. He practically hugged the legs of the Partisan, and received a blow to the head from the butt of the man's rifle.

Still, he recovered and pleaded, "Protect me from her. Please keep her away from me. . . ."

What in the stars . . .

"She brutalized me," he howled. "I gave her all she wanted and she brutalized me, the fiend."

For a moment I stood there in stark disbelief, at last understanding what Tyrus was doing. He was casting his life away. He was saving mine . . . framing our disappearance together as something in the service of their cause.

"Protect me from her. Please. Please, she'll kill me. . . ."

"We'll kill you, Your Pathetic Reverence," roared the Partisan, who shook his legs out of Tyrus's grasp, then delivered a stomp to his ribs.

I stepped forward toward the raised rifles, and my voice rang out: "Stop."

It was authoritative and firm, and these Partisans had to have been told of what I'd done, that I'd absconded with Tyrus. I knew they trusted me not at all, and they kept their weapons aimed at me—but for a moment they ceased to beat Tyrus. He took the opportunity to continue the pitiful display, dragging himself away from me, throwing frightened looks back at me, as though I were a demon come to collect his very soul. As though the Partisans who'd gladly torture and kill him were his sole protection from me.

And despite everything, I felt something in me warming, calming. For yes, I saw what he had done for me. He'd just placed me above suspicion. I would not perish alongside him.

"I have the command authorization codes now," I said calmly. Then I called to the air, "Assemble defensive forces."

Weapons hidden in the walls of the corridor jutted out at my command, and the Partisans all looked up and about with amazement to see what I had done—extracted the prized authorization codes from the captive Emperor through sheer terror.

"We really have the *Alexandria*," said the Partisan who'd stomped

on Tyrus, who was once more shaking off the pitiful Emperor clinging to his legs again—from behind now. "We have the Domitrian
Emperor's ship."

"Yes. It's ours," I said. The Partisans began to lower their
weapons. "Or rather, mine." To the automated weapons: "Sweeping
stunners—1.2 meters!" Then I hurled myself to the floor.

The weapons along the walls blasted the air at 1.2 meters of height,
and those Partisans who had not ducked in time were blasted against
the walls. The few who managed to throw themselves out of the range
of fire were close enough for me to surge at them, to drive their heads
against the ground. The man Tyrus clung to was now in his grasp, and
he drove the other man down beneath him, snaring him in a headlock.

I snared a fallen weapon and raised it to pick off the stragglers
who'd been farthest from us, who were bolting away beneath the wall
of automated fire.

"Cease fire!" I shouted, and the weapons died away into silence.

Tyrus—weakened—was still struggling with the Partisan, who
was about to escape his grasp. I swept over to them and delivered a
blow into the man's temple, knocking him out cold. Tyrus shoved him
aside and the man flopped to the floor, and for a moment we just stood
there looking at each other—I above him, Tyrus on the ground, his
face bloody where he'd struck himself.

"Can you walk?" I said to him.

"Yes," he said, panting, and then his arms buckled as he tried to
shove himself to his feet.

So I seized him and hoisted him up over my shoulder, then stalked
forward down the corridor with my rifle in my free hand.

Between the weapon I carried and the automated bots at my
voice command, the Partisans stood no chance—even with Tyrus's
weight over my shoulder. I couldn't trust him to keep up with me right

now, so I ignored him when he tried to regain his own footing.

I shot our way forward. With one arm, I kept him slung over my shoulder, and with the other I carved a trail of stunners through the Partisans who swarmed in to battle us, until at last I reached the engine core of the *Alexandria*.

Tyrus eased his way back to his feet and caught himself when his legs buckled beneath him. "Well?" he said as he straightened.

I stood aiming my weapon at the bend in the hall. "Well, what?"

"You've gotten us this far. What next?"

"Do I just . . . command it?"

He dipped his head toward the core as a yes.

I barked my order into the air.

The consoles lining the walls pulsed to life as the *Alexandria* recognized my authority and activated full systems. Instantly I ordered every security force field on the ship to be erected, thereby corralling everyone—Neveni and Anguish included—save us.

Then I said, "Take us into hyperspace. Heading: the Chrysanthemum."

Tyrus just watched me in the light of the engine core, so much like the setting on the *Arbiter* where I had ended his life. Where I had nearly doused the flame of his existence for good. For a moment, as we gazed at each other over the humming of the ship's systems, my emotions churned deep within me . . . lingering anger and betrayal at him. The raging hurt of my wounded emotions, that he had done this without me, that he had played his part so readily with me, twisting and manipulating me.

And still, still . . .

There was a white-hot burning current that bound me forever to this man, for I was his and he was mine, and despite all the pain, I knew how much he had done out of love for me.

"You're extraordinary, you know," Tyrus breathed. "I understand if you will forever despise what I have done—"

"Yes. I will." Then I rushed over to him. "Do you know what I hate you for the most? That you never consulted me. If you had, you would have noted a flaw in your thinking, one that is blindingly obvious, yet seems to elude you even now!"

"The possibility that you were too much of an opponent for me?" he said with a pained laugh. "That you'd overcome me prematurely? I considered that. It's the reason for that hair clip."

"And hear that! You assume you know what I'll say."

He caught my face in his hands. "I'm sorry, Nemesis. Tell me what I've missed."

"You forget that you've always been stronger with me."

"I've always known that."

"A tyrant's wife shares his fate, you said." I seized his shoulders. "You didn't think of the possibility that fate might be altered, if I were but there to do this with you. You and I could have done this together, played a pair of deliberate tyrants to topple this Empire from within— and I *still* could have gotten us both out of it alive! This entire galaxy could have crushed in around us, crying for our blood, and *I* would have saved us! I would never let anyone destroy us the way you have."

I seized his face in my hands and looked right into his eyes.

"And Tyrus, I *still* won't."

Then I kissed him.

His surprise translated in the brief stillness of his lips on mine. Then his hands caught my hips and he pulled me hard against him as he kissed me back—desperately, hungrily. He'd been battered, beaten, and I knew it had to hurt him, but Tyrus didn't seem to care, and in that moment, neither did I.

For a long, dizzying moment, I forgot that I had ever known doubt.

His mouth on mine felt like the answer to every question that had ever troubled me. *Of course*, I thought, wonder flooding me—a wonder that felt larger than the two of us, larger than this ship or the battle ahead or the galaxy for which we'd fight. This wonder comprised the miracle of the entire universe, and the fact of existence itself. With gratitude and delight, I thought again, *Of course.*

And then terror edged in, for it was happening, I was slipping away, losing myself in the delirium of the past. I pulled back, but the fever had caught him as well. His arms tightened about me and he claimed my lips again.

My thoughts began to fragment, time slipping its mooring. I was elsewhere . . . in a decompression closet, choking on the thin air, with Tyrus refusing the oxygen mask I meant for him alone. He scorned the mask and his lips plunged to mine, and he said, *See?*

See that I love you? See that I value you more than the very air I breathe? And then I was returning his kiss. My blood lit up. All evil had been undone. He clutched the back of my neck with a rough hand, devouring my mouth, and just before I could sink back into the memory of this, sanity broke through, stark and clear and vivid.

"No!" I cried, and ripped back out of his arms.

Now I was afraid. For I did not understand the magnetic atmosphere in which I—we—were suddenly caught. I could not move. I stared back at him.

Slowly, slowly, he lifted his hand to touch my face. His fingertips framed my cheek, the contact lighter than a breath. But through those small points of contact, I felt the tremor that ran through him again, and I tensed against the urge to answer it.

"I never thought I'd kiss you again," he murmured, his pale eyes intent as they searched mine.

"You . . . you won't." I forced myself back another step, another, raising my arms up to hug my chest, a physical barrier between us. I knew this path. There was too much pain in it. "I can't. I just can't."

His hand sank to his side. His throat bobbed as he swallowed, but I knew I didn't need to explain. He already knew. He understood me as well as I understood myself.

I had to look away from him. "You won't sacrifice me. Nor will I sacrifice you. Whatever happens next, we're in this together. But not that way. I can't endure it."

"Nemesis, I understand."

"You've hurt me."

"I know."

"And you'll do it again. I know you will."

He didn't answer that, the silence resting heavily between us. I found I could not look at him again.

Around us, the *Alexandria* lurched into the dark oblivion of hyperspace, stranding the fleet of the Partisans far behind.

41

I SPENT the next hours securing all the remaining Partisans on the ship in holding cells. Anguish and Neveni, I dared not face alone. I didn't ask Tyrus, for fear he'd claim better health than he had to provide backup.

So I activated the *Alexandria*'s stunners and ordered open the door to the study. As soon as they rushed through, the stunners I'd prepared for them felled them.

Then I dragged them to a secure holding cell.

My control over the *Alexandria* meant I had full access to the surveillance cameras. I was on edge, barely sleeping. Constantly, I used the cameras to check whether Anguish and Neveni remained locked up, and to watch their failed attempts to break themselves out.

I sometimes spotted them in each other's arms and quickly looked away. Other times, the instruments picked up their conversation.

"Are you actually surprised she turned on us?" Neveni said to him. "She's obsessed with him."

"I wouldn't call it that," Anguish returned.

"What would you call it, Anguish? How many times does he have to cut her legs out from under her before she realizes she can't trust him?"

"There must be a reason for this," insisted Anguish.

And his defense of me made me desperately want to go down to him, to tell him the truth of what Tyrus had said.

A fearful thought came to me then. What if they laughed at me for believing his excuses?

Worse—what if they were right?

I passed the restless days and nights in the pitch dark of hyperspace avoiding Tyrus as well. It was simple enough, as his recovering strength limited his ability to rove. Using the surveillance cameras, I could always stay a step ahead of him.

But I spent hours watching his image on the surveillance cameras. . . . He slept as little as I did.

Once he sat in his study, contemplating the burning logs of the fireplace. Another time he stood in the doorway to the high-gravity chamber, gazing inward at it fixedly, and it occurred to me only after a time that he was staring at the workout floor where I'd often thrown myself into conditioning during stays on his ship. As though he were reliving those memories of me, and the wistful look on his face was . . .

The frightening current of realization made me shut off the image, for fear I would take a perilous joy in that.

Three days into our journey, I awoke from a troubled sleep in the middle of the night and checked on the prisoners once more, and then—then I did not resist. I called up Tyrus's image.

And saw him sprawled in a chair, about to do something that made my blood turn to ice in my veins.

I didn't think. I sprinted right to his study and burst through the doors to confront him. . . . He startled to his feet, and I slapped the burning vapor rod out of his hand. Then I screamed at him, right in his face, "Are you *mad*?"

I reached out and snatched the acrid-scented Venalox from the floor, feeling a scream build up in my throat; the horror was devouring me.

"You are using this?" I bellowed at him. "You are *willingly* using this now?"

"It's not what you think." Tyrus's alarm faded, and there was a tiredness to him that goaded me further.

I didn't feel like hearing it. I hurled the Venalox into the fire and rounded on him, anger scorching me. "You have gone mad. You are insane! How could you use this substance?"

"Nemesis, *listen*!" Tyrus roared at me, catching my arms, drawing me close. "I. Am. Not. Using. It."

"You synthesized it for a reason. Why would you do that?"

He let out a groan of frustration, drew me closer so our foreheads were almost touching. "I don't use it. It's the smell. The weight of the phial in my hand. I find it . . . a comfort."

"This is sick. It's wrong."

He released me and paced away, scraping his hand through his coppery hair. "You doubt me? Then make yourself certain of my answer." He turned to me. "Shoot me up with the truth serum, if you like. I will tell you the exact same thing: I didn't synthesize it so I could use it."

But when he suggested it, suspicion reared in me, and I couldn't help it—I was searching every possible nefarious angle to the suggestion.

I folded my arms, turned away to look at the ashen vapor rod scorching amid the flames. "Wouldn't the Venalox remind you of the worst days of your—of our lives?"

"Yes." He let out a long breath. "But the merest smell of it also . . . it also transports me. I've had a distraction since gaining the scepter: the machines. There was always something *not me* in my mind, something other than my own thoughts. It was unending, the sound of them, the feel of them. They gave me something to focus upon, when I didn't wish to think. Now that they are gone, the silence is . . . weighted. I find myself thinking overmuch. Dwelling overmuch."

I looked at him sharply. "Dwelling upon what?"

"My mistakes. Or the possibility of mistakes I have yet to make. With you," he said hollowly. "With the Empire. With this course I've set for us all."

"How can you find comfort in the memory of Venalox? I should think it one of the bitterest memories."

He tilted his head back. "The Venalox was forced upon me repeatedly in the single period of my existence where I was utterly powerless to make decisions, and . . . and at times, especially now, I find myself thinking . . . longingly upon that total lack of responsibility or obligation." Quietly, ashamed, he admitted, "I even miss Alectar at times."

He gave a strangled laugh at the startled look on my face. "Is that not the most . . . disgusting, twisted thing, to miss one's captor?"

"He had total control over you for four years," I said, struggling to understand it. "I suppose he was . . . all you had while I was gone."

Tyrus closed his eyes a moment, and I could almost sense his mortification to bare his truth so with me. I stepped over to him and gently traced my fingers along his arm. The gesture felt strange after being alienated from him so long, but his skin gave a shiver at the contact. . . . It seemed to encourage him to look at me once more.

"What is it you doubt right now?" I whispered. "Is it me?"

I had been avoiding him, so I had no other insight than that.

In truth, I'd been afraid. Fearful of what I still felt for him.

Terrified of all the pain he might cause me yet.

"No." His light blue eyes locked upon mine. "Not you. You've always been my single certainty, even when we were star systems apart." He gently touched a lock of my hair, following the path of his hand with his eyes as though he caressed something sacred. "Even when you were so distant, I wondered if I'd but dreamed of you."

"It's too late to indulge in doubts of anything else," I said simply. "You've chosen a course for this galaxy, it's true, and we're on it now, Tyrus. We're too far in it to change. At this point, doubt is useless. So are false comforts."

He gazed at me a long moment with a sort of tired admiration. "You have always been so strong-willed. You set your mind to a course and then you find a way to make it happen. I make a decision, and then I question it endlessly, to the point where it is maddening." He sank down into the chair again, casting his gaze toward the pitch darkness outside the study's window. "It occurs to me that I never had a chance to tell you the entire story of Anagnoresis."

My eyes narrowed. "The planet where you dwelled as a child. The one destroyed by malignant space."

His shoulders tensed. "You know that much. Yes."

My muscles grew rigid. Had that been a lie? I didn't trust myself to speak.

"And it *was* destroyed by malignant space. Eventually."

"So . . . so what am I missing?"

"Anagnoresis was my greatest mistake," Tyrus murmured. "My worst. For weeks, I watched that scar of light spread across the sky and I *knew* it would be the death of everyone around me. No one would have listened to me, if I—a child—warned of the danger. The Excess never listened to their children. What authority did I have? The Anagnoresians were certain they were safe."

"You should have told them you were a god," I said dryly.

His lips curved up at one side. "I was not an actor yet. I needed years under my grandmother's sharp gaze to hone that skill."

I sank down in front of the blazing hearth. "I know this: you sent word to your uncle to retrieve you. You knew it would result in the death of your father—and it did."

Tyrus darted his gaze toward mine, and then away. "I thought—the trade was necessary. To save thousands of lives, at the cost of one, it would be the right decision, and I would come to live with it. But it was a small province. Randevald decided that none of the Excess there would be missed. He couldn't allow them to carry tales of Domitrian intra-family strife across the Empire, so he ordered Devineé to fire the *Tigris*'s weapons and raze the settlement on Anagnoresis. The entirety of it."

I uncurled my hands. Laid them carefully atop my bent knees. "He killed them all?"

"Yes." Then his eyes shimmered in the firelight. "But what made it worse was the sight when we rose above the atmosphere and I at last saw the malignant space without the cloud cover. Nemesis, it was so *small.* It was so far away! The clouds distorted the light, just as my father told me. . . ."

I caught my breath.

"We'd have had years of safety," he said, "before that malignant space would become a threat to Anagnoresis. Decades, perhaps, to pre-pare for an evacuation. The Excess had *known* this. They had tried to tell me this—to comfort a small boy. By telling him the *truth.*"

I stared at him a long, stunned moment, understanding it. "You were the one who was wrong."

"It was my fault, what happened to them. Malignant space didn't kill them, Nemesis. I did." He let that sit there a long moment, his eyes hazy. "And so for years, I tried not to think about it. I think I must have blocked the memory, successfully, for most of my life. Instead I focused on malignant space itself, on the phenomenon, as though solving that might atone for what I'd done to them. . . . Then I learned of Tarantis and it all came back to me. Suddenly it was staring me in the face: *I* was the problem with this Empire."

And my distrust and hostility melted away and I moved over to him, drawing his calloused hand into mine. "Tyrus, that's not the truth. Surely you can't think that."

"Don't you see?" he said to me, suddenly intent. "Do you know why I didn't believe my father, or the Anagnoresians?"

"Because you were a scared child—"

"Because they were Excess. I was Grandiloquy. I earnestly believed . . . I believed I was better than them."

The words stunned me.

"I took for granted that I knew more than they did. I was a nine-year-old child utterly certain that *I* was in a better position to decide their fates than *they* were."

The naked, brutal honesty of it seemed to scrape the air between us. It had never dawned upon me that Tyrus's egalitarian views were not innate, but learned with time.

"I am Grandiloquy born, and we all regard ourselves this way: as fundamentally better. My mother was more liberal-minded than most, but in truth, I was raised to believe no differently. We associate only with one another or our chosen lackeys among the Excess. We own the media, we own academia, we control the culture and pay the censors who shape public discourse, so where will we ever hear a voice telling us we are just human beings like any other, born to better circumstances? Everything contrives to reinforce this delusion that we fundamentally deserve to preside over others. As a child, I believed in this lie we created for ourselves to justify our power. The very *existence* of what *I* am needs to end if there's to be a better future. I am an embodiment of all that is wrong with this Empire."

And here, here, I could see in total how his thoughts had swerved toward destroying his own Empire rather than reforming it.

"It's impossible," he said, "to have an Empire of this size without a ruling class forming, and rank is blinding to its holders. We exalted few stand so high on our pedestals that we can no longer see the fine detail of the landscape, yet we rule the Excess who *live* among what we can barely perceive. We who do not even understand their existence presume to dictate its terms to them. The solution always had to be an end to the Empire, a total decentralization of power so even the most prominent among each society holds only so much influence, never such an exorbitant amount as I do. . . ."

"So you are doing exactly what you need to do, then. You are breaking up the Empire." I didn't see the problem. "You were in error when you were young, but you don't think that way now."

He gave an ironic smile. "That's exactly it: I, a single person, am arbitrarily making a decision for everyone else in this galaxy that the Empire needs to come to an end—to put a stop to small numbers of people holding exorbitant power. I alone am making this decision. You see where I run into my own hypocrisy. And that's why I cannot halt the doubts. Fundamentally, I am all that I mean to oppose—even in my act of opposition."

I shook my head, impatient. "What's the point of thinking like that? You've told me the rationale. You've clearly thought it over. It's too late to turn back now."

"I could wipe away all that is," Tyrus murmurs, "and perhaps something worse will fester in its place."

"Worse than a repressive tyranny where entire planets are wiped out in a single day?" I pointed out.

"We are not mired in an unending civil war. We are not in a state of universal anarchy. A great number of people live quite contentedly. Every so often I look at the enormity of what I am doing to this galaxy, and I think, 'Stars, what am I doing? What right do I have to do this?' And I cannot shut out those thoughts."

"There could be something worse. That's *always* the risk you take when you seek change," I told him, my voice hard. "But you *do* have the right to do this because this galaxy *has* imbued you with the power of an Emperor. You are exploiting a fundamental flaw in its makeup to destroy it, and if it has that flaw, perhaps it deserves to be destroyed using it. What alternative did you have? Flee with me to a black hole and give it all up, leave a power vacuum for a new tyrant to fill?"

He reached out and took me gently by the arms, drew me closer. "I regret that," he told me hoarsely. "Not a day passes that I don't wish we'd left together."

"Nor for me," I admitted reluctantly, "but that was never an answer. Look at the other choice: You and I ruling together, side by side? The Grandiloquy massed to stop us from making any true change. You had to resemble their form of tyrant for them to support you. You would have had to kill most of the Grandiloquy, and a good number of the Excess imperialists as well, to achieve any substantial reforms . . . but you wouldn't be the Tyrus I know if you were capable of that."

His gaze grew distant. "My mother warned me that our family's power would cost me my soul. I think she was right. It may be impossible to hold the power of an Emperor and remain pure. Even if you and I had ruled and remained . . . noble, all we would have done was reinforce the institution of power we occupied. We'd make the case there *could* be rulers of humanity worthy of holding such influence over the lives of others. Our successors would have ruled on a mandate we helped strengthen, and they might have been devils."

"So there you go," I said, arching my brows. "Those are your alternative decisions, and none of them are better than the choice you've made. So what is the use of doubt now, Tyrus? You've chosen a course, and . . . and if it makes a difference, I think it could work."

He caught my eyes, intent, and it dawned on me that it still mattered immensely to him what I thought of this. "Do you?"

I took his face in my hands, trapping his gaze. "Tyrus, I do."

He sighed and leaned forward, and I surrendered to a dangerous impulse and drew his head onto my shoulder. The sensation of Tyrus so near me, with me once more, felt utterly right.

For was this not the reason we had always been stronger united rather than set against each other? He was my solace and I was his, and here we were sharing our thoughts, our minds once again, deciding together. . . .

Why, this was home.

Not a home as in a place. Not even a home as in my place with Tyrus, but perhaps, in some sense, my home in that I felt I had come back to myself after a long absence. This was more than Nemesis the Diabolic, the human, the Empress. This was the Nemesis who'd felt herself worthy of all those roles . . . the one who could stand at Tyrus's side staring out at the stars and devise and act upon dreams greater than herself.

I'd missed this person. And I'd missed Tyrus. At last I said so to him.

"I fear you will vanish if I take my eyes from you," Tyrus confessed.

For I had been away from him far longer than he had from me. With his raw, vulnerable admission, I finally stopped battling myself.

"I won't leave you again. And Tyrus, I don't want to." Then I raised my gaze to his, and Tyrus read my permission in my eyes, and dipped his lips to mine.

After I met his kiss, he made a low sound in his throat, and his arms swept under me to draw me up across his lap, his arms banding about me in a ferocious hug as though never to release me again. There were tears on his face that I gently kissed away, and he just held me there, nestled in the shelter of his warmth.

There, with the great window looking onto the dark of hyperspace, we held each other, and the last of my doubts melted away.

We were together. We'd returned home at last.

42

OUR NIGHTS were sleepless no more. We passed long hours in a sweet, blissful solitude, not a machine or a Partisan to disturb us in the darkness of hyperspace. It was Tyrus who awoke me at nights with his hand caressing my hair, soothing me after my tormented dreams, and it was I who kissed him awake when he turned to and fro with his own nightmares.

We could not endure to be away from each other.

We talked of everything. We had never been so honest with each other. We spoke of my travels, of sleeping in forests beneath naked skies, of the months passed with Anguish in the wilderness, of the hardships of life on Devil's Shade. Tyrus spoke of the miseries under Pasus, of his doubts and hard-won victories during the isolated, empty years we'd passed apart.

Mostly, we spoke of each other. Revisiting our shared history, we retold it honestly.

It was not easy to relive. Our history was barbed.

Tyrus told of searching surveillance cameras across the Empire for glimpses of me. "In those first months, it crushed me to find you. You looked devastated. Betrayed. By the time we met on Corcyra, your hostility almost came as a comfort—I was glad to see the fire in your eyes again. But then, with what followed . . ."

Pained silences often punctuated our discussion. I could not think of Corcyra with calmness. Hope and dignity shattered, I had almost died.

"You took shelter at the Field Museum," he murmured of that time. "When I realized where you were, I kept the museum closed. I planted a medical bot in reach—just in the next room. But Anguish never looked there. I had the bot ram itself into the wall several times, hoping to attract his attention, but he was too preoccupied. It was unimaginably frustrating."

Remembering the endless painful hours I'd passed in recovery, I was nauseated by this new knowledge. A med bot had been waiting so close by! But Tyrus, trapped by his own deceit, had been powerless to send it directly to me. Anguish and I would have been suspicious.

I had confessions of my own. "I hated myself for failing to kill you on Corcyra," I told Tyrus. "I couldn't do it. I pitied you so—I was sure you were mad."

His lips curled. "If it's any consolation, I suspect I am."

"That was never in question," I said. "Merely the form of the madness." And like that, the solemnity of our discussion was broken, and Tyrus kissed his way down my neck.

"Oh, I will show you something I'm mad about," he vowed, and rolled me onto my back to kiss his way down my body.

The discussions were all medicine—harsh but necessary. With each talk, we lanced and drained old wounds. With each confession, we reawakened the injury and magnified the ache—before curing it.

And as we talked, and as we kissed, we shut our awareness to the calamity in our near future, drawing closer with every day we passed in hyperspace, for soon we would reach the Chrysanthemum. Reality. The harsh future just ahead of us. He had set us on a course, one that he'd always meant to end in his destruction, and I could not allow that. On this one matter—the most crucial matter—I was willing to go to war with him. For he could not survive his scheme, and I would not let it kill him.

A morning came when I reached for Tyrus and found the sheets cold and empty.

I sat up, and my stomach plunged.

Stars gleamed out the windows. We had dropped out of hyperspace into the Eurydicean system.

Little time remained until we reached the Chrysanthemum and the real battle commenced.

Tyrus stood by the window, his tall, disciplined frame silhouetted by silvery starlight, posture rigid and tense. I'd made no noise, but he started at my waking. The tension did not escape him until he felt the press of my body against his side. . . . And then his eyes closed heavily. Soundlessly he leaned against me, drawing strength from me in these final moments we could afford to share in peace.

"Together," I whispered. "Everything we do from here, we do it together."

"It complicates everything," he said. "Now you know the truth."

"I won't consent to your suicide."

"You speak as though I wish to die," he said softly, reaching out to trace his knuckles over my cheek. "I have too much to live and breathe for, especially now that you are come back to me. But, Nemesis, revolutions end with a king's head on a pike."

"Not this one."

The edges of the Chrysanthemum slid into view, the great mass of inactive defensive machines like the teeth of a waiting monster. Then the vast pylons reared into sight, great and shadowy forms in silhouette against the planet of Eurydice.

Tyrus's lie, his pretense to godhood, and his plan to nurture his own downfall had developed their own momentum. Yet the Excess had not risen to overthrow him.

But someone would. Somehow, it would happen. There was too much resentment boiling under the surface, small fragments that would swell into ruptures at this vast lie too many had eagerly swallowed and parroted.

All I knew was that I *would not* play the part he'd designed for me. I would not be the agent of Tyrus's destruction. I had barely survived when I'd believed I had murdered a monster. Now that I understood he intended himself to be a sacrifice for the sake of this galaxy's freedom, harming him was unthinkable.

The main body of the Chrysanthemum filled the window as we drew closer. It looked oddly disordered, the armada of vessels interlinked clumsily without a Domitrian mind serving to unify the vast network of computerized systems. Where his arms wrapped around me, I could feel the slight tremor that ran through Tyrus. Any pretense of peace or serenity was gone. For both of us.

The Chrysanthemum had hosted the worst moments of our lives. Here, he had suffered for four years as a prisoner of Pasus; here, he had set a course to destroy the galaxy as he knew it and ensure his own doom in the process.

Here, he had killed me.

It was Tarantis "the Great" who had first assembled this massive collection of vessels, calling his newly empowered Grandiloquy to him in a royal court, to serve as a centralized fist to project their combined power over the breadth of their galaxy. How hopeful Neveni had looked, at the prospect of deorbiting and destroying this vast superstructure.

A pity I'd cost her that chance. It might have been pleasant to watch this wretched place burn.

As we drew nearer, I saw debris orbiting the Chrysanthemum—detritus composed of thousands of deadened security bots. Others would be littered throughout the corridors of the vessels that composed the great complex. There was no more pretense of safety or security here.

But I would do my best to protect him. In the spirit of our new honesty, I felt compelled to tell him so. "I'm going to keep you alive, Tyrus."

He stroked my hair. "Then we're at an impasse," he said calmly. "For I won't permit you to share my fate. And anyone who aids me will be targeted with me."

I caught his hand, sliding it down so he cupped my cheek. "You have no machines to enforce your will. How do you plan to drive me away?"

He closed his eyes. "What choice is there? Name an alternative."

"There's another way." I kissed his palm—then bit his finger sharply. Startled, he opened his eyes. "We'll pick a new opposition leader." I threaded my fingers through his. "Someone who will moderate the forces that rise against you—someone who can be made to understand the reasons for all you've done—for all *we've* done. He will make sure we're spared."

There was a hint of relief on his face, perhaps because I was clearly speaking of someone who was not Neveni. His eyes searched mine intently. "You have someone in mind."

"I do."

His relief evaporated as soon as I told him:

"Gladdic."

As we pulled in to dock with the *Valor Novus*, a beauty bot worked to transform Tyrus. As I watched his features shift—the cleft in his chin disappearing along with his freckles, his reddish hair lightening to a shade of blond—I fought the gnawing presentiment that *he* was disappearing. That I was losing him once more.

"You already resembled Tarantis," I said. Tyrus and his forebear shared the same pale eyes and sharp cheekbones. "Why emphasize it?"

"For posterity." Tyrus studied the bot's work in a handheld mirror. He had not looked at me in some time. An imperceptible distance was opening between us, which I tried not to mind; we each dealt in our own way with the gravity of the task ahead. "In a thousand years," he said, "when historians look back upon the legendary Tarantis von Domitrian, I wish them to think as well on his monstrous descendant. I want it to be clear to them that the mad, megalomaniac Tyrus was very much a product of Tarantis's line. May they always mention us in the same breath."

He laid down the mirror, giving me a half smile. It was not his smile. Tarantis's upper lip was fuller, more deeply bowed.

"It's a face for a monster of history," he said. "I'll be known for trampling a vast Empire with my delusions of godhood. Known for the mass murder of Luminars—"

"Pasus's deed!"

"I'll take credit for the Sacred City, as well. For more wrongs that still have yet to be known—"

"So the misdeeds of others will be yours. Yet Tarantis is hailed as a hero!" I said bitterly.

"Imagine what passed through his mind those final moments of his existence," murmured Tyrus. "He bought that false legacy of greatness with his very soul, and he still perished as we all do. What does it matter if posterity deems me a Caligula, a Hitler, a Vengerov? I know the truth of myself. I have no fear of that final breath."

He looked at me then, his voice wistful, soft. "And *you* know the truth. It was a torment to be monstrous in your eyes. Only in yours."

It was strange to hear the words as I looked upon his ancestor's face. He'd worn his true features when coming to save me from the Partisans. Expecting to find me tortured and traumatized, he'd disabused himself of all illusions.

But his kindness was a double-edged sword. Now, when I remembered that awful moment when I'd detonated the charge, it was his true face that I saw—his true eyes, stricken and fixed as his heart stopped beating.

May I see that face again one day.

Tyrus waved away the bot and rose smoothly to his feet, sliding into a shin-length oiled-leather coat. I also rose, feeling heavier, somehow, than I had moments ago.

"Nemesis." He paused, studying me with a cool gaze. "If we're to do this, I have a condition of my own."

If I kissed him now, his lips would feel like a stranger's. "Go on."

"You are never to be seen at my side." His voice was remote, formal. "As far as this galaxy knows, you are dead."

"I would have suggested the same." The better for me to be mobile, to slip unremarked through the shadows and keep him alive long enough to complete his task.

And when the reckoning came, and the galaxy finally bent to his will and conspired to destroy him, well . . . I would find a way to direct the chaos so that both of us were spared.

I waved over the beauty bot and typed in a hasty transformation program of my own. A single slice of the laser, and I sheared my white-blond hair to a mere quarter inch. Next, the laser rendered my hair black as pitch. The third pass enlivened my skin with pigment.

As Tyrus watched me, he forgot to pretend indifference. "That becomes you," he murmured.

"You like it?" Before he could touch me, I added, "I don't like yours."

Brows raised, he stepped back. I flicked my fingers over the buttons and gave myself disfiguring growths on my lip and cheek, large enough to distort my own features.

The effect was not flattering.

Tyrus laughed, and I smiled back at him despite myself.

"Come here." Catching me by the waist, he drew me to him. "Lovely," he whispered, brushing his knuckles over my cheek. Slowly, almost reverently, he kissed the corner of my mouth.

"Promise me," he said, and I closed my eyes. Something in me went instinctively rigid at the sight of his false face, which I associated with all the ugliness that had passed between us over the years. But the sound of his unchanged voice reached deep inside me, to a soft and tender place.

"Promise you what?" I murmured.

"Whatever happens, do everything to survive it."

I opened my eyes and looked into his. "Both of us will," I said in a hard voice.

A clattering announced the completion of the docking process. Tyrus's face went oddly blank; he took a long, steady breath, as though gathering himself.

"Don't forget this," he said, pulling away to grab a satchel from a nearby shelf. It was heavy, filled with several books he'd hastily discussed with me this last hour.

I slung it over my shoulder. "Go."

After one last, too-brief kiss, he turned on his heel and walked away. His posture and gait shifted, his smooth prowl becoming a swagger. His shoulders hunched slightly, conjuring an air of abandon. By his third step, he had effortlessly reinhabited the role of the mad Divine Emperor.

As the doors opened, I darted backward, out of sight of the waiting Grandiloquy who'd gathered in the *Valor Novus* to greet his return. Tyrus sauntered directly into the crowd, who erupted in cheers. In response, he flung open his arms. Those nearest him promptly hurled themselves to the ground to prostrate themselves, shouting, "Hail to the Divine Emperor! Hail!"

"Your Divine Emperor is back among you," said Tyrus in a familiar, false, cruel drawl. "He returns from a victory over the venal Partisans, with prisoners in his hold and destruction in his wake. He carries booty plundered from their ships that he wishes to give to his favored few, and yet how is he greeted?" He turned, taking a derisive survey of the groveling Grandiloquy, all of them now rubbing noses with the floor. "Where is the triumphant light show in his honor? Where is the worship for your Divine Emperor's magnificence?"

As they crawled forward, crying praise for him, reaching out to touch the hem of his coat, revulsion weltered in my stomach. I did not know how Tyrus could endure this.

I emerged from my hiding place to follow Tyrus at a distance. The Grandiloquy were too busy crawling after him to notice me, much less remark my "blasphemy" in having failed to fling myself down like the rest of them.

Their distraction gave me an opportunity to scan the grand, high-ceilinged chamber for possible threats. But no danger lurked in the empty balconies that ringed the room. Meanwhile, some of the

Grandiloquy had dared to rise to their knees to ease their shuffling pursuit of Tyrus. Their equanimity astonished me anew. How comfortable they were in worshipping their tyrant! I supposed they'd been bred to it, since for over five hundred years, their ancestors had been obediently placating whichever Domitrian ruled over them.

They must like *it*, I thought. For when Tyrus and I had challenged this group conformity directly, they'd massed to destroy us.

But now that he demanded their mindless submission, they were eager to provide it, never knowing that in doing so, they were bringing on the very extinction they feared.

I fought down the nagging fears and reassured myself with the sight: he was safe here among them. Of course he was. I could afford to leave him.

It would be difficult.

Tyrus was still addressing the crowd in that bombastic, infuriating voice. "Your Divine Emperor sees your every sin—cowardice foremost among them. You craven curs who fled from battle—were you truly so foolish as to believe I had perished?"

Quick murmurs of denial, though the Grandiloquy had no doubt assumed just that. They had, after all, returned from the chaotic gale to a disarranged Chrysanthemum ringed by dead security bots.

"Here is your punishment," Tyrus said scathingly. "Your Divine Emperor has commanded all security bots to stand down. He has willed the Chrysanthemum into disorder. And so it will remain, until you do penance."

As the assembled crowd gamely shifted into proclamations of faith—apparently every one of them had always known he'd return—I quietly slipped past. I aimed myself through familiar corridors, fighting a surreal sense of having slipped back in time as I walked. I'd never expected to set foot in the imperial power center again.

Little had changed. Every face I glimpsed was beautiful, honed to perfection by beauty bots. Every room shone more brightly than the last. I passed diamond-and-crystal windows that winked with prisms, and vast views of the starscape that dizzied those who stared too long. In some rooms, gardens appeared to stretch into a lush, fragrant eternity. Others held makeshift plazas fashioned from jade and malachite, or golden depictions of Domitrians from ages past.

Everything in the Chrysanthemum dazzled the senses. But after years spent among the Excess, the extravagance felt nauseating. I had seen real beauty now—the chaos of planetary weather, untamed animals, flowers growing ragged and wild. The Chrysanthemum drew inspiration from real beauty but concentrated it into overwhelming potency. Flawless faces, sparkling garments, intoxicating scents . . . everywhere one looked, one saw perfection.

Was it any wonder the Grandiloquy were such empty, hollow people? Ordinary people passed their lives rewarded by the occasional brush with sensory delight, and these brief joys motivated them to endure struggles to find further joy, made all the more satisfying for having been hard-won.

The Grandiloquy, on the other hand, led lives saturated by the rewards they unrestrainedly granted themselves, and they struggled not at all. They squandered fortunes, knowing their wealth could not be exhausted. They intoxicated themselves, knowing the damage could be healed. They lived amid intense beauty, but their appreciation of it was dulled by how easily and often they came by it. When everything was gifted, nothing had value.

Only power was rationed here. So the Grandiloquy worked to gain more of it. Whatever the Domitrian dictate might be, they obeyed it to gain an advantage over each other. Once it had been Randevald demanding enthusiasm for animal blood sports and hatred for the sciences. Now it was Tyrus demanding that they revere him as a god. No matter. No wrong could be done, no punishment suffered, so long as one did not displease the Domitrian in power. From the Domitrian, all things flowed.

I trailed to a stop outside the imperial quarters. After a long hesitation, I stepped inside, making my way by memory toward the privy chamber.

Diamond thrones stood side by side beneath an effervescent stenciling that twined elaborately over the ceiling. I walked up to them, my chest oddly hollow as I touched the gleaming arm of the Empress's chair.

Once, we'd planned that I would rule alongside Tyrus—that together, we would lead the Empire into a more just and equitable future.

Instead Tyrus had sat alone, looking down on crowds of vapid and venal courtiers, while he wove a grand and glorious plot to destroy himself. Instead, I had forged through bedraggled crowds of strangers on rundown streets, desperate to preserve Anguish, mustering the will to battle the man I loved.

I wanted to smash them, these stupid chairs. Neither of us had wanted them. Tyrus had felt obligated by his debt to those lost on Anagnoresis. And I had felt obligated to *him*. Stars, *stars*, how I wished we'd aimed for that black hole outside the Sacred City, after all.

Had we taken that course, we'd have forged into a future in which we were unknown. But if Tyrus succeeded now, the future would remember him too well. He would be reviled as the greatest villain of the Domitrian line—the agent of the Empire's destruction.

No one would ever know he'd really been the hero, not the villain.

And I did not know if I could save him—from others, and from himself.

So I let go of the throne and backed out of the room. I retraced my steps through the enchanted halls of the Grandiloquy, until I found the boarding artery that connected the *Valor Novus* with Gladdic von Aton's *Atlas*.

Then, on a bracing breath, I stepped inside to seek my last chance at a kinder fate.

43

"I AM TOLD you are responsible for my rescue."

I spoke as I stepped into Gladdic's study. He cast me a distracted glance, before recognizing me through the disguise. He dropped his tablet and shot to his feet, clutching his chest as though to hold in his heart.

I stopped, dismayed by his obvious fear. "Are you all right?"

"Nemesis!" He flew across the room and grabbed me into a hug. "You're alive! You're all right. Thank the stars. . . ."

As I returned the hug, he spilled a frenzied story into my ear—his panic upon escaping the *Arbiter*, being found by Tyrus's ships before he'd decided what to do next, taken forcibly into custody. . . . "The Emperor paced," he told me, "as I recounted what I'd seen. I tell you, it *distressed* him to know you were in danger. I was certain he would have me hurled out an air lock, or crushed in the gravital chamber, but then . . . he just seemed to forget I existed."

"How lucky for you," I said dryly.

"Lucky!" He drew back, gawking at me. "I felt the farthest thing from *lucky*, let me assure you! His servants brought me back here while he departed with as many vessels as he could muster. When they returned without him, without *you* . . ." His hands were shaking on my shoulders. "Nemesis, I'm so glad you're alive."

"I was never in any danger," I told him.

Tears blurred his bright green eyes. "What? But I—she was going to kill you!"

I gently took his hands, then led him back to his seat at the desk. I'd rehearsed this story several times on my walk here.

"The Partisans didn't kill Anguish," I said. "They . . . they fooled me as well." It seemed more efficient, and also kinder, to persuade him that we'd both been kept in the dark. "You see, they wanted you to get the impression I was in danger so you'd inform the Emperor. In truth, Neveni had prepared a trap for Tyrus. She revealed it to me after you escaped."

"What?" Gladdic knuckled his eyes. "So you weren't . . . harmed?"

"No. When I learned what she had planned, I decided to help her."

"But you're here. The Emperor is here!"

"The plan to defeat the Emperor was only partially successful, Gladdic. But it was *partially*. Surely you can see that." I looked meaningfully out the window, which offered a view of the disorganized arrangement of the Chrysanthemum's vessels.

"Oh," Gladdic murmured. "He . . ." He seemed fearful to say it. "The machines . . . he no longer controls them?"

"He denies it to the Grandiloquy, but yes, he lost his connection to them. Nevertheless, he survived the attack. He captured me. He holds Neveni and Anguish as well. I think he intends to kill them. He . . ." I made a delicate pause. "He believes the best of me. I suspect he is still in love with me."

Gladdic gave a soft laugh. "That became obvious when I told him what had befallen you."

His gaze was tender with compassion for me, and I found myself remembering why I'd chosen Gladdic.

It was this empathetic quality, vanishingly rare among the Grandiloquy, that distinguished him.

He had other strengths too. The time he'd served as Tyrus's propagandist told me he was easily coached and able to convincingly deliver words scripted for him.

The Excess trusted him, though he was Grandiloquy. He was the only member of the elite who could claim widespread support and acceptance among the galactic masses. But he also remained friends with many of his high-born peers. The way he straddled the class divide meant it was unlikely he'd lead or support the Excess in an all-out genocide following the overthrow of the Grandiloquy—something I could not say for Neveni.

He was kind and merciful. He would consider the perspectives of those he fundamentally disagreed with and take time to explain his own position to them too.

Gladdic had no lust for power. He would not use his new stature or exploit his popularity to seize the throne. I knew in my heart he'd turn down any exalted title or position, unlike many who would covet power the moment they overthrew it.

And most importantly, most critical of all:

Gladdic *was not* me.

I did not want to stand before recorders and make a case for liberty. I had no desire to motivate the great multitudes of this galaxy to join together to destroy the man I loved. I did not want to weaponize their anger and hatred against someone I wished to protect, nor did I desire them to scream, "Nemesis lives!" as I issued marching orders for this parody of a conflict, one in which the outcome had already been decided by the ultimate target of its aggression.

I wanted to stay in the shadows, close to Tyrus, watching him weave his own downfall and that of his Empire, while using Gladdic as his puppet. Then, when the winds turned violent, I would seize him and extract him from the eye of his storm. We would escape together and let these people sort out their new galaxy all on their own.

I would not accept, as Tyrus had, that his survival was inevitably *futile*—that he could not transform the galaxy without being destroyed by it. Nor would I reduce myself to a tool for those who hated him, who wanted vengeance for all the wrongs that had warped their lives. Darkness had been gathering for centuries now, and absolutely no part of me wished to catalyze this anger—not after that day at the Clandestine Repository, where I'd had my final brush with pure, unleashed brutality.

There was a better way, one more to my liking.

And stars help me, I had found it.

This responsibility would not be mine.

It would be *Gladdic's*.

It was my private hope that when the time came for Tyrus's downfall, I could leverage my influence with Gladdic to ensure Tyrus's escape. I'd find a way.

"Gladdic," I said now, "sometimes when I was troubled, Sidonia would read to me. I know you did the same for Tyrus when he was indisposed. Would you indulge me now?"

"Of course, Nemesis," he said kindly.

"You'll need to translate. I don't speak the ancient languages myself."

I tugged the satchel off my shoulder and extracted the first of the books Tyrus had given me.

This galaxy is going to need to rediscover the principles of the Enlightenment if we're to move to a freer system, Tyrus told me. *There are certain fundamental ideas in representative government that have been tried and tested in history, so Gladdic needs to be exposed to the intellectual thought that birthed past democracies and republics. Start him with this book.*

"Do you know ancient languages?" I handed him the book.

He had to be familiar with them. The virtual educational programs young Grandiloquy undertook always included Heritage Studies and taught a basic understanding of the dominant tongues spoken by the early settlers. I'd listened to Sidonia practice those unknown syllables for hours on end.

Gladdic took the book from me and flipped through the pages. "Yes, I know this one—English." His brows furrowed. "Where did you get this?"

It took me a moment to think of a believable lie. "From Donia. She told me once this was . . . was the sort of philosophy that should shape the future."

"John Locke. *Two Treatises of Government.*"

I flung myself down onto a nearby divan. "Translate it for me."

"Right now?"

"Yes."

"It's long."

"Start at the beginning. We have time."

Gladdic eyed me uncertainly, and then he settled down next to me and began to translate, reading the original language aloud before roughly interpreting it. He had fallen into a hypnotic rhythm by the time he reached the sentence: "'All peaceful beginnings of government have been laid in the consent of the people . . .'"

Then Gladdic fell silent.

"What's wrong?"

He fingered the corner of the page. "This is a book of democratic thought. The Emperor would not like us reading this."

"He will never know. I told you, he's lost his control of his machines. He isn't watching us now. Keep reading, please."

He considered me for a long, doubtful moment. Then, after a glance out the window at the broken Chrysanthemum to reassure himself, he forged onward shakily.

And I listened to him read, hoping the words were being embedded in his memory. *You do not need to believe these sentiments, Gladdic, or even like them*, I thought to him. *But learn the words and you will be able to speak them.*

By the time he was prepared for his role, he'd have the weapons in hand that could remake an entire galaxy.

It was the first book I made Gladdic read me, but not the last.

Pasus had destroyed many of Tyrus's volumes, so he had to search to unearth works by Thomas Paine, by John Stuart Mill, and other ancients. Most he found in electronic archives and funneled them to me, whereupon I found more reasons "Donia" had been interested in them, and made Gladdic read and discuss them with me.

Some of the works were old national constitutions. Gladdic spent a long evening with me using a service bot to translate the ancient language of French.

"'Declaration of the Rights of Man and of the Citizen' is all well and good, but the French Revolution became a mass slaughter with guillotines," Gladdic remarked to me. "And the American republic eventually morphed into an undeclared oligarchy with a repressive surveillance state."

"It doesn't change the purity of the sentiment that birthed those representative governments," I said to him. "We can repeat what was done correctly in the past without making the same mistakes they did."

Doubt flickered over Gladdic's face, but he read the rest.

So I passed the next weeks, updating Tyrus periodically—but mostly keeping my distance so as to conceal our secrets. Tyrus found me one evening after I'd donned a servant's gear and slipped into the ball dome, posing as a maintenance worker—a necessary function now that his control over the bots was gone. We'd arranged many such discreet meetings, and I updated him on Gladdic's progress.

He floated idly toward me, his back to me. "Well?"

"He is as ready as he will ever be," I said, my eyes on the diamond glass I made a show of scrubbing. "I think if we give him the instructions at the last minute, he'll obey what I tell him to do. I am sure of it."

For a moment, we floated there in the silence, and memories washed over me of the last time we'd been in this place together . . . when Tyrus had fought me. When he'd driven his sword through me.

Such was our own arc of history that we returned here once more—this time to work together.

"If you're certain, then it's time," Tyrus said. "Let's make it happen."

With Gladdic ready for his role, it was time to kindle the flame of resistance. Tyrus ordered the execution of the terrorist Neveni Sagnau and her accomplice, the Diabolic known as Anguish.

The executions would be public, conducted in grand style on Neveni's dead planet of Lumina. We departed with half the Grandiloquy following us, for they'd been promised a raucous party following the execution.

Tyrus had drawn up an impressive list of charges. Neveni had consorted with the rebel Partisans. She had orchestrated the abduction of the Empress after the attack on the *Tigris* and had sent an imposter in the Empress Nemesis's place to defame the Interdict and spread conspiracy theories about the destruction of the Sacred City. She'd abused Gladdic von Aton during his imprisonment with her family. She was a blasphemer and heretic, who indulged in the vilest depravities.

As the darkness of hyperspace enshrouded the *Alexandria*, Tyrus showed me the transmission being circulated across the Empire, the better to draw a wide audience for the live coverage of Neveni's execution. The pompous narrator read out an endless list of offenses, some of which made me laugh softly.

"'Leading youth into depraved debaucheries'?" I echoed. "This is ridiculous."

Tyrus paused the transmission on a still of Neveni's enraged face—a clip taken from some surveillance video. For all I knew, it showed Neveni's displeasure at receiving a poor meal in captivity, but she looked fearsome, her fist uplifted toward the lens, her dark eyes fiery. "I hope she agrees," he said. "With any luck, she'll feel indignant enough to speak out on the scaffold."

"Oh, Neveni's never short on indignation."

Tyrus shrugged. "When faced with death, some become stoic, resigned to their fate. Insulting her pride might forestall that possibility."

"Can you find different footage of her?" Neveni's face looked too convincingly rageful. "Gladdic has a soft spot for those in distress."

Tyrus disagreed. "He'll be likelier to act if he knows he can win a strong ally."

"I can manage to convince him of that." During my time with Gladdic, I had been seeding our conversations with glancing references to Neveni—conjuring a tragic heroine, whose life history illustrated many of the injustices that our reading criticized. I would veer into tales of her ferocity and resourcefulness now as well.

349

"Gladdic concerns me," Tyrus said, not for the first time. "If he proves too fearful to do as we planned . . ."

Then I would have wasted several weeks, making him read books to me. "Neveni will just have to escape without him."

His lips flattened into a line. Tyrus was worried that Neveni might seize control of the resistance we were working to create. Having learned more of ancient history during my evenings with Gladdic, I understood the concern. Tyrus did not wish to create a new Robespierre. And Neveni was certainly capable of taking power too far, given the opportunity.

My hand stole into his and squeezed. "We'll find a way to make it work."

He drew me closer, kissed the crown of my head. I could feel the tension vibrating through his body but did not know how to reassure him. Our plans had backfired so many times. I knew better than to trust luck.

So I gazed out at the pitch black of hyperspace and envisioned those arcs of history, and hoped upon all the stars that we were in the right place, at the right time, for fortune to favor us.

44

LUMINA'S purple atmosphere had enveloped the ship, causing the interiors to glow with a dim, menacing light. Everyone looked bloodless and bruised.

I had stopped by Anguish's cell first, but the betrayal in his eyes was breathtaking, and my words had knotted up in my throat. It tortured me that I could not tell him the reason for my "betrayal," that I had to keep the truth locked inside.

But he knew Tyrus to be an unabashed villain. Even if I had felt able to tell him the truth, he never would have believed it. At best, he would pity me for a deluded fool.

So all I could say was, "I'm sorry."

Then, ashamed, I departed his cell.

Neveni was easier to face.

She was gazing stoically out the window at her home world, her arms crossed. She didn't turn as I entered, but somehow she knew it was me.

"Pathetic," she said pleasantly, as though resuming an ongoing conversation. "I knew you'd run back to him, but I never figured you for spiteful. Or was it his idea to kill me here?"

I could not trust Neveni with the truth either. "I'm sorry," I said. "I thought it would be a comfort, to return home one last time."

"What would you know of it? You never had a true home. Maybe a laboratory somewhere."

She was trying to hurt me. I offered the only kindness I could: "Yes, I suppose that's true."

She turned toward me. Perhaps it was a trick of the violet light spilling through the window, but she looked less angry than resigned. "I'm glad to die with my planet under my feet," she said quietly.

My stomach tightened. So much for kindness—but we needed her angry, not serene. "Anguish will be with you."

She recoiled. "You'd kill him, too? You would actually let Anguish die?"

I said nothing. Even knowing what we had planned, I felt shame swell in me.

Her laugh was bitter. "Of course you would kill him too. We're nothing to you next to Tyrus. Did you plan all along to go back to him?" Her mouth twisted. "No, you didn't, did you? Because he'd be dead right now if I hadn't been stupid enough to want his ship."

That stupidity had been my great good luck. I was so glad she'd wanted the *Alexandria* enough to save his life.

Perhaps she saw it on my face, because contempt flashed in her eyes. She spat at me. "Believe it or not, I never expected any better of you. I knew you'd forgive Tyrus. It's pitiful. At least I'll die with some dignity."

"I wouldn't lose hope so soon."

"Oh, you'd like that, wouldn't you?" She sat heavily on the bench beneath the window. "You'd love it if I stood there cowering, begging him for mercy. Well, you can go fly into a black hole, Nemesis. I'm going to die, and that's fine. I'll hate you both to my last breath. I'll see you in hell."

I paused, then spoke slowly, giving weight to each word. "Save your last words for the execution."

"What?" She went very still. "I'll have a chance to talk?"

"With recorders broadcasting your speech to the galaxy. So I recommend you choose your words wisely."

An ashen resolve filled her face. She hid it, turning away from me toward the window.

I stood there a moment longer, watching her with a heart weighted by grief and old affection. I had known Neveni for a long time now. She would not surprise me on the scaffold.

When she proclaimed our misdeeds to the galaxy, each sin she recited would fuel the burgeoning unrest of the Excess.

I left her then to plan the furious speech that would obliterate us.

Overhead, purple clouds blocked the twin moons of Lumina, casting a shadow across the square where the Grandiloquy had assembled to watch two terrorists die.

Tyrus stood at the center of this square, atop an enormous floating platform surrounded by recorders. The giant screen behind him showed a close-up of his face, contorted now by the crazed smile of a madman.

The live transmission had commenced—his first since that fateful day, years ago, when I'd screamed the truth of the Sacred City to the Empire.

Traditionally, a committee of advisers staged such events. They had issued three recommendations for Neveni's execution.

First: *Do not execute the Luminar on her own planet. It will remind the public of the tragedy that occurred there.*

But Tyrus meant to inspire sympathy. He'd chosen the Central Square for the execution site: a place still littered with the skeletons of Luminars killed by Resolvent Mist.

Second: *Do not put the two prisoners together, lest their connection affect the audience.*

Neveni and Anguish stood side by side, their palms pressed against their respective force fields, only millimeters separating them. The force fields were protecting them from the lingering poisons in the atmosphere, and a series of protective domes shielded those of us looking on. The recorders captured Anguish's doleful face, and the loving tone of Neveni's indistinct whisper.

Above all, Tyrus's advisers had urged him, *Don't give her a chance to speak!*

Tyrus had placed voice amplifiers throughout the Central Square. When Neveni raised her voice, the galaxy would not miss a syllable.

As for the advisers, he'd called them fools and dispatched them back to their home planets—effectively ending their lifetimes of service.

Since I was not officially alive, I stood at a remove with Gladdic, out of sight of the imagers. Gladdic took my arm as Tyrus lifted his hand to an attendant to mark the start of the ceremony.

The force fields' opacity shifted, so that Neveni and Anguish at last perceived their audience. The recorders hummed as they drew closer yet, giving spectators across the Empire an intimate, front-row experience of Neveni's stricken face, her sharp choked gasp.

The machines swiveled to follow her look, panning across the field of Luminar skeletons. They captured Anguish's low, urgent remark—"Neveni. Look at me, only at me"—as he strained toward her, blocked by an invisible barrier.

And above loomed the Emperor Tyrus, visibly enjoying the sight of his prisoners' misery.

"Behold the aftermath of disobedience," he announced imperiously. "You stand amid the ruin of Luminar civilization—a ruin your people brought upon themselves."

"Liar," Neveni hissed.

Tyrus continued. "Your Divine Emperor in his benevolence extended his hand to the people of this planet. He offered them a beautiful new future of scientific growth and learning. But your people were not content with peace. They experimented with bioweapons. They destroyed themselves."

"Liar!" shouted Neveni, her small fists balling at her side. "You *know* that's not true!"

"And you, Neveni Sagnau—you, one of the last survivors of Lumina—*you*, above all, should have repented for these sins. You might have chosen a righteous path, a peaceful path. But what did you do?" Tyrus paused theatrically. "You chose to seed terror across this Empire. You murdered the innocent. You laid waste to the peaceful. You so admired the sins of your people that you strove to outdo them. And so I condemn you to die as they did, in the fatal embrace of Resolvent Mist. This is your last chance to speak, to breathe clean air. Confess your arrogance, your sins. Perhaps if you unburden yourself, your Divine Emperor will be moved to mercy."

Neveni glared at him. "I'll confess."

The force fields merged, imprisoning Neveni and Anguish together. He stepped over to her, a silent wall of strength, and Neveni took his hand, then addressed the Grandiloquy: "Here it is. My confession."

Her words rang over the air, and the Grandiloquy leaned forward around me, eager to hear her grovel and forfeit that fragile dignity.

"My people did not do this to our planet!" Neveni roared. "The Grandiloquy did! And the Emperor *knows* that! He's no god! He's a tyrant! And the Empire is a *lie*!"

Anguish gathered Neveni into his arms as the force field dropped, allowing poisoned air to envelop them.

Within seconds, she began to cough. On other planets, she would already be dead, but Lumina's natural atmosphere and soil diluted the Mist's effects—and made it an even slower, more agonizing way to die.

Gladdic had clutched my arm. "This is terrible," he whispered.

Still coughing, Neveni pulled out of Anguish's grasp. Clutching his hand to her heart, she raised her voice: "Tarantis—Tarantis von Domitrian triggered"—a racking cough—"the great supernova! He . . ." Her knees gave way, and Anguish caught her. The toxic air did not work as quickly on Diabolics, and he remained holding her upright as she gathered her strength to continue. "He used malignant space, just as our Emperor has done! It's not the power of a *god*. The Domitrians have known how to create malignant space for hundreds of years!"

Derisive murmurs from all around us, all the Grandiloquy pretending to find this laughable.

"They stole everything from us!" screamed Neveni. "They have no right to own this galaxy!"

"You are in your last moments," Tyrus mocked, "and you spend them blaspheming your own God."

"YOU ARE NO GOD!" she howled, and doubled over, coughing. The words escaped her, jerky, breathless, urgent: "You are a *MONSTER*!"

Tyrus laughed. His Grandiloquy took the cue and broke into laughter as well, all of them sycophants who knew it to be true but pretended it was not.

"Spirited to the last," Tyrus jeered.

And Neveni just coughed, struggling to breathe.

"I can't watch this," Gladdic muttered.

His eyes had closed. "No," I said sharply. "You have to look."

He shook his head.

"If she can bear it, you can bear to watch it!"

"I can't!"

"Then *save* her," I said.

Gladdic sent me a startled look. "What?"

Neveni had fallen, Anguish kneeling over her.

"Such a brave Partisan," Tyrus jeered. "Fitting you should die strangling on your own lies. Open your eyes, girl. Take your last glimpse of your beloved planet. For it dies with you too."

Neveni forced her head up, and her cheeks were covered in tears of blood.

In the sky above us, a great slash of bright white light tore across Lumina's sky. Neveni screamed as the malignant space opened in the upper atmosphere of her planet.

Cries rose from the crowd, and Gladdic moaned.

My grip fastened on his arm. "Gladdic, you must act. *Save* her. I'll drop the protective dome around us. You will charge out there and defy Tyrus. Publicly."

"He'll kill me."

"No, he won't." I seized his shoulders and turned him to face me fully. I'd removed the growths from my face for this occasion, counting on the inattentiveness of the crowd . . . knowing I needed my true face to look into Gladdic's, to give him this last reassurance.

"I have prepared *everything* in advance for you. Read this."

Then I pulled out the discreet-sheet I'd readied for him, with the entire explanation outlined for him.

The Resolvent Mist antidote waiting on the ship. He would not need it, but Neveni and Anguish would.

And of course, the words he would need to speak before saving Neveni—the ones that would set this galaxy afire.

The location on the ship of every single critical spot Tyrus and I had discovered, the planets where he should venture first—where he could fly unimpeded.

Neveni lay limp now on the ground, Anguish cradling her—two defenseless figures beneath a sky shrouded in death.

Even the Grandiloquy looked sober now, stirring uneasily at the sight unfolding in the sky above them.

Gladdic was frantically reading the discreet-sheet. "There's a neutralizer device!" he exclaimed.

"Here." Pulling open the fold of my gown, I unveiled it, pressed it into his hand. It was the size of a standard rifle. "Do it, my friend. You are ready. All the tools are in your hand."

He gawked at me, and looked back down at the discreet-sheet. *Fire the weapon once into the sky at the malignant space*, he had to be reading. *A second shot, aimed anywhere, will summon your escape pod.*

"We've read of this, Gladdic, and now let's make it happen. You can save Neveni and Anguish, and then the Excess will rise with you to take down the Empire. It takes but one great act of courage to topple a tyrant. Don't you see? You are the key. Liberty and justice, Gladdic!"

The malignant space touched the outermost atmosphere and had a curious effect upon the clouds it contacted. Thunder cracked overhead, gales of lightning forking like branches of a spider's web. Even

Tyrus's composure briefly wavered as he startled at the sound.

He looked out over the crowd, his gaze hunting for me, desperate no doubt to discover whether Gladdic would act while the recorders were yet poised to capture the moment.

But Gladdic was frozen, horrorstruck, and it dawned on me that this would not work, that I had chosen a coward in the desperate hope that he would act and had fooled myself into thinking he would do so.

He will not, I realized, aghast. *He won't do it.*

Then something unexpected happened, for Neveni was crumpled on the ground and my heart wrenched with the realization that she might already be dead. . . . But suddenly, with the last of her strength, she struggled up to her feet.

Blood streamed down her face, and the hatred that blazed there caused the crowd to gasp and reel back. No doubt some wondered how she still lived. But for a lifetime she had chafed at the rule of the Grandiloquy. She had lived and breathed and fueled herself on hatred since losing this planet to the Grandiloquy. She was ready for this.

She opened her mouth and spoke in a feeble whisper—which the speakers caught and amplified. "Nemesis lives," she rasped. "She's alive. It's the truth."

The effort sent her into a coughing fit, yet Neveni endured it, remaining upright as the coughs racked her body. On another desperate, ragged breath, she raised her eyes defiantly and screamed out the words with her last breaths:

"NEMESIS LIVES!"

The last time I had seen her, she had seethed with hatred for me. But I understood that it was not *me* whom she invoked in this final, defiant gesture, as malignant space crackled overhead and the crowd shrieked and hooted. She screamed my name to invoke the hope it conjured: the belief that change was possible.

This cause we shared was greater than the life or death of a single person. Even my life. Even Neveni's.

Even Tyrus's.

There was only one choice.

I crumpled up the discreet-sheet, tore the device back out of Gladdic's grasp, and knocked open the protective dome about us. Shouts rose as I bounded forward, but I paid them no mind. I vaulted up to land on the ground beside Neveni and Anguish.

Then I aimed the device into those bright lashing clouds of malignant space and unleashed its power.

The neutralizer flared out, enveloping the bright malignancy— that token of Tyrus's divine godhood—and crushed it into nothingness.

The ashen skies of Lumina were healed.

A thunderstruck silence fell, disturbed only by the faint buzzing of the recorders sending the live transmission across the Empire. I held still as all eyes focused on me. They recognized me despite my alterations, and my name began to travel from mouth to mouth.

"I do live," I cried, then wheeled on Tyrus. "And you are no god."

I blasted the neutralizer his way, missing intentionally, sending the Grandiloquy scattering. The second shot, we'd agreed, was the signal to power up the vessel buried in the soil behind us. Luminar rock scalded and melted away as the small escape craft surged out of the ground with a deafening rumble.

I seized Anguish and Neveni by their arms and dragged them to their feet, bundling them toward the waiting craft.

"This is a trick!" bellowed Tyrus. "It's another imposter!"

His shout was lost as the craft slammed its bay doors shut behind us, and then we launched into the purple skies above.

Later, on the galactic transmissions, I watched the final seconds of the drama play out. The Divine Emperor Tyrus, flustered and suddenly reduced in his magnificence, stumbled through the remains of his thwarted execution scene, insisting, "That was an imposter, and she told a dreadful lie. I am a god. You surely see—I AM A GOD!"

And he whirled around to cast a thunderous glare at his Grandiloquy, who quickly threw themselves to the ground to grovel before him. How pathetic it looked.

For he had never seemed more lost, and bewildered, and human.

I did not know if that was entirely faked. Up until moments ago, we'd planned on moving forward together, to remaining forever side by side.

But I had to do this. I had to leave.

Inside the escape pod, matters were different.

Neveni hadn't yet been treated by the med bot. She was choking on the blood in her lungs, yet she hurled her arms around me in wild gratitude. Anguish embraced me as well while we rattled away from the destructive chaos.

"I was never going to let you die," I told Neveni hoarsely. "Not either of you. I had to wait for this moment. This gesture. Only the Emperor could have broadcast a message that reached the whole galaxy. I wanted so much to tell you sooner. . . ."

And they both were laughing wildly, delirious with liberation from death.

"We're going to create a new era," I vowed.

Then I plotted our course through hyperspace, to the place Tyrus and I had devised for Gladdic—that first stop in what would be many to spread the words for the ideology of a new day that would allow for no tyrants, no Emperors, no Domitrians.

"And Neveni," I added, "what we do next, what we do from here . . . ?"

She looked at me.

"*I* decide."

They did not question it.

Instead they both grinned at me, and I could not help but smile back—because from here on, we were working together.

45

SIX MONTHS after parting ways with Tyrus, I entered the quarters I'd been sharing with Neveni and Anguish aboard the *Liberty*. It was the small, darting, light ship Tyrus had buried in the soil of Lumina for Gladdic's escape.

From the foul, rubbery scent on the air, it was clear she'd failed once again at trying to duplicate the roasted snake that had been a specialty on Lumina.

"There's something in the heater. I can't call it food," Neveni told me ruefully.

Anguish heroically picked up the body of the snake by his fist and chomped the head in one mouthful. Neveni gasped, hand flying to cover her mouth.

"Anguish, you have to puncture the venom pouch first! Otherwise it tastes . . ."

He chewed and swallowed.

"Really disgusting," Neveni finished.

He looked at us, absolutely expressionless. He rose calmly, a mass of coiled muscle. "Excuse me."

Then aimed right for the washroom.

A retching sound soon followed.

"You'd think he'd know better than to trust your cooking," I murmured.

"I know. . . . Wait. Hey!" Neveni said with a frown.

A smile curled over my lips, but then I caught sight of the projection in the next chamber, tuned into the latest galactic transmissions.

Tyrus.

My heart twisted in my chest. The sound was muted. I stared, looking past the false features, echoes of Tarantis, for those that remained his own. The pale lashes. The steady, cool gaze.

It was a long-awaited Convocation in the Grand Sanctum. In the last months, Neveni, Anguish, and I had been moving from system to system, healing malignant space with the neutralizer I'd used on Lumina.

It was a miraculous device, one that caused an exponential chain reaction. However great the patch of malignancy, it succumbed in a matter of days or weeks to a single shot from the machine. The Excess who witnessed the process were always awestruck, and then, when they learned that the Grandiloquy had been sitting on this technology—*enraged*. Such people were open to the truth of Tarantis, which Neveni and I gladly shared with them.

They were open to the other words I had to say to them—the language taken from the ancient books. I'd meant them for Gladdic to use, but they fell from my lips just as easily.

Perhaps more so—for I believed in them. I believed in what we were doing.

I flatly rejected any suggestion—by any who heard me—that I should claim the throne in my own right.

"Do you imagine you were just unlucky with the Domitrians?" I'd answered more times than I could remember. "If you concentrate power in the hands of one person or one group of people, you are enabling all inheritors to wield that power too! You wish to hand me the power to choose your destinies and limit your speech because I agree with your views—but what happens if my successor does not? The answer is *never* to concentrate power, not into the hands of anyone—however much you trust them. You can endure hateful words spoken by your enemies, when the alternative is worse: your future enemies having the power to silence you when you speak against their injustices! Own your own lives. Take responsibility for ruling yourselves."

Rumors of me would have been unstoppable, even had Tyrus meant to fight them rather than aid in their spread. He played it perfectly on his end. He exhibited just how keenly he could read the currents of the Empire, for he always, *always* took the exact wrong tack when confronted with the rumors in public transmissions.

When gently questioned by earnest, concerned citizens in need of reassurance, Tyrus met them in full imperial garb, threatening them with death and vengeance and fire for daring to doubt him. *"You presume to question your God? What right do you have to ask anything of a Divine Emperor?"*

When brute force was called for with rowdy, hostile crowds, Tyrus appeared to them in broadcasts, ruffled and sheepish: *"Come now, this is silly. These rumors of my wife's return are absurd. They're silly.*

Take some vapors, and just let your betters concern themselves with such things." He all but said *please.*

Today Neveni tuned out the sound of Anguish retching in the washroom and pumped up the volume on the screen so we could hear what Tyrus had to say at this Convocation, a gathering in the Grand Sanctum of the Chrysanthemum for the most prominent personages of the Empire. Public figures had come in person, or as projections in holographic form, from all over the galaxy. No one wondered why he was throwing this one. Tyrus's reputation had suffered from the debacle on Lumina, and from the rumors of my survival that could no longer be quashed.

"Let's hear his excuses today," Neveni muttered, because clearly she expected him to have some elaborate lie ready to rebut the rumors that Nemesis lived, and *she* could cure malignant space.

But that was not his plan. I knew it well.

Tyrus went through the standard greetings to the assembled Grandiloquy and Excess, and then he delved into the subject at hand: *"Lies are being spread that my wife lives. That she has been healing malignant space. This is false news. Nemesis has long been dead, as well you all know, and those who claim to have seen her are lying to you. Do but watch the broadcasts from Eurydice! All the authorities in this Empire have joined me in denouncing this conspiracy theory."*

A cheer rang out from the elites gathered about him, which made Tyrus beam with satisfaction—for the more the prominent figures of this Empire doubled down on the falsehood, the worse they would look in the long run. As for the galactic media on Eurydice, they, too, were spending their credibility reinforcing Tyrus's lies. They'd been the primary propaganda tool for the Domitrians, and with every single breath they wasted parroting words designed to please Tyrus, they eroded the public trust in them further.

I watched with satisfaction that mirrored Tyrus's own.

"I called you together today to offer you consolation," he said. *"As it turns out, your Divine Emperor is indeed gifted with the ability to heal the malignant space in your skies, and I am prepared to do just that all across this Empire!"*

At first the audience of elites rejoiced thunderously to hear it. They had to all feel mounting pressure from restive Excess in their territories, and this development would relieve it.

"So that's what he means to do," Neveni snarled. "He means to undercut us by healing them first."

"Just wait," I murmured to her unthinkingly, certain he had something else in mind. As the cheers at last faded, Tyrus gave a cruel, diamond-hard smile and slouched back in his floating throne, arms spread over the back of the seat. *"Now, I ask the representatives of the Excess: How much are you willing to pay me to do it?"*

Silence lapsed over the chamber.

The Domitrian Emperor just smirked from his throne, all arrogance and power and presumption, tracing his fingers over the gems of his finery.

"I'm not simply doing this for free. A Divine Emperor's time and efforts are most valuable. I expect tribute for this gracious favor," Tyrus said. *"Perhaps you shall all band together to build me another Chrysanthemum, one orbiting a pleasure planet. . . ."*

Neveni cast me a look of bewilderment. I just kept my eyes fixed on the screen.

"Oh, and said pleasure planet, of course," Tyrus went on, *"I wish it to be one where everyone is nude, but of course, the inhabitants must all be screened beforehand so I can ensure they are pleasing to mine eyes. I am sure many patriotic Excess will volunteer their daughters to entertain me. . . ."*

"Is he joking?" Neveni blurted.

With an exaggerated look around him, Tyrus said, *"Why no cheers? Why aren't you hailing me? Many of your colonies have a great and destructive force bearing down on you. Tribute to your God is a small thing to ask. Now hail me."*

With those words, there was a scattering of cheers—first from the Grandiloquy and then from some among the Excess. . . . And I knew that whoever those Excess were, they'd instantly lost all credibility with their own people. Tyrus just smiled as though he'd been hailed as he demanded, though there was true satisfaction in his face.

Why wouldn't there be? In a single gesture, he'd destroyed any illusion that the galaxy's Emperor cared about the well-being of those he ruled.

"He's completely lost his wits!" Neveni declared. She whirled around and stared at me. "Why are you so . . . blasé about this?"

"As you said," I replied, "he's lost his wits."

It was an escalation of Tyrus's damage to his own regime, but certainly not the last. The crippling of the Chrysanthemum's interlinked network of mechanized bots meant a cessation of effective automated censorship—one made total after Tyrus claimed to be "displeased" with the censors he employed to replace them. He threw them all in the most notorious prison vessel in the Empire, the great oblong cityship called the Star Abyss.

As a result, censorship was ripped away overnight. No longer were there any controls filtering the galactic channels of public information, hiding inconvenient truths, banning inflammatory topics; jammers could no longer drown out voices unfriendly to the order of power.

Those first months that I traveled about with the neutralizer, speaking to the Excess on one province, then another, the first few tentative voices reared out of anonymity to make their opinions known. . . .

And then, when those voices were not immediately silenced, the speakers not tortured or killed, a sudden profusion of opinions began to roar into the public sphere.

The opinions had always been there, spoken by those in obscurity on the Empire's many planets, heard only by the most trusted people in earshot—if the speaker was fortunate enough not to end up reported for forbidden, hateful speech.

But every day that passed, more and more rogue transmissions appeared on the galactic frequencies.

Now those voices were amplified, for at last, they could be projected the same way the Domitrian propagandists had been for the last five centuries. Pure and unfiltered speech grew noisier every single day that passed. Neveni kept me apprised of all the new voices gaining prominence, and I cheered to hear their words ringing from one star to another:

"Nemesis lives! She was never an imposter, and she has returned to destroy the Grandiloquy!"

"Don't listen to the media. It's no imposter. I saw her on my very planet, face-to-face, and she spoke of liberty and freedom—"

"The Emperor is mad."

"The Emperor is no divine being."

"The Domitrians are criminals!"

That last sentiment was the most heartening one to hear, for it was the most critical understanding that needed to sink in across this galaxy.

There was one thing above all that had to be eradicated, and obliterated so thoroughly it could never hope to survive: the Domitrians.

There was a notable human weakness. In hard times, one tended to erase the harsh lines of the past. One tended to see the glories of what had been rather than the promise of what was to come.

It was not enough to show the Empire the fallacies of one centralized authority.

The name "Domitrian" had to be poisoned for all time. It was more than a family; it was an idea, it was the foundation of our history. They were cheaters who'd retained an edge the other human beings willingly discarded; they'd become the shortcut to ending all wars, to vanquishing all opposition, and eventually one of them had placed himself on a pedestal at the center of this galaxy. . . . There could be no mythical glory remaining to them. "Domitrian" had to become a swear word on the lips of all who spoke of them.

The truth of Tarantis found fertile ground in the new swelling public mutiny. So, too, did the truth of the Sacred City and the Interdicts.

I had not released that information, but Neveni knew who had.

"The surviving Partisans," she told me in quiet satisfaction, after we overheard a pair of vendors discussing it at a bazaar on the moon Auriga. "I told them all about it, and those who believed me tried to repeat it, but no one used to believe us."

Matters were different in this new era of uncensored information.

Something that once would have been dismissed as a conspiracy theory now rang true. The Interdicts were not immortal, but were kept young due to their residence in a place where gravity slowed time. The Sacred City *had* been destroyed.

And Fustian nan Domitrian was an imposter.

Just as that last rumor gained ground, Tyrus legitimized it on a public transmission of the Chrysanthemum's celebration of Consecration Day.

Tyrus interrupted the publicly broadcast service in the Great

Heliosphere to blurt out, *"I have been troubled by something. There is a hypervelocity star passing near the Armistice Configuration that simply . . . moves too swiftly. Why must the star move? Why doesn't it merely stay in its general location? It strikes me as a blasphemous act of defiance toward me. Does it not strike you that way, Most Ascendant One?"*

Fustian had been in the middle of giving the blessing. Now he gawked at the Emperor, bewildered by him.

"The star just moves as it . . . as it moves," he said. That was all there was to it.

Tyrus looked at him in a way that made Fustian realize the Emperor wanted agreement.

He quickly amended, *"But of course, now that I think of it—our Divine Emperor is correct. There is something amiss about a star that will not settle in a general area."*

"I think we must do something about this," Tyrus vowed.

He declared the first war of his reign: against the hypervelocity star.

At first, when the news spread, it seemed to be a joke, but Tyrus massed his forces against the star itself.

He gave rousing speeches about the ills of the hypervelocity star.

"I perceive in this star the source of all this Empire's strife," Tyrus declared, with the Interdict at his side to give his sacred endorsement. *"I have already spoken to this star—"*

"Spoken . . . to . . . it?" blurted Fustian.

"I commanded it to cease moving, and it declared that it would not. It insults me and my divine authority over the Cosmos. This star plots against my reign, and it must be dealt with."

In his seeming conviction, he inspired some to give uncertain cheers, but it was mostly because they knew they should, rather than because they saw sense in what he was saying. After all, the Emperor couldn't mean to waste firepower attacking a *star*. There was a restive province near there, so he had to intend to attack that, not the actual star.

But no. Tyrus meant to attack the star.

Under the Emperor's ecstatic direction, Tyrus's fleet unleashed salvo upon salvo into the hypervelocity star. The bright weapons streaked repeatedly into the searing hydrogen and helium. He broadcast the attack live, as though this were a true war, and forced Fustian to stand behind him to give his sacred sanction to the action.

"Oh, that strike did it damage," gloried Tyrus, to his confused commanders.

He paced the command nexus of the *Valor Novus* and shouted encouragement to his fleet as they laid weapon fire into that vexing star.

"See how it wilts under the bombardment," proclaimed Tyrus, though the star continued to glow without a trace of damage.

Thus he spent so much of the firepower stored on the Chrysanthemum . . . sinking it into a star. And at last, some spell seemed to have been broken that held the last of the loyalists among the Eurydicean media, for they, too, began to send out broadcasts that subtly undercut the Emperor.

Neveni, Anguish, and I all passed an evening watching a smirking Eurydicean journalist report on the progress of the crusade: *"Today the Divine Emperor made good on that vow of four weeks ago, when his forces mustered to stop the speeding star."*

The image dissolved into footage of Tyrus's fleet firing lasers into the searing mass.

"Experts say the Divine Emperor's new weapons technology is the most powerful in this galaxy's history. But so far, the star has yet to issue a surrender. Some say it never will—including some who once felt differently."

Neveni and Anguish both exclaimed when the view panned to show Fustian nan Domitrian, flushed and stiff as the journalist held out her recorder.

"Interdict," the journalist said, *"you've come here today to publicly withdraw your support from the Divine Emperor's crusade. Can you tell us why?"*

Fustian shook his head. *"It's a farce. It's all a farce, don't you see? The Emperor is no god. He's a madman! As Interdict, I declare him a heretic! An apostate!"*

My eyes narrowed. Of course, Fustian was one of the first loyalist rats to flee the sinking ship. He likely knew the truth about him had been released, and he believed turning on Tyrus first might save him.

"That does it," declared Anguish. "He's lost the Helionics."

"The Helionics who still believe he's holy, yes," Neveni muttered. Then she shifted her gaze to me and watched me in a piercing, suspicious manner, one that made me look at her quizzically.

"So, Nemesis," Neveni said, "want to tell me what the hell is really going on?"

The question startled me. Anguish cast her a knowing look and turned around to plant himself between me and the viewer, tall and looming, his arms crossed. He'd fully recovered his strength. I could no longer defeat him when we sparred.

"What do you mean?" I said.

"We're not fools," Neveni snapped. She jumped to her feet and took her place at Anguish's side. "Tyrus is not an idiot. He's also not totally insane. Well . . . he's insane, but not like this. . . ."

I leaned over to catch a glimpse of words scrolling over the bottom of the screen . . . *Breaking News.* Desperate to escape their scrutiny, I pointed it out to them. "Look!"

Neveni whipped around, and I heard her gasp. For beneath the recording of Fustian, the text announced that the Emperor had ordered the arrest of the Interdict.

Simple words to announce a massive event. I knew this was a major development, for there was no going back from this.

Yet neither Neveni nor Anguish were sufficiently distracted. They turned back to me, accusation on their faces. And a bombardment of evidence poured from their lips:

"We escaped from Lumina too easily."

"Where did you even get that neutralizer? How did you get it without Tyrus realizing it?"

"How haven't we been stopped?" Anguish said. "We are a vulnerable target moving from one destination to another. The Excess always seem to have learned rumors in advance of our coming—we are too public. The Emperor must have sources tracking us. We should have been captured by now."

"Why arrest Fustian and turn all the Helionics against himself rather than announce that he's an imposter?" cried Neveni. "He defeated us in the chaotic gale because he was clever about it, but now . . . He won, and you knew he would—because he's not this stupid! Why, if he *wanted* to be overthrown, I couldn't think of a better . . ."

Then she must have seen something on my face, because she knelt down right in front of me, vibrating all over as though she were holding back the urge to seize me and shake the answers out me. "You're hiding something. Just tell us."

I looked between their faces. Anguish—my brother. Neveni—the combustible friend and enemy who'd shared the best and the worst moments of my life.

Perhaps it was too late to change anything, either for the better or the worse. Events had their own momentum.

And it would be a comfort to share the truth with someone else.

"Tyrus's mind was never damaged," I admitted to them. "Your scans were right on the *Alexandria*. His conscience has always been intact." And then I looked at Anguish. "He's never been a monster. He learned the truth of Tarantis, and then he set out to be overthrown."

They both gawked at me for a long moment.

Then Neveni blurted, *"What?"*

"He set out to be a tyrant so the Excess would rise up and overthrow him. It's why he declared himself a god. He meant to unite all the Grandiloquy and the most socially prominent Excess of this Empire together in repeating a single, ludicrous narrative. All of the Empire's establishment parrots the mistruths of the Domitrians, so he knew he could use that to discredit them forever if they lined up behind the proper falsehood. He's breaking this Empire from within its heart. I learned it on the *Alexandria*. It's why I saved him. We worked together to orchestrate everything that's followed."

Neveni sank down onto the couch next to me, and Anguish still just stared at me, thunderstruck.

"This has all been a sham," he murmured.

"Not a sham," I said fiercely. "It's a revolution, Anguish. The most bloodless possible revolution orchestrated by a regime ensuring its own overthrow."

After all, dictators and oligarchies fought back. They decimated those trying to strip their power.

Not Tyrus. He'd wasted armaments on repeated crusades against the hypervelocity star. He insisted on commanding the forces Grandiloquy marshaled for their Divine Emperor's cause—and always directed them awry.

I could see Neveni's eyes widening as she fit the pieces together in her head . . . that this had all been deliberate.

"Our escape from Lumina was easy because I didn't actually save you from him," I went on. "Nor did I ever endanger you by placing you in his hands to be saved. He was never going to kill you. So there you have it: that's the truth."

They were both totally silent for a weighty moment. And then Neveni reached out, and Anguish soundlessly moved over to take her hand. . . . And my heart gave a curious wrench at the sight of them taking comfort from each other, for I did not know if I would ever have a moment like that with Tyrus again.

"I meant Gladdic to lead this revolution," I told them. "I didn't want to do this."

"It could only be you," Anguish said to me wearily. "You are the one they cry for."

"The one I called for," whispered Neveni. "I was so angry with you, Nemesis, but I think I knew . . . I knew you wouldn't let me die. I knew you'd save me. That's what you do."

And then in a gesture of kindness, she reached her other hand out for mine, offering me a trace of their affection as well. Her soft hand clasped mine tightly, and I realized how desperately I'd craved their understanding.

"I know how it ends," I told her, my eyes jamming shut. Nova blast those tears, threatening me now. My throat felt tight. "I know the truth of this can never be known outside this room—"

"Never," Neveni said.

"Not even if he comes to trial," I said.

The tense silence that answered me confirmed it. How I wished they were inspired in a way I was not. . . . Inspired enough to devise some miraculous alternative to the ending we all approached.

Instead Anguish moved to sit at my other side, his heavy arm draping about my shoulder, and like that, on both sides, I had friends. I was not alone in this.

"I suppose I never really knew him," Neveni offered. "Why is he doing it?"

"He knows he'll be hated for all of history. He accepts it. I think it's his penance," I answered her jaggedly.

"And . . ." Her hand tightened on mine. "And you can accept it?"

I thought of that long-ago day on the *Tigris* when I'd taken Tyrus's fate from him and chosen it for him. Then I forced my eyes open so she would see my resolve. "It's his penance. And I help him—because that's mine."

46

TWO WEEKS later I received a very, very good reason to return to the Chrysanthemum:

The Emperor had invited me to a party.

The message came courtesy of a local Domitrian servant who looked faint with fright when he knocked on the door of our guest lodgings on Atarys. That I answered the door with a weapon slung over my shoulder did not help.

"I don't know what this message contains, but I am to convey it to you with g-greatest compliments," the man stammered, before handing over a slim metal folio fashioned out of diamond-studded platinum. "P-please," he said as he backed away, "inform the Divine Emperor that I did precisely as c-commanded and with total discretion. He promised to release me from service if I conveyed this to you."

I took the message and opened it after his departure. Indeed, it was an invitation. It was time.

I went directly to Anguish and Neveni. "Brace yourself," I warned her gently.

For the party was being held on Lumina. Tyrus meant to move the entirety of the Chrysanthemum into orbit of the planet. The party itself would take place amid the desiccated remains of Neveni's brethren.

"Horrid," she said on a shuddering breath. "He has a true talent for perversity. But why invite you?"

"It's a signal of some kind."

"A signal of what?" Anguish asked. Despite having been told the full truth, he remained skeptical of Tyrus. "For all we know, it's a trap."

"I'm sure it *is* a trap." I spoke steadily, betraying no sign of the turmoil that had electrified me since receiving the invitation. Time was running out. This would all be over soon. Stars pray that I managed to bear the outcome. "It's a trap *he's* setting—for himself."

"Regardless," Anguish said. "We are twelve days away in hyper-space, and this event takes place in ten days."

"The Grandiloquy parties can span days, as you'll remember," I said to him dryly.

"You would never make it in time."

"The timing's deliberate," I said. "The servant who delivered it said as much. So we won't go to Lumina. We'll meet him on his return."

Once we were aboard the *Liberty*, Neveni sent word to the wider network of Excess and Partisans. She alerted them that the Chrysanthemum might soon require occupying forces. This way, we would arrive in advance of the rebel fleets. I did not allow myself to hope for a chance to save Tyrus, but I would not give up on the possibility either.

As we traveled, the party began on Lumina.

The Grandiloquy had been the longest holdouts for Tyrus, with many of them blinded by the bubble of privilege around them. The savvier of them had carefully escaped the Chrysanthemum as soon as the crusade against the hypervelocity star began, but others remained closely attached to the Emperor.

After all, they were victims of their own control over the galaxy's culture. They'd received their information of the growing unrest from the Eurydicean media, and had long learned to discount alternative pathways of information, but Tyrus controlled that media and thus the information that reached their ears. They reinforced one another's belief in their invincibility as a class. They were further blinded by the favors and largesse the Emperor had showered upon them, for Tyrus was willing to spend ruinously nowadays to keep the most avaricious at his side to share his downfall.

For most, it wasn't until the unrest directly affected the provinces they owned that they began to sense danger on the air.

Other Grandiloquy were aware of the danger, but too desperate for the money Tyrus spent liberally, the favors he offered of his dwindling treasury, or the promises of power he offered freely. Still others had treated the Excess on their provinces so cruelly over the years that they had no choice but to cling to the Emperor's side, even as the regime began to sink under its own weight.

For these last loyalists, Tyrus threw his party.

We emerged from hyperspace two days into the revelry, and I tuned in to the galactic transmissions. The party had certainly begun, for Tyrus had stationed recorders all over the planet— unseen by the partyers—broadcasting their antics for all to see. The galactic media played footage around the clock, with commentators alternately marveling and reviling the revelries. "A new standard for depravity," said one. "Nauseating extravagance," opined another. In a time of poverty, the most expensive of light shows raged over the heads and around the celebrants, priceless jewels sparking from their elaborate outfits . . . and yet Tyrus had left the Luminar bodies where they'd fallen, littered amid the dancing and cavorting.

Viewers watched as the last of the regime's loyalists followed their mad Emperor's lead, wildly partaking of substances and behaving with inhuman barbarism. The final sacred Exalteds were used to serve narcotics, their profound innocence witness to the debauchery about them. Tyrus wore naught but a pair of antlers and a mad grin, planted at the center of the celebration like a pied piper leading his Grandiloquy into the most abhorrent antics they could devise. He drank wine from a dead Luminar's skull and loaned fervent encouragement to any lurid spectacle the Grandiloquy partiers could imagine. His gift for inspiring the best in me had this flip side, for he could rouse the very worst in others. The most vile antics of the Grandiloquy were thus displayed for the entire galaxy at the worst possible moment for them.

When a group of partygoers began to dance and simulate sexual acts with the bones of Lumina's dead, I turned off the screen lest Neveni pass by.

This hideous display was certain to be the final blow to the Empire. Even after the horrendous revelations about the Domitrians, Tyrus, the Interdicts, and the nature of malignant space, some Excess had balked at overthrowing the established order. The horrors of the known remained preferable to the dreadful possibilities of the unknown.

But this profane celebration among the dead put an end to all

ambivalence. The last remaining loyal provinces exploded into protest, burning effigies of Tyrus that showed him gnawing on the
bones of dead Luminars.

As we approached the Chrysanthemum, news broke confirming
that Tyrus had disappeared from the party hours before. His loyalists, meanwhile, continued to revel on the planet's surface, utterly
unaware that the Emperor had shared their antics with the galaxy.

We encountered no opposition as the *Liberty* docked with the
Valor Novus. I led Neveni right into the *Valor Novus*, and we did not
encounter a soul. The deserted, brightly lit corridors felt eerily
expectant, like a stage awaiting its players.

Or perhaps they felt haunted.

"Hang back," I told Neveni as we stepped into the heart of the
Chrysanthemum. I sounded so calm. But my stomach was churning.
"Keep Anguish back as well."

"But . . ."

As she looked into my face, she saw, perhaps, more than I meant
to reveal. Her face softened, and she gave me a nod.

"You don't have much time, Nemesis. Make the most of it."

"I will."

Taking a deep breath, I passed through a grand archway, down a
short enameled hallway, and into the presence chamber.

Tyrus sat on his diamond throne, his eyes closed, the bejeweled
robes of a Grande discarded by his feet. The chamber flickered with
eerie light, shed by the purple hue of Lumina, the Chrysanthemum's
new place of orbit.

He was not asleep. Others would think so, but I knew him better.
I knew him like myself.

And I loved him more than ever.

He'd shed Tarantis's face. For the first time since our interlude on the *Alexandria*, he looked like himself again. As I approached, my footsteps announced me. His eyes opened. When he saw me, he rose.

"I received your invitation," I said to him. "Regrettably, I had other plans."

He smiled wearily. "My loyalists don't realize they will soon perish. The least I could do was give them a final party."

I could not help myself. I touched his face, the corner of his mouth, the crease that formed when he smiled. "It *is* almost over," I said huskily.

He turned his head the slightest degree, the eerie light sliding over his dark red hair. His lips found my palm for the briefest moment.

"Good," he said very softly. "Tell me."

"Six thousand vessels are in hyperspace. They'll arrive within the hour."

"Six thousand." His smile now was slow and full of wonder. "How . . . ?"

"Some of the ships were formerly your forces. Others—many others—were built in the last few months . . . by the Excess." His eyes were shining, so I went on. "The technological blueprints that were leaked . . . that *you* leaked?" I paused, and when he nodded once, I smiled and continued. "The Excess were able to make sense of them. All across the Empire, shipbuilders are emerging. The new constructions aren't so fine as the *Alexandria*, but they will do for now."

"Brilliant minds truly are everywhere," he murmured. "And they'll innovate. Better ships will come in time."

"They might never have discovered their potential, had they not been given cause." I wanted to touch him again. To crush him to me, lips and chests and hips, to press against him so hard that the imprint of his body would linger on mine forever.

But he'd withdrawn. Not far. An almost imperceptible distance. But enough to warn me not to touch him.

It was enough, paired with the hungry way he studied my lips, to tell me that his calm was hard-won, and he feared that my touch would undo him.

I hugged myself, trapping my wayward hands, as I continued. "I've been apprised of all the strategy discussions. There are numerous alliances working against you, but they all share a consensus opinion: split up the Empire. Just as you wished. Along hundreds of different fault lines—with one cooperative body of elected representatives to negotiate trade, settle disputes, render assistance. But the legislative bodies will all be local. No laws imposed from afar, not anymore. There will never be another Emperor. The leaders will all be based in the localities they rule—accountable to their voters directly."

"And you?" he asked softly.

"I've been asked to preside as an Empress." I rolled my eyes. "They assured me it would be as a figurehead, no more. I think they've come to realize the folly of that. I've made it clear to them."

He blew out a breath. His hand rose, trembling slightly, as though to touch my face. But at the last moment, his fingers curled into a fist, which he lowered to his side. "You would make a fine Empress," he said steadily.

"No one should ever be an Empress."

He smiled ruefully. "Indeed. I do hope I made that clear to the universe—a single person can never be trusted with such power."

"More than that," I said roughly. "A single person should never be burdened with it." I reached out and grabbed the hand he'd withdrawn and carried it to my lips, kissing it hard. I turned it over to study his palm and kissed that, too. "Tyrus, here is your choice. It's yours to make—and Neveni has agreed to help. We will maintain the story we've created for this galaxy. They will learn of how Nemesis charged in here to confront you"—I paused here to kiss his fingers, one by one, flushing as I heard his sigh—"and how we both then died in the final battle—"

He ripped his hand free. "No," he said harshly. "Nemesis, I—"

"The *Valor Novus* will be in flames," I continued stubbornly. "Our bodies will be incinerated—"

"Damn it, I have *told* you, you will not suffer alongside—"

I kissed his mouth to stop him. Threading my hand through his hair, I kissed him so deeply that the world spun. When at last he ceased to resist me, I felt his tall, muscled body relax. His hands came around my waist to hold me to him, and he began to kiss me back. I pulled away to speak against his ear. "And then, you and I, my love . . . we'll escape. We'll disappear."

He looked at me sidelong, with shadowed eyes. His eyes looked ancient, exhausted. "I wish it were so easy," he said quietly.

My heart sank. But I had expected this.

"The alternative?" he said.

"Wait here. As my prisoner. You'll be tried. Condemned. Executed."

Now it was his turn to kiss my fingers, and then my throat, my chin, my mouth. Burying his face in the crook of my shoulder, he took a deep breath—and then released me. There was something formal, final, in the short step he retreated from me.

"If we disappear," he said, and there was a stiffness to his speech, a stiltedness, that told me how often he'd rehearsed this to himself, "even if we fake our deaths, there will be conspiracy theories for centuries to come. And there will be pretenders, imposters who will take our names to rally others to their cause. And the strife they'll cause might inspire others to look back at us, at our time, through a romantic haze. And then, everything you and I have done will be for naught. *No*," he said adamantly. "Better for there to be an answer to all questions. There must be an execution—a public one."

I stepped toward him. He had nowhere to retreat, for his throne blocked the way. As he realized this, his jaw squared and his eyes narrowed: I saw his intention to harden himself against me.

I cupped his jaw very lightly, for I was done with force. "Will you at least forgive that frightened little boy for his mistake on Anagnoresis? Tyrus, I have to tell you—I've met many children. And none of them have much impressed me with their wisdom."

He laughed. "I think this will do it." His face softened. "And I want to know you are happy, Nemesis. This entire galaxy is yours now. You will be celebrated for the rest of your life. That's what you've earned."

"Earned," I repeated quietly. "And what of you? What have you earned? Not death, Tyrus."

He took a long breath. "I will die for a reason—a *good* reason. It's not a cruel fate, my love. It's a far better death than any Domitrian before me. And you know the truth. The universe can scorn me into perpetuity, so long as you think well of me."

I felt torn between love and helpless anger. "I want to overrule you," I confessed, very low.

"But you won't," he said. "You won't do that."

I would not. I had stripped this choice from him once before. I'd had no right to do it. I had no right now.

"Don't cry," he whispered. For my eyes were stinging.

"I won't," I lied. "Never again, after this."

He smiled crookedly, then brushed his thumb across my lower lip. "Stars, I have been so blessed in this life, to have found you."

My throat closed. I could not speak.

So I kissed him instead, for as long as I dared. Time was running out. Six thousand ships approached. How long? An hour, maybe two.

He, too, seemed to sense the end drawing near. He broke away at last, catching my hand in his. "Let's walk," he said roughly.

Our fingers entwined, we passed through the abandoned halls of our short-lived kingdom, taking in the beauty of this fallen Empire one last time.

As we entered the imperial bedchamber, an idea struck me. I pulled him over to the console, where I quickly keyed in the program to seal a marital union. Our electrodes had burned out during the shock on the *Arbiter*, but we could remarry ourselves. No vicars, no officiants, just the two of us and a synthesizer. We placed our palms onto the device, then pressed them together to activate the new pair of shared electrodes. They blazed to life between us, setting aglow the sparks that had bound us since our first wedding day.

Then, with the little time remaining, Tyrus took me into his arms, and we made love beneath the vast window, under an infinity of stars.

We still lay there, tangled in the sheets and each other, when the window began to fill with the incoming vessels of the fleet.

He watched his own hand trace over my skin, frowning a little in concentration, as though memorizing me.

I swallowed back a convulsion of sorrow. I would not waste our time here with tears.

"Are you afraid?" I asked.

He considered the question a long moment. "Time slows as you approach the black hole. More and more, the closer you draw. I don't perish after my trial. It can be said I will outlive you all. I will still be falling into that abyss at the very end of this universe."

Despite his brave words, I felt his body give the tiniest shiver at the thought. It chilled me as well, that prospect of an eternal separation from the Living Cosmos, the cruelest punishment for a Helionic.

A hideous pain swelled in my chest. "I can't believe this is the only way."

"Life doesn't always give us the choices we want." He pulled me back into his arms, so I pressed myself against his chest.

The frantic thump of his heartbeat betrayed his calm words. He was terrified. He lied to comfort me.

Tears did prick my eyes, then, but I fought them back before they could fall. Everything in me—every inbuilt instinct, and every skill of love and loyalty I had developed in my lifetime—wanted to fight for him. As his breath caressed my hair, I tensed against the overpowering urge to rip him to his feet and carry him out of this place to safety.

Perhaps he sensed my inward battle, for his hand found the base of my neck, massaging the tight muscles, urging them to relax again. "As a child, I dreamed of being a great leader," he murmured, "hailed for guiding this galaxy toward some better future. Those were a child's imaginings, but now . . . Now, what matter if my name won't be honored? I've achieved what I wished and united the people to fight for something better. So many wondrous possibilities lie ahead."

But not for *him*. For *him*, the possibilities were ending.

What good was justice if it did not extend to everyone? Had that quandary not been the inspiration for his great efforts? He had not accepted an order in which justice was reserved only for some.

He deserved justice.

I sat up, determination burning in me. "Tyrus, I do not believe in futility. You don't need to die to make this work. I am going to find a way."

He studied my face intently. "I wish . . . I could make this easier for you. If I had the power to change one thing, it would be that."

Yes. It was an injustice to *me* as well.

"Do you trust me?" I asked.

"Without doubt." He gave a half smile. "And with my life. Several times now."

"Do you trust me to respect you?" I pressed. "To respect your wishes?"

"Yes," he said somberly after a moment.

"Then think on that. And have courage." I kissed him with all the fire in my heart. "Trust me, my love."

"Always," he said.

Neveni's voice came over the intercom: *"Nemesis, it's time."*

When we emerged into the presence chamber of the *Valor Novus*, it was as a prisoner and his jailer. I thrust Tyrus to the floor. The Excess who'd invaded the Chrysanthemum were not only Partisans, but many ordinary civilians who'd joined our rebellion against the Empire, and now the Galactic Emperor was at their feet.

Tyrus played the part of deposed tyrant well.

He got to his feet and cast a cool, arrogant look over the assembled Excess. "Do you Excess truly imagine you can manage without me? The Grandiloquy will reclaim this galaxy and cast you all into a black hole!"

Heated, furious murmurs filled the room. Neveni met my eyes, her raised brows asking a question. Was I up to the task of satisfying our audience?

I answered her by stalking forward and kicking Tyrus's legs out from under him. He slammed back onto the floor.

"The rest of us have groveled to you long enough, Your Supremacy," I said. "Now it's our turn to receive your respect. And your turn to give a pound of flesh."

47

ONE MONTH later, the final Domitrian stood in the center of the Great Heliosphere where, years before, he'd been crowned Emperor.

Today new representatives of republics from all over the former Empire had gathered to watch him be condemned.

As always, Tyrus put on a good show.

"You think to be rid of me?" he jeered after the list of charges was read. "Your republics won't last a single year! Without an iron hand to keep you on course, you'll be brawling among yourselves like dogs. You will *beg* for another Emperor—another Domitrian to rule over you. Mark my words!"

His words were met with defiant roars, hisses, and shouts of "NEVER!" from all assembled. Only I was attuned enough to Tyrus's face to spy the flicker of satisfaction in his eyes. The result of our hard work stood before us, shoulder to shoulder, arm in arm, united in their contempt for a tyrant.

He denied none of the charges. He took credit for the malignant space, and even for misdeeds that were not his doing, such as the atrocities on Lumina.

And in pleading guilty, Tyrus also dragged his last loyal followers down with him.

"Why, yes, my most loyal Grandiloquy partnered with me in deploying Resolvent Mist on Lumina. They rejoiced to see justice done. That's what we were celebrating on Lumina, in fact—the greatness of our deed! 'Carnage,' you call it? Those miscreants died too quickly! They dared to challenge their rightful rulers!"

Witness after witness came forward amid the diamond-and-crystal walls of the Great Heliosphere, each adding new condemnations to his record. Tyrus listened with a brash, unwavering smirk, his posture uncowed. When his accusers cursed him, he laughed.

He only ceased smiling when Gladdic's turn came to speak. Tyrus had done genuine ill to Gladdic, and while he'd had reasons for it, I knew he felt remorse.

"I confess to speaking lies on behalf of the Emperor, despite knowing he was no god," Gladdic said in a whisper.

A humming of hostility arose from the crowd, and no longer was it aimed only at Tyrus. I caught several venomous mentions of Gladdic's name, and as my eyes met Tyrus's, I saw that he, too, had noticed.

Suddenly he lunged forward.

"You traitor!" he roared at Gladdic. "You cur! You were the one who urged Nemesis to defy me—her own natural husband! *You* are the one who conspired to help her oppose me!"

Gladdic blinked a moment. "I—I'm not—"

"This all happened because of *you!*" Tyrus jabbed him with a condemning finger. "I will come back to power and destroy you for it!"

Security hustled forward, driving Tyrus apart from Gladdic. The crowd murmured and shuffled, sounds of hostility transmuting to puzzlement. The faces now angled toward Gladdic showed sympathy, curiosity, goodwill.

When it was my turn to speak, I looked only at Tyrus. His eyes, those pale blue eyes, so sharp with intelligence, so cold when turned on his enemies . . . Could others see how they softened for me? The love in them caused my breath to shorten, my voice to emerge faintly.

"The Emperor is guilty of every charge laid to him."

Only his eyes, tender with understanding, could compel me to speak these hideous lies. There was no changing the course of events now, and so I added my words, the better to hasten these proceedings to their natural conclusion.

"The Emperor deserves more than death for his crimes against this galaxy." I raised my voice. "Cast him into a black hole." And with my gaze, I willed him to hear what I meant: *I love you. I love you to the ends of the universe.*

A thick silence fell over the Great Heliosphere. I had proposed the worst fate available to any Helionic: an eternal separation from the Living Cosmos.

Then a thunderous cheering arose, almost deafening in its intensity. The assembly heartily agreed that the last of the Domitrians deserved such a fate.

I had to bow my head and look away from Tyrus, for I had never expected to play this role.

My entire life had been devoted to saving those I loved, protecting them.

But now, the best thing to do for Tyrus was to destroy him.

Tyrus was transferred to the Star Abyss, a vast oblong prison ship able to accommodate a large viewing audience for his execution. It was powerful enough to endure the turbulence of the Transaturnine System, and it flew through the currents of starlight as we prepared to witness an Emperor's death.

When the hour arrived, Tyrus stood amid the roaring crowd, a solitary figure before their screaming hostility and hatred. He was the tyrant who had ruled them all, and now he was being led toward death, and a crystalline tomb that would witness his final heartbeats.

I'd been accorded an honorary pedestal with a clear view. As he reached the foot of his tomb, he looked up and around, finding me at last.

The hateful noise, the thronging spectators, faded away. We looked at each other, the only two people who existed, connected by our shared gaze and our love.

He drew his bound palms up, and I knew why he splayed his fingers wide over his mouth. He was kissing the place on his palm where his electrode linked him to me.

Unnoticed by all, I lifted my hand and kissed mine as well.

Then he stepped into the crystalline tomb, disappearing from view. It was sealed shut, and with a great blast of supersonic fireworks and a blaring of triumphal music, the tube was shot toward the great dark void of the black hole . . . the same one orbited by the remains of the Sacred City.

Like that, he was gone, cast into the darkest of voids. And the void also seemed to swallow me, for my vision briefly went dark, and I staggered.

Helping hands caught me by my right arm—and two more hands seized my left. Neveni and Anguish stood on either side of me, holding me upright as I swayed.

I nodded tightly to show them I was well. As the festivities swelled about us, jubilant masses celebrating the end of the old order, I spotted

Gladdic stock-still amid the crowd. He was staring fixedly at the former location of the crystalline tomb.

Then, as if he sensed my attention, he looked directly up at me.

His haunted face betrayed his thoughts. He knew what Tyrus had done for him at the trial. Had Tyrus not spoken against him, he, too, might have been in a tomb right now, his course set for the black hole.

There is no futility, whispered my brain. Had my entire existence not proved that, again and again?

The months and years that followed marked the dawn of a new age. There were political struggles as newborn powers tangled over territory. Empowered patriots, at last granted rights over their own lands, found reasons to form new rivalries and hostilities.

But all this time also brought new aspirations, new ideals, new possibilities—just as Tyrus had hoped. For the first time in centuries, the citizens of the galaxy had the power to choose and expel their rulers, and to dictate the laws and policies that shaped their own lives. Scientific knowledge grew apace, and the cure for malignant space spread far and wide. The development of new technologies eradicated famines, and cheapened the price of med bots. Access to medicines expanded. Public transports now served the entirety of the galaxy, with a service corps that spanned the planets. No one was condemned now to perish where they were born if they dreamed of exploring the stars.

Optimism became a galactic trait—and this was Tyrus's doing as well. He had given the people of the galaxy something of infinitely greater value than a skilled leader: he'd given them an evil to overcome, then he'd let them overcome him. And a citizenry that had vanquished a dictator knew itself capable of any aim it pursued. Such people did not understand injustice as an aspect of the natural order, but as a flaw to be fixed through a community's efforts.

For the next six years, I was content to watch Tyrus's legacy reshape the worlds around me. But I had never intended to stay forever. I was only waiting for one more wondrous event.

It came on a warm afternoon, beneath the purple skies of a newly restored Lumina. This was the first of the devastated provinces salvaged after the fall of the Empire. The human remains had long been laid to rest, the toxic fumes of Resolvent Mist at last absorbed. Lumina's Central Square now bloomed with a profusion of flowers.

Neveni turned to me in the sunlight as I inspected her bower dubiously, examining the flowered arch where she'd stand side by side to join with her husband. She gave a laugh at my confusion. "You're wondering why plants. No lights."

"You're not going to link with electrodes?" I said. "Not even one?" Without them, it didn't seem like much of a wedding to me.

"You know I'm traditional. I prefer nature. Flowers in hand, flowers overhead . . ."

I nodded, for she'd delayed their wedding until Lumina at last had its own natural vegetation growing again. I didn't understand the impulse, but I suppose I didn't have to. This wasn't my marriage.

"Anguish doesn't like electricity either."

I snorted. "He also doesn't like insects, but you've talked him into planetary life."

"He talked me into it," she said, laughing. "Living here was his suggestion."

Even Gladdic's role had been an idea of Anguish's.

That Gladdic had become a vicar surprised us all. But he had explained to me that he'd had too many brushes with death not to wonder about the greater mysteries of the Living Cosmos.

He'd learned enough of Neveni's older faith to preside over this ancient ritual, but he still looked very nervous and Gladdic-like as he took his place under the bower. The small crowd of newly settled Luminars fell into a respectful, expectant silence. I recognized some faces among them, people who'd resettled from Devil's Shade when this new colony was formed.

Atmas, fast growing up into a young woman, turned and threw me a vibrant grin. She'd taken well to living under a real sun, on a planet with breezes and an actual sky to gaze upon. I gave her a stern mock frown, for the first strains of music were filling the air. Impishly, she winked and faced front again.

The music was our cue.

I circled around the bank of chairs to retrieve the groom. As we linked arms, I had no need to ask if he was nervous. He was all but vibrating with tension.

"Calm down," I whispered.

"I am utterly calm," Anguish said tersely, but he moved as stiffly as a board as we walked toward Neveni's position beneath the bower. She watched with a broad grin, and I felt Anguish relax as he stared at her.

He became *quite* relaxed, forgetting all procedure and pulling free of me to seize her and draw her into a kiss.

"Afterward!" Neveni chided, laughing as she pulled free.

They turned together to Gladdic, who led them through the vows and then declared them husband and wife. They kissed again—and this time, Neveni did not step away until a few spoilsports in the audience began to clear their throats.

They had asked me to stay on as their guest after the wedding. It was pleasant, at first, to take a holiday from my usual circuit of speeches and lectures. I was much in demand to talk to students and political groups and philosophers about democracy and sovereignty and the overthrow of tyrants. Lately I had begun to feel as though I had nothing left to teach. The whole of the galaxy now agreed with me. The ancient texts were taught in all classrooms. New voices emerged every day, with ideas I could not have imagined myself. Many others now worked to enrich the same histories and philosophies Tyrus and I had revived. They did not merely enrich the ideas, but expanded upon them, and dreamed up new ones.

After an interlude in the company of the newlyweds, I awoke early one morning with a single thought in my mind: *It's time.*

Almost as though they'd anticipated my decision, Neveni and Anguish were already awake. Neveni cast a regretful glance toward the bag slung over my shoulder. "Are you sure about this, Nemesis? We could use your help rebuilding around here."

I shook my head. "You don't need me."

"No," rumbled Anguish's voice as he drew an arm about me. "But we want you to stay."

I smiled at them, these people who had endured and mourned and celebrated and survived so much with me. "Thank you," I said, not because they'd changed my plan, but because they valued me—not as a legend or liberator, but as a friend.

Yet I had to leave.

Wherever I went now, I became a spectacle: the famous Nemesis Impyrean, once Empress, ultimate liberator of the galaxy from the tyranny of her own husband. There were few places I could go without being hounded by crowds, pursued by holographic artists, chased by reporters.

"I'll see what you've made of Lumina soon enough," I assured Neveni, and embraced them both . . . my fellow Diabolic, my brother, and this girl who had been my dearest friend and greatest enemy, too.

I boarded the *Alexandria* and launched into the sky. Neveni and Anguish shrank away far below me as I was carried into the vivid purple atmosphere. My heart felt full as I looked down at this place where Tyrus had drawn me into his arms, where I had first begun to love as no Diabolic should, and where my destiny had changed irrevocably.

Then I aimed the ship on my course, and blasted off into my future.

48

2,500 YEARS LATER

Tyrus filled his mind with her and closed his eyes, grateful for the darkness awaiting him, for he wanted the image of Nemesis to be the last thing he saw.

His mind had dwelled morbidly upon the journey ahead, into the heart of a black hole. He'd convinced Nemesis he was entirely unafraid, but he had never quite convinced himself. Too many superstitious Helionic beliefs of childhood whispered in the back of his mind that this was the very cruelest fate, to be cast to unending darkness. . . . True and eternal separation from the divine Cosmos.

His ancestor, Amon von Domitrian, had unwillingly undertaken this same journey centuries before, and as a child, Tyrus had nightmares about such a fate, falling into an unending blackness from which there was no escape or return. Now he tried to remind himself that this was but a matter of physics. Science. This flight into the black hole would seem like mere minutes for him, while in the rest of the galaxy, centuries and millennia would have passed. He would endure but moments of this plunge before he would be crushed.

Nothing prepared him for the sensation of falling, the way his stomach registered the sensation as though he'd dropped off a great cliff. Tyrus's eyes opened. He'd expected to see only darkness as he passed the event horizon. . . .

But this was not darkness. Far from it.

Skeins of vivid starlight swirled around him, enveloping him on all sides. It struck him that a black hole was only lightless from the outside. To one who could not see past the event horizon, it looked terrifying. But as his crystalline tomb plunged deeper into the hole, all the light that had been drawn in before him and with him also rippled alongside him, heading toward the same point.

Gazing out through the clear walls of the tomb, Tyrus beheld the most vividly beautiful flexures and configurations of starlight he'd ever seen. The sensation of falling faster and faster thrilled through him, his very soul seeming to swell and expand.

Everything—the entirety of his life—rushed through his mind, each sorrow and terrible moment of his abbreviated years, and above all, the torn sky above Anagnoresis.

He had chosen this fate. He had chosen it. He'd made this sacrifice after careful deliberation; it had been the most meaningful use of his existence. Yet tears pricked his eyes as the light rippled faster and faster around him, as together he and the light plunged deeper into the black hole.

Minutes had passed for him, heartbeats. But in the galaxy he'd left, centuries had gone by. Everyone he had known was gone now. Nemesis . . .

He prayed to whatever powers had created the universe that she'd accepted his fate, that she'd found happiness. It was all decided already, done, finished—centuries ago. *Centuries.*

In the silence, his thoughts strayed to his father, and for the first time since Anagnoresis, he felt peace when he thought of Arion. He'd sworn to Arion that he'd fix it. And so he had.

On the whole, his life had been kind. His life had been blessed. He'd found *her.* He'd known Nemesis. How many people knew what it was to love someone as he'd loved her, when she filled his very soul, his every heartbeat? And she loved him in return, and oh stars, how lucky he had been!

"This is not so cruel a fate," he murmured aloud, gazing upon the ripples of light.

The Helionics had been wrong to think this was a place of darkness, of total remove from the universe. He would be shredded and torn apart soon enough—it was inevitable—but for the moment, he gazed out at the expanse of stardust funneling down alongside him and thought it the most wonderous sight he'd ever seen.

A prickling sensation drew his gaze to his palm.

Tyrus spread his hand and watched the electrode light up beneath his skin, in that same spot his lips had caressed before he'd descended into the tomb. He gazed at it with awe. It ignited as though she were here with him. How?

Then a shadow slid over him as something vast and metallic passed overhead, blotting out the view of the stars.

It was the *Alexandria.* Its tethers shot out and seized his tomb, jerked him up into the bright bay of a vessel.

For a moment, heart pounding, breathless, he lay stunned by the gravity abruptly pressing him down. And then the lid to his tomb sheared open, and a hand reached down to retrieve him.

Nemesis appeared over him, a figment of light amid the spill of artificial illumination.

"Come with me," she said.

Was he dreaming?

Her palm touched his, and their twin electrodes crackled.

Still disbelieving, all Tyrus could do was stare. Was he already dead?

If so, death was kind. It was *beautiful.*

But she felt real as she pulled him to his feet, as she led him down the short corridor of a vessel too ungainly and solid to be some ethereal hallucinated carriage. She led him into a windowed command nexus as their vessel twisted and thrust against the currents of light being sucked into the black hole.

Tyrus seemed to awaken in that moment, and fear struck his heart. "You're real. You're here." He seized her, horror unfolding deep within his being, for she would be trapped here as well. She had followed him into hell and she would not escape. "No. No, you can't be here! Nemesis, please, tell me you didn't throw your life away!"

Nemesis trained her beautiful, fierce-eyed gaze on the console before her. "I didn't. Relax, Tyrus. You're not the only one who can devise a secret plan." She touched the controls, her gestures rapid and confident.

The ship bucked violently, shuddered and groaned—and shot directly into the pitch black that for a moment he thought was the depths of the black hole itself . . . and then he realized was hyperspace. *Hyperspace!*

Light could not escape a black hole, but perhaps none before had been reckless, mad, or desperate enough to try leaping into hyperspace from beyond the event horizon of a black hole. A wild laugh escaped him, and then they jolted back out into standard space, slowing to

403

drift serenely amid an infinite array of distant stars, the black hole far behind them.

Nemesis reached her hand up to caress his hair, and said, "Did you really think I'd let you perish that way, my love?"

Amazement washed through Tyrus. He caught her in his arms, grappling for understanding. He touched her beautiful face, stroked his fingers through the bright current of her hair. "I still think I am dreaming. You flew into a black hole for me. What if you hadn't been able to escape?"

"Then we would be together until the end of the universe," Nemesis murmured. "But it seems instead we'll simply share the rest of our lives." She turned her face into his hand, her gaze as direct and clear as ever, her smile dazzling, perhaps a touch gleeful. I spent several years waiting for the right gravital window. I've seen what has become of the new republics. I'm satisfied with their direction. It's time to leave. I told you there was another way."

Wonder flooded his heart. Wonder and gratitude. His gaze dropped to their crackling, interlinked palms. *This* was how she'd found him— by their shared connection. "Why," he realized after a moment, "we must be so far in the future."

"Everyone we knew is long gone. The Empire, Tyrus von Domitrian, Nemesis Impyrean—all a distant memory."

Tyrus framed her face in his hands, drinking in the sight of her. He knew she must be a beautiful hallucination. He drew her into his arms. Their lips met, and his heart seemed to turn over in his chest. "It's you," he whispered against her mouth. It *was* Nemesis . . . offering him another chance at existence.

"You will not be an Emperor, I will not be an Empress. We go into something totally unknown," she murmured. "Are you ready for it?"

He laughed into her hair, laughter that verged oddly on a sob.

Hearing it, she lifted her head, and he answered her questioning frown with a deep, loving kiss.

Joy, true joy, was too complex for a single sound.

But a single word would do. Was he ready? "Always."

They set off through currents of starlight, leaving the curvature of darkness and the distant past far behind them.

They had created a new future. Now they would live in it.

ACKNOWLEDGMENTS

My first thanks is to my readers! I did not intend to make you wait so long after such a cliff-hanger—but I hope it paid off! Thank you for sticking with my characters, and especially thanks to those of you who have been with me since the beginning. It's been a wonderful journey.

My next thanks is to Justin Chanda! I tremble to think of how this book might have turned out if I'd been working with anyone less patient, skilled, and discerning. I've been confident every book I've produced is the best possible work I could have created, and thanks to you, that is still the case with *The Nemesis*. I owe you a debt for that. And to Alyza, for being there every step of the way! And to the whole team at Simon & Schuster for supporting me.

To Holly Root, my fabulous agent, and Dana Spector.

To Meredith, Mom, Dad, Rob, Betsey, Sophia, Grace, Madeleine, and Stella—love you all!

To Jessica and the Persoffs, and Jamie and the Hattens. Todd, Jackie, Lesley, Yae, and all the Illinois crew.

ACKNOWLEDGMENTS

Thanks to Jessica Carlson, for being a wonderful roommate during a tough year.

To Space Camp folks—especially Nicole Wagnon, Morgan Collins, KJ Oliver, Jeff Mazza, Amber Wright, Dillon Spicer, Cody Rieman, Celeste Hird, Matt Jones, and Chris Gorman. Thanks for a great year!

Thanks to Robert Graves, who wrote I, Claudius and inspired Tyrus + this YA sci-fi take on that story. I hope I did it justice!

And last but not least, thank you so much to the booksellers, children's librarians, and bloggers who have passed on word of the Diabolic series to readers! I couldn't do this without your support.